PRAISE FOR
CHRISTOPHER L. BENNETT'S
STAR TREK: EX MACHINA

"Easily one of the best [*Star Trek*] novels in print, *Ex Machina* is the proverbial must-read. . . . Bennett has woven multiple and often conflicting continuity threads in a tour de force that tells a fascinating story with flair, imagination, and weight."

—Megan O'Neill, *TV ZONE*

"Attention to scientific detail is at the forefront of Bennett's tome, as he carefully integrates scientific reality into the framework of the tale. . . . He's got a solid grasp on characterization all the way throughout *Ex Machina*, and no one escapes his watchful eye or is considered insignificant. That's the mark of a great writer, one who makes you care about all of the people in a story, and this is one of Bennett's many strengths."

—Bill Williams, TrekWeb.com

"Thought-provoking stories are one of the hallmarks of *Star Trek,* and stories rarely get more thought provoking than *Ex Machina.* . . . What Christopher L. Bennett has done with *Ex Machina* is to meld together . . . a story [that] cannot help but resonate with anyone who has ever read a history book or a newspaper."

—Jackie Bundy, TrekNation.com

STAR TREK
TITAN™

ORION'S HOUNDS
CHRISTOPHER L. BENNETT

Based upon STAR TREK® and
STAR TREK: THE NEXT GENERATION®
created by Gene Roddenberry

POCKET BOOKS
New York London Toronto Sydney The Proplydian

An *Original* Publication of POCKET BOOKS

POCKET BOOKS, a division of Simon & Schuster, Inc.
1230 Avenue of the Americas, New York, NY 10020

This book is a work of fiction. Names, characters, places and incidents are products of the author's imagination or are used fictitiously. Any resemblance to actual events or locales or persons, living or dead, is entirely coincidental.

ISBN-13: 978-1-4165-0950-9
ISBN-10:   1-4165-0950-X

This Pocket Books paperback edition January 2006

10 9 8 7 6 5 4 3 2 1

POCKET and colophon are registered trademarks of
Simon & Schuster, Inc.

Cover art by Cliff Nielson; background image courtesy of NASA,
ESA, The Hubble Heritage Team (AURA/STcI), and HEIC.

Cover design by John Vairo, Jr.

Manufactured in the United States of America

For information regarding special discounts for bulk purchases,
please contact Simon & Schuster Special Sales at 1-800-456-6798
or business@simonandschuster.com.

To Shadow and Natasha,
predators extraordinaire,
who have saved me
from many menacing pieces of string
and wrapping paper.
Sorry about the "Hounds" thing.

Acknowledgments

I'll try to keep it shorter this time. . . . Thanks first to Marco Palmieri for inviting me to come aboard *Titan,* and to Andy Mangels and Mike Martin for launching it on its way. Thanks also to the various authors whose characters, creatures and ideas I've built upon here, including but not limited to Laurence V. Conley, D. C. Fontana, Maurice Hurley, Robert Lewin, Gene Roddenberry and Jeri Taylor from televised Trek and Keith R.A. DeCandido, Robert Greenberger, David Mack, the aforementioned Martin & Mangels, and John Vornholt from the print side.

For scientific and sociological concepts, I owe inspiration to Thomas J. Barfield, Freeman Dyson, Fred Hoyle, Larry Niven, and Konstantin Tsiolkovsky, among others. Alan Dean Foster also warrants a nod. Thanks to Nigel Henbest and Heather Couper, whose book *The Guide to the Galaxy* has provided much insight into the geography of the real Milky Way, and Geoffrey Mandel, whose book *Star Trek Star Charts* has done the same for the fictitious one. And thanks to the makers of the open-source Celestia astronomy simulator, which not only served as a reference but inspired my descriptions of *Titan*'s stellar cartography lab.

My research was assisted by too many Web sites to

acknowledge, so I'll just thank the whole darn Internet and the folks at Google in particular. Thanks also to the usual suspects at the TrekBBS, Psi Phi, and Ex Isle for technical assistance.

And thanks to Dennis McCarthy for making the star-jellies sing.

HISTORIAN'S NOTE

This tale unfolds from late February to late March, 2380 (Old Calendar).

PART ONE

GIANTS IN THE SKY

Beneath the sky's triumphal arch
This music sounded like a march,
And with its chorus seemed to be
Preluding some great tragedy. . . .
Begirt with many a blazing star,
Stood the great giant Algebar,
Orion, hunter of the beast!
His sword hung gleaming by his side,
And, on his arm, the lion's hide
Scattered across the midnight air
The golden radiance of its hair.

—"The Occultation of Orion,"
by Henry Wadsworth Longfellow

We swim through space, the void's chill brisk against our flesh. We huddle closer, closer, basking in each other's warm glow, in the caress of each other's tendrils [love/kinship/let's play!]. Distant starwarmth beckons from ahead, drawing us toward it [hunger/hope]. Shall we dive beneath space, fold the starpull currents about our bodies to reach it faster? No, our need is not yet great; it is enough to swim [patience/prudence/relax and savor existence!].

Now a cloud of dust impinges, tiny specks of [coldstuff/deadstuff] flaring into briefest life as heat and vapor against our hides [tickles/fizzes!]. We drink the tiny bursts of lifewarmth, [soothing/heightening] our hunger ever so slightly. We spread our tendrils wide, stretching them longer, thinner, growing membranes between them to catch more coldstuff [need/exercise/sheer joy of changing!].

A ripple sensed from below space [curiosity/caution . . . familiarity!]—more kin are coming! Few, but welcome. They breach the surface, the lifewarmth and starpull *eddies of their emergence washing over us, slaking our thirst, and we cry out to them in [greeting to strangers/joy at reunion!].*

But wait—something is wrong [puzzlement/can we help?]. They do not return our calls. They are hardened, sheathed for defense! Are they a threat [defend/flee]? No [disbelief/compassion], they are our own, they must need our help! We cry to them [sympathy/concern], but they are still. No, now they strike out [danger!/where?]—wait, no, they strike at us! This cannot . . . [disbelief/agony] Their stings pierce our hides, burning us. Our breath and fluid-ice bleed out into the void. Our siblings' minds cry out to us, deafening us, then fading to silence. We are dying! [loss/anguish/betrayal/Why?] No time to ask. No time to focus, to armor ourselves, we must flee! [panic/exposed/alone!] We need help! We cry out for other minds [terror/pleading] Someone, anyone! [—who—] Barely felt [real/imagined?]—we cry out again! [—who—] Yes! Help us! [—who are you?—/come/desperation/ grief/ rage/—no—get out—/pain/despair/ —get out of my mind—/dread/dying/why?/NO!/—NO!!—]

CHAPTER ONE

"No!!"

Deanna Troi bolted upright in bed. For a moment she felt adrift in the dark, in a void whose emptiness chilled her bare flesh. She wasn't sure where she was, or even who she was. She felt terrible fear, but did not know why.

But then she felt *his* arms embracing her, bringing her home. Will. Her *imzadi*. Her husband. Her captain. Her anchor. When he touched her, she was never lost.

She relaxed against him, and they stayed that way for a precious moment. Then he spoke softly. "The nightmare again?"

"I'm not sure," she said. "The same sense of . . . intrusion . . . yet different. Not as malevolent." Talking about the recurring nightmare brought unwelcome flashes of memory. It had been over three months since Shinzon of Remus and his viceroy Vkruk had raped her, using Vkruk's telepathy to place themselves in her mind while she made love with Will; yet although the nightmares came less frequently of late, her memory of the event remained as vivid as ever, and she knew it always would. What made it worse was that it had been her second telepathic sexual assault, the first being at the hands of the Ullian historian Jev nearly a dozen years ago. He too had usurped Will Riker's place in her perceptions, forcing her to relive an erotic memory which he twisted into a violation. It was a testament to Deanna's love and faith in Will that she was still able to take joy and comfort from his touch today.

Sometimes it took a little work, though. Reliving those memories intensified the fight-or-flight impulse the dream had triggered, and suddenly she felt a desperate need for personal space. She clambered out of bed and moved to the windows, not stopping to don a gown first. Over the past few months, Will had grown accustomed to her occasional need not to be touched, so he didn't follow. "Not as malevolent?" he asked, his voice gentle. "You seemed pretty scared."

Deanna stared out at the stars, gathering her thoughts. "I don't remember. It was as though . . . something else's fear was being forced into me."

"Something? Not someone?"

"It felt very alien. Yet . . . somehow distantly familiar." She shook her head, giving a slight, nervous chuckle. "Never mind. It was just a dream. A bit of undigested chocolate."

"You sure of that, Ebenezer?" She didn't have to turn to see the smirk on his face. "You've been contacted through dreams before. *Eyes in the dark,*" he intoned in a spooky voice that made her laugh.

"Anything's possible, I suppose, but there's too little to go on." She gazed out at the stars. "Something alien, but familiar . . . probably some symbol my brain pieced together, representing anxiety at the unknown. A natural enough response, considering our mission."

She could feel his excitement at the mission that lay before them, and she shared it even without her empathy. *Titan* and her crew had been meant for pure exploration, but had been forced to defer that mission when Starfleet had assigned them to head a diplomatic task force to Romulus, assisting with the rebuilding efforts following Shinzon's bloody coup and subsequent self-destruction. Right afterward, *Titan*'s aid in the search for a lost Romulan fleet had led to a fall down an extradimensional rabbit hole into the Small Magellanic Cloud, over 200,000 light-years from home. In theory, that had been an explorer's dream come true, but dealing with the destruction caused by the Red King entity and the rescue of the Neyel from their disintegrating homeworld had left no chance for real exploration. And then it had been back to Starbase 185 for two weeks of repairs and debriefing, and another two weeks and change moving out beyond Federation space, past Beta Stromgren, past Kappa Velorum, and finally, last night, past the farthest benchmark laid by *Olympia* on its Beta Quadrant survey eight years ago. From this point on, nobody knew what lay ahead.

It was not an unusual experience for an explorer, of course, and it was a welcome one; yet it naturally brought trepidation too, as any new undertaking did. Perhaps that was all there was behind her sense of alien-yet-familiar dread. Maybe it was heightened because from here on, they were completely on their own—no real-time contact with Starfleet Command, no starbases to offer rest and replenishment, no other starships able to reach them in a hurry. She had gotten a taste of that during their recent sojourn in the galaxy next door. But in an odd way there was something even more daunting about doing it *on purpose*.

She felt Will's gentle skepticism, reminding her that she sometimes overanalyzed, an occupational hazard. "Probably," he said aloud. "But keep a mental eye out, just in case."

Now she did turn to him. "Aye, aye, Captain," she said with an insouciant salute.

He looked her over, reminding her that she was thoroughly out of uniform. "Must be cold over by the windows. Wanna come back to bed?"

"No, thanks," she replied after a moment. Somehow she didn't feel chilled anymore; it must have been a relic of the dream. "I don't think I could get back to sleep right away. Maybe I'll go for a walk to clear my head."

"All right, then." She sensed the disappointment that he quickly reined in. She knew he regretted that he couldn't always be the one to make her feel better, to take care of her. But she also knew he understood how it was for her. Not long before her ordeal with Shinzon, Will had suffered his own ordeal, held hostage and tortured by the dictator Kinchawn of Tezwa. He still had his own occasional nightmares, and though he'd cherished her comfort and support, still there were times that he needed to deal with them on his own. After all, in the wake of being victimized, degraded and depersonalized, it was healthy to reassert one's independence, to find one's own inner strength.

Deanna went to the closet, slipped on a light blue wrap and a pair of sandals, and headed out the door. She sent a light mental caress Will's way, only to find that he'd already drifted off again. Still, his serenity in slumber was a pleasant sendoff.

Strolling the corridors of *Titan* felt somewhat like an exploration in itself. It was still a fairly new environment to her—a new class of ship, a new set of crewmates. More importantly, that crew was the most diverse one in Starfleet's history, including many species Deanna had never personally met before. The Federation had always striven for diversity in principle, but in practice had tended toward fairly segregated crews. It wasn't a formal policy; people generally just preferred to work among those with similar customs, outlooks, and environmental needs. Even in the absence of outright prejudice, segregation tended to result from simple complacency, the unresisted impulse to seek the familiar. So maintaining true equality took conscious effort, and sometimes the effort fell prey to other priorities, or to simple neglect. There had been occasional attempts to challenge that status quo, most notably Willard Decker's *Enterprise* experiment of a century before. But reconciling the needs and attitudes of radically different species posed many challenges, and with the loss of Decker on his crew's maiden voyage, some of the impetus for greater diversity had been lost. The technology for balancing so many species' environmental and medical needs had been less advanced then as well. So over the ensuing years, things had settled back into a less challenging status quo. Certainly some progress had been made; during Deanna's tenure on the *Enterprise*-D and -E, over a dozen species had been represented among the crew. However, it was still fairly unusual for humanoids and nonhumanoids to crew together routinely.

The minds behind *Titan*'s mission had wanted to change that. This new generation of Luna-class explorer ships—a prototype design mothballed when the Dominion War had forced a shift toward more combat-oriented starships—had been revived after war's end, promoted as a reassertion of Starfleet's core ideals of peaceful exploration and diplomacy. For years, Starfleet had been forced to focus on mere survival, and many of its ideals had needed to be compromised in pursuit of that goal. Some had been compromised without so great a need—as Deanna and Will knew better than most, after their experiences on the Ba'ku planet and Tezwa. Many in Starfleet felt it was essential to reaffirm a higher set of values than survival alone, to remind the peoples of the Federation that it was more important to live *for* something than simply to stay alive. Hence the ambitious new mission of *Titan* and its eleven sister ships—emissaries to the unknown, questing out in all directions, hands extended to friends not yet met.

But if these ships were to represent the Federation, it was resolved, then they must represent it in all its diversity. If they stood for peaceful coexistence with future neighbors, then they must stand for peaceful, eager coexistence among the Federation's members. Hence the Great Experiment was spawned, reviving Willard Decker's dream and going it one better—or twelve better.

Will Riker had been a natural choice to carry forward that dream—even aside from the striking similarity of their names and aspects of their life histories. For as long as Deanna had known him, William Thomas Riker had been a passionate xenophile, not merely tolerant of others' differences, but positively delighted by them. He took an unabashed, childlike glee in learning about other cultures, sampling their cuisine, their customs, their music, their art—and in his bachelor days, their sexual customs as well. (Which didn't trouble Deanna in the least; on the contrary, his range of experience in that regard had benefitted her greatly. Though she couldn't always say the same about his experiments with alien music or cuisine.) The chance to captain a crew with so many different species on board, many of which he'd never worked alongside before, had been a dream come true for him.

Will had been a gregarious first officer on the *Enterprise,* popular with his crewmates, organizing poker games, dinner parties, and other crew activities. So far, after a hesitant start and a little prompting from Deanna, he had proven a gregarious captain as well, as fascinated by his crew as by the unknowns that lay outside. It made for high morale among the crew, and Deanna was gratified by that.

However, it also gave her a lot of work. Eager to learn about his crewmates' diversity, and to prove it was an asset to a starship crew, Will had encouraged the expression of cultural idiosyncrasies that a more conservative captain might have discouraged in the name of discipline. To be sure, *Titan*'s personnel were all professionals, all perfectly capable of self-discipline, and did not use that liberty as an excuse for irresponsible or outrageous behavior. Still, with so many different value systems interacting, some friction was bound to arise.

Deanna's wanderings brought her to a case in point: the mess hall. Glancing inside through the windows inset in the doors, she resisted an urge to recoil at the sight within: the predators were feeding. It was hard enough for the members of a single species to agree on what constituted appealing cuisine and acceptable table manners, let alone the members of multiple species. But this was particularly so when several of those species were obligate carnivores.

In the first weeks of *Titan*'s mission, Dr. Ree, the ship's dinosaurlike Pahkwa-thanh chief medical officer, had asserted his predatory identity by putting on flamboyant public displays of his rather savage approach to ingesting large, bloody chunks of raw replicated meat (and sometimes real raw meat, courtesy of the Klingons whose vessels had accompanied *Titan* on the Romulan mission). It was a bold gesture of the kind Deanna would expect from a predator, a forthright assertion: *This is what I am, and if you wish to accept me you must adapt to it.* It was also typical of the doctor's cutting sense of humor, the kind of wit that pulled no punches and shocked people for their own edification. And at first it had just been accepted as one person's eccentricity—although Deanna had noticed that many in the crew took careful note of Ree's routine and sought to schedule their dining at different times.

But then the ship's other predatory crewmembers, including the Caitian lieutenant Rriarr, the Betelgeusian ensign Kuu'iut, the S'ti'ach counselor Huilan, and the Chelon biologist Kekil, had begun to join Ree, making something of a ritual out of it, and a very messy one at that. Among most predatory species it was not only socially acceptable but virtually obligatory to play with one's food; not only was there the instinct to play as practice for the real thing, but the metabolism of a hunter was geared toward a period of intense physical activity prior to feeding. (Back on the *Enterprise,* Data had discovered that playing with his cat Spot before dinnertime often improved her appetite. Worf, who had inherited Spot after Data's death, had adopted the same practice when Deanna had mentioned it to him. Worf had been reluctant to take the cat at first, since Klingons as a rule were not fond of cute, furry things; but lately he seemed to have changed his tune. "The cat's *soft* appearance is deceptive," Worf had told her in a recent letter. "Spot is in fact fierce, cunning, uncompromising, and supremely self-assured. What she wants, she demands, or simply takes. She has the heart of a warrior," he had concluded—high praise indeed from him.) The predators' dining ritual gave literal meaning to the term "mess hall," and made many other crew members increasingly uncomfortable—particularly those from herbivorous species, some of whom saw it as a deliberate act of intimidation.

Huilan himself, one of Deanna's assistant counselors, had worked out a solution, rearranging shifts so that the predators would have their mealtime at the quietest part of the night shift, and have the mess mostly to themselves. It had alleviated the problem, but Deanna wasn't entirely satisfied with it. It seemed too much like the kind of "good fences make good neighbors" policy that this ship and crew were intended to challenge. But there were practical reasons for it, and at least it was an acceptable stopgap until something better came along.

Deanna felt she should stop in for a few minutes and say hello—watch them eat, maybe even try joining in as Will had once or twice. It was something she'd have to do if she wanted to overcome her own revulsion at the sight, and come closer to truly connecting with these crewmates of hers. Yet when she saw them tossing bloody chunks of meat and bone at each other, wrestling them into imagined submission and tearing into them with their fangs and beaks and tusks, it was all she could do not to become physically ill. In the wake of her nightmare, the sight seemed to inspire in her a sense of identification with the prey, a visceral urge to flee and hide. Letting out a shudder, Deanna decided that bonding red in tooth and claw could wait for another time, and briskly strode away. Maybe she was being a bit of a hypocrite, but she was off duty and it was the middle of the night, so that was her prerogative. *Besides,* she thought, *the bloodstains would never come out of this wrap.*

She wandered the corridors aimlessly for a time, greeting crew members when they went by but not seeking conversation. There were more people out than she was used to seeing on a starship's "night" shift; but then, there was a greater range of diurnal cycles represented among the crew. Some species slept only every few standard days; aquatics like Ensign Lavena slept infrequently, generally with only half the brain asleep at a time; and several of the predators were adapted for short-burst activity and needed extended sleep periods. It had been a challenge reconciling duty cycles.

From around an intersection just ahead, coincidentally enough, Deanna heard the distinctive gurgle of water draining from the entrance lock to Lavena's water-filled quarters. Rounding the intersection, she was surprised to see, not the Pacifican flight controller, but Dr. Xin Ra-Havreii, *Titan*'s designer, and now her chief engineer following the death of Nidani Ledrah during the Romulan affair. The Efrosian was wearing a robe and toweling off his long, white, dripping-wet hair and mustache, and Deanna realized he must have been engaged in an affair of another sort. She would have turned away and left him his privacy, but he spotted her and gave a wide, unabashed smile. "Counselor Troi, what a welcome surprise to see you!"

"Doctor," she replied, keeping her tone casual.

"I hope you'll pardon my appearance. Ensign Lavena and I were having the most intriguing ... discussions. Selkies have such lovely speech, don't you think? So musical, so nuanced, much like Efrosian languages. You can't truly appreciate it out of the water."

"Yes, so I've heard." She was not that surprised to see him emerging from a female crew member's quarters; Efrosian sexual ethics did not generally include the concept of monogamy, and he was an attractive, charismatic individual. She was sure that Lavena was not the first to reciprocate his wide-ranging interest in the ship's female

crew members. But she was gratified that Ra-Havreii had
demonstrated a tendency to be discreet about his liaisons;
if she wished to satisfy her curiosity about how an air-
breather could engage in sexual relations with the water-
breathing ensign, she could always ask Will. (Well, that
wasn't quite right; Lavena had been in the amphibious
phase of her life cycle when Will had known her nearly two
decades ago. In a sense, Will had been in a different life
stage then as well, and today he was more uneasy about the
tryst than Deanna was.) That aspect of Ra-Havreii's behavior, at least, was not typical of Efrosians; a people with an
extensive oral tradition, they tended not to consider an
event fully real until they'd spoken of it to someone else.
Ra-Havreii was evidently willing to accommodate more
conventional mores in that respect if not in others. Though
she had no doubt he kept a detailed audio journal of his
encounters.

But that was not something she wished to dwell on.
"Actually I'm glad I caught you," she said. "I'd been hoping we could schedule a talk in the near future."

He spread his hands wide. "I'm at your disposal, Counselor. If you'd like to accompany me back to my quarters,
then once I get changed I can offer you a drink and we can
discuss whatever you like."

"That's very gracious, Doctor, but I was thinking of a
discussion along more formal lines."

Ra-Havreii grimaced, without losing his good humor.
"In your office, no doubt. I saw quite enough of counselors' offices following the *Luna* incident, thank you.
They're all so calculatedly nonthreatening, so self-
conscious in their attempts to put one at ease that they become oppressive." Ra-Havreii, Deanna knew, had blamed
himself for some time after the fatal accident aboard his
prototype ship. For a time she had been concerned that

Ledrah's death from an engine-room explosion would have reignited the doctor's guilt, but instead he seemed to have handled it constructively, embracing his new post as an opportunity to make amends for his past and move forward with his life. The problem now was that it wasn't the only thing he was interested in embracing. "If you wish to discuss my personal life, where better than in my personal abode, where I can truly feel at ease?" he asked in a reasonable yet jaunty tone. "And where I will do my very best to make you feel equally at ease."

Deanna didn't need her empathy to sense the seductive undercurrent in his words. "Doctor, you know perfectly well that I'm a married woman."

"A condition which the Betazoids I've known have been rather flexible about."

"Well, I'm not one of them. And you're not fooling me, you know."

"Ahh, as perceptive as you are beautiful. What am I not fooling you about, my dear?"

"Efrosian or not, you know better than to seriously try to seduce the wife of your own very human captain. You're only trying to distract me."

"Perhaps I'm only trying to distract myself. Even without serious intent, flirtation with a lovely, intelligent lady is a worthy entertainment in its own right."

"If you say so," she told him. "But taken to excess, or where it's unwelcome, it can be disruptive. Lately your flirtations have been growing more frequent, and there have been one or two complaints. From Ensign Panyarachun, for example. She has to work with you every day, and she's told you more than once that she finds your attentions distracting."

"Ahh, but would she be so distracted by them if she weren't intrigued? I've made it clear there's no pressure on her to respond. I'm simply . . . expressing my admiration."

"But she'd like to be admired for more than just her looks."

"And she is! I find her skills to be exemplary. I wouldn't be so intrigued with her otherwise. If I only wanted a beautiful face and body, the holodeck is at my disposal."

"Then if you respect her mind, Doctor, you should respect her wishes as well, and keep your relationship strictly professional."

"As you do with the captain?" At her glare, he said, "I meant no disrespect, dear Counselor—I simply have trouble determining where you think the line should be drawn. It's a strange way of thinking to me. Where I come from, it's considered somewhat rude *not* to flirt with someone of your preferred sex. And the concept of a professional relationship being asexual by definition . . . well, back home we feel very differently. Sex among colleagues is encouraged; it's an excellent way to learn to respect each other's needs and work together for mutual gain."

"It's different for humans like Tasanee Panyarachun. Surely you've been in Starfleet long enough to know that."

"Long enough to find that the lines are more ambiguous than is generally claimed. Besides, isn't this ship all about encouraging cultural exchange, getting past the dominance of human ways of doing things? Who's to say my way isn't worth trying, hmm?" he asked with an impish leer. "It seems to work well enough on the command level."

"Maybe your way would be worth trying, *if* everyone agreed to it. But for now, just leave the ensign alone."

"All right," he agreed grudgingly, "but I guarantee you she'll regret it." He furrowed his snowy brows. "On the other hand, maybe there's something to be said for playing hard to get. It might get her to chase me. And nobody could object to that, could they?"

He stopped at a doorway, which slid open on his approach. "Well. Here we are at my quarters. So either we can end this fascinating discussion on coworker sexual relations, or you can come in so we can explore the issue in greater depth."

"In that case, Doctor, I'll leave you alone with your thoughts."

He clasped her hand in a gentlemanly manner. "Rest assured, my dear, they will be mainly of you."

She smirked. "So long as they're about what I said, not what I'm wearing."

"I daresay clothing will not enter into them at all."

Glaring at him, she extracted her hand from his. "Good *night,* Doctor," she said, and strode away. Once she heard the door slide closed behind her, she dropped the stern act and let out a chuckle. She'd actually found his flirtations rather amusing—purely as entertainment for their own sake, as he'd said—but she hadn't wished to encourage him.

The chuckle turned into a long, massive yawn, and Deanna decided it was time to get back to bed with Will. *I think I'll file this conversation under doctor-patient confidentiality,* she said to herself. Will might be very tolerant of cultural differences, but there were limits.

And this was supposed to be a quiet, late-night stroll, she thought. *Serving on this ship is going to be quite an adventure.*

CHAPTER TWO

STARDATE 57146.4

Melora Pazlar had decided that the stellar cartography lab was her favorite part of the ship. There was no other place on *Titan* where she could feel so free. True, in the privacy of her quarters the Elaysian lieutenant could escape the ship's oppressive gravity, shed her motor-assist armature and cane, and drift in the cozy few centigees of her home-world. But that was a small, enclosed space, comfortably vertical but without the airy openness of home. She'd decorated it with crystal sculptures evoking Gemworld's lapidary spires, but that didn't diminish her awareness of the walls, or of the crushing weight beyond them.

In stellar cartography, though, she routinely left the gravity off completely, the better to soar among the simulated stars. In this holographic realm, the walls and the ship could be completely forgotten, and Melora could drift unencumbered through the heavens, dancing gavottes with planets, bathing in nebular mist, cradling newborn T Tauri stars in her hands, communing with the eloquent silence of space.

Except at times like now. " 'Gum,' " said Kenneth Norellis, breaking her train of thought. "What kind of name for a nebula is 'Gum'?"

Melora sighed and threw a look at the boyish astrobiologist, who stood on the control platform with the Irriol cadet Orilly Malar, both held there by a gravity field about twenty percent of standard. At first, the whole holotank had been routinely kept in freefall for Melora's benefit—except for that two-week stretch when Admiral Akaar had taken it over as a command post prior to the Romulan negotiations—but some crew members had found it difficult to adjust to the free-fall environment, so this refinement had been added. It took advantage of the fact that Starfleet gravity stators emitted virtual gravitons which could be calibrated to decay at short distances, so that starships' internal gravity fields would not disrupt their warp-field geometry. That principle had already enabled her to soar free here or in her quarters unaffected by the gravity from the decks below; it had been simply enough to tweak it so she could do so unaffected by the balcony's local field. "It's named after the human who discovered it. It's just a name, like any other."

"Yeah, but . . . 'Gum.' It's kind of an unimpressive name for something so, so *huge*."

Melora figured she could see his point. The Gum Nebula was one of the largest astronomical landmarks in the Orion Arm. It was a gigantic supernova remnant, a shock front from the death of a star over a million years in the past. It was now over a thousand light-years across and expanding, highly attenuated but still impressive in scale. The volume inside it was large enough to hold the entire

Federation and its neighbors with room to spare—and almost all of it was terra incognita. Its nearer reaches had been ventured into by the Catullans and the Klingons, and impinged on by earlier Starfleet vessels on Beta Quadrant surveys, such as *Excelsior* and *Olympia*. But the majority of this vast bubble of space (she'd heard some crew members joking that it should be the "Bubblegum Nebula," though she'd needed the reference explained) had never been systematically explored—until now. *Titan*'s mission was an open-ended survey of the region within the Gum Nebula—or rather, the coreward half, with her sister ship *Ganymede* taking the rimward half. The ship was now several dozen parsecs past its edge, and the holotank displayed the surrounding space from that vantage point, so that the faint wisps of the Gum Nebula, enhanced for the display, surrounded them in all directions.

Melora had trouble seeing why this region was still uncharted (at close range, that is, rather than telescopically), since it was an astrophysicist's dream. A lively, turbulent region of active star formation, it encompassed numerous lesser supernova remnants, stellar nurseries, HII regions, OB-star associations, cometary globules, the whole celestial bestiary. At its heart was the Vela OB2 Association, one of the biggest, liveliest star-formation zones in the Orion Arm, and the source of the energy which excited the Gum Nebula's hydrogen into luminescence, like the candle inside a Japanese paper lantern. Though she supposed that might make it a bit less of a priority for Starfleet, which was generally more interested in seeking out new life and new civilizations. Star-formation zones were extremely turbulent; the birth processes of stars—and the death throes of the short-lived, supermassive stars that died before they could travel very far from their birthplaces—gave off intense radiation, interstellar-medium shock waves, and subspace disruptions, all of which could prevent habitable planets from forming in the first place or wipe out those nearby biospheres that did happen to form.

Of course, if there was one thing two centuries of Starfleet exploration had proven beyond a doubt, it was that life always proved tougher and more resourceful than science generally supposed, and cropped up in the most unexpected places. Besides, the volume inside the Gum Nebula was immense; even with all those star-formation zones, there was still plenty of room for more hospitable planets. Plus there was a better-than-even chance that exotic life-forms would be found on planets bathed in radiation and racked by cosmic turbulence, employing weird and wonderful strategies to survive. That was why Norellis was here, accompanied by Cadet Orilly, who majored in exobiology. Their assignment was to identify likely places to search for life, and hopefully some less likely but more interesting ones as well.

Melora twisted gracefully about her center of mass, surveying the expanse laid out around them, and reached out to cup Avior in one hand. The simulation actually let her feel warmth from the shrunken red-orange giant. "I don't know," she said. "It doesn't seem so huge from this vantage point. You really should come up here, give it a try."

"If it's all the same to you, Lieutenant, I'd rather keep my feet firmly planted."

"Your choice, Kent. Though I'd have thought you'd learned your lesson about gravity." Shortly before *Titan*'s launch, Norellis and gravity had had a difference of opinion in a vertical Jefferies tube, and as usual, gravity's arguments had carried the greater force, earning the ensign some quality time with the ship's medical staff.

"I did," the human countered. "The lesson is, stay close to the deck."

"Well, how about you, Cadet?" Melora asked, shifting her gaze to Orilly. If anything, the cadet seemed to be having a harder time than Norellis. Even though the Irriol's paws gave her a solid quadrupedal footing on the balcony, the two trunks extending from the base of her wide, thick-necked head clutched the railing tightly with their four-fingered hands. The diamond-shaped armor scales covering her body, which Norellis had likened to those of an Earth animal called a pangolin, were slightly raised as if in alarm.

"No, thank you," Orilly said in her quiet voice, emanating from the rounded mouth between her trunks. "Although this is a marvelous simulation, I am not comfortable with all this . . . space. It reminds me how far I am from . . . home." Her golden-brown scales drooped.

"Come on, Malar, there's more to life than home," Melora said cheerfully.

"Not for Irriol. We are very empathic, with our own, at least. To be severed from the Whole, to be alone, it is . . . difficult." Melora couldn't read her expressions well, but she got the impression that Orilly had pulled back from a stronger word. "No offense to you or the fleet . . . but it is not something we endure by choice."

"So why are you in Starfleet?" Melora asked.

When Orilly didn't answer, Norellis stepped in. "I guess you don't know about Irriol."

Melora shrugged. "Plenty of species out there. Hard to keep track of them all."

"If she's off her world, it means she's . . . well . . ."

"I am an exile," Orilly finished.

"Oh!" She frowned. "Wait a minute . . . if your people can't stand being offworld, then exile must be . . ."

"The worst penalty on their books," Norellis said. "Ir-riol are a nonviolent people. No death penalty, ever."

"No," Orilly said. "Worse."

"So you're a criminal?!"

"Know that I would never do anything to violate my oath or my duty," Orilly said in great earnest. "For only by serving my people well can I hope to be allowed back home."

"Okay, I wasn't questioning that." She knew Starfleet would never have let her in the Academy if her behavior had been suspect. "But . . . can I ask what it was you did?"

Orilly's trunks wriggled. "It is . . . difficult to explain to outsiders. And troubling for me to discuss. But it does not correspond to anything your peoples call a crime."

"Was it some taboo you violated, then?"

"No, much more than that. I did true harm. I did not wish to, but I was foolish and irresponsible and . . . there was much cost to others."

"But you didn't kill anyone."

She lowered her head. "Lives were lost . . . but not in any way that the laws or ethics of other worlds would find me culpable for."

Lucky you, Melora thought. She couldn't say the same about herself. During the crisis on her homeworld four years ago, she had been directly responsible for the death of a leading citizen, Tangre Bertoran. Starfleet had absolved her of wrongdoing, declaring it a defensive act, but Melora had been harder on herself, and had taken a leave of absence to atone in seclusion.

It struck her that Orilly, in her own way, was also aton-ing in seclusion, perhaps in some ways a more profound seclusion than Melora could grasp. She wished she could understand the nature of the offense, the better to offer her support to the troubled-seeming cadet. Maybe with time, she could.

"Well, tell you what," she said. "Let's get to work, take your mind off things. Computer! Overlay sensor data. Display possible biosigns."

The computer complied, breaking down the various biosignature types by color coding and labels: spectroscopic results suggesting molecular oxygen and respiratory gases, thermal signatures and energy curves consistent with life processes, Fourier extractions of possible neural EM signatures, and so forth. *Titan*'s cutting-edge sensors gave them greater clarity over greater distances than Mélora would've thought possible. The virtual sky around them teemed with signatures; even if half of them turned out to be false alarms, there was enough life showing up in this preliminary scan to keep them busy for years.

"Aah!"

The cry came from Norellis. Melora spun to face him. "What is it?"

He looked embarrassed, and pointed at a sensor reading that hovered next to his head. "I turned my head and there it was, right in my face. Startled me."

Melora worked the control padd in her hands, telling the holotank's forcefields to push her gently toward the image. "What is that? There's no planet there. It's very close to us. . . ."

"Maybe a ship!" Norellis peered closer. "Or multiple ships. Hard to make them out."

"Here, let me increase the scale. . . ."

She was interrupted by a keening wail from Orilly. *"No!!"* the Irriol cried, rearing up on her hind legs and stepping back as though in fear. She bumped into the balcony and lost her balance, toppling out into the free-fall zone beyond. It worsened her panic, her six limbs flailing as if in a futile attempt to flee from . . . *something.*

"Cadet!" Melora worked the padd, using the force-fields to catch Orilly and guide her gently back to the balcony. Taking a second to switch on her support armature, she took a deep breath and climbed over the rail into the gravity zone so she could come to Orilly's aid. But the Irriol's flailing trunks made her pull back; her bones were somewhat more fragile than those of beings raised in planetary gravities. Norellis moved in and tried to hold her down, but just got knocked aside for his troubles. "Malar, what is it? What's wrong?" Melora cried, striving to catch her gaze and get through to her.

Orilly met her eyes for a moment, but there seemed to be no recognition there. "Help us!" she cried. "We are dying!"

Will Riker had known something was about to happen before it started.

It wasn't due to any great captain's intuition, though. He just knew Deanna Troi, knew her every nuance of expression better than he knew his own. So when she'd abruptly grown distracted as they engaged in light banter with the rest of the bridge crew (well, all except Tuvok—the middle-aged Vulcan tactical officer wasn't the bantering type), he'd realized that she was sensing something, and readied himself for what she might say or do next.

What he hadn't expected was that Tuvok would be the first to react. Hearing a strangled baritone cry from the tactical station, Riker whirled to see Tuvok gasping and clutching the console for support. His teeth were clenched and he was clearly struggling for control . . . but his eyes showed panic and dread. Glancing over at Deanna, Riker saw the same emotions in her eyes, though she seemed to be controlling it better. "Mr. Tuvok, report," Riker snapped, hoping the appeal to discipline would help him focus.

"I am . . . receiving telepathic impulses . . . raw emotion . . . terror! Pain! Aahh!!" He wrenched his eyes shut, fighting the panic.

As Riker moved closer to Tuvok, Deanna came up behind him. "I sense the same things. Fear, agony, loss . . . also anger."

"Why is it hitting him harder?" Vale asked.

Deanna looked away for a moment. "I've . . . had reason to learn to strengthen my shields against mental intrusion."

Riker winced at the reminder of Shinzon, and of the other mental incursions Deanna had been subjected to over her career. But this was a time for business. "Is this the same thing you sensed the other night? The nightmare?"

"I think so."

Tuvok was still struggling. If anything, he seemed embarrassed by Troi's superior control. "Bridge to sickbay," Riker said. "Dr. Ree, we could use you up here."

"I was just about to call you," came Ree's growling tenor. *"Several crew members have just come down with severe panic attacks. Cadet Orilly, Lieutenant Chamish, even Ensign Savalek and the Lady T'Pel. All psi-sensitives, sir. I imagine Commanders Troi and Tuvok are reacting similarly, are they not?"*

"I'm managing it, Doctor," Deanna told him. "But Tuvok is having a harder time coping."

"If you will have him brought to sickbay, I should be able to suppress his telepathic senses."

"No, Captain," Tuvok said, gathering himself with an effort. "The initial shock . . . has subsided. I am . . . in control."

"I still want the doctor to look at you," Riker said. He had an ulterior motive to the offer, thinking Tuvok might welcome an excuse to be there for his wife, T'Pel. When Tuvok had accepted the post of tactical and second officer, it had been with the provision that his wife be allowed to join him aboard the ship. After being separated from her for seven years by *Voyager*'s abduction to the Delta Quadrant, and facing the prospect of a similar separation twice in recent months (first by imprisonment on Romulus, then by *Titan*'s stranding in the Small Mag Cloud), he had expressed a wish to have her with him aboard the ship, and she had assented to come.

But if Tuvok was concerned for his wife, he showed no outward sign. "No! I . . . believe this to be a distress call. If so, the insights I can provide may be needed. They are only emotions . . . I am their master."

Riker turned to Troi. "Do you agree? A distress call?"

"I do," she answered without hesitation. "Something out there is pleading desperately for help. Something with a very powerful mind."

And what could terrify something that powerful? Riker wondered. Whatever it was, they would need to be ready. He looked over at Tuvok, gauging his mental state. The Vulcan's reputation as one of the fabled *Voyager* survivors had preceded him, but Riker still didn't know the man well enough to tell whether he was really in control or simply putting on a brave front. But he decided to give him the benefit of the doubt. "All right. You're relieved from tactical, Commander—" He cut off Tuvok's protest with a look. "But you can remain on the bridge to advise."

Tuvok nodded stiffly. "Acknowledged."

"Mr. Keru, take over tactical." The big Trill worked his security station's controls, slaving the tactical console to it. Riker turned to the tan-skinned Bajoran at the science station. "Mr. Jaza, scan the area for life signs, psionic energy, any unusual phenomena. Let's see who's trying to spread around their bad mood."

Jaza replied promptly. "Stellar cartography reports strong life signs at bearing 282 mark 20, range point-one-two light-years."

"Is there a star system there?"

"Negative, sir; they're in open space, moving at high impulse. Hold on. . . . I'm getting energy discharges."

"A battle?" Christine Vale asked.

"Hard to tell. The discharges seem bioelectric."

"Let's find out. Ensign Lavena—set an intercept course, warp eight, and engage."

"Aye, Captain. Estimate arrival in three minutes."

As the ship jumped to warp, Riker moved back to Deanna's side. "Do you still get the sense of familiarity?"

"Yes, sir," she said, maintaining proper discipline while they were on the bridge. "It's extremely alien, yet it's something I've been in contact with before . . . a long time ago, I think. I'm trying to remember."

"I believe I can get a visual on long-range sensors," Jaza reported. "Just a moment . . . there."

Riker turned to the screen. At first all he saw was a group of pearlescent blobs of light, little more than pinpoints at this range. They were moving quickly, on erratic, independent courses. As Jaza worked his console, a set of crosshairs targeted the nearest blob and the screen zoomed in, tracking it. It was a translucent, rounded shape, apparently lenticular, with one face turned nearly toward their vantage point. "It reads over a kilometer in diameter," Jaza said. It was illuminated from within by a bluish glow and by numerous points of reddish light arranged in concentric rings. Faint radial striations subdivided its surface into eight wedges. Riker felt the same sense of uncertain familiarity that Deanna described.

Then it angled sideways and Riker recognized it instantly. The eight long, feathery tentacles that trailed behind it, giving it the aspect of a vast jellyfish swimming through the lightless depths of the ocean, made it instantly recognizable. "The Farpoint creatures!"

Vale turned to him. "Sir?"

"We encountered them on our very first mission on the *Enterprise*, Deanna and I," Riker explained. "Sixteen years ago, in the Deneb system. I think we ended up calling them 'star-jellies.' They're shapeshifters, and more than that. They could read thoughts and synthesize any object you could think of, like living replicators. They even have transporter capability."

"They sound more like ships than living beings," Jaza opined.

"They're definitely life-forms," Troi told him. "Immensely powerful telepaths and empaths. I've never felt such overwhelming emotions. That first time, whenever I lowered my mental shields, it was like I became a conduit for their emotions, feeling them as if they were my own, and unable to resist them."

"I can . . . verify that assessment, Commander," Tuvok said stiffly.

"That would explain what's happening to the crew," Vale observed. "But what is it they're so afraid of?"

"There's a smaller cluster of objects closing on the, umm, school," Jaza said. "They read similar to the jellies, but different." He switched the viewscreen to a wider view. Harpoons of purple light were flashing through the school, scattering the star-jellies still further.

"Shields on standby," Riker ordered Keru.

"Shields, aye," the burly, bearded Trill acknowledged. "And weapons, sir?"

"Not yet," Riker said as the attackers came into view. He recognized them as well: gray, lenticular metallic shapes, firing destructive blasts of violet plasma from their central concavities. "They're another form of the star-jellies—apparently their attack mode."

Vale frowned. "Have we stumbled into some kind of civil war?"

"It could simply be competition for food or territory," Jaza suggested.

"Either way," Vale went on, "I don't think it's something we have any business interfering in."

Riker realized she was probably right, though it filled him with regret. There was something ethereally lovely about the star-jellies. He still remembered the sense of awe he'd felt when they'd revealed themselves at Deneb, when the one held captive by the Bandi had shed its imposed disguise as "Farpoint Station" and ascended into space, and reached out to caress its mate's tendrils in a gesture whose simple poignancy transcended species.

"Why don't they fight back?" Keru asked. Riker realized he was right; the attacks were entirely one-sided.

"Maybe they can only fire in the armored mode," Jaza said.

"There's more," Deanna said. "Somehow they just . . . can't. Or won't."

Just then, one of the jellies was struck a dead-on blow to its ventral side, between the tendrils. Two of the wispy appendages broke free and spun away. At the moment of impact, Deanna and Tuvok both convulsed in pain, and Tuvok let out a strangled scream. Vapor erupted from the wound, and the jelly's internal lights flared, flickered and then fell dark, first the blue glow, then the rings.

"Counselor? Mr. Tuvok?"

"Apologies, Captain," Tuvok said. "Not just . . . the creature's death throes. The others . . ."

Deanna nodded. "The grief of the others, combined . . . it's extremely intense. Even with my shields up I felt it."

"Can you sense anything from the attackers?"

She shook her head. "But I can't really probe without lowering my defenses, and I'm hesitant to do that."

"Tuvok?"

"I . . . do not believe there is anything to sense, Captain. The creatures feel the attackers are . . . *wrong* . . . a corruption . . . there is a revulsion, as though toward a corpse."

Deanna nodded. "Yes. These are like dead things to them, and yet they're attacking, menacing. The jellies feel a sense of mortal dread, as though the attackers were . . . well, the closest analogies I can think of are the zombies from old Earth monster movies."

Vale frowned. "Jaza, scan the attackers more closely for biosigns."

"If I remember right," Riker told her, "the *Enterprise*'s sensors couldn't penetrate them. There are substances in their hulls . . . or hides . . . that resist scans."

"We've learned a few new tricks in the past sixteen years, sir," Jaza replied. It was an understatement; the *Luna* class carried prototype sensors beyond anything else in Starfleet. "Uh-huh, those hulls are well shielded, but just give me a moment to calibrate . . . There. The attackers show limited activity in some biosystems, including propulsion and defense . . . but no anabolic processes, and nothing that resembles cognitive activity. The walking dead indeed. But I'm also reading numerous biosignatures inside them."

Riker looked up at him sharply. "What kind of biosignatures?"

"Just a moment, I'm refining resolution. . . . They seem to be endothermic bipeds, about our size."

Riker exchanged a look with Deanna, then turned to Dakal at ops. "Cadet, try hailing them."

"Hailing . . . No response," the young Cardassian said.

"A crew?" Vale asked.

"I've been inside two of these creatures," Riker said. "In at least some of their forms, they contain passages that resemble corridors, with a habitable environment inside. They certainly could be adapted into ships."

"And we've encountered living ships before," Deanna said.

"Except these people don't seem to need them alive," Riker said coldly. "Dakal, keep hailing. Ensign Lavena—put *Titan* between the attackers and the star-jellies. Mr. Keru, shields at maximum." Vale threw him a look, but kept her counsel for the moment.

There were too many ships for *Titan* to block standing still. But she was light, fast, and maneuverable, and her pilot had grown up slaloming through Pacifican coral forests and dodging serpent-rays. Lavena flitted the ship around almost playfully before the attackers' sights, keeping them from getting a clean shot and probably making them dizzy to boot.

"We're receiving a hail," Dakal finally reported. That was a good sign. "Hailing frequencies" were a standard first-contact handshake protocol, allowing two ships' computers to begin with universal physical and mathematical constants and build a translation matrix in seconds, if their databases didn't already have any languages in common. Any warp-capable species with any interest in talking to strangers eventually developed such protocols. The return hail meant that the attackers had at least the willingness to communicate, and that was a good start.

"On screen," said Riker, turning to confront the attackers. When the screen came on, his eyes widened. He hadn't expected them to be beautiful. The screen showed a number of delicate-looking bipeds, slim-boned and decked with downy, green-gold feathers. Hawklike eyes stared from above sharp-toothed, beak-tipped muzzles, and vivid-hued, feathery crests topped many of their heads. Their feathered coats gave them no need for clothing, but they wore protective gear on their joints and vital areas, plus various equipment belts or harnesses and assorted insignia or sigils. Behind them was a passageway of familiar design, triangular and round-cornered, its ribbed, cardboard-brown walls embossed with intricate patterns that seemed neither wholly organic nor wholly artificial.

"Flit off, for your own sake," the one nearest the camera said curtly. He (the translator gave the being a gruff, nasal baritone) was far from the largest of the group, his headcrest was threadbare and faded, and there seemed to be considerable scarring beneath his feathery coat; but he carried himself with a casual yet undeniable authority. *"Our quarry won't linger if they have time to gather their warp fields!"*

"I'm Captain William T. Riker of the starship *Titan*, representing the United Federation of Planets. I don't know the nature of your conflict, but my people aren't inclined to sit idly by when we see sentient beings dying. We don't intend to take sides, but we'd be glad to offer our services as a neutral mediator in your dispute." His voice carried more steel than his words; he only hoped their translators were good enough to render it.

"You talk against the wind," said the avian, his matter-of-fact tone clashing with his poetic phrasing. *"Toy with cosmic fire, and the Spirit's not to blame for your burns. The Hunt must be!"* His image faded, leaving stars.

"Captain, they're firing on the jellies," Keru reported.

"Block it, Lavena! All crew, brace for impact!"

Magenta fire filled the viewer. The blow badly rattled the ship and dimmed the lights. "Shields are holding," Keru reported. "But power systems are being disrupted. I don't know how it's getting through."

Another bolt hit, even harder this time. Riker had to clutch the arms of his chair to stay in it. "The discharges . . ." Tuvok said with difficulty. "Organic rather than technological . . . our shields may not be adequately calibrated." A third hit rammed home the point. Console screens flickered as ship's power systems compensated for an overload somewhere.

"Can we compensate?"

"We may not have to," Jaza said. "The star-jellies have just gone to warp."

"Attackers breaking off," Keru said a moment later.

"Are they in pursuit?"

"Negative, sir. My guess is, they can't track them at warp. Otherwise they wouldn't have been so concerned about them getting away."

Riker could barely imagine how organic beings could enter warp in the first place, though he'd seen it more than once. But there were other priorities. "Damage report!"

Vale was already coordinating the reports on her side console. "Minor casualty reports, nothing serious. We've had EPS blowouts on four decks. Synchronization failure in dorsal shield emitters. Several impulse injectors are fused. Warp is fine, but the navigational deflector's offline. We won't be moving anywhere for a while."

"Bridge to engineering," Riker called. "Estimated repair time for engines and main deflector?"

"At least six hours, depending on whether you want shields back too," came Ra-Havreii's voice. *"Longer if you want me to spend time computing a better estimate."*

"Just do the best you can, Doctor."

As he spoke, a bleep came from Ops. "We're being hailed, sir," Dakal told him. "Same ship as before."

"On screen."

The grizzled avian commander appeared once more. *"I am Qui'hibra, leader of the fleet-clan Qui'Tir'Ieq. We see that you have suffered significant damage. I offer my regret for our part in causing it, but you were warned and chose not to heed. I pray that your misguided actions ended none of your people's lives."*

Riker was taken by surprise; he'd been expecting something more bellicose. "No, thank you, Captain Qui'hibra. But I appreciate your concern."

The avian seemed genuinely relieved, in a stern sort of way. *"That is providential. The Hunt is risky enough for those who seek it willingly, let alone those whose lack of understanding places them in its path. Others have not been so fortunate in the past. You would be wise to keep that in mind in the future."*

"Captain Qui'hibra—"

"For the present, though, your ship needs repair. We will remain in the area for some time while we process our kills. If needed, we can spare the crew and resources of one skymount to assist in your repairs while we do so. But only one."

Riker exchanged a look with Deanna, communing

wordlessly for a moment. "I . . . thank you for the offer, Captain. I'll have my engineering staff coordinate with yours once we determine our needs. In the meantime, I think we should meet and get better acquainted. We're explorers, new to the region and eager to learn about its inhabitants."

"And you have much to learn, it is clear. Very well," Qui'hibra agreed, although he seemed mildly annoyed about it. *"You may send a small party to observe our processing operations if you wish. Just so long as you do not interfere. The Hunt calls still, and makes few allowances. Do you require us to teleport you aboard?"*

"We have our own transporters, thank you. If you'll just provide coordinates . . ."

"Very well. You will stand by. There are rites we must first perform. You will be contacted after, and you will teleport promptly at that time to the coordinates we provide." Qui'hibra cut the transmission without further ceremony.

"All right, then. We'd best get ready," Riker said after a nonplussed moment, and took a few steps in the direction of the turbolift.

Only to find Deanna in his path. "May I ask where the *captain* thinks he's going? Surely this is a job for the diplomatic officer."

Of course she was right. For two decades he'd been reminding Robert DeSoto or Jean-Luc Picard that the captain's place was on the bridge, while his officers went out and took the risks. But those captains had never hesitated to exercise their prerogative to ignore him, and even though he continued to press, he had admired their reluctance to stand by while others stepped into harm's way. When he'd taken command of *Titan,* he'd jokingly promised Picard to ignore his officers' efforts to restrain his wanderlust, and had acted on that promise once already.

But this was Deanna's job, after all. She was an expert in interspecies psychology and sociology, an experienced diplomat and first-contact specialist, and a trained command officer and combat veteran to boot. Who better to take the lead in contact and negotiation with new civilizations? Riker knew all this perfectly well, and assigning her to the post of diplomatic officer had been as much his idea as hers.

In this case, though, he was more reluctant to send her. These hunters had ruthlessly killed a defenseless sentient being before their eyes—who knew how dangerous they were? And he didn't relish the thought of sending Deanna inside one of the corpses they used as ships. He remembered the deep emotional connection she'd made with the star-jellies back at Deneb. To be immersed in their remains, to make diplomatic overtures toward their killers—it wasn't something he wanted her to have to do.

But that was a husband talking, not a captain. They'd both accepted that having Deanna under his command could only work if he kept the two separate. Throwing her a sheepish look, he said, "You're right, of course. I recommend taking Mr. Keru along, though."

"I had him in mind. Mr. Jaza, you as well, please."

"Aye, aye, ma'am."

"And have Dr. Ree meet us in transporter room one. His perspective could be useful. Both as a life scientist and a predator," she added as an aside to Riker. He nodded, approving her choices.

And when I get back, he "heard" in his mind as she strode toward the lift, *you and I will have a little talk about overprotective husbands.*

CHAPTER THREE

The aliens did not seem to be in any hurry to meet with Deanna's away team. She and the others had a long wait in the transporter room while the hunters went about the grisly business of securing their two kills—an operation which the away team observed on a wall monitor. The ships assigned to salvage the kills rotated to approach them ventral side forward—meaning the side opposite the weapon port, bearing a recessed dome in the center. (She recalled that this had been the "top" of the star-jelly ship that had first approached them at Deneb, but only so that its weapon port would be pointed down at the planet. A spacegoing organism would have no absolute sense of up and down.) Deanna watched in grim fascination as each ship's ventral surface shimmered and flowed with cloud-like patterns of energy, dissolving away to reveal the familiar eight tentacles, which slowly uncoiled, reaching outward. Yet at the same time the tentacles were unfamiliar, for they lacked the lambent aura which surrounded the live jellies. Instead they were pasty and fishbelly white, and their movements as they reached out to grapple the dead jellies were stiff and mechanical, with none of the feathery grace of the live tendrils. The partial dematerialization of the armor was also unfamiliar; the star-jelly at Deneb had dissolved its armor completely, or transformed it back into its normal translucent carapace, before extending its tentacles. Indeed, given the creatures' shapechanging abilities, she wasn't sure whether the tentacles were stored beneath the armor or actually transformed into part of the armor itself.

The hunters were thorough in retrieving their spoils; a third ship even retrieved the two tentacles severed in the attack, and the bridge reported that it also beamed aboard as much as it could of the frozen oxygen and fluids that had spilled from the mortally struck jellies.

After the retrieval operation, nothing visibly happened for a time, and Deanna wondered just how involved their rites would be—as much out of impatience as anthropological curiosity. It was nearly ten minutes before they finally received the beaming coordinates. "Umm, you might want to see this, Commander," Ensign Radowski said. Deanna looked over his shoulder at the display. The coordinates were for a chamber at the tip of one of the salvaging ship's tendrils, which had penetrated and sealed the breach in the dead jelly, snaking inward to connect with its internal passageways. Apparently when Qui'hibra had said they could observe the "processing" of their kill, he had meant they would do so in person. She and the others would be beaming inside the body of the magnificent creature whose death she had witnessed—had *experienced*—mere minutes before.

Deanna steeled herself as best she could, recalling all her training in diplomacy and tolerance, before she gave the order to energize. Still, she felt a palpable weight descend on her when she and the others materialized—a coldness, an emptiness echoing with the absence of life.

She caught herself, realizing the sensation was probably her own imagination. Or maybe she was picking up the reactions of the others. She glanced around at them, using her various senses to gauge their reactions. Ranul Keru seemed ill at ease and disapproving; his life experiences had instilled in him a strong, aggressive sympathy for the victims of violence. Jaza Najem was solemn and reverent, like a man at a funeral, yet those feelings warred with an intense scientific curiosity. Only Dr. Ree seemed to take their surroundings entirely in stride.

The chamber was larger than Deanna had expected from the transporter console graphic; she had to remind herself that the star-jellies were over a kilometer across. Its dimly lit walls bore a similar texture to the ones she recalled from Farpoint, but were more rounded and translucent. The whole chamber was slightly askew relative to the local gravity vector, leading Deanna to wonder if the gravity they were feeling came from the corpse around them rather than from the hunters' ship.

A party of avians was approaching the away team, with the alien commander, Qui'hibra, at its head, giving the others instructions about what sounded like routine ship's business. Only Qui'hibra and two others bore colorful headcrests, while the rest had what appeared to be marsupial pouches in their abdomens; presumably the latter group were females. Qui'hibra afforded the new arrivals a disinterested glance. "Welcome to the newest prize of Clan Qui'Tir'Ieq," he said in a not particularly welcoming tone. "I am Qui'hibra, elder of the clan." He indicated a tall, younger female standing next to him. "This is Matriarch Qui'chiri." Deanna sensed strong fatherly affection as he introduced her, but he gave no outward sign of it. "If you will come with us, you may observe our operations."

He and his group resumed walking, leaving the *Titan* party little choice but to follow. "Elder Qui'hibra," Deanna said, "thank you for your welcome. I'm Commander Deanna Troi of the Federation vessel *Titan*. These are Jaza Najem, our science officer; Shenti Yisec Eres Ree, our chief medical officer; and Ranul Keru, our chief of security." Qui'hibra barely acknowledged the introductions. "May I ask what your people are called? What planet you're from?"

"Pardon me, I have my duties." Qui'hibra gestured to one of the other males in the party, who was younger and taller and bore a fiery red-orange crest. "This is Hunter Se'hraqua. I have assigned him as your liaison; please direct your questions to him."

Se'hraqua seemed to have other ideas. "Elder, I still think—" Qui'hibra halted him with a simple stare. Deanna sensed frustration from the younger male, and a resentment divided between Qui'hibra and her own team. The elder remained unaffected by it, his stoic authority unwavering, and soon Se'hraqua bowed to it. "Yes, Elder." He threw a withering glare at the *Titan* party. "Come, try to keep up," he snapped, and strode forward after his commander—or patriarch, perhaps. Se'hraqua reflexively preened his own neck feathers with the small beak at the tip of his muzzle, apparently as a form of composure grooming.

The elder and the matriarch stopped at an irislike portal. "Progress?" Qui'chiri asked one of the other females next to it, who was manipulating the molded shapes on the wall in a way that looked like a cross between working console controls and giving a deep-tissue massage.

"The prize is airtight and nearly equalized," the female reported. "Neural and immune activity confirmed zero."

"A good sign," Qui'hibra murmured.

"The Spirit smiles on us."

"Do not be premature," the elder snapped. "The Spirit does not reward arrogance. Remember that!"

She lowered her head. "My remorse, Elder."

"Hope it will be adequate, cousin. And open the iris."

The female stroked the wall again, and the portal swirled open. A charnel smell poured through, the smell of burned flesh, metal, polymer—maybe all of those, maybe something in between. Whatever it was, it made Troi choke, and Jaza and Keru along with her. Ree flared his nostrils curiously, extended his tongue to taste the air, and mulled it over like a wine connoisseur, although he offered no judgment.

Se'hraqua made a cawing, scoffing sound at the humanoids and spoke to Ree. "Your comrades have no stomach for the kill, it seems."

The doctor tilted his long, lacertilian head. "So it would seem. But these humanoids, they often partake in things they have no stomach for."

The avian studied him, and then the others. But Qui'chiri was already on the move, giving orders. "We need to purge the death toxins faster! Chi'harthi, check the gravitic nodes, ensure their viability. Tir'chuai, see to the motor cortex first thing; I have concerns about feedback trauma from that hit. . . ."

As the matriarch went on assigning the others to their duties, Se'hraqua grudgingly attended to his, leading the away team out into the star-jelly's internal passageways, which were identical to the ones from Farpoint, although without even the dim bioluminescence those had possessed—and without the slow, heartbeat-like sound that had pervaded them. The work teams carried their own lights with them. "To answer your earlier questions," Se'hraqua said stiffly, looking in Deanna's general direction, "our people are the Pa'haquel. We are from no planet; the skymounts are our homes, the Hunt our life and soul."

"Really?" Jaza asked. "Tell me, how long have you lived this way?"

"We have always shared our lives with the skymounts, since the dawn of our civilization."

"Hm. Are they . . . if I may ask, have you engineered them in any way? Their abilities are very . . . unusual for natural creatures. Not to mention their appearance."

"They are as Providence sent them to us."

"But these corridors, the gravity, the interior lighting . . ."

"They are as they are! Do not question their divine perfection!"

Ree interposed himself between them. "Indeed, they are remarkable prey, continuing to serve the Hunt even after their death. My colleagues and I are naturally eager to learn of their many gifts."

Se'hraqua was mollified somewhat. "You are a hunter?"

"By biology and avocation," Ree replied. "I am a doctor by profession, and I am fascinated by these great beings."

"For us, all professions serve the Hunt, and the Hunt serves all our needs."

"I am sure. With these creatures' replication abilities, you can no doubt manufacture anything you need."

"Indeed so." Se'hraqua folded his long, clawed fingers in a pious gesture. "Truly they are the divine source of our lives. They feed us, water us, clothe us, give us homes, give us wings to fly and claws to fight."

"To fight others of their own kind," Keru countered.

Se'hraqua bristled (literally, his crest feathers spreading outward) at Keru's judgmental tone. "Thus is the balance sustained, alien. Do not presume that you speak for the skymounts. You know nothing of them. The Pa'haquel have been bound with them in the Hunt for thousands of generations. You are not the first who have sought to judge us in ignorance."

As they moved along the corridors, Deanna noticed that scattered among the work crews were a number of crew members from other unfamiliar species, including massive red-furred bipeds with feral features and simian tails; delicate, scantily clad humanoids with lavender fur on their scalps and backs; and long-armed, bronze-skinned humanoid variants with a gorilla-like gait. "Pardon me, but may I ask—does the name 'Pa'haquel' refer only to those of your own species, or does it include everyone on your ships?"

Se'hraqua paused, still seeming disinclined to speak amiably with anyone but Ree. "They are valued allies in the Hunt, but they have their own names. They are crew, not clan."

"Thank you." She tapped Ree lightly on the shoulder, and moved in close to his ear membrane. "You seem to be the only one hitting it off with him," she said softly. "Why don't you take the lead?"

"Certainly, Commander."

The honey-colored therapodian went about his task enthusiastically, clearly fascinated by the star-jellies' extraordinary anatomy. The "corridors" turned out to be their respiratory channels; as roomy as they seemed,

Deanna again had to remind herself that for a kilometer-scale creature they were the equivalent of narrow arteries. Although the jellies lived in a vacuum and fed largely on energy, they were still carbon-based life-forms, requiring air, water, and nutrients, which they periodically hoarded from life-bearing worlds, or converted from the raw matter they found in cometary clouds. A parallel set of circulatory conduits carried their equivalent of blood; Se'hraqua explained how they were flushed and converted as a water storage and delivery system for the "skymount" crews. Control of their bodily functions was attained by tapping their nervous systems. Jaza was more interested in learning about their gravitic, warp-drive, and replication/transporter abilities, but Se'hraqua either did not know the details of those systems or did not care to go into them for Jaza's benefit.

"Do you need to take special measures to preserve your kills from decay?" Ree asked.

"A few. Purging the death toxins, halting the metabolic shock from propagating too far—these must be done quickly for a successful reanimation. But they are space-going creatures, after all. At times, if low on energy, they may need to drift for centuries in hibernation before finding a star system to replenish them. It is their nature to be durable."

"But I assume they do not last indefinitely, since you need to replenish them."

"They serve as they are needed." Deanna sensed a predator's reluctance to admit weakness—or simply that of a young, proud male.

Before long, Jaza's tricorder showed them to be traveling into the creature's vast brain. Residual electrochemical potentials were still discharging within its mass, occasionally sending uncomfortable empathic spikes through

Deanna's mind, like being brushed by cold, dead fingers. Qui'hibra's teams were hard at work under her direction; between Se'hraqua's lecture to Ree and Jaza's tricorder scan, it became evident that some teams were tapping into various neurological centers while others were performing efficiently brutal lobotomies, or rather lobectomies, cutting out components they didn't need and having them taken away for later recycling. Deanna stared as fleshy hunks larger than she was were excised and carried away. There went the star-jelly's memories, its galaxy-spanning experiences, its hopes, its capacity for love and delight—all chopped down into handy cubes of meat for easy disposal. Or perhaps consumption?

Diplomatic officer or not, she felt compelled to ask the question. "Are you sure that the skymounts see your . . . relationship in the same way you do? Is it possible they have a different view of being preyed upon?"

Se'hraqua fixed her in his aquiline gaze, blinking once. "Of course they flee the Hunt. All beings strive to live. But we must live as well. Such is the balance of creation. If we succeed in the hunt, the skymounts die. If they succeed in escape, we cannot sustain ourselves, and we die."

"There are other ways of fulfilling your needs," Jaza pointed out.

"It would not be the same. It would not be from *them*." Se'hraqua stroked the wall with reverence.

"But if you cherish the skymounts so much," Deanna asked, "why must you kill them? Is there no way you could cooperate, achieve a symbiosis?"

"You do not begin to understand. We honor their sacrifice. When we strike them down, we do so with deep gratitude and reverence."

"I don't see much reverence around here," Keru interposed.

"This is a time for haste," Se'hraqua snapped. "The rites are performed in their proper time." He returned his gaze to Deanna. "Yes, it would be uplifting if we could share our life-forces, but such is not in the balance. What feeds us drains them. If we occupy them while they live, their immune systems teleport us away."

"How did your . . . relationship with them begin?" Jaza asked. "You must have had another means of space travel before you encountered them."

"Clearly your worlds have not been blessed by the sky-mounts. They breed on planetary surfaces. Quelha was such a world, once. Their sessile young burrowed their roots deep into our world's skin, feeding on its warmth. With their gifts, their granting of desires, they drew in animals to live atop their shells, to roam and swim and fly among their tendrils and membranes." He recited it as though quoting scripture. "When those animals died at the end of rich and happy lives, they gave their flesh unto the skymounts who had sustained them, and thus the mounts grew larger.

"We were savages when we found them, little more than animals with spears, struggling to survive. With their plenty, we were able to build a civilization, to devote ourselves to art and learning. Yet we grew greedy, and demanded too much from them." He closed his eyes. "Many mounts did not survive. Fewer and fewer came from space to lay their eggs. To sustain ourselves, we had to learn to follow those few that remained when their time came to rise to space. While they lived, it could not be. But we were able to redeem their deaths, to make them live again and let us live as well. We found the balance, and thus the Pa'haquel way was born."

Deanna granted him a moment of respectful silence before asking, "And what of Quelha? Do others of your kind still live there?"

"Quelha is long dead. Those who stayed were struck down by divine wrath, because they could not find the balance." Deanna had to wonder: Had the starfaring Pa'haquel taken it upon themselves to be the agents of that wrath?

"Attention!" came a call from Qui'hibra, and Se'hraqua whirled to face his elder. Deanna sensed a twinge of hope that he was about to be assigned a less tiresome duty, but that quickly subsided when it became evident that the elder was addressing the entire crew. "Processing phase complete. All crews, confirm readiness for reanimation!"

One by one, reports came in, confirming their ready status. "Consider yourselves blessed," Se'hraqua told the away team. "But stay silent and do nothing to interfere. This is a holy moment."

The final reports came in. "All crews, stand ready," Qui'hibra said, then spread his arms. "O Spirit of the Hunt, hear me! We pledge this kill to the holy balance. We took its life, not for malice, not for greed, but for the preservation of life, within our clan and among all those whom we protect." His tone was matter-of-fact, not grandiose or florid; but neither was he merely parroting a script. Deanna felt sincerity in him, if not passion. He had done this many times, but it still meant something real to him.

"O spirit of the kill, accept our thanks for your life, and grant us the boon of your body. Let your death serve life, and thus maintain the balance as the Spirit wills. Let this reanimation show us your forgiveness. Our lives to the Spirit," he finished, and all the others echoed it. "Now!"

The Pa'haquel workers squeezed the walls and worked the equipment they had attached to exposed brain tissue. After a moment, the chamber began to shudder, and the gravity fluctuated. Jaza set his tricorder to show an exterior view from *Titan*'s sensors. The star-jelly corpse had moved away from its killer and was accelerating.

Over the next few minutes, the Pa'haquel tested the various systems of their astrocoelenterate zombie, putting it through maneuvers, testing its replication systems, and so forth. They "reeled in" its remaining tentacles, curling them up in a spiral pattern in the ventral recess, and then activated its armored mode. On the tricorder screen, its translucent skin rippled with light and grew slowly opaque, soon achieving the dull metallic hardness of the hunter ships. At Qui'hibra's next order, pulses of magenta light began to flow through its eight meridional fissures, slowly at first but then accelerating. Then a single, sustained burst of energy shot outward into open space.

At that, the other Pa'haquel ships fired bursts of their own in salute. The processing team gave a cheer of joy. Qui'hibra turned to the other male who had been with his party and made a ritual gesture. "Ieq'hairu, loyal cousin, you have the blessings of the Spirit and your kill. I name you elder of this skymount, a status you have earned through loyal service to the clan. May this mount bring you many more kills, in service to life."

The others cheered—all save Se'hraqua. From him, Deanna felt resentment and envy directed at the new elder, as though he wished he were the one accepting command rather than being relegated to public relations. Nonetheless, he kept up a stoic front. "You see?" he said to Deanna. "If the hunt were not in balance, it would fail. Their bodies die, but their souls live on in ours. The transition is painful, yes, but birth is always so. A successful reanimation shows that healing has been achieved, the divine balance preserved."

"There's no doubt of their sincerity," Deanna Troi reported to her crewmates as they sat in the forward observation lounge. From where she sat across the table, Christine Vale could see that Troi was harrowed by her experience within the star-jelly corpse; though her tone was level and professional, her eyes were haunted. "The Pa'haquel and their allies clearly believe that their actions are necessary and righteous, not merely for their own survival but for the sake of divine balance. They believe that without this balance, the universe will collapse into chaos. They express a reverence for their prey, of a sort not uncommon in traditional hunting cultures."

Vale looked down, absorbing her words . . . but she couldn't help being distracted by her reflection in the table. She still wasn't used to seeing herself with black hair. She liked to change her look from time to time; she'd gone through many different lengths and shades over the years, arriving most recently at a short, sandy bob that she'd liked well enough to keep for some time. But once their new mission had begun in earnest, she'd suddenly been struck by the urge to go pure raven, blacker than she'd ever been. The first dye she'd tried had been a bust; although completely black in human-visible light, it appeared a downright ghastly shade to those crew members who saw in ultraviolet. So the ship's stylist had concocted a dye that was guaranteed to absorb every wavelength of light visible to any *Titan* crew member, from terahertz microwaves up to high UV. It let her get through the day without the Caitian, Syrath, and Zaranite crew members laughing uncontrollably (or the equivalent) when she walked by. Yet it seemed to her—though it was most likely just her imagination—that all the EM energy her hair now absorbed was making her head unusually warm.

"That may be," Riker replied, bringing her attention back to the briefing, "but from what you and Tuvok tell me, their prey definitely doesn't see things the same way."

"No. The star-jellies are horrified and confused by this. From what we saw, I don't think they're even capable of attacking their own kind."

"Their failure to return fire is not conclusive," Tuvok said. Now that there were no live jellies in range, Riker had seen fit to return him to duty. "Perhaps, as Mr. Jaza speculated, the astrocoelenterates can only fire while in armored mode. It appears to require significant time and energy to make the transformation—time and energy which they instead chose to focus on generating warp-fields for escape." Vale was amused by his reluctance to call them by such a frivolous name as "star-jellies." Sometimes she was tempted to ask the Vulcans she met where the logic was in wasting breath on so many unnecessary syllables.

"Tuvok," said Troi, "you felt what I felt. Did it seem to you that the jellies were even able to contemplate returning fire?"

"The most I can say is that their emotions were dominated by grief and panic rather than aggression. However, I am not as skilled in the interpretation of emotions as you, Counselor." Though the words were an acknowledgment of deficiency, his voice conveyed it as a point of pride.

"Whatever their reasons," Riker said, "I'm not willing to just stand by and let them be slaughtered. I think what we need to do is establish a dialogue between the species. Maybe if the Pa'haquel can hear directly from their victims, it'll shake up some of their self-righteous assump-

tions. Meanwhile, we should do what we can to defend the
star-jellies from further attacks. We won't destroy any
Pa'haquel vessels, but we'll do whatever else we can to
preserve star-jelly lives."

Vale gave him a sharp look. "But Captain, the Prime
Directive—"

"Does not prevent Starfleet vessels from responding to
distress calls."

"But there's a difference between answering a cry for
help and taking sides in a conflict."

"This isn't a war between sovereign states. This is the
one-sided slaughter of innocent life-forms. Life-forms
which have overtly requested our aid. In my opinion, we
have not only the legal option, but the moral obligation to
intervene."

Vale looked down, pondering his words. Certainly she
sympathized with his desire to help the jellies. She'd been
trained as a peace officer, latest in a long line of Izarian
peace officers, and it was second nature to her to serve and
protect the innocent. And she certainly agreed that the
star-jellies were magnificent, awe-inspiring creatures that
should be cherished, not killed and gutted.

But her Starfleet training told her to be cautious about
even the most well-intentioned interference in others' affairs. By the letter of the law, Riker was correct. The Prime
Directive, as it applied to starfaring powers, only forbade
active interference in unaligned cultures' wars and politics. It didn't forbid giving humanitarian aid to those who
requested it directly, or offering help in negotiating peaceful settlements. It allowed the granting of asylum to political refugees—something that could be construed as
political interference, but was allowed under the Directive
on the principle that it didn't actually force any change on
the foreign state itself, merely removed certain consenting

individuals from that state's influence. (Indeed, on *Titan*'s first mission, a Reman named Mekrikuk, who had helped Tuvok escape from a Romulan prison, had sought asylum and was now living comfortably back in Federation space.) Theoretically, protecting star-jellies from the hunters would be a similar act. Still, it felt more complicated than that.

As if confirming her thoughts, Jaza spoke up. "Can we be sure of that? Clearly the star-jellies can't be entirely natural. Their internal gravity and lights, their warp and replication capabilities . . . even the shape of their internal passageways, the perfectly smooth floors, is too artificial."

Riker furrowed his brow. "I always figured the attacking star-jelly we beamed to sixteen years ago was deliberately mimicking a ship, both inside and out, as some sort of protective camouflage."

"But why would the creature trapped on Deneb have done the same? I read your report—that creature was hoping for rescue, not trying to hide. For that matter, the attacking creature had no reason to mislead you about its true nature. You posed no significant threat to it. And what we've seen here confirms that those corridors are part of their normal anatomy. I think it's clear they've been artificially engineered, modified if not created by beings who wanted to use them as starships."

Vale realized she was smiling at Jaza's endearingly bookish enthusiasm. She immediately assumed a more detached expression and focused her gaze on the captain. She didn't want to go down that road with Jaza again. At least, she hadn't decided yet if she did. After her brush with death in the evacuation of Oghen, she had chosen to seize the moment and taken Jaza to bed. That night, in the warm afterglow, it had seemed so easy—if Riker and Troi could balance career and relationship, then so could she and Jaza. But with the clarity of the next morning had come doubts. Could she really treat the rest of the crew fairly if she had a relationship with him? Could she serve the demands of both her time-consuming job and a blossoming romance without compromising one or the other? And how did she really know Riker and Troi themselves could pull it off? So far they'd managed fairly well, but they hadn't really faced a test yet, a situation requiring a choice between personal and professional priorities.

So after careful thought, and with considerable embarrassment, she'd gone to Jaza and retracted what she'd said to him in bed. She'd asked him to treat it as a one-time thing, with no strings, no hard feelings and no future. He had taken it as well as she could have hoped, expressing regret but telling her he understood, and promising to respect her wishes. It had just made her feel guiltier about reversing course on him like that.

She shook herself, returning her focus to the matter at hand. Reviewing her memory, she was pretty sure Riker had just asked Jaza, "You think the Pa'haquel made them?" or words to that effect.

Now Troi was shaking her head. "They insist that the jellies have been the same since the dawn of their history. If someone did engineer them, it must have been some earlier race."

"History can be rewritten," Keru interposed. "People can forget their true past, or have it deliberately hidden." *I guess a Trill would know,* Vale thought.

"True," Jaza said. "If the Pa'haquel did create the jellies, that makes this an internal matter, and the Prime Directive would apply."

"Would it?" Troi challenged. "Whatever their origins, the jellies now live free, and have a life, a society of their own, separate from the Pa'haquel. These jellies don't even know that their hunters *are* Pa'haquel. They're a separate culture."

"That's open to debate."

"That's right, it is," Riker said. "But that doesn't change anything." He paused, his gaze taking in everyone at the table. "We all understand the risks of intervention. That's what the Prime Directive is for—to make sure we consider those risks, and remember our own limitations. Many of us have seen firsthand what can go wrong when we grow overconfident and meddle too much." He and Vale exchanged a significant look. They both knew the horrific costs of ex-President Zife's clandestine interference on Tezwa. "But we've also seen whole worlds die because we refused to help them—because we thought that somehow a disruption of their worldview was a worse fate than total annihilation. There was a time when I supported that policy myself. But I've seen too much death and devastation in the past decade not to question that. And I think that adhering too slavishly to the letter of the Directive can be an excuse for inaction—for not wanting to deal with the responsibility and the tough decisions that come with trying to help.

"Now, I still believe in the Prime Directive, and I'm still bound by my oath to defend it at all costs. But I will not see it used as an excuse for taking the easy way out, for letting injustices thrive because we decide they aren't our problem. Not on my ship. Not in my crew. Because I trust that this crew can handle that responsibility, can make those tough decisions."

After a moment, he went on. "Either way, what we need to do now is learn more about the situation. We've met with the hunters, now it's time we met with the prey. Mr. Jaza, your first job is to scan for star-jelly life signs and find us the nearest school. Your second job, once we find them, will be to study their biology and learn what you can about their origins." He turned to Troi. "Counselor, hopefully you can do the same. Work on making contact with them, getting more from them than just emotions. Maybe they have long memories, and can give us some answers. But your main job is to learn whatever you can from them, work toward establishing a dialogue—one in which we can hopefully include the Pa'haquel. Try to find a way the two species can coexist peacefully." Troi nodded.

"Mr. Tuvok," Riker went on. The tactical officer looked up sharply. "Your job is to work on recalibrating the shields so they can handle the Pa'haquel's bio-energy bolts more effectively. And work on tactics for defending the jellies from armed attack without resorting to deadly force."

"Acknowledged." Tuvok seemed relieved, Vale thought—probably at not being asked to work with Troi on communicating with the jellies.

"Dr. Ree," Riker said, "your job is to administer telepathic blockers to those crewmembers who can't resist the star-jellies' emotions on their own. I don't want any of our people out of commission when we may need them."

"There is an herbal medicine from my world which I think would do the trick," Ree said. "Some of my people are empathic—though not I, obviously—and there were times in our history when the ability was seen as an aberration, which a drug was devised to 'cure.' With some refinements, it could be adapted to other species."

"Very good. That's it, people—let's go to work."

CHAPTER FOUR

Tuvok stepped through the doors of stellar cartography to find the Horsehead Nebula blocking his path. "Oh, there you are," came Commander Jaza's voice from beyond it. "Never mind that, just step on through." Tuvok did so, adjusting his gait to the lowered gravity of the catwalk, and reminding himself that this seemingly flamboyant mode of presenting data did have its practical value for visualizing spatial relationships. Still, the crew members who spoke of their experiences with the free-fall environment of the holotank tended to describe it in the terms one would use for a recreational contrivance—a "thrill ride," he believed his old crewmate Tom Paris would have called it.

Once he cleared the simulated dust cloud, Tuvok saw Jaza and Lieutenant Pazlar beyond it. Both of them were hovering in freefall, outside the observation platform's localized gravity field. "Feel free to come up and join us, Commander," Jaza said, blithely disregarding the inapplicability of the word "up" to his own current frame of reference.

"No, thank you, Commander. I would prefer to remain here."

"Of course," Pazlar observed. "Vulcans do everything with such gravity."

Tuvok ignored the remark, addressing his comments to the commander. "You wished to see me, Mr. Jaza?"

"Yes, Tuvok, we could use your input," the Bajoran said. "We've been unable to detect any star-jelly schools within sensor range, and we're having trouble tracking the warp trail of the one we encountered before. Something to do with the organic nature of their drives, I suppose."

Tuvok's gaze sharpened. "If you wish me to attempt to sense them telepathically—"

Jaza shook his head. "Don't worry, nothing like that. You see, I realized that the star-jellies can't exist in . . . well, I was about to say 'in a vacuum,' but that would've been a poor choice of words."

"You mean," Tuvok interpreted, "that as living beings they must logically be part of an ecosystem."

"Yes. And I realized the same must be true of all space-going creatures—cosmozoans, to use the technical term. Starfleet vessels over the past two centuries have observed hundreds of such organisms, but their reports have usually described single individuals or monospecies groups in isolation, rarely interactions between multiple species. That's understandable, given the vast distances of interstellar space. But there must be a big picture we're only seeing isolated pieces of.

"So we've been going through all the reported contacts with cosmozoan life-forms, looking for patterns and connections among them. We noticed that *Voyager* encountered more than its share of such creatures in the Delta

Quadrant, so we wanted to consult with you about them. Perhaps learning about the cosmozoans in a different quadrant—essentially a separate ecological region—could help us see some larger patterns."

Tuvok frowned. "Could you not simply have consulted *Voyager*'s logs?"

"We have, but I like to get a more personal perspective when I can. The evidence always comes first, of course, but it can be informative to compare multiple interpretations of the evidence."

Tuvok raised a brow, acknowledging Jaza's logic. "Very well. I will tell you what I can. Keep in mind, however, that my analyses of the cosmozoans *Voyager* encountered were shaped more by tactical considerations than scientific curiosity."

"That's a useful perspective as well. If politics can be a science, as my friend Cadet Dakal would have it, then surely tactics can be as well."

Lieutenant Pazlar smirked. "I've certainly known enough people who treated scientific debate as a form of combat." She entered a set of commands into her handheld padd, and the holographic field of view began to move with disorienting speed. She and Jaza moved to hover alongside him, and the three of them ended up facing a projection of the Delta Quadrant, positioned as though they were looking "down" from galactic north. A familiar jagged line appeared, one which Tuvok had seen many times in debriefings, lectures and documentaries about *Voyager*'s seven-year ordeal: a representation of the starship's course through the quadrant, beginning at the outer rim of the galactic disk in Kazon territory and progressing through leaps and bounds to the Borg transwarp hub in the Three-Kiloparsec Arm, adjacent to the Central Bulge.

They proceeded through *Voyager*'s cosmozoan contacts sequentially, beginning with the nebular life-form encountered on stardate 48546, not long after *Voyager*'s arrival in the Delta Quadrant. "It was *seven* AUs across?!" Pazlar asked in amazement when he recounted that fact.

"That is correct. At first it appeared to be a fairly ordinary nebula aside from the presence of omicron particles and certain organic compounds. Once inside the cloud, we discovered an internal anatomy and biochemistry which indicated it to be a living organism."

"No reason a spacegoing organism, particularly a nebular one, couldn't be that large or larger," Jaza observed. "It's been theorized for centuries that the organic molecules inside the right kind of nebula could potentially be triggered by EM radiation or electrical discharges to organize into life; so the size of such a creature would be largely a function of the size of the original nebula. Seven AUs is tiny as nebulae go."

Tuvok proceeded to the next account, the discovery of a photonic-matter life-form in a protostar on stardate 48693. "I'd discount your 'Grendel' as a cosmozoan," Jaza said. "That species seemed native to its protostar the way we are to planets. We have no evidence it could exist in interstellar space. Let's move on."

Tuvok spoke with some reluctance. "The next relevant encounter was shortly thereafter on stardate 48734. The Komar, a race of trianic-based energy beings inhabiting a dark-matter nebula."

He paused, until Jaza filled in the gap. "According to the reports, one of these beings took you over personally, Commander, and attempted to hijack the ship so its people could feed on your neural energy."

"That is correct," Tuvok admitted. "Fortunately, the Komar inflicted no permanent harm." *Despite my own failure to protect my ship,* he thought.

Pazlar stared. "How could they have a name?"

"Excuse me?" Tuvok asked.

"They were energy beings, right? No mouths. Where'd the name 'Komar' come from?"

"I cannot say. I was not privy to the entity's thought processes. Perhaps some earlier race they contacted gave them the name. Is this relevant, Lieutenant?"

"No. Just curious." She turned to Jaza, and gratifyingly returned to the topic. "But they were native to the nebula, right? So shouldn't we rule them out like the photonic creatures?"

"I don't think so," Jaza said. "The gravity of stars and planets somewhat insulates them from interaction with the interstellar biosphere. The same wouldn't apply to nebular life. I'd count it."

Tuvok recounted what little more he knew about the Komar, and then moved on to the swarm of flagellate organisms encountered on stardate 48921. These creatures, comparable in size to *Voyager,* had employed a form of magnetic propulsion, with their flagellating motions creating the dynamo effect that drove it. But Jaza was more interested in their behavioral patterns. "These were the only cosmozoans in which *Voyager* observed complex social behavior," he explained. "Please tell me all you can remember." Tuvok complied as best he could, while trying to respect the privacy of his then-protegée Kes, in whom the flagellates' EM emissions had induced a premature reproductive cycle.

But Pazlar provided a distraction—fortunately, perhaps, but still annoyingly—by her interest in the creatures' own reproductive behavior. "The big creature thought *Voyager* was trying to *mate* with its partners?" she laughed.

"Correct. It reacted to us as a reproductive rival. We

managed to pacify it by mimicking the submissive behavior of its species."

Pazlar laughed harder. "No wonder I never heard that story. Who'd want to admit a Starfleet ship backed down from a fight?"

Tuvok merely looked at her icily until she subsided. Mercifully, the list was nearing its end. *Voyager* had not encountered any further cosmozoans until the fifth year of its journey, when on stardate 52542 it had been briefly ingested by a two-thousand-kilometer creature which lured in its prey by telepathic projections of their greatest desires. Then in the seventh year there had been two encounters: a gaseous life-form that *Voyager* had inadvertently removed from a J-class nebula on stardate 53569, and the dark-matter entities encountered in a cluster of class-T substellar bodies on stardate 53753.

"That is all I am able to tell you," Tuvok said when he was done. "I am not sure if it will be helpful in tracking the astrocoelenterates."

"It might be," Pazlar said. "Look." She manipulated the padd so that markers appeared at the locations of each of the encounters Tuvok had described: three close together at the outer rim, one in the Crux Arm near the Devore Imperium, and two in the Three-Kiloparsec Arm near the quadrant border. "Look at the regions where you encountered all those creatures. See any common pattern?"

Tuvok studied the display, but was unable to see what she was getting at. "No, I do not, Lieutenant."

She worked the padd to generate three insets which magnified the regions under discussion. "There. See it now?"

He examined the insets, but again had to say no.

"You're kidding. Come on, it's staring you in the face!"

He glared at her. "Clearly it is doing nothing of the kind, Lieutenant, as I do not see it. I suggest you explain."

Shaking her head, she highlighted a cluster of blue stars near *Voyager*'s starting point. "The star-formation region. See? You spent much of your first year in the DQ passing through a long, narrow OB association. It formed a sort of border between Kazon and Vidiian space. A star-formation region that far out on the rim, away from the arms, it's surprising to find. I can't believe you missed it!"

Tuvok was beginning to find her impatience and condescension tiresome. He strove to remain stoic. "As I remarked, Lieutenant, my training is not in the sciences."

"And of course down here in the Three-K Arm, deep in the inner disk—that's the busiest region of star formation in the galaxy. And out here in Crux, where you found that 'pitcher-plant' creature . . . not only star formation, but subspace 'sinkholes' and 'sandbars,' chaotic space—that's got to be the craziest region of space I've ever seen."

"I see," Tuvok said. "And we are also currently in a region of active star formation."

"Well, near one," Jaza said. "The Vela OB2 Association isn't too far away. And this is the common thread of most of the other cosmozoan contacts—they all took place in the approximate vicinity of star-formation regions or other turbulent zones. The star-jellies first encountered by the *Enterprise* were at Deneb—very far from here, but close to a stellar nursery called the Pelican and North American Nebulae." He manipulated his own padd, and the field of view moved to highlight it. "It's actually one nebula with a dark cloud subdividing it as seen from the Federation core worlds. A later survey by the *Hood* detected a few more jellies near there, though they didn't seem interested in communicating.

"Back in the twenty-third century, the *Intrepid* discovered several cosmozoans in its survey of the Scorpius-Centaurus Association—and was ultimately destroyed by a cosmozoan resembling a giant amoeba, although that's generally believed to have been extradimensional in origin. Others have been detected near the Orion Association, the Taurus Dark Cloud, you name it."

"So what is the nature of the connection?"

"It's about what life needs to survive, and to come about in the first place. It needs energy, it needs matter. And it needs a certain amount of turbulence—enough to provide the dynamism and change that an ecosystem needs to form, but not enough to destroy its constituents. On a cosmic scale, star-formation zones are the most turbulent regions, full of intense energy and churning interstellar gases."

"Are they not generally hazardous to life for that reason?"

"To tiny, fragile life-forms like us, yes. But to creatures tough enough to live in interstellar space, powerful enough to journey across light-years? A biosphere made of such creatures would need the kind of energy and rare elements that would be most abundant in those zones."

"So you believe we can find more of the coelenterates if we proceed toward the Vela Association."

"Not just the coelenterates," Jaza said. "I'm hoping to find a whole ecosystem! Something that will reveal more about the common threads tying the known cosmozoan life forms together, the greater processes underlying their creation."

Pazlar appeared skeptical. "But if ecosystems like that exist, why haven't we seen them in other star-formation regions that have been surveyed?"

"We haven't surveyed more than a fraction of the Sco-Cen Cluster, and certainly not its most active region around Rho Ophiuchi."

"But the Betelgeusians have surveyed the Orion and Horsehead Nebula region in detail. There have been isolated cosmozoans found there, but no large-scale ecosystem."

"True. All the more reason to go to Vela and see what we find."

"Keep in mind," Tuvok told him, "that our mission is to find and contact one specific species, not merely to investigate an abstract scientific riddle. What if we do not find the astrocoelenterates at Vela?"

Pazlar shrugged. "Then maybe we can stop and ask for directions."

Tuvok sighed, and for a moment was almost nostalgic for Mr. Neelix.

Captain's Log, Stardate 57148.2

Repairs to the ship's major systems are now completed, without requiring assistance from the Pa'haquel hunters. On recommendation from Commander Jaza, *Titan* has set course for the Vela OB2 Association. The star cluster is over two weeks distant at warp seven, but Jaza advises that if one star-jelly school was found this far from it—not to mention the hunters who follow their migrations—we are likely to encounter others as we draw nearer. He also considers it likely that we will encounter other forms of what he calls "cosmozoan" life, and I have authorized him to use our high-resolution wideband sensor net in his search for such organisms. Perhaps we may discover some nonsentient relative of the star-jellies which the Pa'haquel could be persuaded to hunt instead.

• • •

Ranul Keru was a big man, big enough to be intimidating. That was something he did his best to downplay in his personal life, but readily made use of in his security work. And right now, as he loomed over Torvig Bu-kar-nguv— one of the four Academy seniors serving their work-study tours on *Titan*—he wanted to be intimidating. It should've been easy; the Choblik was diminutive in comparison, a meter-high biped built something like a short-furred ostrich with an herbivore's head, a short neck, and a long, prehensile tail. If not for his bionic arms and sensory organs, the joint enhancements on his legs, the small bionic hand at the tip of his tail, and the polymer-armor plating over his vital areas, Torvig would've looked like the kind of small woodland creature who would dart for the undergrowth at the first sign of a big, bearish omnivore like Keru. Instead, despite all of Keru's best looming and glowering, the engineering cadet merely studied him with the same wide-eyed, analytical curiosity he seemed to apply to everything. If anything, Keru found himself intimidated by that stare—or by the cyber-enhanced eyes that did the staring.

Abandoning the staring-contest idea, Keru went for a more overt confrontation. "The access logs clearly show that your codes were used to tamper with the replicator. Do you know what we found?"

"No, sir," the Choblik said in his flattish, synthetic voice.

A likely story. "We found it had been infested with *nanoprobes*. That it had been programmed to infuse those nanoprobes into the crew's food. Nanoprobes that were designed to latch on to their intestinal walls and remain there indefinitely, doing who knows what once they got there."

"I know what, sir."

Keru did a double take. "You do?"

"Oh, yes, sir. After all, I did design them."

A pause. "Then you admit that you did put them in the replicator."

"Of course, sir. It was the best delivery system for the test."

Test? All in due time. "So why did you just say you didn't know what we found?"

Torvig tilted his head querulously. "I didn't, sir. I knew what was there for you to find, so I hypothesized that they were probably what you found; but I didn't know for a fact that you had found them until you told me—nor did I know how you might have interpreted the discovery. I didn't want to jump to any conclusions, sir." His words didn't have the pedantic tone a Vulcan might have used; rather, he sounded more like an eager student reporting on his research methodology.

"All right, then," Keru went on. "What exactly was it that you were testing for?"

"Exactly, sir? Would you like me to retrieve my detailed notes from my quarters?"

Keru winced at the Choblik's literalism. "All right, approximately, then. What were you testing?"

"Gut feelings, sir."

"Gu—what?!"

"Last week Ensign Panyarachun suggested that I was too analytical in my approach to engineering problems, and told me that humans and other species tend to rely instead on their gut feelings. I didn't understand what relation the gut would have to cognitive decision-making, so I decided to investigate the question."

Keru blinked a number of times. "Um . . . Cadet . . . you do know that's only a figure of speech, don't you?"

"Well, yes, sir, but I was curious about its origins, and I wondered whether it might have a factual basis. The nanites were designed to monitor for neurochemical activity in the humanoid digestive tract."

It would've sounded like a ridiculous excuse to Keru if the cadet didn't already have a habit of formulating such cockamamie hypotheses and means of testing them. He was a devout empiricist, taking nothing for granted, giving fair consideration to any idea no matter how bizarre, and ruling nothing out until he'd tested it for himself. It would be an admirable trait in an explorer, if only he could focus it better. "But why *nanoprobes,* Cadet? Why break half a dozen regulations to deliver them in secret? Why not just, I don't know, ask for volunteers?"

"I figured that since I was investigating the cognitive process, it might contaminate the results if my subjects were aware of the investigation. For all I knew, sir, that could've been the reason why a correlation between intestinal activity and problem-solving had not been verified in earlier studies."

Keru glared at him. He just wasn't getting it. "Didn't it occur to you, Cadet, how people might *feel* about being contaminated with nanoprobes? After all the Borg have inflicted on us over the years, all the grief they've caused," he went on, his voice rising, "did you really think people would take that in stride? That they wouldn't feel outraged, violated, if these probes of yours had actually managed to get into their systems?"

"They would've done no harm, sir. They were made of biodegradable polymers and carbon—"

"That's not the point! This isn't about cold facts and analysis, it's about people's *feelings!* Can't you understand how much people still fear the Borg? How upsetting it would be for them to discover something like this had been done to them, especially by—"

He broke off. Torvig gazed at him for a long moment, then nodded to himself. "I see. By a cyborg like me. Thank you for confirming my secondary thesis, sir."

"What do you mean?"

"It's clear that you've been uncomfortable with me since I came on board, sir. I've found that such reactions are often due to prejudice arising from my species' coincidental similarity to the Borg. Many of us have faced that kind of prejudice, and we're curious to understand the mechanisms behind it. So intolerance is an area of study in which I have an ongoing interest." Keru was aware that Torvig had engaged in discussions and debates about humanoid chauvinism with other members of the crew, including a wager with Lieutenant Eviku that *Titan* would be given a human motto—a wager he'd lost when Riker had chosen the Vulcan creed of "Infinite diversity in infinite combinations" to grace the ship's dedication plaque. But Torvig's eager-student mien rarely wavered, so it was hard to tell whether it reflected a genuine fear of persecution or a simple intellectual curiosity. Keru found himself realizing that, in some odd Choblik way, it might be both. "Aside from their other advantages, the use of nanoprobes allowed me to test how you and/or the rest of the crew would react to their discovery—and therefore what factors shape your reaction to me. Sir." The cadet's voice, while slightly more subdued than before, hadn't wavered from its matter-of-fact tone.

But Keru paused before answering, trying to keep his own tone under control. "You mean you deliberately did this . . . in order to experiment on *me*? To gauge my reactions, my feelings about the Borg, like some amoeba in a test tube?"

"Well, I wouldn't put it that way, sir. For one thing the methodology for examining an amoeba would be completely different."

"Shut up! Just—just tell me *why*. Why experiment on me?"

Torvig looked up at him. "Because you are a crewmate of mine and I want to get to know you better, sir."

Keru's anger deflated, and embarrassment threatened to take its place. But luckily a modicum of irritation remained, though it was more tempered now. Stepping away from Torvig, he took a moment to formulate his words. "Look. I appreciate your interest in learning about your crewmates. But I don't appreciate being learned about by being experimented on, and I doubt anyone else around here does either. If you want to learn about us, there are better ways. Talk to us, socialize with us."

"Better in what sense, sir? I assume they're more comfortable for species like yours; but I'm more comfortable with a practical, empirical approach, with hard, codifiable data. It's what I'm good at."

"But not everything can be codified or empirically explained. Gut feelings, for example. Relationships, for another." *Or fears and resentments.*

"I disagree, sir. You can never conclusively say that something can't be explained—only that it hasn't been explained yet. Well, there is the Incompleteness Principle, of course, but that allows a system to be fully explained within a broader system."

Keru rubbed his temples; this was giving him a headache. "Look. The bottom line is, you broke regulations. You admit it, and you're unrepentant. There will have to be penalties, and there will be a mark on your record for this."

Torvig nodded. "Of course, sir. I anticipated that as a probable outcome. I'm curious to find out what form my discipline will take. There are so many interesting ways of going about it—I hope the captain or Commander Vale will choose one I haven't experienced yet."

Keru couldn't think of a single thing to say to that. "Look. Just . . . for now, you're confined to quarters until further notice. Dismissed."

"Yes, sir. Thank you, sir."

The Choblik turned and strode gracefully from the security office on his long runner's legs, his bionic joints working without a sound. His tail deftly shot forward to avoid the closing door behind him. Keru just stared at the closed door for a moment, then shook his head. *I guess I can't fault him for his enthusiasm, at least,* he thought. Still, he found himself giving a shudder of relief now that the cyborg was gone. He knew, of course, that the well-meaning young Choblik had nothing to do with the monsters who'd killed his beloved Sean.

But how could he convince his gut?

Dr. Huilan Sen'kara, assistant counselor on the *U.S.S. Titan,* reached up to signal at Crewman K'chak'!'op's door and waited. Then that door opened, the Pak'shree emerged, and Huilan still waited. K'chak'!'op—whom most people on the ship called "Chaka," more as a phonetic convenience than an endearment—looked around her and made a rising creak sound with her stridulating mouthparts, which her voder interpreted as "Hello?"

"Down here," Huilan said patiently.

K'chak'!'op moved back a bit, lowered her large round

head until the lower pair of her black cabochon eyes could see him, and then began waving the squidlike tentacles which extended from the sides of her head, six on each side. "Oh, Counselor Huilan, I'm sorry, I didn't see you!" Or so her voder interpreted her tentacular motions, plus the quick stridulation she added to represent his name. The Pak'shree used audible stridulations as their animal forebears had done, to convey things like names, greetings, emotional expression, danger calls and the like, and had later evolved the use of sign language for more sophisticated communication. Huilan's xenoethology studies had shown that many sentient species, including most humanoids, had gone through a similar phase in their evolution, only to shift to spoken language later on. He supposed the Pak'shree had retained their dual system owing to the limitations on stridulation as a form of speech, or simply owing to the sheer versatility of their tentacles.

But none of that was what he was here to discuss. Evolutionary behaviorism was his specialty, but he had come to counsel K'chak'!'op, not to study her. "That's quite all right," he said. "It happens all the time." It was indeed a common occurrence for a not-quite-meter-tall S'ti'ach on a ship full of giants.

"No, it was my fault entirely, you poor dear. Please, please, come in! Make yourself at home! Can I get you anything, sweetie?"

Huilan blinked his large black eyes, amused at being called "sweetie." The S'ti'ach weren't exactly known for their sweet disposition—at least, not by the prey animals of S'ti'ach'aas.

Still, he graciously followed K'chak'!'op into her quarters, noting how extensively she had personalized them. Indeed, with help from the deceased Chief Engineer Ledrah, she had essentially transformed them into a replica of the earthen architecture of her homeworld. The walls, floor, and ceiling were almost totally covered in replicated clay, wood, and stone, held together by a secretion of her own body, which the humans liked to call "silk" by analogy with their arachnids but which was really more of an organic cement. The only openings left were for the doors, wall console, and replicator, and there was no furniture save for a couple of low, wide mounds of earth. Yet the walls were intricately textured, a loving exercise in Pak'shree tactile art, although Huilan was not qualified to judge whether the patterns represented actual talent or mere enthusiasm. Still, it was a striking space to occupy. "Your quarters are lovely. It's no wonder you like to spend so much time here."

"Aha," she stridulated. "I expected that was why you came, Counselor. Everybody's so kind with their concerns about me, holed up here in my quarters all the time. But I'm fine here, really I am. Please, have a seat," she added, lowering her four-segmented, six-legged body onto one of the mounds, and brushing some padds off of it with some of her tentacles while she spoke with the rest. Pak'shree language was structured to allow them to "talk with their hands full."

Huilan just let his middle pair of limbs rest on the ground, assuming the centaurlike stance which was his equivalent of sitting, at least in this ship's low gravity. Actually K'chak'!'op's quarters maintained a higher gravity than the rest of the ship, but it was still a bit light for him. "Oh, I know you are. Everyone's been so concerned about you staying in here all the time, wondering if you're agoraphobic or xenophobic or something. Although of course they know you couldn't have gotten through Starfleet training that way, so they wonder if something's happened recently to traumatize you, and they're just ever so concerned," he said with a touch of mischief.

His dark-adapted eyes picked up the HUD images in her contact lenses, which were translating his speech into simulated tentacle motions. "Yes," she signed back, "it's so very sweet of them to worry. I hope you can reassure them, dear."

"Oh, I understand perfectly, Chaka. It's not about phobias or antisocial tendencies or anything like that." He ambled closer, looking up at her with his eyes wide, flattening out his dorsal spikes and wagging his short, wide tail, doing everything he could to maximize his blue-teddy-bear cuteness and put her at ease. "The simple fact is that it's just too *small* for you out there, isn't it?"

K'chak'!'op twisted her tentacles together, the equivalent of clamping her mouth shut. Huilan went on. "The doors are too narrow, the workspaces too cramped, the ceilings too low. And the turbolifts—"

"Ohh, don't talk to me about the turbolifts," she replied, though her voder rendered it in a light-hearted tone. "Don't misunderstand, dear, I'm not a claustrophobe; it's just so uncomfortable. I can't let myself stretch out, and there's so little room for my tentacles that I don't feel free to express myself. I have to keep my words all small and cramped, and there's no music in that! Besides, in such a tight space with endoskeletal people, I'm afraid to move around for fear I'll crush somebody."

"It's not easy for me either," Huilan commiserated. "You're the biggest one on the ship, I'm the smallest— except for little Totyarguil, of course." That was the baby of Olivia and Axel Bolaji. Born four months prematurely, he'd spent the past two months in an incubator in sickbay, and had been essentially adopted by the whole crew as they followed the tiny, helpless creature's development toward viability. It amazed Huilan that something human could be so small. "I'm constantly having to strain upward to reach things, get special chairs to sit on, even ask for help sometimes—which isn't easy for a S'ti'ach. On our world we're top of the food chain, undisputed. It's an ocean world, all islands. Resources and room are limited, so life stays small. It was quite a shock to the S'ti'ach ego to discover the galaxy populated by giants, let me tell you." The process had been eased somewhat, Huilan reflected, by the Federation's sensitivity in its choice of ambassadors. The first UFP representative to their world, Alexander, had been a humanoid no taller than a S'ti'ach, as well as a man of great wisdom and sensitivity. A member of an extraordinarily long-lived (and generally human-sized) race, he had been a Federation diplomat for over a century, since a Starfleet crew had rescued him from the persecution he'd faced on his own world, Platonius. He had been pivotal in convincing the S'ti'ach that they could participate in the Federation as equals.

"Ohh, you poor dear," K'chak'!'op signed, with a commiserating crackle of her mouthparts. "I hadn't thought that it could be hard for you too."

"But what I don't understand," Huilan went on, "is why you wouldn't just tell anyone. Why have you dodged the issue every time it's been raised?"

Her tendrils twirled, but no translation came; it must have simply been a nervous gesture. "Well," she finally said, "it's just that . . . well, Captain Riker and Dr. Ra-Havreii, they're both so proud of this ship of theirs, and I just . . . I didn't want to hurt their feelings. Especially that charming young Dr. Ra-Havreii—he did design the ship, and it was very clever of him, and I don't want him to be disappointed."

Huilan suppressed a snicker. "Now, Chaka. You know perfectly well that humanoid males are fully grown adults. They don't expect to be coddled, and they don't need to be."

"Yes, I know that. And I know they're my superior officers, I respect the chain of command and all that. But males just bring out the mother in me. Especially males who actually act, well, responsible and adult! It's just so charming to see a male with something on his mind other than sex."

You don't know humanoids very well, do you? Huilan joked to himself. *Particularly Ra-Havreii.* But she had a point; since Pak'shree were only male for the decade or so between their immature neuter stage and their mature female stage, that was their only window to mate and ensure procreation, so they essentially spent their entire male stage fixated on mating. "I'm a male too, you know."

"Ohh, yes, and you're completely adorable. I hope you don't think that's rude of me, Captain Riker didn't seem too amused when I called him adorable, but you're just so irresistibly cute I can't help myself."

"Cute I may be, but I'm ruthless when I need to be. I won't keep your little secret, because the captain deserves to know why you don't like to leave your quarters. He's a big boy, and so is Dr. Ra-Havreii, and they can handle it. The question is, what can *you* handle?"

"I can go out when I need to, really. I just don't *like* to. I'm tired of bumping my head on doorframes. This ship just isn't *comfortable.* You understand that, right, dear? As you said, it isn't comfortable for you either."

Huilan pondered. "No, I suppose you have a point. A ship like this—it isn't really comfortable for anyone, is it? Everything's a compromise. Everything's designed to be a reasonable average. The temperature, the humidity, the gravity, the diurnal cycle, all calibrated to strike a balance between different species' needs. Those of us with really different needs—Zaranites, Selkies, Elaysians—must wear special, uncomfortable suits during the day and know that our guests will never be fully comfortable in our own quarters. But there's a human saying about compromise— it's a solution that makes everyone equally unhappy. The conditions of this ship aren't really ideal for any one species, and so nobody's really comfortable. It's an awkward way to live. It has been whenever it's been tried in the past. Indeed, there are some who say that's one reason why mixed-crew starships like this haven't generally succeeded in the past—that it's just too much trouble for species with such different needs to try to coexist in a single, closed environment. They say it's just too much to ask."

"Well, that doesn't make a lot of sense," K'chak'!'op said. "I mean, we're space explorers, aren't we? We seek out alien environments, often visit worlds much harsher than this."

"True, true. But the claim is that when we come back to our home ships, the places where we spend most of our time, we want them to be comfortable and familiar."

"Maybe so, but that's no reason to abandon the whole concept! If people think that way, how far are they from deciding that it's not worth listening to ideas they aren't comfortable with? That way of thinking, it's so shallow, it's immature, it's—"

"Male?"

K'chak'!'op gave off the equivalent of a laugh. "Sweetheart, our males can't be bothered to think about such questions at all. But it's not the way a responsible adult should think."

"I agree."

"Good for you, dear."

"So why are you still in this room?"

There was a long pause. "Ohh, you're very good! That was very smart the way you led me to that, sweetie. You deserve a pastry for that, would you like me to get you one?"

Huilan cackled. "Only if you obtain it from the mess hall."

She stridulated a laugh of her own. "Ohh, all right. Come along." She led him out into the corridor. "At least the lift won't be too crowded if it's just you and me. Still, I wish there were a more comfortable way to get there. You know what this ship should've been designed with? Ramps between decks. Maybe if they'd built the corridors in a continuous spiral, connecting each level to the next. . . ."

"Oh, yes, I'd like that," Huilan replied. "Then I could ride a scooter to where I needed to be, save myself a lot of walking. Maybe we could propose it for the ship's next refit."

"What a good idea! Yes, we really should. Let's see, what else could we propose? How about replacing the seats with holographic projections that could be reshaped for each user?"

"Why not make the whole bridge a holodeck, adjustable for any use?"

"Oh, that's good! And how about this. . . ."

Chapter Five

It was four days before *Titan* made another cosmozoan sighting, though what they found was not a star-jelly. Rather, it was a Black Cloud—a living dark nebula of the type theorized in the twentieth-century fiction of Earth astronomer Fred Hoyle. "We detect radio emissions and shaped magnetic fields throughout the Cloud," Jaza reported in a briefing, "linking thousands of point sources into a network. These are probably clumps of particulate matter, small asteroids and planetesimals, with organic molecules laid down in complex chains. Collectively they make up its brain."

"Is it intelligent?" Vale asked.

Jaza shook his head. "The neural activity is too simple. Little more than stimulus-response and motor control. The magnetic fields shape its interior structure, giving it a gaseous anatomy of sorts for transporting nutrients and waste through its 'body.' They can change its shape, too. In fact, we discovered it that way, by comparing our subspace sensor scans of its current shape with the visible-light image through an optical telescope, showing how it looked over a decade ago." He displayed the images side by side on the obs lounge monitor. "See how it's taken on a spindle shape, oriented radially outward from that proto-star nearby? At first we thought it was just a conventional cometary globule until we saw how quickly it's changed shape—and I should add that for a living nebula drifting through interstellar space without warp drive, a dozen years or so is very quick. It's actually reshaped itself to present the smallest possible profile to the protostar, to minimize erosion from its T Tauri winds."

Riker smiled at Jaza's enthusiasm, but said, "That's all very interesting, Commander, but does it help us find any star-jellies?"

"No, I suppose not. But it does suggest we're on the right track. The closer we get to the Vela Association, the more species we'll probably see."

Indeed, it was only another day before their next find. At first it seemed like they might have found a star-jelly, since the sensors detected similar compounds in the crea-ture's hide. But as *Titan* grew closer and refined its scans, the creature turned out to be a spheroid mass only a few hundred meters in diameter, seemingly inert, although sensors detected faint biological activity inside it. Jaza concluded it was hibernating for its interstellar journey, and backtracked it to a nearby blue star. On approaching that star system, Jaza's people discovered numerous other creatures of the same species occupying the cometary disk around it. By observing numerous individuals in different phases, they were able to reconstruct their life cycle fairly quickly. "When they drift into a system," Jaza explained, demonstrating with sensor images and computer anima-tion on the obs lounge monitor, "they open up and deploy vast solar sails to collect energy. They also use the light pressure to maneuver through the system. They latch onto the cometary chunks and mine them for CHON."

Riker had read enough science officers' logs to recognize the shorthand for carbon, hydrogen, oxygen, and nitrogen, the essential building blocks of carbon-based life. "In simpler terms, they feed on them."

"Yes, but more like a plant drawing nutrients from the soil, with the solar sails analogous to photosynthetic leaves. They use the CHON and the solar energy to reproduce themselves. Once the offspring are grown, they break off and deploy their solar sails, using them to accelerate out of the system, as well as to save up energy for the long journey ahead. Like Bajoran sailseeds spilling out into the wind. They seem to point themselves toward the brightest stars in the sky—which makes sense, since those are either the nearest or the most energetic."

"Why would they evolve that way?" Vale wondered. "Why not just stay in one star system, where they know there's enough energy and matter to live on?"

"Well, they don't seem to be anywhere near intelligent—"

"Pardon my anthropomorphizing," Vale said.

"But I'd assume it's because in a turbulent region like this, a given star system could be struck by disaster at any time. Cosmozoans that evolved interstellar migratory behavior would thus have a survival edge."

"What about the star-jelly-like compounds in their shells?" Riker asked. "Are there any other signs that the species are related?"

"Hard to say for sure. I'd say they're related in the sense of being part of the overall ecosystem of the Orion Arm. So it stands to reason they'd be made of similar stuff. Also as spacegoing creatures that procreate in star systems, they may have evolved similar shell chemistry for similar needs. I don't yet have enough information to say if they're directly related."

"All right, then, how about this: if the 'sailseeds' contain compounds the star-jellies need, is it possible the jellies might feed on them? If we follow them, could they lead us to the jellies?"

Jaza mulled it over. "Cosmozoans generally live very far apart, at least this far out from the core star-formation region. It would be fairly unusual for one to come across another, for the same reason that Starfleet encounters with them have been fairly infrequent. So I doubt we'd see them feeding on one another very much, at least not until we get closer—assuming I'm right that there's a fuller ecosystem at Vela.

"Since they can travel at warp, star-jellies would be better off just hopping to the nearest inhabited planet to find biomass—and given their replication abilities, they could convert CHON from comets directly just as the sailseeds do." He pondered. "Still . . . species with similar needs might seek out similar conditions. So tracking sailseeds might help us find our way deeper into the biosphere, which would increase our chances."

Vale sighed. "Maybe instead we should find some Pa'haquel and ask how *they* track the jellies down."

"Somehow," Riker said, "I don't think they'd tell us."

"Probably," Jaza suggested, "they're more familiar with the jellies' habits and migration patterns. Or maybe they can scan for some kind of 'spoor' we don't know how to recognize."

"Or maybe they can tap into some sensory ability of the jellies they kill and inhabit."

Jaza pondered the captain's suggestion. "Perhaps. Some kind of empathic center in the brain, possibly."

Riker looked at him sharply. "So to find an empath . . ."

"Maybe it takes an empath."

Deanna was very quiet for a while after he made the suggestion. "I was hoping it wouldn't come to that," she finally said.

Riker sat next to her on the couch, close but not too close, trying to remind himself that he was speaking as her captain, not her husband. That was why he'd come to her in her office. "You must have known that we'd need your empathy when the time came. Your own reports said that emotion seemed to be their primary form of communication."

"I know, Will . . . I've just been hoping to avoid it."

He paused, choosing his words. "You told me, back on the *Enterprise,* that contact with the jellies was a beautiful experience. Exhilarating, you called it."

"When they were happy, yes. But even then it was overpowering. And I was a different person then." She looked inward. "You can't know what it's like . . . having another being's emotions forced into you like that. Even though it's not intentional or malicious, it's still . . . like being inundated, swept away in a flood. Being totally helpless to control or resist it . . ."

To hell with protocol, Will thought, and took her in his arms. *"Imzadi,"* he said, and then nothing more for a moment. Then he pulled back and met her eyes. "Deanna . . . your ability to, to connect with others . . . to share in their feelings, accept them inside yourself and help others understand them . . . it's your gift. You've used it to heal minds, to build bridges, to prevent wars and save lives. It's your strength, Deanna. Your strength has always come from letting others in, not blocking them out." He stroked her cheek. "Don't let Shinzon take that away from you."

She gazed at him for a long moment, a smile gradually growing. "You're not so bad a healer yourself, you know."

"Just something that rubbed off from my wife."

"Hey, no rubbing during work hours."

"Ahh . . . there's the rub."

After Will left, Deanna darkened the room, meditated for a few minutes to center herself, and then opened her mind. Her awareness expanded, letting in the emotional voices/flavors/colors of the rest of the crew (all except Dr. Bralik, of course, since she couldn't read Ferengi). She took a moment to acknowledge them, acclimate to them, and filter them out of her perceptions. Along the way, she noted a faint twinge of awareness that she had sensed growing stronger over the past weeks—little Totyarguil down in sickbay. Such a pure little voice, all feeling, no thought, no taint of damage from the world yet, the empathic equivalent of untrodden snow—save for the vaguely registered trauma of his mother's accident, the premature labor, the transporter surgery. But the turmoil had been brief and quickly eased by the comforting conditions of his artificial womb, and his still-forming mind had all but forgotten it. Now there was only a vague sense of incongruity about his existence, but one within the bounds of comfort: *This is not my home. This is different. But it will do.*

Deanna latched on to that pure tone as a model, willed her own mental state to the same smoothness, the same blankness open to input from the world. White snow, white paper, white light, racing outward unencumbered by mass or time, her awareness spreading through space, pervading it, a cosmic background immanence. *Here I am,* she declared by being—white snow, paper, light, awaiting footprints, writing, silhouettes. Diaphanous silhouettes, dancing shadow puppets trailing wispy, waving tendrils— *here I am, awaiting you.*

But nothing came. Time was subjective in this state, but the *duration* of the silence became palpably greater. Deanna looked at herself from without, asking herself if her timidity, her fear of losing control was holding her back. She searched her mind for self-sabotaging doubts and fears, did her best to smooth them out and leave only pure white. But still nothing came, and at length, on opening her eyes and existing within her skull once again, she had to conclude that the problem was perhaps not with her mind, but with her brain. Although the star-jellies were powerful transmitters, perhaps her Betazoid-sized brain was too small and weak a receiver at this range, and too weak a transmitter to catch their attention. She needed amplification.

Which brought her to Orilly Malar. "Thank you for seeing me, Cadet," she said when the Irriol arrived in response to her page. She shook Orilly's trunk in greeting and invited her in. "Please, sit," she said, offering her a low floor cushion. The quadrupedal cadet thanked her and settled down on her haunches, then blinked her big black eyes inquisitively at the counselor. Deanna took a moment to drink in the Irriol's features, her rounded head and golden pangolin scales, and found herself with a sudden craving for pineapples.

Deanna explained her problem, then said to the cadet, "I think that your people's gestalt abilities could be helpful here. You could join me and the ship's other psi-sensitives into a larger network of sorts, like an array of telescopes, and together we'd be more sensitive than I can be alone. Perhaps we could be strong enough to send a signal that would get the star-jellies' attention and bring them to us."

Orilly fidgeted, twisting her trunks together. "What you ask . . . it would be better if you had another Irriol. I am . . . not someone you should trust with a gestalt."

"I know you're an exile, a criminal by your people's laws. But your service to Starfleet has been exemplary. I know you can be trusted." She knew, indeed, that even the most malicious Irriol criminal could be trusted to serve Irriol interests offworld in order to earn points toward freedom from exile, since the desire to return home was an instinctive need, overriding all other concerns. But there was nothing in Orilly's psych profile to indicate any malicious drives, and the nature of her crime was still unclear to Deanna.

"Not with this, I cannot," Orilly said. "Failure of gestalt . . . it is at the heart of my crime."

"Can you try to explain to me what your crime was?"

"It is not easy. Perhaps as an empath, though, you can understand better. I will try."

Orilly explained as best she could, with both words and empathic impressions. She strove to convey to Deanna what life was like on Lru-Irr. It was not only the Irriol themselves who shared the empathic gestalt; it was *all* the life of their world, everything sophisticated enough to have a nervous system—and, many Irriol believed, even the simplest plants and microbes, even the planet itself. All the life-forms of Lru-Irr sensed each other, knew each other, cooperated in an intricate, symbiotic dance of life and death, predation and submission, dependence and giving. The Irriol had never considered themselves above nature, but a part of it, the mind within Lru-Irr's body, giving awareness to the whole and tending its needs. It was the embodiment of the old Gaia principle, Deanna recognized, a biosphere as a cooperating whole, almost a single organism. Animals didn't quite fling themselves into their predators' jaws, but the sick and elderly of a pack would often choose not to flee, sacrificing themselves for their fellows and also serving to feed their predators. Yet this happened less often when the predators were fuller and stronger. The needs of the whole and the interests of the one were given equal consideration—although that made it sound more conscious than it was. The creatures of Lru-Irr simply *felt* what was called for, felt how the patterns of the gestalt combined and affected the moment, and reacted as much in response to that as to their own individual drives—which were, after all, only part of the Whole.

The catch was intelligence. Sapient beings had more power of choice, a more complex range of responses than creatures of instinct. Irriol felt the gestalt as much as any animal, and it influenced their choices even when they did not know why; but sometimes choices were made in defiance of gestalt, and the balance was disrupted.

Orilly told Deanna of a day when she and her little sister were on a trip to the islands, and fell in a ravine while out exploring. She sprained a trunk, while her sister broke a leg and several ribs. A *voliro,* a local predator, came near, and she *felt* its need, its place in the gestalt. She filled in what she could for Deanna, contextualizing her instinctive awareness with specific knowledge she'd gained after the fact. The island's ecosystem had been damaged by shifts in the climate which brought heavy storms and unwonted cold. The *voliro* was one of the last of its kind on the island. It was pregnant, but half-starved; one meal would make the difference between its litter's life and death. If the litter died, there would not be enough of the animals left to limit the population of a small rodentlike creature. Out of control, the rodents would consume the roots of the local flora, killing them. Other species in the gestalt would normally feel the imbalance and react to restore it; but it was isolated, out of reach of other predators. The Irriol would do what they could, but only so many resources could be spared. If the *voliro*'s litter died, the region's ecology would be damaged. Many creatures of multiple species would die. The local Irriol village, a community of hundreds, would also have to relocate in time.

Orilly had not known these specifics at the time, but she had felt the gist of it in her bones, and known that at that moment, the predator's rights were weighted more heavily in the gestalt than her own or her sister's. Her sister felt it too, and gave up trying to stand on her broken leg, simply laying there for the predator to take. "But I didn't want her to die," Orilly said. "I didn't want to die either. So I . . . I threw rocks at the *voliro* until it ran. And I put my sister on my back and carried her to safety."

At home, she went on, her family was disturbed, sensing that she'd violated gestalt. "Did they punish you?" Deanna asked.

Orilly seemed bewildered by the question. "The gestalt is punishment enough. I felt the wound I caused, felt it grow and spread. The mother's babies died unborn. Within months, the rodents had overrun the area, the plants were dying. So many were starving." She shuddered. "But my crime was worse than I knew. With the plants gone, the roots were gone, and when the next storm season came . . . there was a mudslide. The village was buried. Hundreds died." She gazed up plaintively at Deanna. "I am a mass murderer, Counselor. The pain of it . . . feeling the gaping wound I tore in the Whole . . . in some ways, exiling me for my crime was almost an act of mercy."

Deanna chose her words carefully. "I won't presume to judge your people's ways. But you did what you did out of love, to save your sister. And you couldn't have known, even with the gestalt, that the indirect consequences would be so great. If anyone could have predicted the mudslide, it would have been prevented, or the village evacuated."

"It does not matter. I knew that depriving the *voliro* and her babies would cost many lives—Irriol lives or others, it makes little difference. I heard the gestalt and I chose to ignore it . . . and others paid the price." She lowered herself to all fours, resting her head sadly on her forepaws, and wrapping her trunks around them. "My sister was ready to give herself. She understood what I could not. And she did not forgive me for making her the reason for my crime."

It was a while before Deanna spoke. "I had an older sister once. Her name was Kestra. And she died before I was old enough to remember her. I would give anything if she could be alive today, even if she hated me." She slid out of her chair and to her knees, to meet Orilly on her own level. "Malar . . . you had a difficult choice to make. Either choice would have been just as painful, for you and for others. But either choice would have saved lives as well as cost them. The choice you made was made out of love, and the desire to help another being."

"No. I was selfish. I could have given myself to the *voliro*."

"Then who would have carried your sister to safety? You made the right decision for *your* gestalt—the smaller one that was your family. So I know I can trust you with this small gestalt I'm asking you to help me form."

She leaned forward, made sure to catch Orilly's eyes. "I won't tell you your sense of guilt isn't valid. In fact, I think it's extraordinary that your people can care so deeply for your world, feel such a profound bond to its life. If anything, Malar, the guilt you feel is a testament to the strength of your empathy. And that strength is what I need.

"So will you help me?"

Orilly tilted her head and spoke slowly. "You could order me."

"I need you to choose this. To open yourself willingly. That's the only way it'll work."

The cadet drew in a long, shuddering breath and sighed. "Very well. I will try."

Aili Lavena fidgeted within her hydration suit as she headed back to her quarters after a long shift at the helm. The Selkie appreciated the garment for allowing her to function in Starfleet, to interact with air-breathers in a way she no longer could on her own, now that she'd outgrown her amphibious phase. But being enclosed in it for hours at a time could grow uncomfortable. She didn't like the way her twin gill-crests, which started atop her smooth head and continued down her back, had to stay sandwiched within the stiff fins on the suit's back, confined within the porous layers that kept oxygenated water circulating across their surfaces. Every day at end of shift, she was eager to get back to her water-filled quarters, strip fully nude and luxuriate in the freedom of it. It was often even nicer when she had someone to join her in luxuriating, but today she was just as happy to have some solitude. Arranging sex with an air-breathing partner could get complicated and strenuous. Aili *liked* complicated and strenuous sex, but right now she was feeling too lazy.

As she neared her quarters, she saw Dr. Bralik, the Ferengi geologist, approaching from the other direction. She waved absently to the small-eared female, intending to leave it at that, but Bralik seemed to have other ideas. "Ensign Lavena!" she crowed in her loud, nasal voice, whose grating qualities were only slightly muffled by the air-water interface between it and Aili's dainty seal-like ears. "You know, I've been hoping to have a talk with you."

Lavena stopped, accepting that comfort would have to wait. "Hello, Dr. Bralik. What can I help you with?"

"Oh, just a matter of curiosity, if you can spare a few minutes."

"I'm glad to help, if I can."

"Good, good. Now, let me see, if I've got this straight, you Selkies, you can't breathe out of the water, right? I mean, of course, you've got that suit on and all, but is it just a convenience or do you need it all the time?"

It was a question she'd gotten many times, and she didn't mind satisfying the Ferengi's curiosity about her species. "In this phase of my life, I'm fully aquatic," she said. "In the first phase of our lives, we're amphibious, able to breathe on land at least part of the time, though we need to stay near water so our gills don't dry out. Later in life, after childbearing, our lungs can no longer sustain us, so we live in the water full-time."

"But you still have lungs, right? I mean, you're talking to me."

Aili smiled. "My lung is smaller than it was, and has changed in structure. It serves as a flotation sac, nothing more. And my voice is produced by muscle vibration, not airflow."

"Hm. I'm no biologist, but that seems kind of an odd evolutionary twist."

"We don't have much land on Pacifica," Aili explained. "We go out to the sea so we don't use up resources our young need to grow. As humanoids we need to develop at least partly on land."

"Okay. I'll take your word for that. Still there's one thing, though, one other matter I'm wondering about."

"Yes?"

"So if you can't breathe air even for a little while . . . how exactly did you *frinx* with Dr. Ra-Havreii last week?"

Aili gaped at her, speechless. Bralik shrugged and added, "That is, unless Efrosians can breathe water. I asked Ravvy about that at lunch the other day, but he didn't want to go into detail."

"He . . . he *told* you?" The bastard had insisted he'd be discreet!

"Oh, I'm sorry, are you, did I upset you? Didn't mean to, honey, really. I mean, I thought Selkies were pretty liberal about such things. Judging from the gossip I've heard from Ferengi males, though you can't always believe that."

"No, it's . . . I'm certainly not a prude," Aili insisted forcefully. Being thought of as a prude was perhaps the one thing more embarrassing to an aquatic Selkie than . . . well, the other thing her people thought of her. "It's just . . . other species, you know, and their standards . . . I'd just really rather appreciate it if you didn't talk about my liaisons to others. And I'm going to have a talk with Dr. Ra-Havreii about that, too."

"Oh, don't worry, Ravvy didn't tell me."

"He didn't? Then, how—"

Bralik tapped one of her ears. "I may not hear as well as a male, but my quarters are nearby. I overheard Ravvy talking to Counselor Troi when he left your quarters."

Oh, Abyss! "Troi?" Aili gasped. "You mean—she saw him leaving . . . she knows about . . . oh, no." She was almost tempted to rip her suit open right here and drown herself in the air.

"Say, what's the problem? No reason she'd be jealous. It's not like Ravvy was *frinxing* her too—though not for want of trying, I can tell you."

"Look, just—please, don't tell anyone else, okay?" Without waiting for an answer, Aili moved on and hastened to her quarters. Now more than ever, she needed to be alone.

"Just to be clear," Deanna explained in the next morning's briefing, "the gestalt is not like a mind-meld. The ship's telepaths and empaths will be linked together, but only to share psionic sensitivity and power, not thoughts or knowledge. We will be . . . *aware* of each other's presence, affected by each other's responses and needs, but on a visceral level, not a cognitive one." Riker was glad to hear that. He didn't want every telepath on the ship to share in Deanna's memories of last night, or any given night.

"It will be necessary for Dr. Ree to neutralize the telepathic suppressants he administered before," Deanna added. "We may need every psi-sensitive mind the ship has. The larger the gestalt, the better."

Tuvok seemed uneasy. "What you propose will be difficult for . . . the Vulcans on board. Once we make contact, the influx of intense emotion will prove difficult to endure." Riker didn't need to be a telepath to know Tuvok was concerned on a personal level, not just a tactical one. Most Vulcans weren't nearly as good at hiding their feelings as they liked to think—a discrepancy which had served Riker well in many a poker game.

"Your role in the gestalt," Deanna explained, "and that of the others, will be mostly passive. You'll essentially serve as psionic amplifiers for Cadet Orilly and myself, allowing us to broadcast more strongly. Hopefully once we have the star-jellies' attention and can open communications, the gestalt won't be necessary any longer—they'll be able to read my thoughts and send theirs back to me."

"Hopefully," Tuvok repeated.

"Even if not, Orilly and I will bear the brunt of their communication. That may shield the rest of you from the full effects."

"But again you cannot say so with certainty."

"Mr. Tuvok," Riker asked with a touch of steel, "will you be able to perform this duty or not?"

The Vulcan met his gaze evenly, though he was very closed off. "Yes, sir, I will."

"Good. Counselor, proceed."

Deanna chose to assemble the group in stellar cartography, adrift in free fall, in order to help them find the right state of mind to communicate with beings who lived most of their lives that way. She knew it was an uncomfortable environment for Orilly, but it was important for the Irriol to accept it, to open herself to it, if this was to work. The cadet understood that and was making a brave effort, though her legs and trunks were still flailing some and she kept putting herself into a slight spin. Fortunately, Lieutenant Chamish was nearby and used his low-level telekinesis to halt it. The simian-featured Kazarite was an ecologist, his telepathy limited to communion with animals, since higher cognitive functions interfered with it somehow. Deanna was hoping that wouldn't reduce his usefulness here, since he was serving mainly as a conduit. Then again, the jellies' emotions had affected him before, even though they were sentient beings. That anomaly might be worth exploring later on, but for now it was simply convenient. At least he was comfortable with floating; the Kazarites could use their TK abilities to levitate for short distances, a useful skill in their mountainous homeland.

The others here were all Vulcan—Tuvok, T'Pel, Savalek—except for Ree. He was here mainly to monitor the others' health, but Deanna was hoping that, although he lacked the active empathy of some Pahkwa-thanh, he might have some latent sensitivity that could contribute to the gestalt.

Deanna realized that she hadn't yet had much chance to get acquainted with Tuvok's wife T'Pel, even though she'd been aboard for weeks now. She was a civilian with no scientific credentials, and thus had no formal shipboard duties requiring interaction with others. She had kept largely to herself so far, and Tuvok had shown no interest in discussing his personal life with his crewmates. When T'Pel had arrived in cartography, Deanna had apologized for imposing on her. T'Pel had simply stated that Tuvok had briefed her on what was expected and she was ready to serve. Deanna sensed a tentativeness in both her and Tuvok, and perhaps between them as well, but maybe it was just their unease at the situation.

Ree handled himself unexpectedly well in free fall, using his heavy tail to maneuver about his center of mass gracefully, almost like a cat. He scanned each person present with his medical tricorder, and bringing himself to a halt facing Deanna, reported, "The psi-suppressant has been fully purged from all your systems. All your psi indices read nominal. Sadly, mine is also at its normal, immeasurably small level."

"Then we're ready," Deanna said, and turned her head to Orilly. Reaching out to take the cadet's trunk-hand, she caught her gaze and said, "It's time, Malar."

Ree tilted his head at them. "Should we all join hands?"

Orilly looked puzzled. "Why?"

"Oh. Never mind, then."

"Just try to relax and clear your mind," Deanna told him. "Like meditation."

Ree sighed. "I knew I should have eaten first. Anyone willing to volunteer a limb?"

Orilly winced. "Please, Doctor," Deanna said. "Not all of us find your sense of humor relaxing."

"Sorry."

After that, things grew quiet. With a little physical and empathic handholding from Deanna, Orilly was able to calm herself and begin reaching out with her mind. At first, there seemed to be no effect. But gradually Deanna recognized a change in her awareness. There were no other thoughts impinging on her mind, no subsuming of her identity; but she seemed to feel her own mind *expanding* in scope and perspective. It was like she was opening up, freeing herself from constraints she hadn't even been aware of, as though the full range of her senses before had only been tunnel vision. The rest of the universe seemed *closer* than it had before, clearer to discern.

She reached out her senses, listening for familiar voices, sending out a probe: *We are here. Speak to us.* It seemed to echo now, her mental voice/presence; it was stronger, more resonant than before. She knew it would carry farther.

And indeed, before long there was a return echo, a faint impression on the edge of awareness: acknowledgment, curiosity. *We are also here; where are you?* Or so it would be if it were in words, rather than emotions and impressions.

Here. Deanna opened her eyes, taking in stellar cartography's display of the heavens around the ship. Six others were with her, but she saw only the cosmos. Stars—*founts of lifewarmth*—watering holes. Dust clouds—*ticklish softness, nourishment*—grazing fields. Emission nebulae—*invigorating, soothing*—cool breeze. Stellar nurseries—*turbulent lifewarmth [too much/careful you don't get burned/whee, let's do it again!]*—swimming the rapids.

Yet there was more than she could see, and now she saw it. Fields of energy: gamma, radio, tetryon, psi *[how's the weather?/let's ask it!]*. Contours of *[starpull]* gravity, hills and vales in spacetime. All of it a veneer atop the fathomless depths of subspace *[we dive, but not too deep!/mustn't lose our way]*.

They saw what she saw, and she felt attention focus upon her, engulfing her—gentle curiosity, but that of a child's hand cupping a ladybug, not threatening but still overpowering. *We greet you, but you are not-us [wary/caution/curious]. How do you know us?*

We have met your kind before, Deanna sent back, *a long way from here in space and time.* She looked around, found Deneb in the sky and focused her attention on it. *There,* she thought, and gave them her memories of Farpoint.

Yes—our cousins sang of you! Listener and Liberator [great joy/gratitude]. Not so far from here, though.

We wish to get to know you, be your friends, she projected. She hesitated to send the next thought, since it might commit her a bit too much; but this was a bond of emotion, and it just felt right. *We believe we can help you with a problem.*

CHAPTER SIX

Christine Vale had been staring at Jaza Najem for over a minute now, while he stared in turn at his console. The Bajoran was so enthralled in his studies that he didn't even realize she was studying him—his warm coffee-colored skin, his wide dark eyes, his high, intelligent forehead, his expressive lips, the way the ridges between his eyebrows gave him a perpetually thoughtful look.

Knock it off, she thought. Yes, he was handsome. Yes, he was intelligent and thoughtful, and an extremely generous lover . . . *Stop that.* That was something that needed to remain in the past, and not affect her job. She was the first officer, he was the science officer, and that was all there was to it. So if she wanted to go up to him and ask for an update on his researches, she should just do so. As simple as that.

Sure.

So she just stood there and kept staring.

"You don't have to feel guilty, you know."

Jaza didn't even look up from his console, so it took Vale a second to realize he was addressing her. "What?" she asked, coming close enough that they could talk in private.

Now he did look up, and smiled. "I told you I understood, and I meant it. I don't begrudge you going back on an impulsive promise made in the heat of passion. I'm a scientist, remember—which means not only that I place a premium on rational thought, but that I understand the value of admitting one's mistakes. So it's not a problem."

"Well . . . good. Of course. Didn't need to be said." He smiled and nodded. After a second, she sidled closer. "Not that I think it was a mistake to . . . do it at all. Just . . ."

"Right. To follow up on it."

"And it's not like I don't *want* to, you understand. Not that I wouldn't like to."

"I get it."

"It just wouldn't really . . ."

"Work, right. And I respect that."

"Good." She cleared her throat. "So . . . you seemed pretty enthralled by those energy-beings just now." A short time ago, while Counselor Troi and the others had been starting their seance or whatever it was in stellar cartography, Jaza had detected yet another new cosmozoan species in a small HII region half a light-year away. The bright magenta cloud of excited hydrogen was inhabited by thousands of discrete plasma-energy matrices which demonstrated lifelike behavior. They fed off the hydrogen-band energy emissions in the cloud, competing for the best feeding locations, on the side facing the young A-type giant star whose radiation fuelled the emissions, but not so close to the surface of the cloud as to be disrupted by that radiation. "Are they showing any signs of intelligence?"

"No, not a trace. But I've discovered a secondary feeding behavior. They can disrupt the molecular bonds in carbonaceous asteroids, absorbing the released binding energy."

"Oh. That's . . . very interesting."

Jaza smiled. "I suppose it doesn't sound that way. It's just that . . . well, it's somewhat unusual in the annals of Starfleet to come across energy beings that can be studied at leisure rather than trying to kill you, take over your body or subject *you* to testing."

They shared a laugh, which was bigger than the comment deserved but then trailed off into an uneasy silence. After a moment, Vale found herself speaking in spite of herself. "So . . . do *you* want to? I mean . . . would you, if it weren't . . ."

He smiled at her, knowing she wasn't talking about studying incorporeal beings. "Of course I would. But . . . most of all, I don't want you to feel we can't be friends."

That made her blush more than the rest of the conversation had. He deserved better than the silent treatment. But just as she opened her mouth to speak, Jaza's console began beeping. "What is it?"

He studied the data. "A school of armored star-jellies has just come out of warp next to the HII region." After another moment, his eyes widened. "They're firing on the creatures."

Vale tapped her combadge. "Captain Riker, to the bridge, please."

A moment later, Riker emerged from his ready room. "Report."

"A group of armored star-jellies has engaged the energy beings in the nebula, sir."

"On screen," Riker ordered. Jaza hit the transfer controls to uplink his console readouts to the main viewer.

The bridge crew watched for a moment as the distant saucers flew into the hydrogen cloud, lighting it up with their plasma stings, whose color almost matched its own. The energy beings, localized shimmers of light within the depths of the cloud, grew more frenetic in their movements. Soon there were brighter discharges of light within the cloud, vast searing arcs that struck the saucers.

"The energy beings are harnessing the cloud's electrostatic potential as a defense," Jaza said. "The potential energy contained in a nebula is immense—it makes for a devastating weapon. The attackers are taking significant damage despite their armor. One of them is spinning away out of control, leaking air and fluids . . . it's done for."

"Are they Pa'haquel or live jellies?" Riker wanted to know.

"Hard to get bioreadings at this range," Jaza said. "But looking at the subspace emission spectra from their warp emergence . . . yes, there's a subtle difference in their warp signatures. It wouldn't be detectable with standard sensors, but yes, these are Pa'haquel ships."

Ensign Kuu'iut spoke from tactical, his voder interpreting his chirping speech. "Judging by their number, sizes, and surface details," the Betelgeusian said, "it's the same pack that we encountered before. Including their recent kills."

"Did they follow us?" Riker asked.

"Their warp emergence vectors suggest they came from 308 mark 41, sir."

"More or less ahead of us," Vale interpreted.

Kuu'iut's hairless blue head nodded. "Yes, ma'am."

"More than likely," Jaza said, "they just thought the same way we did—the closer to Vela, the more cosmozoans they're likely to find."

"But why attack the energy beings?" Vale wondered aloud. "What possible use could they have for them?"

"Hard to say," Jaza said. "The beings they kill lose cohesion—their energy dissipates into the cloud. Maybe they intend to use the energy as a fuel source. Live jellies feed on energy, after all. But I see no sign that they're absorbing the dissipated energy. Maybe that comes later."

"Or maybe they just do it for sport," Riker said coldly.

"Either way, they're winning," said Kuu'iut. His feeding mouth snarled in excitement as he spoke through his beaklike upper mouth. "They've disrupted hundreds of the creatures and they aren't slowing down. I don't think they intend to leave any of them alive."

Riker stared at the screen for a moment. "Could that be why we haven't found this kind of spacegoing ecosystem in other star-formation zones?" he said heavily. "Because somebody hunted the life there to extinction?"

Just then the turbolift doors slid open and Counselor Troi emerged, followed by Tuvok and Ree. Vale saw Troi stare at the viewscreen for a moment and then meet Riker's eyes. It seemed to Vale as though there was more passing between them than a significant look. "How far are they?" Troi asked at last, seeming to confirm that impression. Vale frowned slightly.

"About half a light-year," Riker replied.

The counselor shook her head. "We have to move," she said emphatically, coming down to Riker's level of the bridge. "The star-jellies are coming to meet us."

"You made contact."

"Yes. They're wary, but they've heard of what we did for them at Deneb, so they're willing to talk."

Riker raised his brows. "Always nice to have good references."

"But we can't rendezvous this close to a Pa'haquel fleet. We need to get out of here, meet them en route."

The captain nodded, accepting her urgency. "Do you have a course?"

"They're coming in from the protostar cluster at 54 mark 223. They should be here within half an hour."

"Helm, you heard. Set an intercept course and engage at warp six."

"Aye, sir," Lavena said, and bent to it.

"In the meantime, you can report on what you learned. Senior staff to the observation lounge," he ordered.

Most of the senior staffers were already on the bridge, save only Keru and Ra-Havreii, so it didn't take them long to assemble. Vale took a moment to get a cup of coffee before the meeting started, and sipped it absently as Troi began her report. "The gestalt technique was a success, but it shouldn't be necessary anymore. Now that I've gotten their attention, they can read my thoughts and send theirs to me. I should be able to interpret for them."

"In that case," Tuvok asked, "I suggest the doctor readminister his telepathic suppressants, lest we again become overwhelmed by their emotions."

"It will take a few more hours for the counteragent to clear from your systems," Ree said.

"Don't worry, Tuvok," said Troi. "Their normal emotions are far more . . . pleasant than what we experienced during the attack."

"Emotions of any kind are distasteful to me, Counselor—including worry," he added pointedly.

"Is there any chance of programming the UT to translate their thoughts directly?" Vale asked. "It's been done before."

"The *Hood* tried that sixteen years ago during their attempt to study the jellies," Troi told her. "It wasn't successful. I suspect the problem is that their communication is more emotional than verbal."

"More like animals?"

Troi mulled it over. "They're very intelligent. Clear thinkers with long, detailed memories and knowledge spanning half a galaxy. But yes, in some ways they are very animal-like. Intelligent but wild, like dolphins or Betazoid pachyderms. They live for the moment, act on instinct. I suppose that's why Mr. Chamish is sensitive to them, even though Kazarite telepathy generally only works with animals.

"They're very open, uncomplicated creatures—childlike, in a way, but with centuries of life experience and a perception that dwarfs ours. They're very honest and forthright; they share everything telepathically, so they have no secrets in their society—much like Betazoids, only more so. Indeed, they have a strongly communal sense of identity."

"A group mind?" Vale asked.

Troi shook her head. "No, they are individuals. They just don't entirely think of themselves that way, and rarely act that way. Their emotional and social bonds with their schoolmates are so strong that they feel an intense sense of identification, a blurring of their definitions of self and other. Not unlike the bonds I've often felt between new mothers and their babies. Remember when Noah Powell was a baby?" she asked the captain. "How Alyssa spoke of Noah as 'we' all the time, as though they were a single person? And it wasn't an affectation. She didn't even realize she was doing it." Riker grinned. "It's the same with the jellies, only intensified by their telepathy and empathy.

"They're so close to each other that they can't even contemplate harming one another. They can defend themselves against other species—we saw the one at Deneb attack the Bandi who'd imprisoned its schoolmate—but they can't cause each other pain without sharing in it. The idea of attacking one another is inconceivable to them.

"That's why the Pa'haquel's attacks are so horrifying to them, so devastating. As I thought, they don't know that the 'zombies' attacking them are manned by living beings. Apparently their senses can't penetrate the Pa'haquel's armor or shielding. They think they're being attacked by members of their own kind who have somehow risen from the dead and turned destructive. And they can't bring themselves to attack their own."

"Even when they're dead?" Keru asked.

"Perhaps especially then. It would be seen as a desecration. They believe that violating the dead, even in self-defense, would bring down a fate even worse than this. So they're helpless against the attacks when they come. And they have no warning, since they can't tell the difference between live and dead jellies until they attack."

"They're telepathic, aren't they?" Vale asked. "Can't they tell by the lack of thought activity? Or by the fact that they're armored? Hell, if this has been going on for millennia like the Pa'haquel claim, shouldn't every jelly in the galaxy know by now to go on the alert whenever they detect a warp emergence?"

"The attacks are comparatively rare on a galactic scale," Troi explained. "Ninety-nine percent of the time, if they detect jellies coming out of warp, it'll be a friendly contact. And if they do come out armored, or aren't broadcasting telepathically, then they could be live jellies who are injured or in danger. The jellies can't just ignore that possibility, no matter what the risk. It's simply not in their nature to reject contact with others of their kind—not if there's the slightest chance that they are live jellies in need."

"There is a detectable difference in their warp signatures," Jaza told her. "We just discovered it with our wide-band sensors—which were also what allowed us to break through the Pa'haquel's shielding and read them inside. I guess the jellies don't have anything equivalent. If we shared the knowledge with them, they could replicate our sensor tech for themselves."

"That would let them detect the hunters and evade them," Vale said, "but what would that do to the hunters' way of life? They need these things to live on."

"These 'things' are living, feeling creatures," Troi protested, but Riker quieted her with a look.

"She's right," he said. "I don't want to save one species by endangering another." Troi subsided, her expression conceding the point.

"So you didn't tell them about the Pa'haquel?" Vale asked, then chose to rephrase it. "They didn't take the information from your mind?"

Troi faced her. "I wouldn't have made that decision unilaterally, Christine. And they wouldn't take anything from my mind that I didn't share."

"But if they have no concept of privacy—"

"The link doesn't work that way. As I said, it's primarily empathic. For me at least, conveying factual information takes a little more . . . interpretation."

"But your reports from Farpoint said they could replicate anything a person thought of, telepath or no. How do we know they can't just take the knowledge from any of our minds?"

"They only seem able to read from nontelepaths within a very short range."

Jaza leaned forward. "You say they don't realize the attackers are piloted as ships. So they have no awareness of having been engineered for that purpose? No memory or history of serving that role?"

"I didn't explore the question with them in detail. But I get no sense that they've ever been anything other than wild creatures. And—"

The comm interrupted. "Bridge to Captain Riker," came Kuu'iut's voice.

"Riker here."

"You should get out here, sir. We've picked up the star-jellies on approach . . . but it looks like the Pa'haquel have too. They've broken off from the nebula and are headed after the jellies."

"Damn. Adjourned," Riker said, and rushed to the bridge. Vale and the other bridge officers were close behind.

"We should warn the jellies, tell them to raise their armor," Troi said to the captain. He looked to be on the verge of agreeing, so Vale spoke.

"We shouldn't. Then they'd want to know how we can tell the attackers aren't star-jellies. If we're not prepared to give them that ability, we can't let them know we have it."

Riker grimaced. "You're right. We'll just have to protect them ourselves until they can armor up or warp out."

"Should we really be getting involved?"

He glared at Vale fiercely. "They came here to meet us. It's our fault they're under attack." *My fault,* she saw on his face, and the same was mirrored on Troi's. "Shields up! Weapons on standby. Put us directly in the hunters' path."

"Tuvok," Troi said, "I suggest doing what you can to raise your own mental shields. This may get rough."

"And Mr. Kuu'iut, take over tactical again," Riker added. "Tuvok, if you'd prefer to return to quarters, be with your wife—"

"I would rather stay, sir. I believe I will be better able to handle it this time."

Riker stared at him for a second. "All right. Are your countermeasures ready?"

"The shields have been recalibrated for bio-energy. The warp core is rigged to emit a series of magneton pulses which should somewhat deflect and dissipate their plasma bolts for several kilometers around the ship."

"Excellent."

Once the hunters dropped out of warp, Lavena began her blocking maneuvers again. On the screen, the jellies scattered as the shooting began, and their panic reflected on Troi's face, though she kept it under control. Vale looked to Tuvok, and saw it there too. On screen, she saw the Pa'haquel's blasts go astray under the influence of Tuvok's magneton pulses—meaning that Lavena didn't have to move quite so fast to block them all.

Soon a hail came, and Elder Qui'hibra appeared on the screen. *"Move aside, Titan. We have lost a skymount today and must take another."*

"They don't seem to want to help you, Qui'hibra. I suggest you consider other options."

"You have chosen a foolish course, Riker. You fight against the balance, and it must be restored—at your expense, if the Spirit wills."

"I don't see balance in your relationship with these creatures, Qui'hibra. I see parasitism. Maybe once you had a healthy symbiosis, I don't know, but now you're exploiting these beings, terrorizing them. I think the Pa'haquel are capable of being better than that. I'm still willing to help you and the 'skymounts' negotiate a peace, but I will not—"

"You would destroy what we are, and far more—more than you begin to understand. If you understood, you would stay out of this. But I have no time to explain it to

you. Your loss." The screen went dark—only to light up with weapons fire.

"Aili, block it!"

"No need," Lavena said. "It's aimed at us!"

Against a dead-on weapon blast, the outward push of the magneton pulses only slowed and weakened the bolt, so most of the hits connected. Tuvok's shield recalibrations held, but the ride was bumpy. Several Pa'haquel saucers ganged up on *Titan,* trying to herd it aside so the others could pursue the star-jellies. "Should we return fire?" Kuu'iut asked.

Vale saw the dilemma play out on Riker's face. He didn't want to make an enemy of the Pa'haquel, but he had to protect his ship. Then an idea struck him. "Put ship's phasers on stun," he said. "Their ships were life-forms once—maybe we can knock them out temporarily."

Kuu'iut let out a whistle at the unusual order, but complied as he did so. A few dull orange beams lanced out at the attacking ships, with no apparent effect. "No good," Kuu'iut reported. "Either their armor is too strong or it's because they're already dead."

But Lavena had just about managed to wriggle free of the herding group. She flew after the rest of the pack, struggling to get the ship back between the hunters and their fleeing quarry. But despite her best efforts, *Titan* was still only one ship. And the Pa'haquel gunners were swiftly learning to compensate for the magneton deflection. A number of energy bolts got through, and jellies began to be struck. Troi and Tuvok gasped with the pain of every blow. When Tuvok screamed and Deanna sobbed in agony, it was clear that another jelly had taken a mortal hit.

"Deanna?" Riker asked.

She held her hands to her head. "Too much . . . overpowering, the grief . . . how could we let this happen?"

Something in her tone, her face, made Vale realize that she was interpreting the jellies' thoughts. "We told them we could help . . . yet we brought them here . . . betrayal!"

"Tell them we did mean to help, this wasn't supposed to happen."

"Help . . . how? Tell us!"

"There is a way," said Tuvok, and he lunged toward the science station, shoving Jaza aside.

Vale realized what was happening. "Jaza, stop him! If he gets that warp-signature data—"

But Jaza was already on him, trying to pull him from the console. With a surge of Vulcan strength, Tuvok threw him off, knocking him into the approaching Keru so that both men fell into a tangle of limbs and Keru's half-drawn phaser went clattering across the deck. Vale dove for it . . . but just then a honey-brown blur whipped through the air, took Tuvok in the chest, and knocked him to the deck. After a moment, Vale realized it had been Dr. Ree's tail. The therapodian leapt over the console to straddle Tuvok and injected him with a hypospray. "Apologies, Commander," he said. "But I broke nothing I can't easily fix."

Once the commotion died down, Lavena turned to the captain. "The jellies have gone to warp, sir. The hunters have broken off their attacks on us."

"Good. Dr. Ree, get Tuvok to sickbay, and get him back on that suppressant as soon as you safely can." But Riker said this while facing the screen, on which the slowly spinning corpse of the Pa'haquel's kill was displayed. The hunters' ships were already moving in on it, deploying their tentacles. "No," Riker said. "Not this time." He strode forward. "Lavena, take us in. Tactical, I want a tractor beam on that star-jelly. Once it's locked, fire wide-beam phasers at the Pa'haquel ships to blind their sensors, then helm, engage at warp eight, course at your discretion."

Vale glared at him, but said nothing as the crew carried out his orders. The ship shook a bit as it strained to drag the jelly's huge mass forward, and again as the warp field tried to compensate for its presence. "Any sign of pursuit?" Riker asked after a moment.

"No, sir," Kuu'iut said. "They must need time to build energy for warp, like the jellies. They are hailing, though."

"Ignore them. Let our actions speak for us." He exchanged a look with Troi; her expression was one of deep gratitude. But there were no more jellies nearby for her to channel.

Vale stepped between them. "Captain, may I speak to you in your ready room, please?" she asked stiffly.

He studied her for a moment. "Very well. Commander Troi, you have the bridge."

"Uhh, Captain?" Lavena asked. "How long do we continue towing . . . that?"

Riker gave it a moment's thought. "Give it twenty minutes, and if there's still no sign of pursuit, drop to impulse."

"Aye, sir."

"I think taking the star-jelly away was unwise, Will," Vale said without preamble once they were alone. "The Pa'haquel are sure to see it as a gratuitous, hostile act."

All right, I can't fault her for candor, Riker thought, although he wasn't in the mood to accept her argument. "I couldn't just stand by and let them desecrate another corpse," he told her emphatically.

"As they see it, you've probably committed a desecration. Made its sacrifice meaningless."

"The Aztecs thought they had to cut out human hearts

to make the sun rise every morning," Riker said. "Some sacrifices are meaningless to begin with."

"It's not our place to decide that—"

"Not our *place*? Christine, it's our *fault* that star-jelly got killed! We invited it here."

"Like you said, Will, intervention carries risks. You made the choice to intervene, this is one of the consequences. But how far are you willing to escalate that intervention? And when did we decide to take the star-jellies' side in this?"

"I haven't taken sides. If I had, I'd have let Tuvok give them that sensor data. But I had to do something to show that we hadn't sided against the jellies either. Think of this as a show of good faith."

"Was that what you had in mind when you gave the order, or did you only just come up with it now? Sir?" That last was spoken more softly, a concession that she'd gone a bit too far. But it was unnecessary; Riker had to concede that she was right about that. She saw as much in his face, and went on. "You were acting on impulse, Will. On emotion. Frankly, I don't think you're being objective about this. It's obvious that Deanna has formed a strong bond with these creatures. What hurts them hurts her, and you can't bear to see her hurt."

He looked at her sharply. "When I offered you this job, I gave you my word that I would never let my personal feelings for Deanna affect my command judgment."

"And you offered me the job because you knew I wouldn't hesitate to call you on it if you ever did. Because you knew you needed me to help you keep that promise. Well, here I am."

Riker met her gaze for a long moment. "You're right. And I appreciate it. I do need you as a check on my conscience, Christine. But you're off-base about this. Yes, this is personal to me, but it's not about Deanna. Not mainly, anyway."

"Then what?"

He began to pace, gathering his thoughts. "You know as well as I do that the Federation's been through some dark times lately. Our principles, our ideals, they've taken a beating in the name of survival. The Ba'ku incident . . . the attempted genocide of the Founders . . ."

Vale nodded. "And Tezwa."

"And Tezwa," he confirmed with a heavy sigh. For a split second he was back in that dank, stinking cell beneath the floor, screaming from Kinchawn's tortures. A part of him would always be there. And it was his own president, a man he'd voted for, who had made Kinchawn happen. "All of us who were there, who know what happened, Christine—we all made the decision that it had to end. That we wouldn't accept any more compromises. That we had to regain the moral high ground, stand firm on our principles from now on."

"I'm with you there, of course," Vale said. "But what's that got to do with this? How does meddling in a conflict we don't understand reaffirm our values?"

"There's more to it than that, Christine." He turned to the window, gazed at the prismatic streaks of starlight warping past. "All this time we've assumed that the corruption rose out of the desperation of the past ten years . . . the Borg attacks, the Klingon conflict, the Dominion War. That we never would've compromised our ethics if we hadn't been driven to it, if our spirits hadn't been beaten down by all the horror and destruction."

"Okay." She waited for the rest.

"But the first time we encountered a star-jelly . . . sixteen years ago, back in the Golden Age," he said with sarcasm, "it was being tortured, exploited. The Bandi starved it and brutalized it into obedience, forced it to transform into a starbase and replicate anything its occupants craved. And they did it for *us*, Christine. For the Federation."

"We didn't know that's what they were doing."

He whirled. "And why not? Why didn't we? When this simple, primitive agricultural society, a people with a tiny population and no industry, came to us and told us they could produce a state-of-the-art facility in sixteen months, it was obviously too good to be true. But we shrugged our shoulders and told them 'sure, go right ahead,' when we should've been demanding to know more about how they proposed to achieve this miraculous feat."

"Starfleet sent the *Enterprise* to investigate. They sent you."

"But not until 'Farpoint Station' was already completed! Why did we wait so long?"

"Deneb is a remote world. Not much Starfleet traffic gets out that way. Not until we knew there was going to be a staging facility there for us to use, anyway."

"That's just it. It was a dream offer. A whole luxury frontier outpost built to order, prefab and ready to use without us having to lift a finger. A perfect launching point for opening up a whole new region of the Alpha Quadrant to exploration. We weren't willing to look that closely, didn't ask the questions we should've asked, because we didn't want to jeopardize that prize. And so we allowed an innocent star-jelly to be tortured and abused for *sixteen months,* when we could've done something to prevent it.

"We were selfish, Christine. We knew something didn't smell right, but we looked the other way because it suited our interests. And we didn't even have the excuse of fighting a war! The Cardassian border wars had fizzled out, the Tzenkethi War was over, things were as peaceful as they ever got. Opening up the Cygnus Reach was going to be a bold adventure, a reaffirmation of our grand ideals of peace and learning—a lot like *Titan*'s mission is meant to be. And we started it out with an act of callous neglect for another being's suffering."

Out of breath, he paused to gather himself, then spoke again more quietly. "At times, I've wondered why Q chose Farpoint Station as a test case for whether humans had outgrown savagery. Why he chose that place and time to challenge our right to expand further into space, when we'd already been at it for centuries. Maybe he was trying to show us that we weren't as evolved as we thought. Maybe he put us on trial *because* of the exploitation of that creature—and judged us on whether we chose to end it or sanction it."

"If so, we passed the test. We made the right choice."

"Picard made the right choice. The Federation—I'm not so sure." He shook his head. "The hell of it is, we never really did that much exploring of the Cygnus Reach anyway. The *Enterprise* was supposed to be the flagship of this new long-term venture into the unknown . . . but after the Farpoint incident, with no base that far out, it never really took off. The Bandi tried to rebuild Farpoint, but they just weren't up to the task. Then Starfleet's priorities shifted and the *Enterprise* spent most of its tour closer to home, conducting diplomatic or relief missions. In the end, everything that creature suffered, it was all for nothing. We compromised our principles for nothing, and all in the name of an ideal.

"Well, not this time, Christine. Not again. This is our second chance, and we have to learn the lessons of the first. We let the star-jellies down the last time, and we let ourselves down in the process. It can't happen again."

Vale took it in, nodding in acknowledgment. "Okay,

Will," she said, crossing her arms, "so what, then? Do we destroy the Pa'haquel's whole way of life just to assuage Starfleet's collective guilt? Or yours?"

He threw her a disbelieving look. "Giving up one custom doesn't destroy an entire culture. I'm descended from people who built their nation on slavery and genocide, but giving those up didn't destroy our culture—if anything, it brought it closer to its ideals."

"Your ancestral culture also had a bad habit of telling other people how to live, saying it was for their own good, and practically wrecking their civilizations in the process. That's part of why we have a Prime Directive in the first place."

"So we should slink away and leave the star-jellies to their fate?"

Vale spread her arms. "You want the Pa'haquel to adapt—maybe it's the jellies who need to adapt. Only their taboo about firing on their own is keeping them from evening the odds."

"And how much would that change *their* culture? Christine, the last thing I want is to start another interstellar shooting match!"

"You think I do? I just don't want to see more of my people get killed in someone else's crossfire!"

That brought them both to silence. Riker was reminded of how many members of Vale's *Enterprise* security staff had died in recent months, on Delta Sigma IV and Tezwa. A pall hung over the ready room for a moment. "Sorry," Riker said, and Vale's apology overlapped it. He gave her a small, sheepish smile before starting again. "Look. These are both intelligent species. That means they're both capable of acting on more than instinct and raw survival. I believe there must be some way they can reach peaceful coexistence. Everything I believe, everything this ship is about tells me that there has to be. If this mission is to mean anything, I say we need to try to help them find that path, rather than abandoning them to bloodshed."

Vale absorbed his words. "Okay. Granted, your motives are valid."

"And I'll grant that maybe my approach has been a little one-sided. Maybe I am commanding too much from the heart in this case . . . and I'd be a liar if I said that seeing Deanna in so much pain didn't have at least a little to do with that." He smiled. "So I'm grateful to have such a cold and logical exec."

She glared at him, and they shared a chuckle, the tension fading. "Glad I could help. I still think you're wrong, though."

"And I think you're wrong," he replied in equally amiable tones. "So maybe between us we can hammer out a compromise both species can live with."

CHAPTER SEVEN

Jaza Najem realized it would be inappropriate to regard the violent death of a star-jelly as a stroke of good luck. But with the jelly's corpse only a few dozen meters away in *Titan*'s tractor beam, Jaza had his best opportunity yet for a detailed sensor scan of the creature's anatomy. It would have been better to have a live creature whose biological functions he could observe in action, but having a static subject to scan at leisure allowed him to build up a clearer picture of its anatomy. And since this one was in its translucent-shelled default mode rather than armored up, its innards were much easier to scan. To take full advantage of the opportunity, he'd moved from the bridge to the exobiology lab, where he could consult with its staff.

The jelly's anatomy, as displayed in the lab's main holotank, followed a basically toroidal structure, a series of concentric rings. The central core apparently contained the creature's brain—"comparable in size to *Titan*'s whole saucer section," Lieutenant Eviku had said with awe.

There were sensory organs at both ends of the axis, close to the brain. The dorsal one took the form of a parabolic dish with a central spike, and also served as the weapon emitter, though it was covered by the translucent shell in the creature's default mode. The ventral sensory organ was a dome at the center of the larger concavity in which the tentacles could rest. The scans suggested it bore some similarities to a transporter scanner/emitter, as well as a subspace transceiver. "Maybe we should have an engineer here too," Kent Norellis muttered.

The two rings of red lights, one halfway out, the other along the outer rim, seemed to be analogous to warp reactors. It was hard to tell in a dead creature, but their residual activity and sensor profile revealed a fair amount. They were apparently the jelly's main sources of metabolic energy, and also served as continuum-distortion generators, producing the gravitic and subspace fields which the creatures used to go to warp and maneuver at impulse. A network of wave guides within the creature, wispy and invisible on this scale like its respiratory and circulatory networks, distributed its internal gravitic fields into a planar shape; essentially anything above or below the equatorial plane would be pulled "down" toward it. The two hemispheres of its body would have opposite gravitational vectors, and any conduits right along the equatorial plane would be in free fall—not unlike the "sweet spots" of early starships' gravity fields. Jaza felt it would be an interesting environment to live in, though Norellis wasn't so sanguine.

The young human was more concerned with other issues, though. "These have got to be artificial creatures," Norellis said. "Why else would they have internal gravity?"

"It seems to be a side effect of their propulsion systems," Jaza said. "A kind of gravitic leakage that's shaped by the wave guides."

"But why shape it to be planar like a planet's gravity?"

Eviku tilted his long, tapering head thoughtfully. "They do have a sessile phase on planetary surfaces," the Arkenite pointed out. "It stands to reason that their metabolism might require a gravity field aligned that way. It could have evolved naturally."

Norellis studied the image skeptically. "It sure *looks* artificial. The way the distortion generators are arranged in regular rings."

"I've seen deep-sea organisms on Arken and Earth with similar arrays of lights."

Cadet Orilly reared up onto her hind legs for a moment to get a different angle on the holotank display. It wasn't something Jaza saw her do very often, except to fit into a turbolift. "The generators themselves are clearly organic."

"True," Jaza said. "And they don't function like any warp engines I know about." How they actually did work was still something of a mystery, as with most of the cosmozoans that possessed FTL or subspace capabilities.

"But how could warp drive evolve naturally?"

Jaza pursed his lips. "Our findings as we approach Vela support the hypothesis that cosmozoans originate in star-formation zones. Those zones can be turbulent in subspace as well as normal space, and that can weaken the boundary between the domains. It's possible some lifeforms could evolve to take advantage of those conditions." Some cosmozoans seemed to exist partly in subspace to begin with. There were some, like the "vampire cloud" that had destroyed the *Farragut* in the 2250s and a similar creature battled by the Klingons in the 2310s, which had the ability to change mass and composition, implying that they extended into higher dimensions. For a being that existed partly or mostly in subspace, evolving warp capability didn't seem quite so implausible. Jaza was still skeptical, but he had to admit his initial certainty was starting to waver.

"But what's the evolutionary incentive for warp drive?" Norellis asked.

"It would give a clear survival advantage," Eviku said. "Cosmozoans need energy and matter to feed on, and that means star systems, which are light-years apart. And it allows much faster escape from cosmic disasters."

Jaza worked the controls for the multispatial sensor array, studying its readings. "It looks as though the distortion generators extend partly into subspace. Although the rest of the star-jellies are strictly three-dimensional."

"Could the generators once have been autonomous organisms that the jellies incorporated into their anatomy?" Orilly asked. "Like the mitochondria in humanoid cells?"

"Or they could've been added by someone later," Norellis countered. "I mean, that's obviously the more likely answer."

"Too many wrong ideas have been called obvious in the past, Kent," said Jaza. "It's not a word I like to hear in my department. We should at least consider possible natural explanations for their traits before we assume they must be artificial."

"Yeah, okay," the human said, mildly chastened—but not silenced. "Still, what kind of natural explanation could there be for evolving transporters and replicators?"

"Well, let's consider that possibility." Jaza brought up his scans from aboard the Pa'haquel ship and during the battles, and compared them with readings from the *Enterprise*-D's encounter at Deneb. "There—that looks like a telekinetic component in their transporter signature. During their transformations, too."

"I suppose," Orilly said, "that a sufficiently advanced telekinetic brain could be able to manipulate matter on a molecular level."

"Particularly when it's as large as a starship's saucer," Eviku added.

"Yes. And if it had the ability to harness subspace fields, couldn't it telekinetically transmit matter through subspace and achieve teleportation?"

Jaza raised a brow. "We can't rule out the possibility."

"Still, it doesn't seem very probable, does it?" Norellis asked.

"Well, how about this," said Eviku. "Given their ability to transform their own bodies as needed, it's possible that ancient star-jellies could have observed starships performing such tasks as teleportation and warp propulsion and then created their own equivalents. Even if these traits are artificial, it doesn't mean someone designed them to serve as ships."

Norellis mulled that over. "I guess that's possible. But then, how do you explain the smooth floors, and the corridor lights?"

"They're naturally bioluminescent," Eviku said. "It's only natural that the light could be seen through translucent internal membranes. As for the floors . . . hmm, maybe they're smooth to facilitate the purging of contaminants—so that nothing gets stuck in a depression where it can linger and cause damage."

"It's a stretch."

"Yes, it is." The Arkenite sighed and turned to Jaza. "The star-jellies have a strong taboo against desecrating the dead, right?"

"Quite right."

"I don't suppose there's any chance that taboo would include an exception for autopsies done in the name of scientific enlightenment?"

"No, I rather doubt it."

"We could at least beam over and take a closer look, couldn't we?" Norellis asked. "Maybe take a few little tissue samples? They wouldn't have to know."

"It wouldn't be proper," Jaza said firmly. "Science is no excuse for disrespect toward others' spiritual beliefs."

"So it's all right to stay ignorant? That doesn't sound like science-officer thinking."

Jaza smiled. "I believe that science and faith are compatible quests for enlightenment. There's always a way to serve them both." At the moment, though, he had to admit he couldn't think of one. He could sympathize with Norellis's temptation to autopsy the star-jelly from the inside. "Hm. Maybe if we try a—"

Just then, the captain's voice came over the intercom. *"Lieutenant Commander Jaza, report to the bridge, please."*

He tapped his combadge. "Jaza here. What's happening?"

"Deanna's been contacted by the jellies. It seems they want their body back."

When the star-jelly pod emerged from warp, several million kilometers off *Titan*'s bow, its fourteen members were fully armored. Riker at first wondered if the Pa'haquel had tracked them, until Jaza identified their warp-emergence signatures. That didn't entirely put him at ease, though. "Why are they armored? Do they still blame us for luring them into an ambush?"

"We should raise shields," Kuu'iut advised.

"Wait," Deanna said, her attention focused elsewhere. After a moment, she turned to Riker. "They don't blame us anymore. They can see the truth in my thoughts. They know we meant them no harm. Still, they're timid, hesitant. They need to assert their strength, and we need to show submission to put them at ease."

"You heard the lady, Mr. Kuu'iut. Shields down—and think friendly thoughts."

"We should release the tractor beam as well," Deanna added, "and back away respectfully from the corpse."

Riker nodded. "Disengage tractor," he said evenly, trying to maintain a calm and properly solemn state of mind and project as much to his crew. "Helm, thrusters aft, five hundred meters per second. Then resume station at one hundred klicks."

"Thrusters aft, aye," Lavena acknowledged, her voice appropriately muted. Riker recalled that she'd always been good at responding to his moods; then he quashed that thought as it brought an amused glare from Deanna.

By now, the jellies' shells were starting to ripple with cloudy white light, while discrete blobs of purple flowed through their meridional fissures in the opposite direction. Then, nearly in synch with each other, the jellies began to flip over and fade into translucence, a maneuver he recalled from the Deneb encounter. "Why the rotation?" Jaza asked.

"I think it's a form of display," Deanna told him. "To show your full face and confirm that you are dropping your defenses. Also to aim your tentacles at whatever your weapon emitter was aimed at before."

Once the jellies had de-armored and deployed their tentacles, they drew into formation around their slain comrade. Two of them cradled it gently while a third took its limp, trailing tentacles and ceremonially furled them back into their ventral depression. As they did so, Riker stood to attention. A moment later, the rest of the bridge crew followed, and they silently paid tribute to the fallen.

When the furling was done, the two bearers grasped the corpse more tightly, drawing closer. A tear rolling down her cheek, Deanna spoke. "They offer us deep gratitude for our reverence toward their lost sibling, and for rescuing it from desecration. We have proven ourselves their friends, and in return they wish to invite us to accompany them."

"Accompany them where?"

"I think . . . yes . . . to the world where it was born. They wish to return it there. Here," she said, moving over to the helm, "they've given me the location."

She consulted with Lavena for a moment, locating the proper star on her helm display. "It should be a two-day journey at warp seven," Lavena said.

Riker looked from her to Deanna. "Tell them . . . we'd be honored."

Ree clucked his tongue as he studied Tuvok's neurological scans. "You're certain that the jellies are still making contact with you?"

"Yes, Doctor. It is unquestionably they. The telepathic inhibitor is proving insufficient."

"Only on you, it seems. Your wife, Orilly, and the others are all adequately inhibited."

"But they are targeting me specifically for contact. When I—" He hesitated, out of the embarrassment which Vulcans supposedly didn't feel. Ree had to admire the Vulcans for their sense of irony—imagine, pretending to be emotionless, and then pretending the pretense was logical! And of course anyone who could smell their pheromones could tell how flimsy their facade of dispassion truly was. "When I attempted to transmit the sensor information to the star-jellies . . . although I did not obtain the information, the attempt did reveal to them the knowledge that such information exists." Ree noted that he wasn't calling them by their scientific name anymore. Did that perhaps denote a growing sympathy toward them? "Since then, they have made attempts to persuade me to share the data about the warp signatures, and the specifications for our sensor technology."

"Persuade? Are these attempts coercive?"

"I do not believe they are intended to be, but that is the effect. The . . . emotions . . . feel like one's own. Without the inhibitor, I share their desire for rescue from the Pa'haquel as profoundly as they. Even with the inhibitor, I am concerned that they may be able to influence me unduly if they bring enough effort to bear upon me. You must increase the inhibitor dosage if I am to return to duty."

"I fear it is not so simple, Mr. Tuvok." Ree's tail began to twitch as it did when he was wrestling with a problem whose neck eluded his jaws. "There are limits to the efficacy of medication. It can only modify the brain's chemistry so much, and its structure barely at all. And your brain, Mr. Tuvok . . ." *It's a real mess,* he wanted to say. "It has been through an inordinate amount of strain over the past decade. Let me see," he said, reviewing Tuvok's file. "Brainwashing by a Maquis operative . . . thermal damage from a telekinetic accident . . . limbic-system imbalance following a meld with a Betazoid sociopath . . . decades-long infection by a dormant memory virus . . . extensive brain damage and memory loss from neuroleptic shock . . . temporary Borg assimilation . . . and the onset of the preliminary stages of *fal-tor-voh.*"

"All of those conditions were corrected," Tuvok insisted.

"Yes, but they left their scars. As did the extensive torture and hardship you recently endured at Romulan hands. You are still in the process of healing from that; your emotional control was tenuous for a Vulcan even before we encountered the jellies." Tuvok said nothing, but he didn't need to; his shame was redolent. "And even if you had mastered the emotional trauma completely, it would still have left a physical spoor in your neurochemistry, as did all the other neurological traumas you've experienced. Your mind, my friend, bears a proud and admirable catalog of scars. You are a survivor, and should be esteemed for that, but being a survivor carries its costs. In this case, the inhibitor is simply limited in its ability to affect your particular neurochemistry. A purer, more innocent brain than yours, I could protect from the jellies' passions. But with experience comes pain, Mr. Tuvok, and I cannot spare you from all of theirs. You will simply have to endure it. As you have endured far worse in your time."

Tuvok's eyes were hard to read, but his scent was an odd mix of gratitude and disappointment. "In that case, I have no choice but to remain relieved of duty."

"Or you could simply accept the passions into you and bend them to your will."

The Vulcan looked at him oddly. "I wish it could be that easy, Doctor."

"Deanna, wait up!"

Troi held the lift doors and allowed Christine Vale to step in. "Bridge?" she asked.

"Yeah." The car started into motion, but Vale spoke up.

"Do you mind if we hold the lift for a moment? I've been meaning to talk to you."

"Not at all. Computer, hold."

The lift came to a stop, and Vale spoke. "I wanted to apologize for the briefing the other day. I was a bit . . . confrontational toward you. Implying that you might've given sensitive information to the star-jellies. I know you wouldn't really do that."

Troi raised her brows. "How do you know I wouldn't? Tuvok almost did."

Vale stared at her. "Are you saying you might?"

"That's not the question. The question is whether you think I might. If you feel there's a legitimate concern, Christine, you shouldn't deny it to protect my feelings."

"Okay," Vale said after a moment. "Frankly I did have some concern about that. But it's the way I think. It's my training—I worry about security risks. I knew you wouldn't betray your duties under normal circumstances, but from what I understood about the power of their emotions, how strongly they make you identify with them, I couldn't be sure."

"Of course."

"But it was Tuvok who broke, not you. That's actually . . . well, pretty impressive. To have more control than a Vulcan. So I'm not worried about you anymore."

"Except on general principles," Troi said.

Vale stared. "What do you mean? Deanna, I don't . . ."

"It's all right, I understand. You see it as part of your job to make sure my relationship with Will doesn't affect his command decisions. To be a balance to my influence, if necessary."

"Yeah. Right. That's just it," Vale said, nodding. "I'm glad you understand. I just wanted it to be clear that there's nothing personal about it."

Yet that brought a disapproving look from Troi. "You're doing it again, Christine."

"Doing what?"

"Hiding what you really feel. If we're to have a viable relationship, you mustn't hesitate to be honest with me."

"What—you think it *is* personal? Come on, Deanna, we're friends. I like you, you know that."

"I do, of course. And it's mutual. But that doesn't mean there can't be tensions. Jealousies."

Vale gaped at her. "You don't mean—Deanna, I do *not* feel that way about Will Riker!"

Deanna laughed. "Oh, no! No, of course not, that's not what I meant. Believe me, I'd know if you did." Vale was at once relieved and confused. "But you do feel that way about Jaza Najem, don't you?"

Vale glared. "You know, those powers of yours can be a little invasive at times."

"Christine, the only power I need to discern that is eyesight. And experience at observing humanoid behavior," she added. "Don't worry—I don't think it's obvious to everyone that you've slept together."

Now she blushed. *Just those who've seen us in the same room, I bet.* "It was only the one time."

Deanna studied her. "Why do you feel guilty about it?"

"I don't! I'm not . . . We worked it out. It was a one-time thing, no strings, we're both okay with that. It's behind us."

"So why does the subject make you so defensive?"

Vale started to protest, but realized that Deanna would coax it out of her with her relentless Socratic approach anyway. So she gathered herself and tried to think about it, to get ahead of Deanna and take an honest look at her motives. The counselor waited patiently as she did so. "Okay. I guess maybe I'm not entirely sure I *want* it to be behind me. It was . . . if we weren't coworkers, it was something I definitely would've pursued. So I can't help wondering if I should pursue it anyway."

"And how does that make you feel?"

"Well . . . a little scared. Dating a coworker . . . it's risky. There's so much that can go wrong. So many ways it can mess up the relationship, or the job. It's a hard balance at best."

Deanna nodded. "So I guess those risks are occupying your thoughts lately. The danger of a conflict of interest, of a relationship interfering with your professionalism."

"Yeah." She saw where Troi was going. "And you think I'm projecting that onto you and Will. Being hard on you because of it."

"What do you think?"

Vale let out a frustrated puff of breath. "I think, frankly, Deanna, that I get a little tired of your smug certainty that you have all the answers. Of how—of how easy you make it look. Your job, your marriage, making them work together. Yeah, I am a little jealous of that. Every day I have to compete with you, and I don't feel like I'm ahead of the game."

"Compete with me?" This time her question actually seemed surprised, not just a therapist's prompt. "What do you mean?"

"I mean that six months ago I was a lieutenant, a security chief. I never expected to be on the command track, let alone to be a first officer so soon. But here I am, thrust into it practically out of nowhere. That leaves me with a lot to prove. To myself, to my crewmates, to Starfleet. I'm still figuring out how to do this job, let alone how to balance it with a relationship.

"But a lot of the things that are supposed to be part of my job—managing the crew's affairs, leading away missions—you have a hand in those too. I rarely feel like I'm doing any of it on my own. And you've known Will so much longer, have decades of experience with him. I'm the first officer, I'm supposed to be Will's partner . . . but you've been his partner a lot longer, in a much deeper way. You automatically have his ear—hell, you have his *mind's* ear. A lot of the time, on the bridge, when he's trying to make a decision, he looks to you before he looks to me. And if I didn't know better, I'd swear you were literally communing telepathically."

For the first time in this conversation, Deanna looked uneasy. "To be honest . . . that's exactly what we're doing."

"I didn't know you could do that!"

"Normally I can't with a non-Betazoid. But Will and I . . . partly it's the intimacy of our bond, and partly just that our minds have somehow always been more in tune than most. It's something that's gotten stronger since we were married."

Vale absorbed it. "Well. I appreciate you telling me. Now will you tell me how I'm supposed to compete with that?"

Deanna touched her arm reassuringly. "It's just another form of communication, Christine. You have as much power to influence his decisions as I do. Probably more, because he strives to keep the proper chain of command in mind when he's on the bridge. All else being equal, he'd probably choose to give your advice more weight than mine at any given time."

"Okay," Vale said. "But what am I supposed to do when you and he have a consultation I'm not even privy to?"

"That's a valid point. I'll talk to Will about it—we'll both make more of an effort to avoid that in the future."

Deanna's gentle, wise openness defused Vale's anger

. . . although a part of her still envied how easy Deanna made everything look. "Okay."

"And keep one more thing in mind, Christine: Will Riker chose you. He pushed for you, courted you until you said yes. He arranged for that fast promotion because he felt there was no one better suited for this job. He values you as his first officer, his partner. And take it from me: He's very committed to his partnerships."

Vale smiled, heartened by her words. "I'll remember that. Thank you, Deanna."

"My pleasure." She looked up. "Computer, resume."

The lift went on its way again, and the two women stood there in companionable silence for a moment. Then Vale said, "So, uh, what do you think I should do about Jaza?"

"I can't tell you what to do. . . ."

"I know, but if you have any thoughts . . ."

"Computer, hold," Deanna said, and the lift stopped again. "I think it's important to find your comfort level. If you're unsure of yourself right now, if you want to find balance in your career, then maybe this isn't the time to pursue a relationship. It isn't always necessary to rush into what you want. My relationship with Will didn't go smoothly the first time, because we were both young and unsure of what we wanted. But on the *Enterprise,* we had the time to grow together, to build the foundation of a strong personal and professional partnership, and our love eventually grew from that."

Vale nodded. "Okay. But on the other hand," she said, remembering how she'd felt after Oghen, "either one of us could get killed at any time, and then we'd have missed our chance."

"That's true too. There isn't always a simple answer. Some relationships do require time and patience, but there's no guarantee of getting it. Whichever way you go, it's a risk."

"Great. So you're saying there's no way to decide."

"I'm saying that maybe the decision comes down to your other priorities. If your career is what's most important to you right now, and if you feel a relationship with Jaza would disrupt that, then that's a perfectly valid choice to make." Deanna touched her shoulder. "What matters is that you make the choice based on the factors in your life and Jaza's. It shouldn't be about Will and me, or you and me."

Vale took a moment to absorb that. "Okay, then. Thanks for the talk."

"Anytime. Computer, resume."

Another companionable silence arose, to be broken again by Vale. "Um, what I said about your decades of experience . . . I wasn't calling you old or anything."

"No, of course not. I understand."

"I just meant—"

"I know."

"A little maturity, it's very becoming on a woman."

"Certainly."

"You're definitely still hot."

Deanna threw her a sidelong look. "You better believe it, kiddo."

The jellies' destination was a star system with a G8 primary, smallish and yellow-orange, surrounded by five planets and a brown dwarf which orbited at about sixteen AUs. The dwarf's gravity had perturbed any outer planets out of the system, but had also cleared the inner system of most of the asteroidal and cometary debris which could have posed an impact hazard to its planets. The second world had a nice low-eccentricity orbit right in the heart of the star's habitable zone. The star itself was stable, with minimal flare activity, and it was comfortably far from any potential supernova stars, pulsars, stellar nurseries, or other celestial hazards. All told, it was one of the safest abodes of life they were likely to find this close to the Vela Association.

"So what do we call it?"

Riker turned to Deanna and quirked an eyebrow at her question. "Don't the star-jellies have a name for it?"

"Nothing that translates into words," she answered with a shrug. "Just a general sense of safety, family, nurturing. Perhaps 'Nursery,' but that's more its category than a name for the particular place. So you're free to call it whatever you want."

He grinned at her. "Captain's prerogative, eh?"

"It's one of the perks of the job. So what's the first place name that Captain Will Riker adds to the almanacs?"

"Oh, that's easy. Deanna's Star, of course."

She blushed, laughed. "Oh, no. Will, please, no. That would be too embarrassing." She exchanged a look with Vale. "And not entirely appropriate."

"All right, then, how about I let you name it instead? What would you like to call it?"

Deanna again looked at Vale, as if for approval. The younger woman shrugged assentingly. Deanna gazed at the star on the viewscreen for a moment. "How about Kestra?"

They exchanged a long, meaningful look. That would be an even better gift to Deanna, he thought. "Kestra it is, then. Mr. Jaza, please log it as such."

"Aye, sir."

Although the planet—which he could now call Kestra II, Riker supposed—was a fairly safe place as far as cosmic hazards were concerned, it was still girded by a cordon of star-jellies, dozens of them patrolling its orbital space in armored mode. Below them, scans revealed other, unarmored jellies at various altitudes, apparently keeping watch over their sessile young on the surface.

"The planet is fairly active geologically," Jaza reported. "I'm reading star-jelly-like biosignatures congregating around zones of hydrothermal activity—hot springs, alkali lakes, and the like."

"That fits with what Se'hraqua said about them burrowing their roots to feed off their planet's warmth," Deanna said.

Jaza nodded. "And the Bandi sustained their captive jelly with geothermal energy. It must be their preferred energy source during their sessile phase."

"That might be why the wounded jelly came to their world in the first place," said Riker, remembering that geothermal energy had been the one resource Deneb IV had possessed in abundance.

"One thing puzzles me," said Vale. "If the Pa'haquel have been hunting them for millennia, they should've been able to find this world by now. Why haven't they attacked it?"

"I've been wondering that too," Jaza said. "For that matter, why haven't the Pa'haquel come to one of these breeding worlds and domesticated its jellies, rather than going to the trouble of hunting them in the wild?"

Riker frowned. "You saw how much their culture revolves around the hunt."

"That wouldn't explain it," Deanna told him. "Even the most ideologically driven cultures, when you get right down to it, base their ideologies on their practical needs. If those needs then change, the culture may cling to its traditions for a while, but eventually later generations will grow up seeing more harm than good in them and rebel, replacing them with a reformist ideology that suits their needs better. So there must be some other reason why the Pa'haquel have kept their hunting traditions."

"Well, whatever it is," Vale said, "we'll have to ask them. I doubt we'll find it here."

"We never know until we look," Riker reminded her.

Soon *Titan* and the jellies' funeral procession had reached the orbital cordon. They passed through it without incident; no doubt the defender jellies had been advised of *Titan*'s friendly status. However, one armored jelly broke formation and took station several dozen kilometers off their stern, keeping unobtrusive guard. The other armored jellies in visual range signalled with their meridional chaser lights in acknowledgment of the bereaved school.

Soon the school settled into a low orbit above Kestra II, with *Titan* and its shadow following suit. The pallbearers released their charge and let it float free. This continued for a full orbit, taking over an hour. Those jellies above and below, tending to their duties, blinked their lights and commiserated telepathically (so Deanna reported) as the procession went by. Those that could spare the time flew up alongside and exchanged solemn tendril-caresses with the grieving school, although they left the corpse untouched. Deanna narrated the whole affair in somber tones, her tears flowing freely. After a while, concerned at the sheer volume of grief she must be processing, Riker leaned over and whispered, "Can't you block out some of what they're feeling?"

Her eyes widened. "I can . . . but this should be acknowledged." She clasped his hand. "I'll be all right. It's . . . cathartic. A healing grief."

Once a full orbit had been completed, the school took up a new formation around its lost member, essentially stacking themselves into a column with it in the middle, keeping a few hundred meters between them. The rings of red lights within their bodies, normally almost washed out by their overall glow, began to shine brighter. "They seem to be . . . drawing residual energy from the dead one's distortion generators," Jaza reported. "Sharing it among themselves."

Vale was startled. "That seems . . . a bit vampiric."

"No," Deanna said. "They're preserving a part of its life essence, making sure it endures within the school."

"It also makes practical sense," Jaza added, "if they mean to inter the body on the planet. Even lifeless, those generators contain massive amounts of energy—enough to warp space. They'd have to either drain them or remove them first, if they didn't want to risk serious environmental damage in the event of a rupture." He furrowed his brow. "I suppose the sessile young don't fully charge theirs until they leave the surface."

"Or else they don't grow in until adulthood," Vale countered.

"Maybe. But they'd need gravity manipulation to be able to lift their own mass into orbit."

"Unless the adults carry them there."

"People," Riker advised, "could we curb the scientific speculation for now, out of respect?"

Vale bowed her head. "Sorry, sir."

Once the energy transfer was complete, the two pallbearer jellies took hold of the corpse once more, and the school began a deorbit maneuver. *Titan* followed suit for part of the way, until they began drawing too close to the atmosphere. "Their destination appears to be a cluster of wide, deep hydrothermal lakes in the southern hemisphere," Jaza reported. "I'm reading what must be sessile jellies in various stages of growth, living in the lakes. Of course—I should have realized. Living things that huge, they'd need to live in water to avoid being crushed in planetary gravity—at least until their gravity-control systems are mature."

"Helm," Riker ordered, "maintain orbit over those lakes at current altitude."

"Maintaining, aye," Lavena said, entering the commands for the forced orbit.

Meanwhile, Jaza was checking his scans. "The other regions of heavy geothermal activity on the planet . . . I'm reading very similar lake complexes at each of them. There's little chance of that happening naturally, with such regularity all over the planet. The jellies must engage in . . . I don't know whether to call it nesting or terraforming. Amazing. Seeing them out in space, it's easy to lose your sense of scale about these creatures. They need to transform whole ecosystems just to nurture their young."

"Mr. Jaza," Riker cautioned. "I don't want to repeat myself."

"Sorry, Captain. But this *is* how I show reverence for the universe—by trying to understand its truths. The more I learn about them, the more I can appreciate their beauty."

Deanna touched his arm. "It's all right, Will. They're a curious people themselves. They appreciate our inquisitiveness toward them. Even now. It's a sad time, yes, but it's also a time of renewal, of growth. Once they inter their sibling in the nesting ground, its biomass will sustain the ecology that in turn sustains the growing jellies. And the energy they drew from it . . ." She drew her brows together. "I'm having trouble interpreting what they're telling me, but they say it will bring new life as well. In fact, I think that will be the final part of the ceremony."

Soon the jellies reached the largest lake in the cluster and hovered above it. Jaza put a magnified overhead view on the main screen. Around the rim of the lake were a number of shapes that had to be immature jellies, half-submerged in the water. From above they appeared as eight-pointed starbursts, consisting of eight narrow radial vanes with lobes growing outward between them from their central masses. The lobes were different in color from the adult jellies; if not for their regular shapes he would have assumed they were islands. It appeared they had plants and soil atop them, and presumably animals living upon them as well, much as the Pa'haquel had described.

Something bleeped on Jaza's console, and he looked at the readouts in amazement. "Prophets. Sir, I'm reading huge amounts of transporter activity down there. Directed beneath the lake." Even as he spoke, the deceased jelly began to glow with a watery purple-white shimmer which Riker had seen—and experienced firsthand—before. "Of course," Jaza breathed. "Any other way of trying to bury a creature a kilometer wide would massively disrupt the ecosystem. They're beaming out a space for it beneath the lakebed, then beaming it in quickly before the bed collapses."

"What are they doing with the excavated earth?" Vale wanted to know.

"It's being stored inside one of the jellies."

Now the jellies, their grim burden delivered to rest at last, hovered in slow circles above the nesting grounds. "They're communing with the children," Deanna said. "Explaining to them what's happened, sharing their memories and emotions. Assuring them that the cycle of life continues . . . that after death there is new birth." She gasped, and just then the jellies began to circle faster, spiraling upward into the sky. "Oh my God," Deanna breathed, though it was with excitement and wonder. "They're starting."

"What?"

She beamed at him. "Something wonderful."

The jellies' helical dance carried them up into orbital space, past *Titan* and beyond. The pattern twisted, evolved, and came to center around one jelly, now glowing more brightly than the rest. "It's the one that took in the clay and soil," Jaza said. "There's something happening inside it now . . . some kind of matter transformation."

Deanna met Riker's eyes with wonder. "Conception!" she said. "After death . . . comes new birth."

Riker stared at the screen. "This one . . . just happened to be ready to conceive? Or are they always ready?"

"It makes sense," Jaza said. "With their ability to transmute matter, synthesize anything, they could create an ovum whenever they wanted. Or maybe 'bud' is a better term for it. Asexual reproduction."

Deanna shook her head. "No. Well, not entirely. What I'm feeling . . . it's decidedly not 'asexual.' " Indeed, she was breathing hard, and Riker noted a familiar flush in her cheeks. He stared at her. She reached out and took his hand, but otherwise seemed only distantly aware of his presence. "The others . . . the whole school, we're all part of it." *We?* "This is just the beginning . . . oh!"

"Transporter activity," Jaza said. "The, uhh, embryo, it's been beamed into another jelly!"

"It passes through every one," Deanna said, as the on-screen dance shifted to center on a different jelly, presumably the embryo's recipient. "Each one contributes something . . . each one helps craft the final form. It passes through all until a consensus is reached . . . until it reflects them all, their essences, their visions. It's . . ." She shook herself, and gave an abashed chuckle at herself for getting so carried away. "It feels as much like . . . a creative collaboration, a group sculpture or performance piece, as a sexual act."

"If they can make an egg from scratch," Vale said, "they can remake it. Rewrite its genes, edit them into whatever form they want."

"Eugenics," Keru said, disapprovingly. "Choosing every trait about your baby . . . it seems so cold and calculating."

"It's not like that at all," Deanna said. "There's no set of preconceived notions behind it, no attempt to give themselves greater power or limit their diversity. What I'm sensing . . . there must be a more scientific way of putting it, but I'm feeling it like a work of art. Learning the right techniques, the right basic forms to use, making sure they're free of error . . . but once you have them laid down, there's still so much freedom, and getting them right is what gives you that freedom."

"Error-checking," Jaza said. "The environment cosmozoans live in—all the hard radiation, the quantum distortions—they'd need a means to guard against harmful mutations. But one that at the same time would leave them free to evolve and maintain a healthy level of diversity. This kind of conscious design and revision of their genome—it's perfect for that."

"Yes, that's it. That's what I'm feeling from them. They sense that balance on an instinctive level. They only want what's best for the baby. And so they try to give it the best of all of themselves, and the best of the kin they've lost." She beamed, her eyes glistening. "There is such bittersweet joy in this."

"Maybe this is why the Pa'haquel haven't tried to domesticate the jellies," Jaza mused. "Any attempt they made to reengineer them could be consciously undone during procreation. They have no choice but to take them from the wild."

And so it continued for some time, the jellies transferring the embryo between them one by one, until all fourteen members of the school had left their mark on it. Then it was returned to the originator, but Jaza reported more replicator-like activity from inside it. "Second-draft revisions?" Vale suggested.

"Essentially," Deanna said, still breathless. "They're nearing consensus . . . very nearly . . . Yes," she said, though it seemed she was holding herself back from shouting it. Riker had long since stopped watching the viewscreen, though the others on the bridge remained studiously focussed on their consoles. She grinned at Riker, eyes wide with wonder. "And now the quickening."

"That would be an energy transfer," Jaza interpreted. "They're feeding energy into the embryo . . . its biosigns are growing stronger, stabilizing." On the screen, the "mother" jelly, at the center of another column formation, glowed brighter, especially near its core, where a separate light seemed to be growing within it.

"We share the essence of our lost sibling," Deanna said, falling into the first person plural once again.

"Or what's left of it," Jaza said. "Most of that energy was used in the conception process."

Now the jellies completed their dance, each of them giving the "mother" a final caress. The others continued swirling around while the gravid jelly descended back to the nesting ground. "Permission to launch a probe, sir," Jaza asked. "Just to get a better look at this."

Deanna nodded briefly, indicating that the jellies wouldn't be offended. "Granted," Riker said.

Once the "mother" reached the hydrothermal lakes, the

probe allowed them to watch from below and to the side as it reached up into its ventral cavity with all eight tentacles. Gingerly, it extracted the embryo, a glowing pod resembling a mother-of-pearl pumpkin, and lowered it slowly into the lake. Despite the delicacy of the action, it was still over forty meters wide, and the water displacement produced a set of prodigious but gentle waves radiating out across the lake.

Soon the pod was completely submerged, but Jaza reported its biosigns were still healthy and strong. "It's extruding eight small anchors into the lakebed," he said, reading sensor data from the probe. "I suppose those will grow into its geothermal roots. Eventually it'll grow large enough to breach the surface again."

The "mother" creature lingered for a few moments, and then rose up to join the others again. "Do they just leave them there?" Vale asked.

"They keep watch from orbit," Deanna told her. "The young are fairly self-sufficient, and there's little that can hurt them . . . short of a volcanic eruption, I'd say. And the adult jellies can speak to them telepathically, teach and nurture them that way . . . so in a sense they're always together."

"Even when this school is away?"

"They have a very communal sense of parenting. The children belong to them all."

Jaza cleared his throat. "So . . . if they feel the young are safe . . . would they have any objection to us sending down an away team to study them?"

Deanna laughed, somewhat breathlessly after the extended wash of emotions she'd endured. "They would have no objections, Najem. But I would if you intend it to be anytime before morning. I'm exhausted." She looked at the chronometer on her armside console. "And I hadn't realized how far past end of shift it is."

"All right," Riker said. "Let's all get some rest, and we'll arrange a survey in the morning." He and the others turned over their stations to the gamma-shift personnel who'd been waiting patiently, then made their way to the turbolifts.

But when Vale tried to get into the lift after Riker and Deanna, the counselor stopped her. "Would you mind?" Vale looked between them, then nodded and stepped back, allowing the doors to close. Deanna sighed heavily and fell against Riker. "Ohh, thank goodness." She pulled him down to her and kissed him passionately.

When it finally ended, he grinned. "I thought you were exhausted."

"From all the emotions of the mating. Which," she added, "I really, really need to get out of my system as soon as possible."

His grin widened. "Can you hold out until we get to our quarters?"

"I don't know." She had him pushed against the wall now. "Maybe you'd better have us beamed there."

CHAPTER EIGHT

Elder Qui'hibra studied the sensation feeds with mixed feelings. The displays projected on the control atrium's wall showed him the telltale signatures of a successful mating. On the one hand, he was glad the mating had gone well; he hoped the embryo would grow into a large, powerful skymount which would serve the Pa'haquel in generations to come. But it was frustrating that the energy fueling the mating had come from a kill that should have been serving his clan in the here and now. Those fools in their little metal toy of a starship had proven more of a nuisance than he'd expected, and would need to be taught the error of their ways soon, one way or another, lest they bring more disruption to the balance.

Next to him, Qui'chiri shivered. Qui'hibra allowed himself a private moment of amusement at his daughter's melodramatic gesture. He knew that by now her hide had grown as tough as his; she'd inherited that from him, along with her mother's beauty and genius for fleet management. She was simply offering a critique of his tactic: hiding the fleet in the breeding system's outer cometary belt, one sky-mount at each of the most likely departure vectors, their shells camouflaged as ice and with internal heat reduced to minimum. It was not a particularly comfortable tactic, and he had overheard some griping, mainly among the young Pa'haquel males and the Vomnin and Shizadam crew members. (The Rianconi never complained about anything, though Qui'hibra suspected the cold was most troubling to their dainty, half-bare bodies. Conversely, the Fethetrit were prone to complain about everything, but their thick red fur gave them an edge here.) But if Qui'chiri's only concern were her own comfort, she would not have wasted his time or her own with such weakness.

As he expected, a moment later she followed the gesture with words. "I still question the wisdom of this, Father," she said. "To attack them so close to a breeding world . . ."

"So long as we do not make a pattern of it, the risk is manageable," he replied. "And you know what is at stake, probably better than I. We lost a mighty mount to the cloud-shimmers, and several brave families. Our numbers are even more badly depleted than before. We must replenish them in time for the Great Hounding."

She bowed her head briefly at the reminder, but then spoke impatiently. "You know that we will never get there in time, no matter how hard you wish it."

"True." It was hard for him to admit, but the numbers were undeniable. "But such a massive Hounding will result in many losses among the other fleet-clans. I want us strong enough to fill the void, so the balance may be kept. Not to mention the balance within our own fleet," he reminded her.

"Yes, yes, we still have too many fertile females and

unwed males to pair off, and they need somewhere to go."
She parroted the familiar argument in singsong tones.
Neither of them mentioned the unthinkable: lose too many
more skymounts and they would have to be absorbed into
another fleet, shamed and subordinate. The shame of
missing the Great Hounding would make it even worse.
"Spirit deliver us from an excess of young males impatient
to start their own families. The regular number is bad
enough." Qui'hibra let out a tiny laugh, one that probably
only Qui'chiri knew him well enough to recognize as
such. That youthful ambition had served him well, had let
him win a prime mate and build this proud fleet-clan; but
he was glad to have outgrown that contentious phase. He
too had needed to wait for his chance to split off from his
birth-skymount and start a subclan of his own, and his impatience had made him a major discipline problem for the
elder of his small, struggling fleet.

"But at least that is a risk we can cope with," Qui'chiri
went on. "If we were to drive the skymounts from a breeding world this fine, it could cause a major population drop
for generations to come."

"But since it is such a fine world, they would not abandon it easily. And we will not attack too close to the system. When a departing school is spotted, we will trail it for
as long as we can."

"At the risk of losing it."

"Another manageable risk."

"Like allowing that *Titan* ship to continue meddling?"

"Others have meddled in the Hunt before. The Hunt
continues. The balance is kept."

"These seem to have a closer rapport with the skymounts than most. They concern me."

"Their intentions are good, if arrogant and ignorant. I
do not wish them harm if I can avoid it."

"Nice to say in theory. I am a female, I have no time for abstractions. And as you say, we have little margin for error, this close to a Hounding. I say kill them mercifully quick, commend their souls to the Spirit, and move on to the next crisis." That was Qui'chiri—reliably pragmatic to the end, an ideal female. It was what he cherished about her. When his last wife—a competent matriarch, but nowhere near the level of his first, Qui'chiri's mother—had died, Qui'chiri, as the most senior surviving female of the Qui'ha line, had been forced into the role of clan matriarch well before her time, but had borne the responsibility magnificently. If only he had the luxury, he would dote over her shamelessly and devote himself to singing her praises. Instead, most of their conversations were about the business of the clan and the hunt. But that was the language they both spoke best, so it was better that way.

"It is an option," Qui'hibra told her. "But the Hunt is for their good as well, even if they do not accept it."

"And if they disrupt the balance and the chaos takes hold, they will die just the same, and many others with them. Better they die for the right reasons."

"Better still if we can make them see wisdom. Then they could prove an ally."

"All right," Qui'chiri said. "That is practical, I can support it. But the moment it becomes a choice between killing them and losing another skymount—"

"They die, of course."

"Of course." She gave his neck feathers a quick, affectionate preening. "I had no doubt. Good to have it said, though."

Just then, the Shizadam crew member monitoring communications turned to him. "Elder, we have a hue and cry from Skymount Tir'Shi. A school is nearing the system on a vector within their field."

"Inbound, you say? Not outbound?" he asked.

"Verified. A school of thirteen members, inbound at sublight." Qui'hibra was irrationally disappointed. He'd been hoping for a rematch with the school they had fought before. Of course it was natural to expect that school to remain in-system for a time, recharging its energies and ensuring that its offspring settled in well. Still, that school owed him blood, and he wouldn't feel the balance had been truly restored until he could claim it.

But the fleet needed new mounts now, regardless of their pedigree. "Very well," he said aloud. "Continue tracking, then follow them at the edge of sensation range. Once a comfortable distance has been gained, the rest of the fleet will warp to meet you and we will attack."

"So . . . why do you hate Cadet Torvig?"

Ranul Keru glared at the tall, atypically slim Tellarite across from him. For the umpteenth time, he cautioned himself not to rise to the bait. "I don't hate him," he replied in a level tone.

"Liar. How else do you explain these absurdly harsh discipline recommendations you made, hmm? Confinement to quarters? Revoking of security clearances? Possible transfer? What do you think this is, the Spanish Inquisition?" Counselor Pral glasch Haaj didn't conduct his sessions like any other therapist Keru had ever known. One would think that the argumentative approach favored by Tellarites would serve to put patients on the defensive, making it harder for them to trust their counselor and open up about their problems. But Haaj had a way of making it work—of exposing people's mind games and preconceptions, deflating their illusions, and maneuvering them into self-contradictions that forced them to question their assumptions. And he did it without the noisy bluster of the stereotypical Tellarite, though with just as much arrogance. Rather than shouting in anger, he delivered his barbs with withering dryness in a smooth, cultured tenor voice.

"What he did was serious," Keru countered. "And he doesn't seem to care that it was wrong."

"Wrong? How? No harm would've come of it."

"That's not the point. It was incredibly thoughtless of him to attempt to infest people with, with *nanoprobes* without considering their reactions."

"Oho. *Nanoprobes,* is it? *Naa-no-prrobes,*" Haaj said, mocking Keru's weighty delivery. "Not simply nanites, which everyone knows have been routinely used in medicine and research practically since the Dark Ages. No, these were *naa-no-prrobes.* I can practically hear the italics. Tell me, Mr. Keru, what exactly was it about these microscopic monstrosities of Mr. Torvig's that warranted such melodrama?"

Keru glared at him. "You think this is about him being a cyborg? That I'm treating him unfairly because he reminds me of the Borg? Counselor, I'm not a bigot."

"Well, you're certainly not a smallot." Haaj looked over his massive frame. "Good grief, I'm amazed you were never joined. A whole family of symbionts could've set up house in there with room for guests. I'm sorry, that was small of me. Well, proportionately. Now where were we?"

"You were calling me a bigot."

"Excuse me, *who* called you that? I'm sure the word never crossed *my* lips. But since you bring it up . . ."

Keru sighed. "All right, I admit, the sight of Torvig makes me uncomfortable. Frankly it makes a lot of people uncomfortable, and he's well aware of it. Yet he deliberately chose to take an action that would provoke that very unease."

"Ohh, I see. Well, we can't have that. Challenging people's prejudices? That way lies madness, surely. Better to conform, to downplay your uniqueness and just try to fit in. After all, that's how the Trill did it up until a decade or so ago, right? And we all know how well that worked out for you lot."

That struck a nerve. For centuries, the joined Trill had kept the existence of their symbionts a secret from the rest of the galaxy, afraid that other humanoids would see them as parasites holding their humanoid hosts in thrall, or as inferior creatures to be exploited or dissected. The truth had come out about a dozen years ago, and had been better accepted than the Trill had feared. But keeping secrets was a longtime habit of the joined Trill leadership, stretching back to an ancient and horrible act of genocide thousands of years in the past, one which the Trill elites had tried to erase entirely from their history out of the shame they felt at the act. More recently, they had concealed the fact that half the humanoid population was fit for joining rather than a tiny fraction, for fear that the many would covet the symbionts of the few, steal and trade them as commodities, and hate and persecute their possessors. Three years ago, the weight of all the secrets had reached the breaking point, culminating in a violent uprising by a radical unjoined faction, the exposure of all those buried secrets, and the murder of the majority of the symbionts. So Keru had to concede that trying to conceal one's true nature for fear of how others would respond was not a very healthy thing to do.

"Okay," he said. "That's not what I meant to say. What I meant was, there are better ways to assert your individuality than deliberately provoking others. Maybe that kind of, I don't know, activism has its place, but not on a Starfleet vessel. I can't sanction deliberately disruptive behavior no matter what its motives. And that's still true regardless of my Borg issues. I admit I don't exactly have warm and fuzzy feelings about cyborgs, but I'm not letting that affect my work. You should know that. I've dealt with those issues."

"No, you haven't."

"Yes, I have."

Haaj shook his head. "Haven't."

"Look, we've been talking about it for the past few weeks!"

"Talking about what?"

"About . . . about Oghen. About T'Lirin."

"T'Lirin was a Borg? Imagine my surprise."

"No, no!" He reined in his frustration. "About having to leave her behind. Having to admit that, that sometimes you have to make that choice. Like Worf did with Sean." For years, Keru had resented the Klingon for what he'd done, for killing Keru's lifemate rather than trying to save him from Borg assimilation, as Picard had been saved, as Tuvok's former shipmate Annika Hansen had been. The events during the evacuation of Oghen, in which Keru had been forced to leave Lieutenant T'Lirin to die in order to save the rest of his team and a number of refugees, had forced him to reconsider those beliefs, and to reevaluate his bitterness toward Worf.

At first, he had been reluctant to seek help in this from *Titan*'s counseling staff. He had chosen instead to talk it out with his best friend, Alyssa Ogawa. But Alyssa was a medic, and had insisted that she wouldn't serve him as well as another professional, one trained for such services. "If your leg is broken, you don't go to your friend, you go to a doctor," she'd told him. "This is no different. The mind needs maintenance and care just like any other part of the body, and if you're smart, you'll get it from someone who's qualified to provide it. The best way I can help you, Ranul, is by sending you to them." She had convinced him, but he hadn't been sure which counselor to talk to. Deanna Troi, having been Worf's former lover, was too close to the issue. And Keru had trouble taking the toylike Huilan seriously. He realized that was a prejudice in itself, a hangup he needed to overcome, but dealing with that could get in the way of his other problem. So he'd chosen Haaj. After the first session, he'd wondered if he'd made a mistake; yet he'd kept coming back regardless. There was something draining yet refreshing about his contentious sessions with Haaj, not unlike sparring in the gym.

"So you've dealt with that, have you?" Haaj said now, in his usual skeptical tone.

"Yes, I have."

"You're all right with having to leave someone behind to die."

"If I have to, yes."

"And when do you have to?"

"When it's for the greater good. When it has to be done to save more lives."

"Ahh, I see. So you'll sacrifice the individual for the good of the whole."

"If necessary."

"Oh, so *that's* what you mean by dealing with your Borg issues! You've decided that the individual really is irrelevant after all, that only the collective matters. Well done, lad, you've convinced me. Where do we sign up to be assimilated?"

Keru gaped at him. "No! God, no! What I'm saying, it's entirely different! What happened on Oghen—I didn't just casually throw T'Lirin's life away like some cog in a machine. I *agonized* over that decision."

"But you made it anyway."

"Yes," he said, wincing.

"After swearing to yourself that you'd never, ever contemplate such an act, because that's the way the Borg do things. Well, that tells us what your word is worth, doesn't it?"

"I—" Keru realized he had no ready answer. He sat silently for a time under Haaj's querulous stare, contemplating what had been said. "So . . . you think I'm taking my own guilt out on Torvig? Treating him like a Borg because I'm afraid I'm turning into one myself?"

"Don't ask me. We've been talking about what *you* think."

Again Keru was slow to answer. "Maybe . . . I don't know. I guess that's something I need to think about."

"Finally. Something penetrates that thick skull. I was starting to wonder if you could hear me from way up there."

"But it doesn't change my job. Torvig is a discipline problem. He violated numerous regs, and I offered a recommendation on how to penalize him. But it was just a recommendation. The final decision was up to Riker and Vale, and they went with a lighter discipline. So whatever biases I may have . . . they're just my problem, because they don't determine the kid's fate."

"I see. So because you don't make the decisions, it's all right for you to project your self-loathing onto him. Well, I'm sure he'll be glad to hear that."

"I didn't say that! I said it isn't about how I do my job."

"So? Why should I care how you do your job? Do I look like the first officer? You came here to deal with what's going on in your mind."

"But you were the one who brought Torvig up!"

"And you were the one who gave me reason to."

Keru glared at Haaj, forced to admit that, as usual, he had a point. He had let his state of mind influence his discipline recommendation, and that was what had brought it into Haaj's purview. "All right. So I have a problem, and I need to deal with it. Where do I start?"

"Well, that's not my problem. Not till next week, anyway. Your hour's up. Go on, shoo! I've got other patients waiting, and with you in here there's barely room enough for *me.*"

Once the door shut behind Keru, he had the realization that it hadn't been a full hour. And he was fairly sure he was Haaj's last patient of the day. But after a moment, he realized there was method to Haaj's meanness. Now that he'd made a discovery about himself, Haaj was giving him time to process it. The wiry Tellarite had taken the action that helped his patient the most, just as he always did.

Keru smirked, realizing how much he liked the guy.

Aili Lavena swam beneath a star-jelly, feeling more alive than she had in months. Kestra II's hydrothermal lakes were warm and comforting, rich in oxygen, and just alkaline enough to lend an interesting tartness to their water.

And at last Aili was able to do her job without needing that horrid hydration suit. She didn't have the pleasure of being nude, though; she was on duty, and thus wore a minimal uniform, a halter-style swimsuit held on by shoulder straps so as to leave her dorsal crests free. But it was still a delight, at last being able to join an away mission that made use of her species' particular gifts.

And the realm in which she swam was amazing, too. This sessile young jelly was less than half-grown, and maybe about a century old. The eight nodes that made up its body at this age formed an island half a kilometer across, atop which had grown a lush ecosystem. The rest of Commander Troi's away team was surveying it now, with its consent; though still young, the jelly had reached full sentience and learned much of the universe from its starfaring elders. But Aili alone was getting to see its underside. Eviku, who descended from aquatic ancestors, was also doing his part to survey the lake, but he couldn't dive as deep or last as long without oxygen as she could.

Well, perhaps "underside" was an exaggeration, for the true underside floated only slightly above the lakebed, and the space underneath was choked with thousands of tendrils in addition to the eight immense geothermal taproots that bored deep into the magma flows below. Aili was exploring more off to the side, though still within the bounds of what the creature's ultimate size would be. Indeed, she could legitimately say she was within the jelly itself. Extending from the island, forming the framework of its ultimate saucer shape, were eight radial vanes of staggering size. The vanes consisted of a dense lattice of tendrils of all sizes, catching matter from the winds as well as providing a framework for vines, small animals and avians to climb on. Between them grew a tangle of fibers and struts, growing out across the water's surface and down below it, further anchoring the growing creature and extending the reach of its self-sustained ecosystem. Beneath the water, the network of its growing body had become the basis of a complex ecology like that of a coral reef or a deep-sea thermal vent on Pacifica or Earth. Schools of fish darted among its tendrils, and Lavena playfully chased after some of them, leaving her wrist-mounted tricorder to work on its own. They proved elusive, though, and darted through a narrow gap which she couldn't swerve in time to avoid. Her shoulders wedged into it, and she struggled to break free.

To her surprise, though, after a moment one of the tendrils shimmered with magenta ripples and dematerialized, setting her free. "Thank you," she said, sobered by the reminder that this was a self-aware ecosystem, conscious of the needs of everything that inhabited it and acting to provide for them. It was how the jellies drew so many species to live among them, an irresistible lure. Nearby, she could see more purplish shimmers, almost looking like reflections of light in the water, as the jelly provided plants for a group of whirling starfish-like creatures to dine on. Such a thing could be the perfect trap, Lavena realized—it could draw in animals with their heart's desire, then beam their constituent molecules into itself as raw material for its growth. But the jellies grew so slowly, or so Jaza had explained, that they could easily wait for the animals to die and decay naturally.

More than that, though, they seemed to genuinely care about their nests, feeling a responsibility—even in youth—to give back to the ecology that nursed them. Thinking about it left Aili feeling abashed, and she decided to swim to the surface and get her mind off of it.

But when she breached the surface and got her bearings, she found Deanna Troi nearby, sitting on one of the jelly's tendrils with her boots beside her, dangling her bare feet in the water. "Hello, Aili," she said. "The water is marvelously warm, isn't it?"

"Yes," Aili replied. She tried to hide her unease from the commander, but knew it would be futile. "Commander . . . I need to tell you something. About . . . what you saw . . . with Dr. Ra-Havreii . . ."

Troi studied her. "Ensign, I don't pry needlessly into the private lives of my crewmates."

"Of course not," Aili was quick to say. "But . . . I just didn't want you to think that I was . . . flaunting my sexual activities before you. I have no intention of doing that, of doing anything to make you or . . . or the captain uneasy with me."

Deanna smiled. "Aili, I have no reason to be uneasy about it. You and Will had a harmless fling two decades ago. If that sort of thing bothered me, I never would've married him." She lowered herself languidly onto one side, propping up her head with one fist, to bring herself closer to Aili's eye level. "I think we both know that I'm not the one who's bothered. I think we both know what Captain Riker doesn't—about the difference between amphibious and fully aquatic Selkies."

Aili stared at her, motionless except for her gill-crests, which reflexively undulated to maintain waterflow across them. "Then . . . you know?"

"I know that in your amphibious phase, you're supposed to devote yourselves to procreation and parenting. That purely recreational sex is something you're supposed to save for your aquatic phase, once you've discharged those obligations. I also know it doesn't always work that way in practice."

"Yes," Aili said in a small voice. "Especially where offworlders are involved. They find us more alluring in amphibious phase . . . because they can mate with us more easily in the air, and because our breasts are enlarged then." She gestured toward her own four small breasts, which no longer needed to produce milk and had thus flattened out to enhance her streamlining. "Often they don't understand the difference between our phases . . . and we're often content not to tell them."

"Understandable," Troi said. "To be expected to be so responsible all the time . . . then to look at your aquatic elders and see them free to romp and play, to be totally free in their sexuality . . . it's a natural temptation. Not just the desire to be free from responsibility, but the desire to 'act grown-up,' as it were."

"But giving into that temptation is . . . somewhat scandalous."

"But does that actually stop anyone from doing it anyway?"

"Rarely," Aili admitted. "After all, they're offworlders. They'll go away and no one will be the wiser. And you never have to see them again."

"Unless you decide to join Starfleet . . . and end up on a ship commanded by one of them."

"Well, there's that." Aili looked away. "It's just that . . . it was inappropriate. Not for him—I was an adult, fully mature by human standards—but for a Selkie it was improper and irresponsible, to spend my energies on a human lover rather than my children. And if it were known that Will . . . that the captain had participated in my impropriety, it would reflect badly on him. And I don't want that, ma'am."

Troi smiled. "I understand. Will's former partners tend to remember him very fondly."

"Well . . . truth be told, I don't remember him that clearly at all."

"Really!" Troi seemed mildly offended on her husband's behalf, though there was humor in it.

"It's just . . . there were so many. I was . . . very irresponsible back then. More than most. I was a poor mother, a poor caregiver. I wanted to put that behind me, to make up for it. That's why I joined Starfleet. Even though I knew I might encounter . . . various old partners again. I'm a different person now, I figured I could handle that. But to have the captain himself be one of my . . . I'm just concerned how it would reflect on him."

Deanna reached out and clasped Aili's shoulder. "Well, your secret is safe with me. No one else needs to know you were intimate with Will, and Will doesn't need to know about the . . . inappropriateness of it. After all," she said with steel in her voice, "it's not like he's ever going to try it again."

Aili would have sighed if she still breathed. "Thank you, Commander. I'm so relieved that you understand." She smiled. "Would you like to join me for a swim? You were right, the water's wonderful."

But Deanna had suddenly grown distracted, looking skyward. A shadow passed across the sun, and Aili looked upward. Above them, a gigantic star-jelly hovered, a vast dark cloud with a halo of refracted light limning its edges. Wispy tendrils extended downward from it like rays of sunlight breaking through clouds. "Oh, no," the commander breathed. Then she tapped her combadge and scrambled to pull her boots back on. "Troi to *Titan.*"

"Go ahead."

"Will, I've just been informed—another school of jellies is being attacked."

Riker had been just about to order the away team beamed aboard when, with a shimmer of purple, they materialized on the bridge. All but one, that is. Deanna's eyes scanned the others—Jaza, Eviku, Chamish, Rriarr—and she struck her combadge. "Troi to Lavena. Are you aboard?"

"Yes, Commander, in my quarters," came her response a moment later, her voice oddly modified by the underwater acoustics. *"They beamed up my drysuit too."*

"Report to the bridge, Ensign," Riker said, then turned to Deanna, barely hearing the Selkie's acknowledgment. She spoke in response to his questioning look.

"The jellies are impatient. They want us out there as quickly as possible."

"Out where? Coordinates of the attack, Mr. Jaza?"

The Bajoran was already at his console, scanning. "Three-two-one mark 42, point-eight light-years distant. A school of thirteen under attack by . . . looks like most of Qui'hibra's fleet. Yes, the rest are on their way to intercept."

Riker turned to Axel Bolaji at the conn. "Chief, time to intercept, best speed?"

"Fourteen minutes, sir. The brown dwarf's gravity complicates departure angles at warp."

"Damn. All we can do is watch." By now Jaza had a high-magnification image on the screen, courtesy of long-range sensors. "Take us out of orbit anyway, helm, best speed to intercept. Lieutenant Rager, try hailing the Pa'haquel fleet."

"Hailing . . . no response, sir."

On screen, the jellies began withdrawing their tentacles, flipping over and materializing their armor. "Have they decided to fight instead of run?" Riker asked, knowing it was unlikely.

"They still can't bring themselves to attack," Deanna told him. "They know now that something else is controlling the corpses—thanks to us." *Thanks to Tuvok,* Riker amended, though he knew the Vulcan was not to blame for letting the information slip. "The school comes from outside the system, but the news has been spread telepathically. But they still can't desecrate them. They have a wounded member who can't go to warp, and they're staying to try to protect it."

Before long, the only way to tell the groups of armored jellies apart visually was by their behavior—whether they fired or not, whether they defended or menaced the injured, unarmored member. "Is their armor protecting them?" Riker asked as he studied the one-sided battle.

"Only some," Jaza said. "In fact, the armor's composition seems to be in flux . . . like they're improving their defense against the plasma stings as they go." A pause. "But the Pa'haquel are adjusting the stings to compensate, upping their intensity." And they clearly knew the most vulnerable points to strike—apparently along the meridional seams in the armor. Riker and the crew watched helplessly as several hunter ships focused their blasts along a single seam in one jelly's armor until it split, spilling a roseate cloud of plasma.

Deanna and Chamish both gasped at that moment, and Deanna sagged against him. "Dead?" Riker asked with sympathy.

"Yes. I'm . . . doing my best to block out the pain . . . but there are hundreds of jellies in the system, and they *want* me to share in it. They want us to do something, to tell them what we know so they can see these attacks coming and get away in time. They don't understand why we won't help them. They're begging us, Will." Her voice was rough despite her best efforts to block out the emotional onslaught.

But Riker realized something, and turned to Chamish. "Lieutenant, you feel it too?"

The Kazarite widened his dark eyes, and spoke in a gentle voice that belied his somewhat feral, simian appearance. "Yes, sir. Perhaps the inhibitor is less effective on my species."

"Or maybe it just isn't strong enough." He turned to

Vale. "Commander, contact all the telepaths on board, find out if they're being affected too."

"I've already gotten calls from Savalek and Orilly, confirming it. Sickbay reports T'Pel is reacting too."

"How bad is it?" Riker asked Chamish.

"Not severe yet . . . but they are pressing . . . *aah!*" On the viewer, another jelly's armor shell cracked open. With the defense formation scattered, enough shots got through to finish the defenseless jelly as well. "Please, Captain . . . they want me to . . . *I* want to help them . . . I advise you to relieve me of duty, sir."

Riker turned to the security station. "Mr. Keru, I want escorts on all psi-sensitive crew members. I don't want any of them getting access to that warp-signature data."

"Aye, sir. Does that include Commander Troi?"

Riker exchanged a look with her. "I think it should," Deanna said, "just in case."

"All right. Commander, Mr. Chamish," Keru went on, "I'd like to ask you to leave the bridge, please. You'll be met when you leave the turbolift and escorted to your quarters."

"Of course, sir. Thank you." The soft-spoken ecologist turned to Riker. "But please, Captain, if there is a way you can help them . . ."

Riker nodded at him reassuringly, and the Kazarite smiled and meekly left the bridge, Deanna just behind him. *Not that I have the slightest idea how to stop this massacre,* Riker admitted to himself. "Rager, try hailing again. Damm it, isn't three enough?" The attack showed no sign of stopping.

Jaza's voice was subdued. "The injured one, the unarmored one . . . it seems it was hit too many times. It lost too much structural integrity . . . I guess it's past salvaging."

"Sir!" Keru spoke with some alarm. Riker looked up sharply.

"What is it?"

"Security reports . . . they can't find Mr. Tuvok, sir."

Tuvok had to make the anguish stop. Nothing else mattered.

No—he knew that other things still mattered. He knew that what he was about to do was unethical and immoral, that it violated his duty as an officer and his principles as a Vulcan, and would probably end his Starfleet career. He just didn't care. The pain, the grief—feeling the jellies die, feeling the agony of losing a loved one multiplied a thousand times over—it was too much to control, too much to *want* to control. The sheer need to feel it, to act on it, overrode everything else. If it were T'Pel, if it were his children dying out there, would not even a Vulcan throw discipline to the winds before seeing them slaughtered? And right now, as far as he was concerned, it *was* his family dying out there. He felt it as they felt it. He loved them, and had to give them what they needed to save themselves.

And yet even now, even in the throes of uncontrollable emotion, somehow he retained his intellect, his cunning. Vulcan philosophy taught that emotion clouded the judgment, left one in a fog of animal impulses. Yet now his perceptions, his decisions seemed clearer than they had ever been in his life. The confusion came from fighting against emotion—and right now he had no wish to fight it. So there was no doubt, no ambiguity. He knew exactly what he needed to do, and was preternaturally alert to anything that could stand in his way. He remembered every detail of *Titan*'s Jefferies-tube network, of the patterns of its security forces. He recalled exactly how to reprogram a tricorder to mask his life signs from the sensors. He knew it all because he *had* to know it. Far from hampering him, the passion inspired him, guided him.

It had been this way before, he knew. In the prison on Romulus. Seven weeks of torture, starvation, and degradation. Feigning death to escape, a healing trance. Awakened in time to hear the guard preparing to scan him, risking exposure. There had been only one option left to him by his circumstances, his need to survive, his sheer rage. He had chosen, then as now, to set everything else aside, to save his shame and disgust for later and do what he had to do. He had killed four Romulans and mortally wounded another, forced himself into the fifth man's mind before he died. He had abandoned Surak, given into rage and hate and killing, and he had chosen not to care until afterward.

But he couldn't think about that now. He couldn't care about that now. He was here—the science department. Someone here would have the access codes to the warp-signature data. His were blocked. He had tried a backdoor access already, but wasn't familiar enough with these computers, with the cybersecurity protocols which Commander Jaza had devised based on principles from the Bajoran underground. He had recognized similarities to Maquis protocols, could have cracked the codes in time, but he had no such time. He needed viable codes *now*. And he needed an authorized voice to speak them.

The main, general-use lab space was cluttered as such spaces tended to be, full of components and consoles and tables that got shoved around at the whims of whatever inspirations struck the scientists who shared it. This was deficient from a security standpoint, since the Jefferies-tube access panel was hidden from ready view.

Tuvok slipped out through the panel soundlessly and

peered around the portable holotank that someone had placed in the middle of the floor. Few were present in the common lab right now; that was fortunate. One was a security guard, a large, dark human named Okafor. He was escorting Cadet Orilly toward the exit. Tuvok could see that Orilly was agitated, feeling the jellies' deaths as he did, feeling their urgings for help; yet she went along meekly with the guard. Her head turned toward him, as though she knew just where to look. Her eyes locked with his, yet she said nothing to the guard.

But there—on the other side of the lab, conversing with K'chak'!'op, was Melora Pazlar. Tuvok felt a thrill of pent-up irritation at the tiresome Elaysian. She was irreverent, rude, arrogant. Yet he knew she would have the codes he needed. How perfect.

Tuvok leapt at her, was on her in a second. She fell to the ground under his momentum. He heard several snaps of bone, heard her cry out. He didn't care. His hands went to her temples.

Strong, slick tentacles entangled him, pulled him back. K'chak'!'op. He struggled against them. "Please stop, little one," came the sound of the Pak'shree's voder. "You're so fragile, I don't want to risk hurting you!" But Pazlar was writhing on the floor, trying to back away, but helpless. Perhaps her motor-assist armature had shorted out. It was perfect, but he had to get free, get to her. Out of the corner of his eye, he saw Okafor with phaser drawn, trying to get a clear shot. He fought harder, but more tentacles now entangled him.

But then Orilly leapt into motion. One trunk knocked Okafor's phaser away while the other swept against him and knocked him through the open doorway. She kicked his feet out of the doorway with her paw and slapped the lock panel. Then she spun and charged K'chak'!'op, rearing up on her hind paws. The Irriol's weight slammed into the Pak'shree, knocking her over and breaking most of her tentacles' grip on Tuvok. With a triumphant surge, he pulled free of the rest and fell upon Pazlar once again. She struggled feebly as his hands clutched her temples. "My mind to your mind," he rasped. "Your thoughts to my thoughts!"

"Nn*no!*"

"Our minds are becoming . . ."

"One!" they finished together. Yes—he had her voice. Now where was the code? The access code. She couldn't hide it from herself.

"Computer!" she said, Tuvok's puppet. "Display wide-band sensor specifications. Include specific calibrations and readings for Pa'haquel biosigns and warp-signature data. Authorization Pazlar, Gamma Nine, Emerald."

The computer chirped obedience, and the data came up on the nearest wall screen. Tuvok drank it in, and the jellies knew it as he did. Along with it he sent his own knowledge of deflector shields and how to calibrate them against the bio-energy stings of the hunters. He sagged with relief. Already he felt their triumph, shared in it. *Now they will be safe.*

And then the guilt began to sink in.

INTERLUDE

CLAN CHE'HITH'RHA LEAD SKYMOUNT, STARDATE 57175.3

Elder Che'sethri had grown tired of the Hunt. Sacred duty or no, the unrelenting grind of it left its wear on an aged body and mind. There were times that Che'sethri wished he could emulate the elders of other species, those who lived in blissful ignorance or neglect of the cosmic mission which drove the Pa'haquel, and who could afford to indulge in leisure, comfort and simple inactivity.

Yet a vista like the one spread before him on the sensation wall was enough to fire what remained of his predatory spirit, to get him excited about the Hunt once more, for a little while at least. For before him was the largest assemblage of skymount schools he had beheld in many a year. They had been drawn by a rare and novel phenomenon: a protostar had collided with a tachyon stream, and their interaction had somehow triggered a subspace vortex. The gravitational suction from the vortex drew in the protostar's hydrogen, compressing and fusing it, and the resultant energy fed and perpetuated the vortex, while also radiating outward in a flood of wide-spectrum energies, heavy nuclei, and exotic particles. As such, it was a veritable feast for starfaring creatures. The sensation feeds revealed five different schools of skymounts, turned toward the fount with their tentacles spread wide, sails grown between them to catch the nourishing outpour. They were not alone; a few of the diaphanous sail-sylphs that rode the tachyon currents had spilled wind and fallen to normal space in order to feast. Some branchers were present as well on the far side of the system, though the skymounts and sylphs kept their distance from those.

But they were of no interest to him now. The five schools offered an unprecedented opportunity; with luck and cunning, he could make the biggest kill of his career. Some in his clan complained of being too far antispinward to reach the upcoming Great Hounding. But to Che'sethri, there was just as much glory to be had here, and with no need to share it with others. Maybe his fleet would add enough skymounts to require splitting it in two, and allowing his eldest son to take his place at the lead of one. With other great fleets depleted by the Hounding, he could swoop in with two mighty fleets in its wake and instantly become a force to be reckoned with. Other fleets would be eager to make alliance with his, giving many nubile females in marriage to boost his fleet's numbers. Perhaps some of the high and mighty fleets, like that overbearing fossil Aq'hareq's, would be so badly depleted that he could absorb their shamed survivors into his as a ready labor force.

Such a triumph, he imagined, might win him enough esteem that he could get away with turning both fleets over to his sons and retiring into leisure. He chuckled to himself. More likely, a hunt that successful would fire him up too much to enjoy retirement. Perhaps the best-case scenario would be if he died gloriously in the struggle and left the triumph and prestige as a legacy to his sons. But what struggle could there ever be with skymounts? Perhaps when he was done with them he would go after the branchers.

Huntsmistress Rha'djemi jogged up to him, bowing her head briefly, though her attempt at humility made little headway against her lust for action. "We stand ready, Elder. All mounts report their stings are hot and ready to fire. We are poised to strike all five at once, three ships emerging in the midst of each school. We will take them unaware, all fat and gorged and slow—my Elder, if we wished we could slay every last one!" She finished with a laugh of savage glee.

Che'sethri chuckled at her zeal. "Calm yourself, Huntsmistress. Remember the balance. Kill too many, and what will our grandchildren have to kill?"

"Of course, Elder. I just meant—imagine if we could."

"Yes." Not that he could blame her. Rha'djemi's enthusiasm for the hunt was what made her indispensible to him, what had brought her to her rank and kept her there. Raised without a mother or sisters, the girl had always been more interested in combat and hunting than in the maintenance of skymounts, resources and personnel. Her fierce competence had brought her quickly to authority, and quickly silenced those few foolish young males whose pride made them resent taking combat orders from a female (and the Fethetrit, whose pride made them resent taking anyone's orders). If anything, she'd had more friction with his wife, who wasn't accustomed to dealing with a female under his command instead of hers. But Rha'djemi had won the matriarch's grudging respect, if not her love. The huntsmistress, far more than Che'sethri himself, had kept this fleet a viable hunting force over the past few years. And he supposed he had himself to blame for her lack of regard for future generations. He had done all he could to discourage her suitors, not wishing to lose her to another mount or fleet through marriage. Unfortunately there were no eligible males on this mount that were distant enough relations for her to wed. And she could not remain a huntsmistress if she were mount-wed and obliged to serve the needs of her skymount. He would marry her himself just to keep her onboard, if his wife would ever allow it.

He noticed that Rha'djemi was staring at him, almost trembling with bloodlust, and he realized he'd wandered off into thought like the senile old fool he was. He bowed to her. "May the Spirit bless our hunt this day, and may the prey forgive us for what pain we cause," he intoned ritually. "Proceed with the strike."

Rha'djemi rolled her eyes; she had no interest in religion, and *liked* inflicting pain. But she made no comment, being too eager to begin the strike. "Yes, Elder," she said in a hurry, already whirling to address the crews. "Communication teams, confirm synch! Propulsion teams, ready for dewarp! Stinger teams, keep them hot but keep them focused! Ready . . . ready . . . *strike!*"

But even as she spoke, Che'sethri began to realize something was wrong. The skymounts were already starting to move, away from where the subfleets would emerge. It was almost as if they knew an attack was coming. But that was not possible.

The sensation wall blurred as the warpfield collapsed. After a moment, it cleared again . . . and by now it was definite that the skymounts were fleeing. "Fire, fire! Compensate, do not let them slip away!" Rha'djemi was calling. He heard surprise in her voice, but she kept it firm and steady, focusing the crews, keeping them from losing their rhythm in the face of this unexpected turn.

But the skymounts had already picked up a fair amount of speed and were pulling away. "Pursue, best speed!" the huntsmistress snapped. "Divert energy to sublight propulsion!" Now the quarry began to tumble and shimmer, their armor slowly materializing. By the time the attacking mounts drew close enough, the armor was in place, the stings absorbed.

"Keep firing!" Rha'djemi cried. "The armor cannot hold long!"

But something strange was happening. The sting blasts were not even reaching the armor; instead they splashed off of shield envelopes that shimmered just above the prey's skin. Rha'djemi emitted a squawk of surprise, but promptly swallowed it and rallied herself. "Compensate for that! Scan for the shield frequency, recalibrate the stings! Maybe we can pierce them!" She had enough experience battling Fethet raiders and planet-dwellers' fleets (always so protective of their imaginary borders) to be able to cope with deflector shields.

He sensed her frustration, shared it. This was to have been a triumph, the hunt of a lifetime, and now they'd be lucky to bag two or three before the rest warped away. What had happened? How had it gone so wrong so quickly?

"Concentrate on the weak spots! Be bold, draw close, remember they will not fire back!" Despite her dismay, Rha'djemi kept her focus, and the determination in her voice brought Che'sethri renewed confidence. Perhaps this would not be the kill of a lifetime, but it could still be a good kill, and that was what mattered. They had a duty, a sacred task to perform, and with Rha'djemi guiding the hunt there was no question of success.

But then he saw Rha'djemi shimmer with violet light and disappear, her voice falling silent in midcommand. He looked around wildly, saw the others shimmering out along with her. A moment later, the violet glow engulfed him.

Then he saw Rha'djemi's form before him once again, and he was relieved. Except in the next moment, he realized that behind her, all around her, was open space. Her mouth moved, but he heard nothing. Her eyes were wide with a fear he'd never seen in them before. The sight was even more painful to him than the rush of air torn out of his lungs in the next moment.

At least, Che'sethri reflected in his final moments, he had managed to keep her with him until the end.

PART TWO

TITANOMACHY

Thus moving on, with silent pace,
And triumph in her sweet, pale face,
She reached the station of Orion.
Aghast he stood in strange alarm!
And suddenly from his outstretched arm
Down fell the red skin of the lion
Into the river at his feet.
His mighty club no longer beat
The forehead of the bull; but he
Reeled as of yore beside the sea,
When, blinded by Oenopion,
He sought the blacksmith at his forge,
And, climbing up the mountain gorge,
Fixed his blank eyes upon the sun.

—"The Occultation of Orion"

CHAPTER NINE

When Will Riker had gotten his promotion to full commander, nearly two decades ago back on the *Hood*, Captain DeSoto had taken him into his ready room for a private talk. "At this rate," he'd said, neither of them recognizing the irony at the time, "you'll be a captain within five years. I don't know if you'll still be on this ship when the time arrives, so I figure there are some things I should let you in on now."

The list had been short but insightful, typical of Robert DeSoto. But the last item had been the most important, he had stressed. "When you get your own ship, and go on your first mission . . . you will make a serious mistake, one that will have lasting consequences. Not 'could,' not 'might'—will. Or 'shall,' I guess," he amended with a smirk, to make it clear he wasn't addressing Will by name. "Don't misunderstand, I'm not saying I lack faith in you. It happens to every captain. It's how people learn, it's necessary. The catch is, the mistakes you make as a captain can do a hell of a lot more harm than the mistakes of commanders, lieutenants, and other mere mortals."

"And there's nothing you can do about it?" Riker had asked.

"You will make the mistake, that can't be helped. But if you remember that, if you accept it, then you can probably keep the mistake from being too big."

Now, today, Riker was wondering if too much time had passed since he'd heard that advice. Already, only a few months into his first command, he'd made more than one mistake of truly epic proportions. In the Small Magellanic Cloud, his decision to purge the Red King's intelligence from the Romulan fleet it had taken over had forced its energy matrix back into the substrate of surrounding space-time, triggering an expanding spatial distortion which had destroyed the Neyel homeworld of Oghen and snuffed out its population of two billion—and possibly the populations of several other worlds to boot, if the subsequent closure of the interspatial rift had not damped out the distortion wave as theorized. True, if Riker and his crew had not intervened, the emergence of the Red King's protouniverse would have wiped out those worlds anyway, along with most of the rest of the SMC, in a sort of localized ekpyrotic Big Bang. But the thought still haunted him that if he'd acted less precipitously, gathered more information before attempting to interfere with an unknown and profoundly alien phenomenon, two billion deaths might have been averted. Starfleet and Deanna had assured him there was nothing he could have done differently, as had Picard when he'd sought his former captain's advice over subspace. And intellectually he knew they were right. But he still couldn't help wondering.

And now, on his very next mission, he'd made another mistake which could devastate an entire civilization. The species itself would presumably adjust, but its culture would be changed forever. Whatever he may have thought of the Pa'haquel's way of life, he couldn't see its forced abandonment due to his precipitate actions as anything but a catastrophe.

On a smaller scale, Riker's mistake had caused serious damage to at least one member of his crew, probably more. Melora Pazlar was in sickbay with numerous broken bones and other physical traumas, her fragile, low-gravity frame badly damaged by Tuvok's attack. The damage to her mind by the forced meld had not yet been assessed; Dr. Ree did not believe there would be neurological damage, but the psychological was harder to assess. As for the damage to Tuvok's career as a Starfleet officer, or Orilly Malar's, it was too early to judge. Others had been under the jellies' emotional influence and had not acted upon it. At the moment Riker was more inclined to blame himself than either of them, though.

As soon as Tuvok had accessed the sensor data and transmitted it to the jellies, Deanna had called the bridge to pass along their triumph and gratitude. Within minutes, they had begun replicating the new sensor components, incorporating them into their anatomy. They began instructing their young to do the same, and sending out the word through their telepathic channels. More than likely, Jaza had surmised, they would write it into the genes of new embryos, and the ability to detect and evade the Pa'haquel would become a permanent part of their species.

But Qui'hibra's hunting fleet had already left by the time Riker learned of this. Shortly after their fourth kill, they had wrapped their trophies in their tentacles and warped away, even taking the remains of the one they couldn't use as a ship (for scrap parts, perhaps—or was "allografts" a better word?). Deanna had guessed that they were taking a risk by striking so close to a breeding world, not wishing to chance scaring them away from it, and thus had chosen to process their kills away from the jellies' sensory range.

Yet Riker had chosen to set off in pursuit. Jaza still hadn't figured out how to track star-jellies at warp beyond a certain distance, but Riker ordered Lavena to set course based on their warp-entry vector. It was necessary, he had resolved, to inform the Pa'haquel of exactly what had happened, and to offer what assistance he could in dealing with the consequences.

"Is that such a good idea?" Vale had asked in the privacy of his ready room. "Maybe we've already done enough damage with our good intentions."

"So we just walk away? Wash our hands of the consequences? You can't really believe that, Christine."

"I don't know. You're right, I don't want to leave our mess for someone else to clean up. Of course I want to help fix it if we can. But it was wanting to help that started this in the first place. That's why there's a Prime Directive."

He had paused, considering her words. It had been the horrors on Tezwa, as well as Delta Sigma IV and Oghen, that had led him to reject the idea of the Prime Directive as an excuse for turning a blind eye to suffering. But Tezwa's horrors had resulted from President Zife's abandonment of the Prime Directive, his self-serving interference in the planet's political affairs. Did Riker run the risk of becoming the very thing he was trying so hard to fight against?

No—he wouldn't accept that. He'd forced nothing on anyone. He'd gone to help where he'd been specifically asked, and had tried to engage in a dialogue with the other side, imposing nothing on them. His decision to tow away the jelly's corpse may have been damaging to relations with the Pa'haquel, but not to their way of life. His mistake had been in failing to anticipate the influence the jellies would have over members of his crew. That had not been a Tezwa-sized mistake, and it was one he was willing to do his best to remedy.

"I stand by what I said before, Christine," he had declared. "The Prime Directive isn't an excuse to avoid responsibility. Responsibility means being aware that you can and will make mistakes, and should do everything you can to minimize and correct them. It doesn't mean being so afraid to make mistakes that you avoid taking on any responsibility at all. Mistakes happen. They're a part of the process of getting anything done. So they're no excuse not to try.

"In a case like this, the Prime Directive means that we can't impose our values or solutions on the Pa'haquel. We can't dictate to them how to solve the problem we've helped bring about. But that doesn't mean we can't assist them in finding their own solutions."

It was now the next day, and the Pa'haquel fleet had tracked *Titan* down, coming up alongside them at warp and surrounding them in a formation that said "pull over" in no uncertain terms. As Riker gave the order to drop to impulse, he decided that they probably wouldn't be all that interested in his "assistance" right about now. But at least they deserved answers.

Moments later, Qui'hibra appeared on the main viewer. *"Riker of* Titan," he said. His tone was calm, quiet, coldly furious. He stood utterly still, his hawklike eyes fixated on Riker, unblinking, unwavering, like a raptor studying a field mouse. Will felt a flash of gratitude that there was a viewscreen, raised shields and dozens of kilometers of vacuum between them. *"I know that what has happened is somehow your doing. You will explain to me precisely what you have done."*

"Elder Qui'hibra. That's exactly what I've been meaning to discuss with you. If you'd care to beam aboard, we can—"

"Understand something, Riker. Thousands of Pa'haquel have died in the past day. Our hulls no longer shield us from the skymounts' senses. They are teleporting entire crews into vacuum. We cannot retaliate because they suddenly have shields like yours, and can suddenly sense us coming and be ready for us before we exit warp. The word to suspend hunting skymounts has been spread as fast as it can be, but the Pa'haquel are spread wide and many did not get the warning in time. You have murdered whole clans, Riker. My desire for an explanation from you is the only reason you are not currently a cloud of atoms dissipating into space. You will give me that explanation now, and if you wish to have any chance of avoiding that fate, you will include the means of reversing what you have done."

Riker was horrified. He had expected that the jellies would simply flee from the hunters, leaving them unable to make new kills, forcing them to gradually give up their nomadic lifestyle, or at least switch to constructed starships, as their "skymounts" wore out or were lost. Since the jellies were incapable of firing on their own kind, he'd assumed that retaliation would not be an option. He hadn't considered that they would target their attacks against the crews inside. And he was so accustomed to combat in the age of deflector shields that he hadn't considered the use of teleportation as a weapon. In retrospect, it seemed obvious—the jellies would not want to leave the bodies of their dead to be further desecrated. They would want to cleanse them of infestation and return them to their native soil at long last.

"Elder Qui'hibra . . ." He hesitated. "I assure you, I had no knowledge or intention that anything of the kind would happen. What's taken place here was an accident, not a deliberate act."

"You are still not explaining."

"Very well. We were able to use our sensors to scan inside your ships and detect your presence. We also found a way to distinguish your warp signatures from those of live, er, skymounts."

"There are no such ways. We shield our inner hulls specifically to preclude detection."

"Our sensors are a prototype design. And it was difficult even for them to detect you."

"Go on." His voice remained level, yet the fury in it was deeper than ever.

"We had no intention of sharing this information with the skymounts. We did not take sides. However, the skymounts are powerful telepaths, and they were able to influence those members of our crew with similar abilities. We attempted to repress our crewmembers' telepathic senses, but when you attacked near the breeding world, the sheer quantity of terrified emotions was overwhelming. Two of our crewmembers, acting under the creatures' influence, gave them access to our sensor information and shield calibrations, and the specifications for replicating the necessary components for themselves."

Qui'hibra's stare still didn't waver. *"And as a result we can no longer approach the skymounts without losing an entire clan and its homes."*

"Let me convey my deepest regrets for the loss of life. If there is anything we can do to help—"

"The first thing you can do is to deliver those telepaths of yours to us for retribution."

Riker took a step forward. "That's not going to happen, Qui'hibra. I alone am responsible for what happens aboard this ship. And will vengeance accomplish anything? Will it help your people survive? Think about it. My people had the technology to scan through your hulls. Maybe we have technology that can protect you as well. For instance, do you have any sort of shield technology which can block transporters?"

Qui'hibra growled, but he seemed to be contemplating Riker's words. *"They have been able to compensate for our existing shielding methods. Our allies are already at work on devising alternatives. But even once we gain such shielding, the skymounts will still be able to flee from our attacks. The Hunt will end, the balance will be broken, and chaos will overtake us all."*

"With all respect to your beliefs, Elder . . . surely there are other species you can hunt. We've seen that you already do. And if necessary, you could travel in ships like ours. It would be an adjustment, I know, but—"

"Hrrha! *You have not the slightest comprehension of what is at stake, do you? That will teach me to give an idiot like Se'hraqua the task of explaining it to you. But who knew a tiny pest like you could topple the whole balance?"* Qui'hibra hissed to himself, thinking. *"Then you should know. You will follow us, Riker, and we will show you the full magnitude of what you have wrought. I would not destroy you before you knew the full anguish of your guilt. You will follow, you will see, and you will know my horror and my sorrow—not merely for the Pa'haquel, but for all who live within the balance. And then you will either show me technical miracles to repair it all—or you will embrace your death in the knowledge that it is richly deserved."*

Deanna hated having to bring the latest news to Orilly Malar. The cadet was already devastated enough by her participation in the data theft, but before, her guilt had been mollified by the belief that at least she had helped save lives. Now she had to learn that the lives she had saved had in turn taken thousands of others using the knowledge she had helped give them. It was not something Deanna wanted to burden her with. But she was bound to find out, and Deanna wished to break it to her as gently as possible, and to be there to help her cope with it.

Indeed, the news hit the gentle Irriol hard. Even though Deanna strove to soften the blow as much as possible, Orilly swiftly broke down and curled herself up into a pineconelike ball, shuddering gently. If Deanna could have found a soft spot to stroke, she would have done so. As it was, she had to settle for projecting a soothing empathic aura. She had been afraid this would happen. Confinement to quarters was unduly arduous for one of Orilly's gregarious species, and Deanna had urged Will not to impose it, but he had seen no other choice under the circumstances. He had granted her broad visitation rights, though, and Deanna had made a point of checking in on her two times a day. After this news, she decided, she would have to add another daily visit.

Finally Orilly reached a point where she was able to speak again, though she remained mostly curled up and her voice was muffled. "It has happened again. Once again I acted on impulse to help someone, and many more have paid the price for it. I curse everything I touch."

"No, Malar. No one can predict the long-range consequences of their actions. All you can do is choose what seems right in a given situation."

"But I did not even do that!"

"Yes, you did. You were motivated by compassion, by the desire to save lives."

"At the cost of my duty, Counselor. My duty to my ship, to my crew. My duty to my people! After this they will never let me return to Lru-Irr," she wailed. "I will never feel the embrace of the Whole again. I will be doomed to live as one forever."

"I don't believe that. If the rest of your people are anything like you, Malar, then they're a kind and compassionate people. They will understand that you were controlled by an outside influence."

"That does not matter. My people have few exiles to represent them offworld. Few commit crimes as hideous as mine. We must serve their interests perfectly if we ever wish to return home."

Deanna frowned. "Perfection is an impossible standard. Malar, tell me—how many exiles do you know of that have been allowed to return home?"

A moment's silence. "I do not remember. Very few."

"Do you know of any for sure?"

"I am sure there have been some."

She spoke carefully. "Has it ever occurred to you . . . that if you do serve your people that well offworld, and if there are so few of you to do it, that it's in their best interest to keep you in exile indefinitely? How do you know they will ever let you return at all?" This could be a risky path to take—undermining her faith in the one thing that kept her going. But if that were a false hope, a fixation that kept her from finding other things to live for, it would be best to wean her from it.

"I have wondered that, yes," Orilly said. "But they would not do that to a sister Irriol. They would not condemn one of their own to live in solitude any longer than she deserved. If they were capable of that, then they would be the ones in exile. No, Counselor—if I am doomed to exile forever, it will be my own fault."

Deanna had her doubts. If they considered her a heinous enough criminal to exclude her from the gestalt at all, that implied they were able to see her as less than Irriol, not deserving of the compassion they would extend to others—much as cultures possessing capital punishment thought of those they executed. Orilly's deep and instinctive need for the gestalt might be blinding her; the idea that it might be unattainable, that she might not be allowed to return home no matter what she did to earn it, would be too unbearable to contemplate. Many species had such irrational blind spots when it came to the pursuit of their instinctive needs and passions. (Which explained some of her mother's choices in husbands, she thought wryly.)

But perhaps Orilly was right. As Deanna had just said, she had trouble believing that the race which had spawned this gentle soul could be prone to such callousness. Maybe they could be persuaded to let her rejoin them after all. Maybe, after what Orilly was going through now, they could be persuaded that she'd suffered long enough. Deanna would certainly do what she could to argue that case to them, she decided—even if it meant depriving Starfleet of a promising young scientist. For now, though, there was little more she could do to comfort the cadet. Orilly needed to work through her guilt and grief; Deanna simply had to make sure the process did not become self-destructive. The suicide rate among Irriol exiles was disquieting.

Deanna's concerns about Tuvok were different. Although he was unlikely to become suicidal, his resistance to dealing with the personal consequences of his actions was troubling. It was not just a "Vulcan thing;" she understood that counseling Vulcans required a distinct approach, and she was trained in their therapeutic techniques. She also understood that Vulcans generally preferred to manage their psychological issues in private. This was not necessarily unhealthy, since Vulcans were well-trained in self-contemplation and behavior management. The goals they aspired to differed from the ones she valued, since rather than seeking to reconcile with their emotions, they sought to minimize them, to emphasize systemizing behavior over empathizing and approach a cognitive state that in most species would approximate high-function autism. (Indeed, she sometimes wondered if Surak might have had the Vulcan equivalent of Asperger's syndrome, and turned it to his and his people's advantage.) But it was not her place to reject the validity of that approach.

However, she was unconvinced that Tuvok was managing to cope with his actions even in a healthy Vulcan way. She sensed turmoil in his mind, a shame as intense as Orilly's, and it did not seem to her that his meditative efforts to process it were gaining any ground—at least, not based on the disordered jumble of *keethara* blocks and *kal-toh* sticks which she glimpsed over his shoulder when he declined to invite her into his quarters. She did not know Tuvok that well; although she had spent time with many of *Voyager*'s crew as they adjusted to their return home, Tuvok had remained aloof. But it was clear enough that he was as stubborn as any Vulcan she had ever met. In this case, though, she feared that his stubbornness was being applied to self-recrimination. She needed to find a way to help him redirect that obstinacy in his favor, use it to drive his recovery process rather than hindering it. But for now she couldn't even get in the door.

Attempting to recruit Tuvok's wife to help gained her little. "He has not spoken to me about it," T'Pel told Deanna when they met in the latter's office. "Indeed, we have spoken of little in recent days. He prefers his solitude."

"You're his *wife*, T'Pel. He can't shut you out if you don't let him. And he needs you to be there for him."

T'Pel gave no outward reaction. "Tuvok has always been self-reliant. We have spent many years apart, and he has done well enough without my presence."

"Maybe," Deanna said. "But he asked to be allowed to have you join him on *Titan*. His acceptance of a post on this vessel was contingent on that request. Doesn't that suggest that he wants to change that aspect of your relationship?"

The older, chocolate-skinned woman pondered for a moment. "Perhaps. But what he has been subjected to . . . what we have both been subjected to . . . it is a distasteful matter. And Tuvok is a proud man. He does not wish to be seen in his . . . compromised state." Deanna almost smiled. Tuvok had just been reunited with his wife after a long absence, had invited her to join him in a part of his life she had not shared before. She imagined that even a Vulcan would wish to be appealing to her in those conditions. To be made to appear weak, emotional and un-Vulcan would have been an embarrassment indeed. But she didn't want to add to his embarrassment by saying as much to T'Pel.

"Besides," T'Pel went on, "there is nothing I can offer him. I am not a healer. I know no mental discipline techniques with which my husband is not already familiar; indeed, I know far fewer, for I have not required the mental training of a Starfleet security officer."

Underneath T'Pel's words, Deanna sensed an undercurrent of mild frustration, or at least uncertainty. T'Pel not only felt that she had nothing to offer Tuvok; she seemed unsure what she had to offer anyone. Deanna could deduce the reason easily enough. T'Pel had spent most of her adult life raising her children and managing the affairs of her household, and had never studied for any other career. But now all her children were grown, and joining her husband on *Titan* had meant leaving her household's affairs in the hands of her eldest. It had also meant coming into an environment which did not require any of her particular skills. After being so invaluable to her family and household, it must have been quite a step down to feel so superfluous.

It was an issue Deanna would keep in mind for the future. For now, though, she tried to offer something that could at least begin to help both T'Pel and Tuvok. "What you have to offer, T'Pel, is what he brought you here to share with him: your companionship, your support. Tuvok is no doubt fee—*experiencing* uncertainty about his worth. It would help him for you to simply show him that he has value to you. That you accept him as he is, even when he's vulnerable. He can take strength from that knowledge."

"That is not a very Vulcan sentiment, Counselor."

"Isn't it? What about the ship's own motto? 'Infinite diversity in infinite combinations.' Surak himself taught that we're stronger when we join together with others— that the interaction of different beings, different minds, can produce unexpected and valuable synergies. You and Tuvok may both be Vulcans, but you're still different people, and that in itself gives you something to offer him. You just have to reach out and share it with him."

T'Pel raised a brow. "That is an unconventional interpretation of Surak. However, I find it logical. I shall endeavor to follow your advice."

"Thank you, T'Pel." *At least it's a start,* Deanna thought. But she expected it would take more than that to help Tuvok deal with his guilt. *Tuvok, Orilly, Will . . . self-flagellation is becoming entirely too common a pastime around here.*

"Bridge to Captain Riker."

As a Starfleet officer, Will Riker was trained to wake from a sound sleep at a moment's notice. Over twenty years of experience had enabled him to hone the skill. Unfortunately, neither training nor experience could make him enjoy it. The late-night call from Hachesa on the bridge meant he'd have to give up having Deanna comfortably spooned within his arms. It meant he'd have to get up and endure some strong replicator coffee to shock himself into a ready state. It meant he'd pay for the sleep deprivation at a later time.

Most of all, it meant there was trouble. "Riker here," he said reluctantly, feeling Deanna stir against him. "Go ahead."

"We having intruders on the bridge, sir. Captain Qui'hibra and two others have just beam aboard without warning. He is demand to speak with you at oncely, sir."

Riker groaned softly, as much at the gamma shift commander's mangled syntax as his unwelcome news. ("It wouldn't be so bad," Deanna had said to him one night, "if only there were some consistent *pattern* to it." If Hachesa's grammatical idiosyncrasies corresponded to any rules of Kobliad syntax, the rest of the crew had yet to figure out what they were.) Sitting up, he put some steel in his tone. This was his ship, and it was time to remind Qui'hibra of that. "Raise the shields. Have security escort our *guests* to the observation lounge. I'll meet—"

Qui'hibra's voice overrode him. *"I will not play games, Riker. There is no time. What I have brought you to see is beginning now. I have come to your ship because you claim your long-range sensors are superior to ours. I had hoped to be closer before it began, but if we are doomed only to watch, we must see as clearly as we can. And you will come in haste, Riker, for the onset is mere moments away. Either agree now or my clan will batter down your shields and have you teleported to this bridge. Remember that you are in* our *territory and still breathe only at my indulgence."*

Riker exchanged a look with Deanna, who was sitting up now too. *He's* very *serious, Will,* she thought to him. *Better play along.*

Though he was tempted to drag his feet as a show of protest, Riker was eager to get answers, so he dressed and made his way to the bridge as quickly as possible, Deanna right beside him. The rest of the main bridge crew was also in the process of assembling as he arrived, presumably summoned by Hachesa.

"Elder Qui'hibra," he greeted his intruder curtly, then looked at the others behind him, another male and a crestless female. "And these are?"

"My clan matriarch and daughter, Qui'chiri. And Hunter Se'hraqua, who is here to witness the cost of his negligence. There is no time for pleasantries, Riker—the Great Hounding has begun."

Qui'hibra gestured at the screen with a small tilt of his head; clearly he was not one for melodrama. Riker stepped down to the center of the bridge for a better view—and his eyes widened.

On the screen, hundreds of Pa'haquel ships were swarming around something . . . *immense*. It was cylindrical, rounded, pocked like an asteroid, yet it was under thrust, firing discrete blasts of blue-hot plasma from a sort of rocket nozzle at the far end, and expelling jets from side openings to maneuver. Some of the jets seemed to be aimed at the attackers. Seven enormous spines extended outward from its body, each one the stem for a vast sail; the sails overlapped like flower petals to form a wide, diaphanous skirt around the creature's body. It was clearly a living thing, and the Pa'haquel were clearly trying to change that, barraging it with heavy fire. No, not just the Pa'haquel—Riker realized that some of the attacking ships were different in design, not armored jellies but more conventional starships. But they were like wasps swarming around an elephant. He winced as a maneuvering jet hit a hunter skymount dead-on. The saucer was blasted away into an uncontrolled spin, leaking fluids into space. This was the Great Hounding? Some kind of mighty hunt to prove themselves? Why drag him all this way to show him this?

But then he noticed the rest of the picture. In the background, behind the raging battle, was a beautiful blue-green planet, clearly M-class. Tactical markers superimposed atop it pointed to ships that were too small to see at this range—ships that seemed to be swarming off the planet in droves. The sight was agonizingly familiar. It struck Riker that the asteroid-size creature seemed to be rotating, its plasma exhaust port slowly moving to point toward the planet. "Mr. Jaza . . . tell me what we're looking at."

"It's taking place in an F9 star system six light-years

ahead, sir. The creature is making course for the planet, using some kind of collimated plasma bursts for decelerational thrust. It reads eighty-three kilometers along the long axis, sir."

"How much damage are the Pa'haquel doing to it?"

"Not much, sir. Its hide is ablating under the impacts, and the sails are taking substantial damage, but there are some extremely dense crystalline compounds in it. They'll probably kill it eventually, but not without sustaining heavy losses. And, I think, not in time."

Riker was beginning to realize what he meant. "Mr. Jaza . . . how many people are on that planet?"

"I estimate over two hundred million sentient life readings, sir. Maybe a few tens of thousands on the ships." Only a tenth the population of Oghen . . . but that didn't make it any easier.

"The ships belong to allies of ours," Qui'hibra said. "Rianconi, Vomnin, Shizadam. Still more are on the planet, assisting in the evacuation. The Fethetrit aid us in the attack itself."

Six light-years . . . there's nothing we can do. "There won't be enough, will there?"

"Not unless the Hounding can stop it in the next few moments."

Indeed, it looked as if some progress was being made against the leviathan. A concerted attack upon one of the sail-petals, its sail already badly shredded, cracked it near the base of its stem. A whole cluster of Pa'haquel ships extended their tentacles to grasp it and break it fully free, long sheets of torn membraneous material trailing behind it. "Yes," Qui'hibra muttered. "Now use it as a lance! Get around and drive it into the maw!"

But the leviathan was retaliating against the motes that had wounded it, firing maneuvering jets at them. Some were damaged, others—mostly the Fethetrit starships—destroyed outright. Riker contemplated the sheer amount of power that would be necessary to maneuver such an enormous mass through Newtonian reaction, and understood how those jets could be such devastating weapons. But they were feeble compared to its main plasma thruster. A thruster that was now aimed directly at the planet ahead.

"There's . . . a massive energy buildup inside that thing," Jaza reported in a rough voice. "But it isn't firing the main jet . . . it's letting the pressure build . . . oh, Prophets, here it comes. . . ."

"Get the sail-spine into the maw," Qui'hibra was chanting. "Foul the nozzle, at least knock off its vector!" But the remaining ships were struggling to maneuver the massive spine, barely even retaining their grip.

Then it happened. A flare of blinding blue plasma blasted forth from the leviathan's maw, shot toward the planet at terrible speed. "It's . . . an extremely dense mass of plasma," Jaza said. "Traveling at . . . over one point two million kph. Impact in seven minutes."

Riker turned to Qui'hibra. "Is there any way your people can deflect it? Dissipate it?"

"They will try" was all the elder said. He and the others watched raptly as several fleets broke off their attack on the leviathan to chase down the plasma projectile. But it took them time to catch up, and with each passing moment, the necessary angle of deflection to miss the planet became that much greater, that much harder to achieve. And since it was not solid, deflecting the entire mass would be even more difficult.

Once the ships caught up, they blasted at the plasma mass with their own stings, trying to disperse what they could of it. "The Fethetrit ships are firing tractor beams,"

Jaza reported after a moment, "wide-beam, attempting to draw away some of the mass. Transporter activity . . . they're beaming parts of it into their buffers . . . like bailing a lake with a bucket."

"Everything helps," Qui'hibra murmured, though he didn't sound as though he believed it. "We fight the chaos every way we can, until one or the other falls."

But the plasma mass drew ever closer to the planet. Eventually the skymounts broke off their attack and flew ahead, forming themselves into an array which they positioned in the plasma's path. "They're generating an intense magnetic field," Jaza reported. "The energy readings I'm getting . . ."

"They are putting everything they have left into it," Qui'hibra said.

Riker stared at him. "Then if this doesn't work . . ."

"Until one or the other falls, Riker."

As powerful as the magnetic field was, the plasma just had too much kinetic energy. The mass flattened out somewhat as it hit the field, but plowed through with no significant change in direction. The ships it directly engulfed simply ceased to exist; those on the periphery were swept along in the plasma's magnetic wake, tumbling out of control. Riker had no idea if their inertial damping was strong enough for the crew to survive the acceleration . . . but they did not appear to be under intelligent guidance anymore.

After that, there was an agonizing wait. No one said a word. Riker barely remembered to breathe.

Then the plasma mass hit the planet.

The flare of light made his eyes water, but he couldn't look away. What followed happened in agonizing slow motion. A vast cloud of ejecta, larger than nations, spewed into space at an angle; the impact had apparently been on a bias, digging a long gouge into the planetary crust, leaving a yellow-hot skid of molten land, molten homes, molten lives. Outward from the impact streak, a shock wave expanded visibly through the atmosphere, shoving clouds and weather systems aside, leaving dust and ash and fires in its wake. A nearby ocean was swept away, vaporized into steam, leaving bare ocean floor. A fireball roiled, blasting backward out through the swath of vacuum punched in the air by the plasma mass. Dozens of ships in orbit thrust madly to escape it; some failed, their telltales blinking out on the screen.

Perhaps they were the lucky ones. In one moment, this world had ended. The shock wave, Riker knew, would propagate around the planet at supersonic speed, blasting everything in its wake, scalding it with superheated steam. The dust and debris would form a dense cloud around the planet, blotting out its sun. Most of its life would go extinct, with only the meek surviving to inherit: the small animals and insects, the creatures that could survive with little food and could reproduce and evolve fast enough to adapt to the changes.

Then the leviathan fired another blast, and Riker realized that soon, nothing at all would remain alive on this world.

"The harvesters," Qui'hibra explained in a subdued tone, seeing the crew's shock, "feed by bombarding planets with enough force to blast their crustal matter and oceans into orbit. Once they have done this to a planet, they take up polar orbit and collect the water, minerals and organic compounds in their feeding sails." He turned from the screen to face Riker directly. "They always target inhabited planets, for only those contain the concentration of water and organics that they need."

The female, Qui'chiri, touched his arm. "Elder."

He turned back to the screen. In the foreground of the image, the Hounding fleet had finally managed to get control of the sail-spine. They had retreated to a considerable distance, and were now charging in at high speed, tilting at this immense windmill with one of its own vanes. They drove the spine into the maw at an angle, and it blew a hole clear through the side and shattered, its tip vaporized to plasma by the force of the impact. The harvester tried a moment later to let off a third burst against the planet, but it was feeble and uneven, with part of it blowing out the hole in the side and pushing the monster off trajectory. The stream would miss the planet and was too diffuse to matter.

But then the second plasma bolt struck, hitting head-on and causing even more devastation than the first. Any beings still alive on that planet, Riker knew, would soon enough be caught between two expanding waves of destruction. The fact that their killer was joining them in death was small consolation.

Two hundred million lives. It was still too much to grasp. *Is this the way it's always going to be? Will this entire mission be marked by death on a planetary scale? Is there no way to escape it?*

Qui'chiri gently preened her father's head feathers with her claws. "We could not have made a difference had we been there, Father. This harvester was too old, too strong. At least it will slaughter no more worlds, bear no more young."

"Tell that to the Shalra who have seen their world die today." Again he faced Riker, strode toward him. Qui'hibra was small for his species, the top of his crest barely reaching Riker's eye level, but he loomed large nonetheless. "Tell it to the thousands of other worlds that will die when there are no more skymount fleets to defend them.

"This is only a sample, Riker. I can show you more. Mr. Jaza. Have your screen display the second set of coordinates I gave you to scan. Use your maximum magnification."

Jaza looked to Riker, who nodded slowly after a moment. The screen image jumped to another part of the sky, zoomed in on a star surrounded by sheets of expelled hydrogen and eructating vast jets of plasma. "A T Tauri star?" Riker asked.

"No," Jaza said. "Indicators suggest it's a G6 main-sequence star—or used to be."

"This is the handiwork of starpeelers," Qui'hibra explained. "Photonic beings, made of coherent energy fields sustained in plasma matrices. They travel from star to star, peeling away their atmospheres to give themselves vessels of plasma to travel in."

Riker frowned. "Are they intelligent?"

"Who can say? If they have minds or purpose, we cannot comprehend either. They seem driven purely by the need to propagate. And they have no concern for the inhabited worlds whose climates are destroyed, whose surfaces are irradiated as a result of their labors. This time we were fortunate; only primitive microbes have paid the price in that system. But as soon as the starpeelers begin to leave the system for others, the Pa'haquel will be there to eradicate them—if there are any skymounts left for us to fight with. Mr. Jaza, the third coordinate set now. Full spectral imaging."

The image changed again, settled on a distant puff of darkness. The screen cycled through false-color depictions of various spectra, and it became evident to Riker that the dark, ellipsoid cloud engulfed a star and its inner planets. "This is a system we were too late to save, two generations ago. A great civilization walked there, a race of poets and builders. Then the cloud came. It is not a predator, not a hunter; it is a simple phototroph, a mindless thing drawn to light and warmth. But its mass blocked the star's light from reaching its planets, and its friction stripped away the poets' atmosphere by degrees. They slowly froze and suffocated . . . until the captured sunlight heated the cloud and burned whatever remained alive. All their great works, their mighty structures, are melting and eroding away. We only know of them through the radio messages they sent out before the end.

"Many strange and glorious creatures roam the stars, Riker. Most of them are not hunters. But they are vast and powerful, and even the innocuous among them can destroy worlds if they are allowed to. We are insects, crawling underfoot as giants roam the skies. If we wish to survive—either their malice or their neglect—we must battle them. We must hunt them, and hound them from our worlds, and kill them as fast as they breed, or else they would overrun the galaxy in time. They would devour your worlds, as they once did ours."

Deanna stared at the elder. "Se'hraqua told us that your world . . . was struck down by divine wrath."

Qui'hibra threw the younger male an irritated glare. "Se'hraqua has a mystical streak. He was *supposed* to explain all this to you, but chose to make vague pronouncements instead."

Se'hraqua bristled. "We do not need to justify the Hunt to these weaklings. It is our holy tradition; that is reason enough to continue it. The rest is incidental."

Vale gaped at him. "It's incidental if whole worlds die?"

"They die if we fail in maintaining the divine balance. The balance is the point. And now you have shattered the balance." He turned to Qui'hibra. "Elder, why do we waste time pandering to these fools? They have seen the magnitude of their crimes, now let them die! The balance demands it!"

"You think snuffing out one tiny ship will restore the balance? Fool! We need solutions. These aliens found a way to help the skymounts fight us and flee us—perhaps they have a way to help us fight back."

Riker took a step forward. "Elder Qui'hibra—what you've shown us here is . . . horrific, to be sure. I appreciate what's at stake here. My people have had to face destruction on this scale before." *Too recently, and too often.* "And of course we will do whatever we can, within reason, to help defend inhabited worlds against this kind of menace. But surely you have other options besides hunting star-jellies. Your allies clearly have the technology to build starships and weapons of their own."

Qui'chiri scoffed. "You will find none as effective as the skymounts," the matriarch said proudly. "The mounts are faster and stronger than any ship I have ever seen. Their metamorphic and generative abilities make them adaptable and easy to repair. Their organic nature makes superb camouflage. And as living, breeding, self-sustaining creatures, they require no massive infrastructure to support them. You cannot hunt starbeasts while tied down to a planet—especially when planets are often their favorite food. To hunt we must live free, migrate among the stars with the very prey we battle."

"Our allies contribute much," Qui'hibra said, "but many of them are worldless too, by tragedy or by choice. They depend on our skymounts to generate replacement parts for their ships, food for their bellies. The mounts do not wage the Hunt alone . . . but without them, there can be no Hunt, or too feeble a hunt to hold the balance."

"Even so, the jellies are intelligent beings. I can't

accept that there's no alternative to murdering them in order to save others."

Qui'hibra strode closer, coming beak-to-nose with Riker. "And I will not accept seeing more billions die for the sake of hundreds. Yes, we kill skymounts, but their species thrives, because we fight to preserve it along with all the others. All their knowledge is shared, and we never take a whole school, so nothing is lost. If we did not prey on them, others would. If a school of skymounts had flown into the nebula where you saw us battle before, the cloud-shimmers would have fed on them all, dissolving their organic molecules and feeding on the released energy. And they would have spared none, just as they spare no living thing when they swarm over planets or invade starships. At least when we kill them, it serves a higher purpose."

He thrust his head forward further into Riker's face, puffing out his feathers. "But if you cannot help us restore the balance, then there will be no purpose to anything anymore and I will kill you simply because you deserve it."

Chapter Ten

The young Fethet was staring at Deanna again with hunger in his eyes. She couldn't clearly sense whether that hunger was sexual or literal, and didn't know which prospect would trouble her less.

The battle against the cosmozoans made strange bedfellows, it seemed, but everyone did their part. The Fethetrit—massive red-furred bipeds with bear-wolf features, Ferengi-like ears, and vicious, hooked claws extending from their knuckles—were a race of warriors and conquerors, or so they had told her incessantly over the past two days; but here and now their task was to aid with the Shalra refugees. It was no doubt something they had done on numerous other occasions, and knew their part in quite well, but still they found it necessary to bluster and complain about how far beneath them it was. The other races in the alliance just indulged them and didn't talk back, and Deanna had opted to follow their lead.

After all, there were more important uses of her flagging energy. Thousands of refugees still needed processing, still waited for places to be found for them to sleep. There was no question that a nomadic society had an edge when it came to battling spacegoing behemoths, but when it came to finding new homes for tens of thousands of refugees, their abilities were somewhat more limited. Will had readily volunteered *Titan*'s crew and and resources to assist in the effort, only to be told by Qui'hibra that they would have been impressed into helping anyway.

But the Pa'haquel and Shizadam supervisors were driving the crew extremely hard, and Deanna could sense that although necessity demanded no less, many of them saw it as punishment. Word had gotten out that *Titan*'s people were responsible for the star-jellies' newfound ability to fight back, and although the supervisors and guards nominally protected them from retaliation, some were not as conscientious as they should be. A number of *Titan* crew members had needed Dr. Ree's care after sustaining various "accidents." Such incidents had diminished, though, after one attack had been attempted in Ree's presence and the doctor had summarily bitten the Pa'haquel attacker's forearm off. (When Riker had questioned his tactics, Ree had stated that he was simply doing what was necessary to safeguard the health of his crew— and besides, he already had the attacker down in sickbay with the limb being reattached. Most of the time, Ree was gentle as a lamb with his fellow crew members, but lately he had shown himself to be somewhat ruthless toward those who threatened them—first Tuvok, now this Pa'haquel. But in both cases he had hastened to repair the damage he'd inflicted. Troi was starting to wonder if he interpreted the Hippocratic Oath to mean "First, do no *permanent* harm.")

Still, Deanna was grateful that Oderi seemed to have

taken her under her wing. The Rianconi was not an intimidating presence by any means; she was a dainty humanoid with pale lavender fur atop her head, down her back and along the outsides of her arms and legs, and like most of her people, she wore nothing but a thong, footwear and a few equipment-bearing arm and leg bands. But she was a calming presence nonetheless. The Rianconi, a quiet, nonconfrontational race of herbivores, seemed an odd member of this community of hunters, but they had evidently made themselves indispensable. They tended to the needs of the other species in many ways, including medical and psychological treatment, food and recreation services, and even sexual services, which they considered an integral part of health care. ("A most enlightened people," Ra-Havreii had predictably said upon learning of this.)

"We have traveled with the Pa'haquel for millennia," Oderi had told her when Deanna had first asked about her people, during brief breaks in the refugee work. "Our world was near another major starbirth zone, the one to rimward of here. It was a place of glories, with great luminous nebulae whose like is unmatched in all the Arm."

Deanna had recognized it from her description. "We call it the Orion Association. I've been there myself once—the near end, though, a star called Mintaka, only partway to the great nebulae. But you're right, it is a magnificent place, so bright and beautiful that my father's people named this whole arm of the galaxy after it. It's very far from our home space, even farther than we are now, but we found it irresistible to travel to."

"You are fortunate, then," Oderi sighed. "To my people it is a memory only."

"Is that where the Pa'haquel and the skymounts are originally from?"

"The Pa'haquel, yes. I cannot say about the skymounts. But when our world was destroyed by starbeasts, the Pa'haquel saved many of us. We were frightened of them at first, as they are predators, and at first they saw us as a burden. They hunted alone then, and only wished to hunt, not to tend to the needs of the helpless. They spoke of abandoning us on another planet—but once we knew that planets could be destroyed, we had no wish to be left on one. So we chose to be helpful rather than helpless."

"Why did you migrate from Orion to here?" Deanna had asked. "My people have found few starbeasts there. Did the Pa'haquel wipe them out?"

"No, but we harried them from it, drove them to seek other feeding grounds. We followed their migration for hundreds of generations, and in time they led us here, where we found another hunting ground as rich as the one we had first known."

In modern times, the Pa'haquel alliance had clearly developed a more systematic and charitable approach to dealing with refugees, and Deanna wondered how much the Rianconi had had to do with that. There were certainly other voices in the alliance, but each species seemed to have its favored niche. The Pa'haquel and Fethetrit were the hunters and fighters. The Vomnin—long-armed, knuckle-walking quasihumanoids with bronze skin and wide, flat faces—were the scientists and engineers. The Shizadam—crocodile-scaled centauroids with small, weak forearms—were the bureaucrats and record-keepers. There was no strict species segregation, and these rules had exceptions, but they were few. The Rianconi, though, were the oldest of the Pa'haquel's current allies, and those most committed to the alliance. They were never found in any role save the support and care of others, but Deanna suspected they had managed to wield considerable influence in their unassuming way.

Deanna feared, though, that the newest refugees would not be as successful at finding a place in the alliance. The Shalra were essentially large gastropods with long, ridged shells. Emerging from the front of each was a flower of four tentacular arms and four cabochon eyes around a four-beaked mouth. They were a people with minimal technology, no scientific knowledge and little physical prowess. Their culture consisted largely of intricate songs, linguistic experimentation, and abstract mathematical games, beautiful to hear and intrigung to Deanna as a student of alien cultures, but useless to the alliance. The consensus, Oderi had told her, was that there was nothing they could contribute to the Hunt. Most likely the Vomnin would find a place to settle them on one of their colony worlds. Unlike most of the alliance members, the Vomnin were not nomads or refugees, but an independent, multiworld civilization which had chosen to ally with the hunters against the cosmozoan threat.

But if nothing else, Deanna thought, the Shalra had demonstrated great resilience and adaptability. Certainly they were devastated by the loss of their world; even though they had known little of the world beyond their local bounds, they had still lost everything they had known, and many had lost family and friends. They were grieving as much as any being in similar circumstances. But the strangeness of their new environment did not seem to add unduly to their psychological burden. Two days ago they had not known of other worlds, had not even known the extent and nature of their own. By conventional Prime-Directive wisdom, they should have been so culture-shocked as to have been thrown into collective catatonia, if not racial suicide. But the Shalra were forcing Deanna to question that conventional wisdom, and her own kneejerk acceptance of it in the past. True, they had believed they lived in a world of magic and divine mysteries, but if anything that had made it *easier* for them to accept the existence of aliens and other worlds. To them, most of the world was already an unknown, a realm beyond their comprehension where new discoveries could lurk over every hill. So accepting new wonders such as starships and aliens was relatively easy for them. Perhaps young societies, like young people, were better able to adapt to new ideas because they had not yet grown complacent in the conceit that they understood the world.

True, the Shalra were still inclined to see technology as magic and the aliens as supernatural beings; but the Pa'haquel and their allies made no attempt to persuade them otherwise, merely letting them define things however they wished. "Is it right to let them think of you as gods?" Deanna had asked Oderi.

"If that is what makes them comfortable, why not?" the Rianconi had answered. "Should it not be up to them to decide how to fit us into their worldview? If they call us deities, it is because deities are something they understand and know how to cope with. It gives them the power to manage contact with us, to define it in their own terms, rather than being forced to accept our definitions of ourselves, based on concepts they have no idea how to manage."

"But if they believe you're gods, it gives you the power to dominate them."

Oderi had smiled. "I have found that most beings get upset when their gods do not do what is expected of them. And when that happens, they tend to overthrow them as false gods. Believe me, the alliance has learned better than to try it." Deanna had reflected on what had happened to James Cook in Hawaii—and what had almost happened to James Kirk on Miramanee's World—and realized the Rianconi had a point. Perhaps the Prime Directive was as much about protecting the explorer as the natives. And perhaps its assumptions about the fragility of pre-warp cultures were somewhat condescending.

Now, Deanna studied the flowerlike faces of the Shalra who waited in line for her handouts of food, breathed in the heady aroma of their grief, anxiety and determination to survive, and reflected that if Starfleet had been in charge and had followed the letter of the Prime Directive, all of them would be dead now, along with their whole beautiful, intangible culture. But on the other hand, Will's refusal to abandon the star-jellies to their fate may have placed countless more worlds in jeopardy. Both the choice and the refusal to intervene had an impact.

So which would be the least damaging option here, she wondered: To help the Pa'haquel regain their ability to hunt and kill star-jellies? To abandon them to work it out for themselves and hope for the best? To require them to adopt a different way of life, if a viable one could even be found? There seemed to be no option that would not result in devastating loss of life on at least one species' part. But was it right to sacrifice the needs of the few for the needs of the many? Deanna recalled Jean-Luc Picard's impassioned opinion on the subject: "I refuse to let arithmetic decide questions like that!"

At the moment, she was glad to leave that question for a later time. Right now she had people to help on an individual level, Shalra who knew nothing of these larger issues but were concerned simply with where they would live, whether they could obtain enough food, or whether they would ever see their mating-circle partners and children again. *And one Vulcan,* Deanna added. T'Pel was here too, at Deanna's recommendation, and she was a dynamo. Having charges to take care of again had given her a renewed sense of purpose. She tended to the refugees with great efficiency and unwavering calm, but with a gentle and reassuring touch and unexpected patience for their emotional distress. It was not what Deanna would have expected of Vulcan motherhood . . . but on reflection she felt that it was what she *should* have expected. Compassion was a logical trait in a caregiver.

A heavy growl from nearby disrupted her reverie. The Fethet's patience had finally run out, it seemed. His tail twitching violently, he shot to his feet and upended the table of nutritional supplements he was meant to be handing out. The Shalra slithered back from the disruption as best they could, but there was little room to spare. "This is intolerable!" the Sasquatchian youth bellowed. "The Fethetrit are not meant to *serve* the needs of primitive slugs! You, all of you, should serve us!" He swung his head and hands around to encompass everyone in the spacious chamber. "Once we ruled this sector! We raped worlds until they screamed for mercy, then we raped them harder until they begged for death! We gnawed on the bones of their kings and philosophers! We turned the likes of you into our livestock, devoured your worlds till nothing was left, then cast the husks aside and found new worlds to feed on!"

The Pa'haquel supervisor was not intimidated by his bluster. The lanky avian strode over to the twice-as-massive Fethet, puffed his feathers to their fullest and barked, "Sit back down and clean up your mess."

"I am a Fethet! I do not take orders from birds like a mewling Rianconi. I devour them as my dinner!" Deanna had heard boasts like this before. The Fethetrit bantered about sophontophagy even more than Dr. Ree did, and unlike him, many seemed sincere in the desire. But this time it went beyond boasting. The angry male clenched his fists, bringing his knuckle-claws into position, and swung at the Pa'haquel. Even without the claws, the mass of his fist alone would have been enough to cave in the supervisor's skull, if the latter hadn't been alert and dodged the blow. But one claw struck glancingly and tore a livid gash in the side of his head. Feathers broke free and fluttered heavily to the ground, weighted by blood. The Pa'haquel ignored the injury and lashed out with a kick, his own splayed talons taking the Fethet in the gut. But the Fethet's dense red fur cushioned him, and the blow was not serious. He caught the supervisor's leg and squeezed. Deanna heard several loud cracks.

But she was too busy moving to think about it—moving swiftly and silently behind the Fethet, positioning herself for a disabling kick at the back of his left knee, which she delivered with precision. She'd studied *mok'bara* under Worf for years, and fought against Jem'Hadar in the years since; it had been a long time since she'd needed to rely on breaking pots over people's heads.

But the Fethet merely staggered and let out a roar of pain. He was limping, his left leg barely responding, but that didn't stop him from whirling around and beginning a lunge at Deanna. Fleetingly, she wished there had been a pot handy after all.

Then a flash of light hit the Fethet from behind. He staggered and toppled, and she rolled aside before his weight crushed her. Behind him, she saw a Vomnin female in a tripedal pose, one arm still with its knuckles on the ground while the other held a disruptor. Deanna was about to thank her when the Fethet stirred again. Clambering to hands and knees, he prepared to lunge at his newest assailant. The Vomnin changed the weapon's setting one-handed, and before Deanna could say anything, blasted the Fethet's face off.

"No!" the supervisor cried, but it was too late. "You . . . should not have done that," he gasped through the pain of his shattered leg. "We need all our strength."

"We are stronger without a monster like that," the Vomnin cried. "And you are in no position to dictate to me, Pa'haquel." She aimed her weapon at the supervisor's intact leg, and the avian clenched his teeth and bowed his head in acceptance. The Vomnin holstered her weapon and strode proudly away on all fours. Silence and the stench of burned fur remained in her wake.

Reinforcements arrived just then and took charge of the wounded supervisor. Deanna merely sat there quietly for a time, head in her hands; then she let Oderi lead her away. "The alliance . . . isn't always this tenuous, is it?"

Oderi shook her furry head, blinked her huge loris-like eyes. "Now that no more skymounts can be taken . . . the others begin to fear that the Pa'haquel will no longer be able to protect them. Their fear makes them angry. And there are many old tensions. The Fethetrit's boasts are not entirely bluster. They did conquer and enslave dozens of worlds before starbeasts shattered their power, and some were Vomnin worlds. And the Vomnin feel they should be in the lead; they see nomads as rather primitive. But the skymounts have always given the Pa'haquel the edge."

Deanna nodded. "Alliances based solely on a common enemy are always tenuous. They never resolve the preexisting conflicts, only repress them and let them fester. I—"

A piercing alarm began to sound, interrupting her. Wincing, Troi turned to Oderi, who was back on her feet and consulting the status-display band she wore about her wrist. "What is it? What's going on."

"The station is under attack by branchers."

"Branchers?"

"A very, very deadly form of starbeast. Huge living crystals. They fire beams that disintegrate living matter and absorb its bio-energy. They—"

"Oh, my God. Can you show me an image?"

Oderi nodded and tweaked her status band to project a small hologram of the scene outside the station. Deanna gasped at the sight of the familiar, ramified blue forms closing in on their position. They were the same kind of Crystalline Entity that had destroyed Data's homeworld decades ago.

And there were three of them.

"Shields up!"

The words came unbidden to Riker's lips the moment he glimpsed the approaching Crystalline Entities on the viewer. The sight awakened painful memories of Melona IV, a nascent colony destroyed before it had even gotten started, when the Crystalline Entity—or rather, *a* Crystalline Entity—had swept down upon it shortly after the *Enterprise* had dropped off the first set of colonists. Most of the colonists, along with Riker's away team, had survived by retreating into caves lined with protective refractory materials. But two had not. Carmen Davila had not. Riker had grown close to her during the journey to Melona; the charming engineer and he had shared a love of fine cuisine, as well as numerous intimate "desserts." He had been drawn to her courage and generosity. But those same qualities had led to her death, when she'd gone back to try to help an older man reach the caves. She and the old man had been reduced to ash before Riker's eyes.

Now he stared at the screen. "Arm phasers and torpedoes."

"Sir," said the ensign at security, "we still have people on the station."

"I'm aware of that!" Riker snapped. *Imzadi*, he sent, and felt an echo back. *Don't worry about me*, came her thoughts. *Protect the ship.*

Still, Riker turned to Qui'hibra, who had been aboard to consult with him (or dictate to him—opinions still differed) about the relief operations. "Can the station's shields handle those things?"

"If we do our part defending it," the elder said. On the screen, several fleets of Pa'haquel skymounts were already moving to engage the Entities, along with the few Fethetrit ships that had deigned to assist with the refugees rather than flying off in search of battle or plunder elsewhere. "Lower your shields, Riker! I must return to my skymount."

"I'm sorry, Elder, but I will not compromise the safety of my own ship. You'll just have to monitor from here."

Qui'hibra didn't waste time arguing. "Very well. I trust my daughter and Huntsmaster to manage." He spoke into his communicator for a moment, advising Qui'chiri to proceed without him. Then he turned back to Riker. "I take it you will join the battle?"

The temptation was strong, but he held back. "Not yet. Not unless it becomes necessary to protect the station."

"Very well. With you on station defense, it frees one more skymount for the battle. You may yet be needed, though. The branchers are a mighty foe, hard indeed to kill. In some ways they are worse than the harvesters; at least those take generations to travel between worlds. The branchers are fast, elusive, cunning. And they are more often the hunters than the hunted." He said it with a hint of admiration. "But I doubt your phasers would do much good. Break one in two and you only double the number of your enemies. Break it into a hundred and you win the day, but the fragments will grow into a hundred more to menace you in years ahead. The only way to beat them is to pound at them until every last growth node is destroyed. You must practically grind them into powder."

Onscreen, the skymounts and Fethetrit ships were matching their actions to his words, firing dense barrages at the Entities. The vast crystal life-forms rolled like sapphire tumbleweeds to dodge the attacks, and fired back with their familiar disintegrator beams. "My people have encountered one of these creatures in the past," Riker said. "I never knew they travelled in groups."

"Normally they do not, but they are canny beasts, and drawn to the scent of blood. They must have come in response to the Hounding, to feed on the organic matter blown into orbit and on the carrion we left. But first they wish to finish us off, so they may feed freely. They know we are weakened by the Hounding. But my fleet is still fresh and near full strength," he finished with pride.

The Fethetrit's shields fluctuated and sparked under the impact of the disintegrator beams, but held for now. When the beams struck skymount armor, they left gouges that looked shallow, but must have been meters deep. The struck ships shimmered, their armor re-forming, but Riker knew they could only do that so many times before running out of biomass.

"Extraordinary," Jaza said. "Those beams, they somehow convert the chemical energy of carbon bonds into EM form and channel it into the Entities' bodies. It's not unlike how the cloud-shimmers feed."

"They are too fragile to land on planets, so they leech their life-force from the skies," Qui'hibra growled. "They can strip a whole planet bare in hours."

"I know," Riker said, his voice hard. "I've seen it happen."

The elder studied him. "You bear a grudge. Good—if you channel it well. By your survival I take it you have effective weapons against the branchers?"

Riker recalled a vision of the Crystalline Entity shattering like a wineglass, shaken apart by the graviton beam which Data had designed as a means to communicate, but which Dr. Kyla Marr had turned into a weapon to avenge her son. The beam had shattered the creature uniformly, leaving nothing behind that could regenerate. To his Starfleet principles it had been horrific, an act of murder rather than self-defense. But nonetheless he had felt satisfaction at seeing Carmen avenged. And this time it would be self-defense, and defense of his crew, his wife. . . .

No, Imzadi. Her presence, still in his mind, cautioning him, calming him. She was right, of course. He wasn't about to hand over any more knowledge which could affect the local balance of power—not before he had more information about its consequences. He'd done enough damage already.

"We relied mainly on our shields for defense. And . . . we made attempts to communicate with it. To make peaceful contact."

Qui'hibra gave a curt, squawking laugh, the first hint of humor he'd ever evinced in Riker's knowledge. "Branchers are not interested in discourse with their meals. They are gluttonous beasts, needing much energy to sustain their life processes, to power them into warp. Sources of bio-energy are sparse in the void, so they must take whatever they can find, and there is no talking them out of it. It is instinct, the overriding need to survive and grow. If you survived your encounter with this brancher without killing it, then it must have only recently fed and been sated enough not to press its attack. We will not be so fortunate today." He gestured to the screen, where two of the Entities were ganging up on a skymount, bombarding it from both sides until its hull ruptured at last. Other ships were systematically blasting away at them, breaking off snowflake chunks and pounding them into fragments, but they were only small pieces of the whole. Once the skymount was inert, the Entities made short work of it, disintegrating it until only a diffuse cloud of dust remained. Qui'hibra's timeworn crest drooped, but his voice remained level. He had just lost family, Riker realized, but it was a loss he knew from long experience how to bear. "See how they coordinate their efforts. They must have only recently split off from each other, to be so inclined to cooperate rather than vie for advantage. Mitosis depletes their energy, so they will be ravenous. More of my clan will surely die today. But we will make sure the branchers die as well." He stepped away, issuing more instructions into his communicator.

If anything, Riker thought, it seemed the Fethetrit ships had the edge over the Pa'haquel, since they had shields, and their torpedoes rivalled the skymounts' plasma stings in power. But the Entities' blasts wore away at their shields until they started to give way. The viewscreen tracked one ship as its shields gave out entirely and the feeding beam played across it. The ship, being inorganic in construction, did not explode or vaporize, but once the beam had passed, it appeared to coast along on momentum alone. "Zero life signs registering aboard," Jaza reported. "Even the polymers have been disintegrated."

"Tactical, assessment of the Fethetrit shields," Riker ordered.

Kuu'iut was at Tactical, since Tuvok was still confined to quarters. "Inferior to ours, sir," the Betelgeusian replied. "Perhaps fifty to sixty percent of our shields' power at maximum, and at least seventy percent less energy-efficient."

"Fethetrit prize attack over defense," Qui'hibra said. "Look at them. See how they throw themselves headlong into battle, no caution, no judgment, just berserker fury. See there!" He gestured as a Fethetrit ship accelerated headlong into a feeding beam until its shields flared out, then continued as a ballistic projectile until it slammed into the Entity and exploded, fragmenting it into three large chunks and thousands of shards. "They throw their lives away at every chance, it seems. Yet they seem to like it that way. And better for us, perhaps, that they keep their numbers low. Still, we commend their souls to the Spirit just the same, though Spirit only knows whether It would want them."

"I take it that the fragments are still a threat?" Riker asked.

"It will only take them a moment to adjust to the separation, and then their hunger will drive them again. But they are smaller now, and weaker. And the more of them there are, the more chance there is of one slipping through our lines. Keep your weapons hot, Riker."

In quick succession, two more Fethetrit ships were wiped clean of life, and one skymount had a chunk sliced off its edge and quickly digested by the beams. It continued to move under intelligent direction, though; presumably it had a means of sealing off the damaged section. "Have them retreat to station defense," Qui'hibra ordered his huntsmaster. "Send out mount Ieq'Fha to take their place."

"Is it wise to send organic ships up against these things?" Riker asked. "It just gives them more sustenance, more energy to fight back with."

"Only if they catch us. And we are taking more from them than we are giving up."

Indeed, the two remaining intact Entities were significantly smaller than before, their branches robbed of symmetry as though trimmed by a blind-drunk topiarist. But they continued to fight cannily, and Riker realized one was using its beams to herd the last Fethetrit ship toward the other. "Order them to veer off!" Qui'hibra instructed his people, but apparently the Fethetrit were not inclined to listen. *"Rrraa.* All their fellows have died and they are jealous. At least tell them to die usefully!" he added into his communicator.

But his huntsmaster apparently had other ideas. Qui'hibra's own mount—Riker realized he was starting to be able to tell them apart—swooped in and fired a barrage of stings at the Entity's core, snapping it in two. Coordinating with the Fethetrit, they proceeded to dissect the halves further, rather than chipping away at them from the outside as before. *"Let us cut them down to harmless size first,"* came the huntsmaster's voice. *"We can then crush the fragments at our leisure."*

But the Fethetrit were not as careful in their aim and were less successful in breaking off fragments. And one that they did break off, given momentum by the Entity half's rotation, flew right into them, the collision damaging their shields and leaving them vulnerable. They dove almost eagerly into a kamikaze run, but the Entity dodged and took only a glancing blow. The impact was enough to destroy the last of the Fethetrit, however. "Useless fools," Qui'hibra cursed-but he muttered a prayer for them anyway.

It seemed the Entity half was retreating now, perhaps spooked by the efficiency with which Qui'hibra's mount was chopping up the rest of its former self. But the remaining Entities—one large, three small—continued to keep the rest of the Pa'haquel fleet at bay. One of the small ones managed to slip through the line and made a dash for the station. "Block it!" Riker ordered Lavena. "Tactical, fire a warning shot, try to scare it off."

"You cannot think that will work after what you have seen?" Qui'hibra demanded.

"Unlike you, I'm not willing to kill what might be a sentient being without trying the alternatives first. Is there any way to incapacitate it?" he went on, not allowing the elder to argue the point. "Any sensory organs we can blind, weapon emitters we can cripple?"

"No, they are too redundant. Blow away one node and they shunt the beams to the next."

Riker had a memory from the Farpoint mission. "Jaza, can you calibrate the deflector array to emit the kind of energy it feeds on? Maybe we can satisfy its hunger for now—or at least lure it away from the station."

"On it, sir."

"Your sentiment is foolish, Riker," Qui'hibra said. "Know that even if you drive it away alive, we will hunt it down and pulverize it if we can. More likely it will outrace us and escape, and another planet may die because of your 'mercy.' "

Riker took a moment to absorb that. "That may be," he said. "But the bottom line is, *Titan* is a science vessel, not a warship. I'm just playing to our strengths."

"The deflector is ready, sir," Jaza announced.

"Activate the beam."

The viewscreen showed a false-color wash of light illuminating the Entity. It paused, rotating uncertainly in place, and then changed course toward *Titan*. "Helm, thrusters aft full. Lead it away from the station."

"Thrusters aft, aye."

But the Entity's propulsion system, whatever it was, packed significantly more punch than thrusters. In moments, it was upon them, bumping up against their shields, backing away at the sting of them and then trying again. "The beam isn't sating it," Jaza said. "I think we've just whetted its appetite." Now the feeding beam fired, battering against the shields, and the Entity continued to push against them physically, making the ship shudder. "I'd say that's definite."

"Shields are holding," Kuu'iut reported, "but I can't be sure that will last. The energy beam is taking up a lot of our power."

Suddenly the ship shook harder and the power fluctuated. "Report!"

"It just figured out where the bio-energy beam was coming from," Jaza said with some alarm. "It's fired a feeding beam directly into the deflector array, taking advantage of the same frequency window that lets the beam exit the shields. Sir, it's sucking energy right out of the ship! The conduits aren't designed to transfer power at this rate."

"Shut down the deflector array!"

"I have been trying, sir. It's not working."

"Shield energy is falling," Kuu'iut said. "Down to seventy percent." Another shudder. "Sixty-four!"

"This is what your kindness brings, Riker," said Qui'hibra. "Will you die for your Federation ethics?"

Riker glared at him. "If I have to. But not today." He

whirled to Kuu'iut. "Concentrate torpedoes on the stem. Break it in two. Maybe the halves will be too weak to press the attack."

A row of miniature sunbursts flew out from the bottom of the screen, striking the Entity at its core and cleaving it like a jeweler's chisel. "Helm, push between them at full impulse. Knock them apart."

Titan surged forward, shaking as the halves collided with its shields; but at this close range, the impulse engines had not had time to accelerate the ship very much, so the collision was comparatively gentle on both ends. Still, the tactical display showed that the two Entity pieces were knocked away spinning, like billiard balls on a table. Before long they regained control, but headed off in opposite directions rather than resuming their attack. Riker realized that several of Qui'hibra's ships were closing in on them, and the remaining Entities had all been broken up or driven away.

"Harry them!" Qui'hibra cried into his communicator. "Do not let them go to warp!"

Riker kept an eye on the pursuit while he gathered damage reports. *Titan* was in relatively good shape, needing only some replacements and repairs to the deflector array power conduits and a couple of shield capacitors.

But soon Qui'hibra approached him grimly. "Three of the partial branchers escaped into warp. Even so small, they are too fast to overtake. I only pray other hunters find them before they find other peopled worlds or ships."

Riker spoke tentatively. "I'm sorry. I wish there had been more we could do."

The elder shook his head. "I do not blame you for this. There were too many; some would have gotten away regardless. You did what you could when it came down to it. And you showed innovation in your tactics; I can respect you for that, if not for your squeamishness. Most importantly, you put yourself at risk to protect the innocents on the station." Qui'hibra clasped him on the shoulder. "That, in the end, is what the Hunt is all about."

Riker met Qui'hibra's gaze, gratified that some degree of trust had been established. Still, he was unable to shake the thought that he had not done all he could. He could have easily destroyed all three of the Crystalline Entities in moments. True, they had some intelligence, and were only wild creatures trying to survive, as they had a right to. But was their right to life worth sacrificing worlds for?

Was the Pa'haquel's side the right one after all?

CHAPTER ELEVEN

Dr. Ree had been butting heads with Wangliaph, the female Fethet assigned to the station's medical-wing security, for hours now. Almost from the moment they had met, they had been exchanging insults and threats, challenging each other's authority, and coming close to exchanging blows.

It had been the most fun he'd had since last he'd been on the homeworld.

Even back home, Pahkwa-thanh females weren't often inclined to play this way with him. Though he was seen as massive and physically intimidating by his *Titan* crewmates, he was not large or strong by his own people's standards, nowhere near the alpha or even beta-male status that held the interest of females. He had gone into medicine so that he could contribute to society in another way, one to which he had proven well suited; but partly he had hoped that professional and economic success would draw the females he had been unable to attract with physical prowess. Those plans had been somewhat sidetracked two decades ago when the Pahkwa-thanh had joined the Federation and a whole new hunting ground of alien diseases had been opened to him, daring him to chase them down and wrestle them into submission. The intellectual thrill of that particular hunt had diverted him from the hunt for mates ever since, and he was largely satisfied with that. Among the frail humanoids he had found himself closer to an alpha, respected for his strength and skill, his gregarious instincts serving him well once he had found an audience inclined to listen. Many had been slow to warm to him, intimidated by his appearance or eating habits, but in Starfleet, most made the effort to overcome such reactions and accept him as he was. So he had not lacked for social contact either. Still, he did find himself feeling lonely at times, and was grateful for a holodeck where he could distract himself with chasing across the open plains and ripping into moist, pliant throats.

From the way she looked at his Shalra patients, it seemed Wangliaph had similar taste in recreation and little interest in settling for holodecks. "Just look at them," she had said to him in a rare quiet moment between insults and posturings. "Vast, slow-moving hunks of soft, juicy meat. Don't you just yearn to snap open those shells and feast? At least bite off some arms or eyes to see if they'll grow back?"

"Perhaps you need your prey to be so slow and helpless," Ree had teased, "but I prefer more of a challenge. Besides—it would be rude."

Before the Fethet could muster a comeback, Captain Riker had come in, with Lieutenant Commander Keru accompanying him. Counselor Troi was already present, helping Ree tend to the patients. Riker had come to brief them on the situation; Ree appreciated that he had come to them rather than requiring them to leave their work with the refugees. He continued to move around the ward, monitoring patients' vital signs, as Riker related the tale of the battle with the Crystalline Entities, and pondered aloud what it signified. Wangliaph muttered something about the smell of omnivore breath and lumbered away into the next ward.

"This situation just gets less and less clear-cut," he said. "Not that it ever was to begin with, but now . . ."

"Now neither side is abstract to you," Troi said. "You already sympathized with the star-jellies—we all do—but you also have personal grounds for identifying with the victims of the Crystalline Entities."

"You think seeing another whole planet destroyed before my eyes didn't affect me personally?"

"Of course it affected you, but it was still remote, abstract. A tragedy on that scale can be too large to process. Will, I'm not criticizing. It's good that you can identify with both sides now."

"Is it? It just makes it harder to sort this whole thing out. Obviously what the Pa'haquel are doing serves a valuable purpose—maybe even an essential one. We didn't know how lucky we had it in the Federation. There are places in the galaxy far more dangerous than we ever knew. Perhaps we even owe the Pa'haquel our thanks for keeping the cosmozoan population from growing out of control, overwhelming known space.

"But I still can't accept that slaughtering innocent, sentient life forms is the only way to do it. If they were just . . . very useful animals, it would be one thing. But hunting thinking creatures, surviving at the expense of other sentient beings . . . there's a fundamental difference there that any civilized people should recognize."

Ree looked up in surprise at that, and must have made

some sound, because he caught the others' attention. "You have a thought on that, Doctor?" Riker asked.

"I simply find it an odd sentiment, Captain. And, if I may be so bold, a false distinction."

"What do you mean?"

"Simply that my people have always regarded our prey as sentient."

Riker and Keru appeared shocked. Troi was simply inquisitive. Ree went on. "I suppose I understand why peoples like yourselves, from agrarian and industrial backgrounds, would think of animals as mere objects, resources to be harvested. But to a hunting people, you must understand, the prey is a powerful, complex entity with a will of its own. To bring it down, we must respect and understand its behavior—its personality. We must be able to judge its moods, guard against its anger.

"And as often as not, sir, the prey wins. Hunting packs routinely come back empty-handed. Sometimes they come back smaller than they started. So to us, the prey is anything but an inferior. It is a mighty force on whom our very survival depends. How could we not believe it has a mind and a soul?"

"I thought," the captain said uneasily after a moment, "that Pahkwa-thanh had clear-cut taboos about killing sentient beings."

"Civilized beings, yes." At their puzzlement, he explained. "Civilized beings tend to consider themselves in control of nature, exempt from its cycles. They do not think of themselves as prey. So to treat them as such would not be . . . polite. We Pahkwa-thanh always strive to be polite. Even in our insults, there is a proper social protocol." He gave a hissing chuckle at the humanoids' fidgeting. "Rest assured I have never been faulted for my etiquette. As long as you do not consider yourselves fair game, I would never dream of treating you as such—although I'm sure you would all be quite succulent. Particularly you, my dear Counselor."

She stifled an uneasy laugh. "Why, thank you."

"But wild peoples . . . let me try to think of an example relevant to yourselves. I know. Have you read Dr. Gillian Taylor's monographs on humpback whale psychology? Or listened to the oral histories of dolphins?" Troi showed recognition, but her husband shook his head. "You should. They are most insightful and witty. The whales were hunted to extinction by your people, brought back only through temporal intervention. The dolphins fared better, but still suffered much from human fishing nets and pollution. But they never blamed you for killing them. They never declared war on you or sought to exact retribution. Because they did not have the civilized being's conceit of being above the food chain. They were wild peoples who knew and accepted that survival was a day-to-day matter, and that any creature could become food for another at any time. They accepted the risk as part of life, and never condemned their predators."

Riker took a moment to absorb his words. "That's very interesting, Doctor, but I'm not sure it applies here. We know that the star-jellies don't see it that way. That they're horrified by what's been happening to them, outraged at the Pa'haquel for doing it to them."

"Respectfully, sir, I disagree. They were horrified when they did not understand it. They saw it as something unnatural, not a normal cycle of predation."

"But now they're turning on the Pa'haquel, killing them en masse."

"They are protecting their fallen siblings from desecration. And they will do what they must to achieve that, even kill, just as any animal would kill to survive. But I do not believe that killing is itself the goal. That kind of vengeance is not the way of the wild. You kill to survive, to feed or to escape becoming food. We do not hate our prey, and it does not hate us. We simply play our parts in the dance of life and death."

Riker remained unconvinced. "The star-jelly at Farpoint station tortured the Bandi leader. I saw it with my own eyes. Deanna, you said it felt satisfaction."

Troi furrowed her brows. "No, Will, I think Ree's right. That jelly only tortured Zorn because it wanted him to free its schoolmate. There was anger, yes, but its satisfaction was more about coming closer to its goal. The pain it inflicted was only a means to an end. It didn't mean the jelly was motivated by sadism." She fidgeted; something about this line of discussion made Troi uneasy. Ree imagined there might have been times in her Starfleet career when she had been forced to use harsher interrogation techniques than she would have liked.

Riker fell silent for a time, thinking. Ree returned to checking patients' vitals, but cocked his head to listen once Riker spoke up again. "If what Ree says is true, then maybe there is a way out of this. The Pa'haquel need the star-jellies to do what they do . . . but the jellies haven't understood the situation, so the Pa'haquel have had to use force to get their way. What if we explained the big picture to the star-jellies? Told them how valuable they could be in protecting the galaxy from dangerous cosmozoans? What if we could persuade them to work *with* the Pa'haquel? To allow themselves to be used as ships while they're still alive? We know it's possible. The Farpoint jelly allowed us aboard it, it didn't expel us. If they could be convinced to let the Pa'haquel live inside them, then the

Pa'haquel wouldn't have to kill them any longer. They might even be stronger for it. Live star-jellies can probably do things that dead ones can't even approach."

By now Troi was staring at Riker in disbelief. "So let me get this straight, Will. You're asking me to negotiate a treaty between hunters and their prey."

"If Ree is right, it should be a lot easier than some of the treaties you've negotiated."

"I'm not so sure. Even if they don't hold grudges, convincing them to change such a—*primal* way of defining one another won't be easy."

Riker stroked his wife's arm, and Ree felt a twinge of envy at the obvious depth of love they shared. "Deanna, my faith in you knows no bounds."

She rolled her eyes. "Just my luck."

"Madness!"

"Impossible!"

"Blasphemy!"

Riker had spoken to Deanna about persuading the jellies to work with the Pa'haquel, but had soon realized that the reverse might be just as hard. Now that he had actually proposed it to the Conclave of Elders, an assembly of the leaders of the various Pa'haquel fleet-clans in the area, he realized it would probably be even harder. He wished Deanna were here with him, in this large meeting chamber on the senior clan's lead skymount, to make the case. But they had only authorized one representative to speak on Starfleet's behalf.

However, he noted that Qui'hibra himself had not joined in the chorus of objections. He was nearly the only one who had not—the other being his daughter Qui'chiri. Only the ship elders and the senior males of their subordi-

nate families had formal voting status in the Conclave—
with their votes weighted in proportion to their place in
the hierarchy—but all the elders were accompanied by
their matriarchs, who served as advisors and were free to
participate in debate if not voting. A few non-Pa'haquel
were present as aides, but none had status on the Conclave. Qui'hibra seemed to hold a high standing in this
council, if only because his fleet-clan was now one of the
largest and strongest in attendance due to the attrition the
others had suffered in the Hounding and against the Crystalline Entities. The key role Clan Qui'Tir'Ieq had played
in defeating the Entities had also boosted their status.
Given that, it was an encouraging sign that Qui'hibra and
his daughter seemed receptive.

Beyond that, though, they had given Riker no cause for
optimism. Qui'chiri said nothing but appeared openly
skeptical, while the elder himself maintained his usual
statuelike calm, pinning Riker with that cold hawkish gaze
that made some primal part of him want to scurry away
into the underbrush.

Not that the others were reticent about speaking for
him. "You would have us betray our most sacred traditions," said Aq'hareq, the senior fleet-clan's elder, an ancient, wiry, battle-scarred male with almost as many
bionic parts as Torvig. "Such a thing could not restore the
balance, only worsen it! The Hunt is the struggle for survival! For one to live, the other must die, that is the balance! That is the will of the Spirit!"

"More than that," Qui'chiri said, turning to Riker to explain. "If we do not prey on the skymounts, what keeps
their population from growing out of control like any
other starbeast?"

"They're intelligent beings," Riker said. "If they understand the ecological dangers of their overpopulation,

maybe they can be persuaded to limit their procreation. Besides, you're not the only thing that preys on them, are you?"

Qui'chiri conceded the point. "True. Indeed, they would still lose many if they joined us in the Hunt." Riker found he couldn't share her detachment at the prospect. Even if he did bring about this peace, he realized, it wouldn't mean an end to the dying. But at least he could give the jellies a choice in the matter.

"It would never work," objected a third elder, Rhi'thath. "How can we hunt with mounts that have wills of their own? What if they wish to chase sailseeds or dive in nebulae when we tell them to attack branchers? What if they panic and flee?"

"Do not speak of them with such disdain!" The others whirled. The cry had come from Se'hraqua. Riker had been surprised to see him on the Conclave, since he had seemed to be a fairly unimportant member of Qui'hibra's fleet. But apparently he had been abruptly catapulted to the head of his family by the loss of its elder males in some recent battle, so he was entitled to be here, if only in a subordinate standing.

"Mind your place," Qui'hibra warned. But Se'hraqua did not subside.

"Forgive me, Elders, for my disrespect to one of higher station, but I cannot abide his disrespect, his blasphemy toward the skymounts. Let alone that proposed by this alien Riker. The very idea of this disgusts me. The thought of—of *taming* these glorious souls, reducing them to beasts of burden, it is an outrage!"

"More so than killing them and living in their corpses?" Riker had to ask.

"You understand nothing, human. We do them honor by taking them in glorious struggle, freeing their souls to join the Spirit and taking only what they leave behind. We *earn* their bodies as our prizes, as a legacy of the honored dead. We have no right to their bodies while they live!" Most of the elders nodded or squawked in agreement.

"All right," Qui'hibra said, his voice rising slightly. "You have made your point. But have they not now won a great and decisive victory over us? Surely that wins them everlasting honor that we cannot take away."

"No, that is not the way of the Spirit!"

There were gasps around the table. "Silence!" cried Rhi'thath. "Do not presume to lecture your Elder on the ways of the Spirit, you arrogant whelp!"

"Again, my apologies." Se'hraqua fell silent, still seething.

"Impertinent or not, he has a point," Aq'hareq said. "It would be an affront to the skymounts' dignity to tend them like livestock. Just as it would be an affront to ours to tend livestock. We are hunters! We earn mastery over beasts by tooth and claw. That is the way of the strong."

"Adaptability is also the way of the strong," Riker said. "A human thinker called it survival of the fittest. Whatever qualities, whatever behaviors are best suited to a particular environment will win out over others. If the environment changes, if the needs of survival change, then the species that don't change with it are no longer fit to survive."

His words were met with thoughtful silence, so he went on. "I also want to make it clear that nobody's talking about enslaving or domesticating the skymounts. What I'm proposing is a partnership, the two species working together—just as you work with Vomnin or Rianconi or Shizadam." He looked around the meeting chamber, choosing his words carefully. "Clearly you all have great reverence for the skymounts' power, for their skill and cunning at evading you. Recently you've discovered how dangerous they can be, how ruthless and efficient they are against their enemies. If anything, I'm sure that makes you respect them all the more." Many of the elders and matriarchs were nodding now. "If you respect them that much as adversaries, imagine how valuable they could be as allies. Imagine that power, skill and cunning working alongside yours instead of against it."

"But it would be a risky partnership," Qui'chiri said. "We would be dependent on their willingness to cooperate, answerable to their whims. It would be a struggle to convince them to go along with our wishes."

"Isn't life a struggle already? Isn't that what the Great Hunt is all about? You'll just be pursuing the same struggle in a different way. Maybe it carries more risks, but it also promises greater rewards. How is that not worthy of a hunter?"

Qui'chiri looked around to see the males nodding, looking intrigued. "I am a matriarch, not a hunter. Your words are pretty, but someone must deal with the practical matters. And I would much rather work aboard a nice, well-behaved dead skymount that does not object to my ripping its guts out to install living quarters."

The matriarchs nodded and laughed in agreement. The males glared at them, shaking their heads and muttering about disrespect and the inability of females to grasp higher spiritual matters. Qui'hibra, though, merely looked amused. "If anyone can talk a live skymount into letting her rip its guts out, daughter, it is you. Curse me for it all you like, but I know you will meet the challenge and triumph over it."

Aq'hareq looked at him sharply. "Then you say we should accede to this mad plan of the human's?"

"I see no choice but to try," Qui'hibra said, addressing the whole chamber. "There is far more at stake here than our pride or our traditions or our convenience. We teeter on the brink of chaos, and must find a way to restore the balance. If that means changing how we live, then we will change it. Because the one thing that must not change . . . is that the Pa'haquel lead the charge against the chaos. No matter where the chase takes us, no matter what it costs us, we are the ones who hold it at bay, who keep it from consuming more than its due. We are the ones with our beaks at chaos's throat through all eternity, as the Spirit of the Hunt created us to be. We do not serve our own convenience, our own habits, our own bloodlust. We are the Spirit's hounds. Remember that."

As the elder spoke, Riker could tell that he was winning them over. Some remained skeptical, and others seemed uneasy but realistic about the need for new solutions. Once Qui'hibra finished, a vote was called, and the proposal passed by a narrow majority. Aq'hareq and Se'hraqua were among the dissenters, unsurprisingly. With the proposal passed, Qui'hibra turned to Riker. "Now—how do you propose we proceed?"

After the Conclave session ended, Se'hraqua attempted to leave hastily and speak to no one. He had no wish to be reminded of his humiliation, of being forced to submit meekly to chastisement by that weak old bird Qui'hibra. By all rights he should have sat on the Conclave as an equal by now, with his own skymount to command. That the Spirit had spared him, of all the adult males in the Se'ha line, was proof enough that he was worthy and fated for something more than subordinate standing. But Qui'hibra had refused to trust in his worth, keeping him on menial duties and denying him the opportunity to make a kill he could claim as his prize, a mount of his own where he could rebuild the Se'ha line and bring it glory and prestige in the Hunt.

And then the faithless fools on *Titan* had thrown off the balance, perhaps cheating him of any further chance of making his kill. They had offered this mad scheme of cooperation with the skymounts, but Se'hraqua could never bear to desecrate the holy beasts so by forcing them into slavery while they lived. The skymounts must live free and die free; the Pa'haquel had the right to master only their bodies, not their souls. That was the way of the Hunt, and Se'hraqua could not imagine participating in the corruption Riker proposed, even if it meant he would never have his own mount. But to his disgust, the Conclave had acceded to this madness, and now he wished only to get them out of his sight.

Before he could make his break, however, he found himself waylaid by Elder Aq'hareq. "I would speak with you, Hunter."

Se'hraqua lowered his head respectfully. Aq'hareq had voted against Riker's scheme and thus was still worthy of respect. "Please, Elder. I apologize again for my offense."

The elder placed a gnarled, half-bionic hand on his shoulder. "To me you gave no offense. You spoke eloquently and with true reverence for the Spirit and the skymounts. You show a commitment to our traditions which is rare in one so young."

Se'hraqua stared. "Thank you, Elder! Such words from such a celebrated veteran bring great honor indeed." To be in Aq'hareq's favor could bring many rewards, he realized. If he cultivated that favor well enough, perhaps he would be asked to join the Aq'Tri'Hhe fleet-clan as it sought to rebuild from the Hounding. Even if no new mounts would be forthcoming, there might still be posts of real responsibility needing to be filled, and perhaps he could rise to eldership of a mount if its current elder fell in combat and he acquitted himself well. So although his esteem for Aq'hareq was sincere, he was not blind to the benefits of expressing it.

Aq'hareq brushed off his praise, though. "I am but a hound of the Spirit, as Qui'hibra said. Although I do not share his opinions about what that means." He grimaced. "He has never been one of strong faith. To him, the great balance is but a mundane thing, a matter of ecology and population control."

"The Elder is a loyal servant of the Spirit." For appearance's sake, Se'hraqua judged that he should defend his elder. Just not too emphatically.

"But not an inspired one. Not one who understands the deeper meaning of the Hunt, the core of our traditions. We do not hunt to keep the ecology in balance! That is but a secondary effect."

"Yes," Se'hraqua said. "We hunt to give reverence to the Spirit, to serve as the Spirit created us. We pledge our blood and our lives in Its service."

"True, my young friend, true. Death affirms life, death feeds life. That is the balance. To think that will change just because of a temporary setback to the Hunt—that is folly."

"I agree, Elder."

"Good, good. Because I would request something of you."

"Anything, Elder!"

"Do not be so quick to pounce on this. I make it a request only, for I would be ashamed to make it more. I would like you to volunteer for Qui'hibra and Riker's mission to . . . *negotiate* with the skymounts."

Aq'hareq spoke the word with the same distaste Se'hraqua felt on hearing it. To dare to speak with skymounts as equals, to trespass upon their holy flesh without having won the right in the trial of the Hunt? "Elder, why would you ask me to participate in such blasphemy?"

"I doubt the skymounts will allow the blasphemy to occur at all. If they do, then it is part of the Spirit's plan anyway. But either way, we need an observer present who can offer . . . a dissenting perspective. Who can evaluate the events from a clearer vantage. Qui'hibra and Riker's plan is not the solution to our crisis, of this I am sure. But by observing and learning, young one, perhaps you can scout out a path to a real solution." The elder leaned closer, lowering his voice. "For instance, perhaps you could discover the means *Titan* used to distinguish our warp signatures from the skymounts'. If we could compensate for the difference, it would restore our advantage of surprise."

Se'hraqua felt a thrill of hope at the prospect, but skepticism tempered it. "The prey could still teleport us from our own mounts."

"We can devise defenses against that. Besides, think how much worthier the Hunt for skymounts will be if they actually fight back! At times I wonder if the Hunt has not grown too easy, made us soft. Looking at Qui'hibra's weakness, and how easily he swayed the Conclave, it is hard to doubt. Perhaps this whole crisis is the Spirit's way of challenging us to become stronger, worthier servants."

Se'hraqua nodded slowly. The elder was wise indeed. Surely the hardships the Spirit had inflicted on his own family were just such a trial, and it was his task to prove himself strong enough, worthy enough, by playing a role in helping the Pa'haquel regain their strength. Could he have a destiny even greater than winning his own mount and leading the Se'ha line to renewed prosperity?

There was only one way to find out. He had to follow

this spoor wherever it led, and be ready to strike at the right moment. "I will do as you ask, Elder. And proudly."

"Excellent. Together, and with the others who think as we do, we will see to it that the Hunt endures. As it always has, and as it always shall."

"Counselor, I have told you before that I do not desire your assistance."

Deanna met Tuvok's eyes evenly as he stood in his doorway, stiff as a statue. "I appreciate that, Commander. But I'm not here to offer counseling. I'm here because I want *your* assistance on an important matter. May I come in?"

Tuvok hesitated. But T'Pel came up behind him and said, "Husband, simple courtesy dictates that we invite her in and hear her proposal."

He seemed to soften fractionally. "Very well." He stepped aside and let her enter. T'Pel invited her to sit and undertook to prepare tea for them all. But Deanna knew Vulcans had little interest in wasting time on social niceties, so she went right to business, explaining Riker's plan.

Unsurprisingly, Tuvok reacted with puzzlement and discomfort. "Surely you cannot think I would be of use to you in this assignment," he said. "My actions prove that I cannot resist the astrocoelenterates' emotional influence."

"Your actions are precisely what make you most useful to me, Tuvok. If the jellies are to be convinced to work with their age-old predators as allies, the proposal needs to come from someone they trust. Even if Dr. Ree is right that they don't hold grudges, they would still be wary of traps and deceptions. They're most likely to trust the pro-

posal if it has the backing of someone they consider to be
on their side, someone who's helped them against the
Pa'haquel and clearly has no agenda in the Pa'haquel's
favor."

" 'Only Soval could go to Andoria,' " T'Pel quoted as
she poured the tea. Deanna recognized the Vulcan prov-
erb, though she was more used to the human "translation"
which substituted different historical referents.

"That's right. And if this plan does work, if we are able
to get the two species cooperating in the defense of inhabited planets against other cosmozoans, then they'll need to
learn how to work together—how to fight together. It
would help greatly if the jellies had access to the thoughts
of an experienced tactician such as yourself, Tuvok."

He avoided his wife's gaze. "How am I to help convince them to accept our agenda when I am so easily made
a puppet of their wishes, their impulses? I would be a lia-
bility to you, Counselor, not an aid."

T'Pel handed him his tea. "Logically, husband, she
would not be here if she believed that to be the case."

Deanna appreciated her support. "I am able to resist
acting on their emotions. I have shielding techniques I
could teach you, more advanced than standard mental
shields."

Tuvok shook his head. "I doubt they would be effective. Dr. Ree believes that my mental shielding may be
permanently impaired by the neurological traumas I sustained in the Delta Quadrant and Vikr'l Prison."

Deanna smirked. "Tuvok, mental shields aren't like de-
flectors on a ship. The brain is more adaptable than that,
more plastic. As with any other part of the body, its weak-
nesses or injuries can be compensated for with training
and exercise."

"Within limits. Do you not think, Commander, that I

have been engaged in such exercises of my own since I came aboard *Titan?*" He snapped out the words, then paused and grimaced. T'Pel touched her fingers to his, calming him somewhat. "You can see for yourself that they have not been effective. My ability to manage even my own emotions is tenuous at best."

"That's perfectly understandable, Tuvok, after what you've been through these past few months."

He was shaking his head before she finished the sentence. "You do not understand."

But she had sensed his reaction to her words "these past few months." That pointed her in the right direction. "You don't believe this is a recent problem, do you? What I'm sensing from you is that you see it as an intrinsic character flaw." His refusal to meet her eyes or T'Pel's confirmed it. In spite of herself, she let out a chuckle. "Tuvok—*you* think of yourself as overemotional?"

"I am pleased that you find my personal failings amusing."

"No, that's not it, Tuvok. It's just—I got to know some of your *Voyager* crewmates somewhat while you were adjusting to your return home. And most of them agreed . . ." She hesitated, but then realized he'd probably take it as a compliment. "They thought you were the stiffest, most humorless Vulcan they'd ever met. They liked you, of course, and respected you, but they certainly didn't think of you as emotional."

"Perhaps not under normal circumstances, Counselor. Even a weak fortification will hold when it is not assailed." He went on reluctantly. "But when I have been exposed to . . . external sources of strong emotion . . . I have never been able to manage them successfully. You are aware of my meld with Lieutenant Lon Suder, I assume."

She nodded. During her work counseling the returned

Voyager crew, she had become acquainted with most of their adventures. Suder had been a Betazoid, one of the Maquis rebels who had been integrated into *Voyager*'s crew. A violent sociopath, he had murdered another crewman. Since life imprisonment in the brig was not an option, Tuvok had attempted to rehabilitate Suder, using a mind-meld to teach him Vulcan control. In turn he had taken Suder's violent emotions into himself and had difficulty controlling them. "You can't blame yourself for that, Tuvok. Suder was a fellow telepath, and a dangerously unstable personality. There was no way of predicting the side effects."

"Still, my inability to cope with his violent emotions endangered the crew. And there have been other instances." Another long pause.

"Go on," T'Pel told him softly. "It is all right."

Deanna felt him take strength from her. "Such as when Mr. Neelix and I were . . . joined into Tuvix."

Her eyes widened. She knew from the records that Tuvok and the ship's boisterous native guide had been merged by a freakish transporter accident into a single being, integrating both psyches into a distinctive third one. Deanna had found it an extraordinary case study, although to this day she couldn't begin to understand—or at least believe—the science involved. Yet few of her interviewees had spoken much about the incident. It had clearly been a very painful set of events. The crew had grown fond of the unified being, who called himself "Tuvix." But his continued existence would have ended Tuvok's and Neelix's lives. The choice between the one and the two had been wrenching for the crew, and they had been reluctant to speak of it afterward. Tuvok, to all indications, had never acknowledged that he remembered the incident at all, and even the talkative Neelix had respected his privacy. For him to bring it up now was striking.

"I—Tuvix was prepared to condemn both myself and Mr. Neelix to oblivion," he said, "so that he could live on. In his fear, his selfishness, he was willing to sacrifice two other lives, and to jeopardize the morale and stability of *Voyager*'s crew." Deanna understood what he meant. Had Tuvix remained merged, the crew's lingering hostility would have severely disrupted morale. And on a ship stranded in the wilds of space, perhaps for a lifetime, morale was crucial to survival.

Still, she met Tuvok's eyes and spoke comfortingly. "How can you blame yourself for that? Tuvix was a unique entity, the result of the synergy between you and Mr. Neelix. You can't attribute any of his actions, his choices, to either of you uniquely."

"Perhaps. And for a time I was inclined to assume that Tuvix's resistance to self-sacrifice came from Mr. Neelix. He always possessed . . . a healthy fear response. However, he repeatedly demonstrated an instinctive regard for others, a willingness to subsume his own needs to those of his shipmates."

"And you haven't? Service to others, to the greater good, is a Vulcan ideal."

"It is a logical ideal, and when I am governed by logic I am able to make that choice. But as part of Tuvix, I was an emotional being—just as much as I am when under the star-jellies' influence. And I coped poorly with the emotions of fear and self-preservation, making a selfish and irresponsible choice.

"It has been the same ever since. My control is too easily compromised, and when it is, my judgment is dangerously unreliable." He fell into memory, shaking his head slowly. She sensed he was contemplating the horrors of his imprisonment on Romulus, but he did not choose to address it. But he gripped his wife's hand more firmly. "When I felt the jellies' anguish, their need . . . I knew I was out of control, but I did not *want* to regain it. I chose to betray my duty, Counselor. I chose to assault and injure Lieutenant Pazlar, to violate her mind. I knew it was wrong and I did not care."

"Your priorities were distorted by the jellies' influence. That's all."

"And it is enough to prove that I cannot help you. What if I fall under their influence again? What if I were to force a meld onto T'Pel, or onto you?"

It was no random example, Deanna knew. She had made no effort to keep Shinzon's assault on her a secret. That would have been giving into shame; it would have been a surrender. Still, she didn't appreciate Tuvok using it to try to scare her off. Rather than letting it show, though, she just raised an eyebrow in an almost Vulcan way and said, "Mr. Tuvok, I'd just like to see you try it. I can handle myself."

"As can I," T'Pel told him with confidence.

"And I can help you do the same, if you'll let me. Even if, for the sake of argument, you're right about having less emotional control than most Vulcans, maybe the problem is that you've been relying on Vulcan techniques—techniques which are designed to set aside emotion, rather than accepting its presence and letting it inform your judgment constructively. Maybe you could benefit from a more Betazoid approach."

Tuvok pondered her words, but remained unconvinced. "Even if your training could help me, it would take time to master. Months, possibly years. It is not a feasible option in the current situation."

Deanna hesitated. "There may be a shortcut." At his warily inquisitive look, she went on. "I once dealt with a case where an elderly Vulcan suffering from Bendii's Syndrome melded minds with a human who was . . . known for his stoicism." Out of respect for their privacy, she kept the names of Sarek and Picard to herself. "It gave the Vulcan the control he needed to perform at his peak for one vital mission, while the human bore the brunt of the Vulcan's uncontrolled passions. I suppose it was analogous to your meld with Mr. Suder, only in reverse." She took a breath. "If you meld with me, then you will be able to call on my shielding disciplines to block the star-jellies' emotions from your mind."

Tuvok frowned. "But if that portion of your mind is so occupied . . . then it will not be available to you. You will not be able to block their mental pressure."

She fidgeted. "I know."

"You would be . . . helpless against mental intrusion."

"Yes." *Stop rubbing it in, or I might change my mind.* Even though she found the star-jellies' minds pleasant enough, the prospect of having no control over their access to her mind left her feeling very vulnerable. A touch that was enjoyable when invited could be unbearable when one could not refuse it, as Deanna knew all too well.

T'Pel saw her unease. "Perhaps I could be the one to meld with him."

"Thank you, T'Pel, but no. Neither you nor any of the other psi-sensitives in the crew has the necessary training in shielding techniques. And you're all on the inhibitor drug. It has to be me," she finished, a bit shakily.

Tuvok studied her quizzically. "You would do this for me?"

"I would." Of course it was for the mission as well. But diplomatic officer or no, she was still a therapist first.

"That is . . . most generous of you, Counselor. But are you certain it would be safe? My last meld with a Betazoid . . ."

Deanna glared. "Was with a homicidal sociopath. I can't say I'm flattered by the comparison." She smirked. "Don't worry, Tuvok. My only unhealthy obsession is chocolate."

Tuvok quirked a brow. He exchanged a look with his wife, who simply nodded. "In that case, I agree. And I hope Dr. Ree is also a skilled dentist."

CHAPTER TWELVE

Melora Pazlar stood at the workstation in her quarters, studying astrometric scan data on pre-main-sequence stars in the RCW-33 region. She had been standing there for hours, enjoying the freedom to do so. Here, in her native gravity, standing was as comfortable as any other posture. Gravity was little more than a handy reference vector, a way to ensure that loose objects would eventually settle themselves against a single surface. The deck was just a convenient perch, kissing her feet with only the gentlest pressure to say "Here I am," ready to serve as a pushing-off surface when needed but otherwise not imposing. In here the deck would never be forced up against her, compressing her spine and her joints, making her stiff, making her ache all over. In here it would never rise up to slam into her with enough force to smash her bones.

In here it could not attack her. And neither could anyone else.

The door chime sounded, and Melora jumped, the

small convulsion of startlement enough to launch her slowly upward. She caught herself on a handhold and sighed. "Yes, who is it?"

After a moment a voder-generated voice came over the intercom. *"It's K'chak'!'op, Lieutenant. I was wondering if I could come in for a moment."*

"Uhh, I'm kind of busy right now. What's it about?"

"Well, I brought over those new cosmozoan-tracking subroutines I was working on for stellar cartography. I thought you might want to take a look at them before our new guests come aboard. I know you're still on light duty, but I'm sure you must be bored with it by now."

Indeed, she was bored out of her skull, but she hesitated. "Couldn't you have just uploaded those to me?"

"Well . . . yes . . . but the truth is, I wanted to see how you were doing. I . . . well, I feel terrible that I wasn't able to do more to prevent your injuries, and—"

"All right! All right, just—just a moment." She pushed off the wall and drifted in a low arc toward the door, catching herself on the modified antigrav sled that rested there, and throwing a resentful glare at it as she did. Dr. Ree had mended her bones as best he could, but he had told her that the regeneration process could only be accelerated so much. An osteostimulator took only minutes to restore a broken bone to sufficient strength to function in the gravity it had evolved for, but getting it strong enough to function in substantially higher gravity took substantially more time. A week after the attack, she was still undergoing daily stimulator treatments along with low-*g* physical therapy in sickbay, and was under medical orders to stay off her feet in ship-normal gravity for at least another few days. Taking a cue from *Enterprise*'s mission to Dokaalan last year, Dr. Ree had had an antigrav cargo sled modified for her as a makeshift hoverchair. She hated the thing. She had always hated having to be seen dependent on a chair, unable to move under her own power. She couldn't stand to appear helpless. She had thought that over the past dozen years or so she had reached the point where that didn't bother her so much anymore. But that was before she really had been rendered helpless. Before she had been smashed to the deck, flopping uselessly like a dying fish, unable to prevent Tuvok from wrenching control of her mind and body away from her and forcing her to give up secrets she was sworn to protect.

She didn't hate Tuvok for what he had done. She couldn't blame him, any more than she could blame sensitive little Orilly for helping him. But she hated herself for the shudder of panic that went through her every time she was reminded of the assault, of the violation—of her true and inescapable helplessness.

Taking deep breaths, Melora gathered herself, and hit the door panel. Despite herself, she couldn't help pulling back a bit at the sight of the massive Pak'shree looming in her doorframe, tentacles writhing, mouthparts gnashing. "Ahh, there you are! Mind if I—whoa!" K'chak'!'op made a move to come in, but reared back as her forward segments crossed the threshold into the centigravity field.

Melora realized she'd retreated behind the antigrav sled, and cursed herself for it. Nonetheless, she said, "Maybe it'd be better if we talked like this."

"Oh, yes. I'd be helpless in there. I wouldn't want to smash into you by accident."

"Uhh, look, you said you had those subroutines for me?" A fringe effect from the corridor's gravity was pulling her gently toward the door, she realized. She caught herself on the sled, again resenting the need to depend on it.

"Ahh, yes." A tentacle reached back and retrieved a

padd from the utility pouch she wore attached to the back of her carapace. An exoskeletal being, she wore no clothes, instead having her forward body segment painted in sciences blue. "But I also wanted to make sure you were feeling all right, and ask if there was anything I could do for you. I've been meaning to see you ever since the accident, but you're so hard to find. When you're not in sickbay you're always cooped up here in your quarters."

"Is that so bad?" Melora challenged. "It seems to work pretty well for you."

"Well, I thought so before, but it does get rather lonely. Just me and my fears."

Melora stared. "Fears? You mean like claustrophobia?" When K'chak'!' op had finally emerged from her seclusion a couple of weeks ago, she had explained to Melora how cramped the ship made her feel.

"Well, that was part of it, but it wasn't my real fear. Mainly I was afraid of hurting someone. You little endoskeletals, you're just so fragile."

Melora snatched the padd from her tentacles. "I'm not fragile!"

"Oh, no more fragile than any other endoskeletal. It's all relative of course. Why, if Vale or Troi or, Goddesses forbid, dear Captain Riker or Mr. Tuvok were to fall down in my planet's gravity, they'd shatter too. It's simply a matter of physics."

"Okay, I get what you're trying to do, Chaka. But I'm not afraid. I'm just giving myself—giving my body time to heal in its natural environment."

"Nonsense. You're trying to cut yourself off from other people again, deal with your problems in seclusion, just like you always do."

Melora gaped. "What brought that on? What happened to Miss Nice and Considerate?"

"I don't mother grown females, Melora. You're strong enough to take the truth. Or you should be. Maybe it will take a little time for you to rebuild that strength, but I know you have it in you. So I intend to help you build it up again. Why don't we start by going to the mess hall for a bite to eat?"

Melora threw a look at the sled. "I'd really rather not."

"Why? Because you don't like being dependent on a machine? Look at me. Listen to me. We couldn't even communicate without this machine I'm wearing. And we couldn't breathe without the machine we're standing in. Or floating in, as the case may be."

Melora realized that the big crustacean wasn't going to let her off the hook. But she admitted to herself that Chaka had a point. "All right. Let's go to the mess, talk over these subroutines." She began clambering into the sled. "But why are you taking such an interest in me, anyway?"

"Oh . . . just passing a favor forward."

"So—how are our guests settling in?"

Christine Vale chewed on a forkful of eggs while she formulated her response to the captain's question. Riker had invited her to breakfast (which he cooked himself), since Troi had an early appointment with the Pa'haquel delegation. The group consisted of a few dozen clan and crew members, mostly from Qui'hibra's fleet-clan, which would serve as a skeleton crew for the attempt to coexist with a star-jelly, if an agreement was reached. (A live star-jelly, that is; she found herself and others starting to fall into the habit of using "star-jelly" for the live beasts and "skymount" for the reanimated dead ones.) This morning, Qui'hibra had summoned Troi to discuss—or rather, argue about—the fine details of the negotiations they were preparing to attempt with the jellies. Riker hadn't been happy about the scheduling, but the Pa'haquel were impatient, and he and Troi both wished to avoid alienating them when their relationship was tenuous enough already.

"It's a mixed bag," she finally said. "The Vomnin envoys are friendly enough; I think they're mainly curious about our technology. A lot of theirs is just as good, but they seem eager to learn for its own sake."

"Good."

"And the Rianconi, well, they're just eager to please. Enough said there." Certainly the scantily clad humanoids had drawn considerable attention from the crew when they had come aboard, and had done nothing to discourage it. One of the males, observing that Vale seemed tense, had even offered to provide for her needs on an overnight basis. She had politely declined. Not that she had any great problem letting a man wait on her hand and foot (and in between), if he freely chose such service and saw dignity in it; she'd done as much on Risa and Argelius in her day. But when she did so, she preferred the man to be less dainty and fragile than these Rianconi were, so that she didn't feel she was taking advantage. Well, and for other, more shallow reasons. Besides, a lot of her tension involved her uncertainty about Jaza, and taking another male to bed when she would rather be with him hadn't struck her as the best way to relieve it.

"But the Pa'haquel . . . well, they don't like us, they don't trust us, and they insist on acting like they own the place. A lot of the crew aren't happy with the way they think they can boss us around."

"Neither am I," Riker said. "But let's face it—we're the visitors, they're the home team. They're the ones who understand this part of space—and if it comes to that, they're the ones who can call for backup and blow us out of the sky. We're a long way from the Sixth Fleet." He nursed his coffee. "Maybe it'll do the crew some good to be reminded of that. Out here maybe it's best if we learn a little humility."

"Maybe. But on the other hand . . ."

"On the other hand?" Riker prompted when she opted to have a slice of melon instead of finishing her sentence.

When she was ready, she went on. "I'm just not so sure about what we're doing. I know I was the one saying we shouldn't interfere in their way of life, and I'd defend to the death their right to, et cetera, et cetera. But I'm not crazy about actively helping them perpetuate it either. To tell you the truth, Will, I hate hunting. Back on Izar, you know, there's a sizeable sect of traditionalists, descendants of the early colonists who had to live off the land. And they think it's this grand, noble tradition to carry on the ways of the first settlers. Which they think means hunting for sport and having the unrestricted license to own archaic, lethal weapons—plasma rifles, projectile weapons, crossbows, anything without a stun setting. Never mind that they live in cushy houses with replicators and tended lawns and don't need to hunt for their food or defend themselves against predators in the bush. It's all about 'tradition' and 'pride' to them. But to me, as a cop, as the daughter of a cop, it was more about having to call in the coroner when somebody wasn't careful enough with the damn things and blew their kids' heads off. Or when somebody lost their temper or got scared, and pulled a trigger before they had a chance to think about it, to stop themselves. I lost family to those weapons, to the 'noble hunting traditions' that kept them legal.

"Now, I freely admit that makes me biased. Looking at it objectively, I understand that in some cultures, some environments, you have to hunt to survive. I understand that humans did it for a million years or more. And of course I can't deny that the things the Pa'haquel are hunting—monsters like that harvester. . . ." She blinked; the image of the Shalra homeworld's demise was still seared on her retinas, right on top of Oghen's. "Well, something has to be done to stop them from destroying whole inhabited worlds.

"But it still doesn't seem right to me, what we're doing." Will just watched her patiently as she went on. "I mean, we're going to try to make the star-jellies into their hunting dogs. To take these beautiful, sensitive creatures and make them into weapons. It doesn't seem right. Violence as a first resort . . . that shouldn't be the Starfleet way, not anymore. Even the harvesters or the Crystalline Entities, they're just animals following their instincts. Killing them for it—that's just not the Starfleet I signed up for."

Riker tilted his head in acknowledgment, clearly not offended. But he did offer a counterpoint. "Starfleet has its rules, but so does nature. Letting animals do what comes naturally—that means killing, and being killed. It's no different for the star-jellies. They're wild animals, Christine. They already have to fight to survive. And we've seen they have no qualms about killing when they have to."

"When they have to. But to make a whole lifestyle of it. . . ." She shook her head. "It just seems like suddenly we've taken the Pa'haquel's side here, trying to change the jellies to be like them."

"Weren't you the one who suggested that the jellies needed to change?"

"I don't know, I guess so. As a rhetorical device, I guess. Hell, let's face it, I'm all over the map on this. I wanted to stay out of it because I don't *know* what the right side is. I think everyone's entitled to their own way of life, ideally, but when it starts to hurt other people then I'm not so sure. How do we know the Pa'haquel can be trusted with the power that live star-jellies could give them? How can we say they're the ones best qualified to deal with the cosmozoan threat? How do we know they'll only use that power against cosmozoans? And what about the other intelligent cosmozoans out there? The Pa'haquel don't seem to discriminate much where their targets are concerned."

Riker grimaced. "I don't know. I don't know, Christine. I don't think this is an ideal solution either. But it's what I've got right now. At the moment, my top priority is to help end the conflict between the star-jellies and the Pa'haquel. The jellies asked for our help, then we let them take it from us, and as a result another species' way of life is endangered. I want to fix *those* problems, the ones I'm directly responsible for. Dealing with the bigger issues, that comes later." He shrugged. "Who knows? If this works, the star-jellies will have a say in the alliance too. Maybe they can add some compassion to it, offer some alternative solutions."

"Except they have no qualms about killing when they have to," she echoed.

"There is that." Riker furrowed his brow. "Maybe that's the whole problem here. The reason we've had so much trouble figuring out what to do according to the Prime Directive or Starfleet policy. Those policies are geared toward dealing with technical civilizations, structured governments, laws and treaties—maybe it doesn't prepare us well for dealing with the wilder kinds of intelligent life. Beings that only live by the laws of survival and need. So this is something we're making up as we go."

Vale nodded, finishing up her eggs. "And right now, *our*

continued survival depends on not ticking off the Pa'ha-quel too badly. So we're pretty much acting out of necessity too."

"Right. But I'm hoping to find a way to move beyond that. Successful negotiations between the Pa'haquel and the jellies—even if it does mean turning the jellies into fighters, it still means that former mortal enemies will have learned to work together, will have found an alternative to killing each other. And that's a good start. Maybe it's the first step toward a world of cushy houses and manicured lawns where deadly force is an anachronism."

"Maybe." Vale saw the Shalra world again, saw her aunt's coffin being lowered into the ground with full police honors. "But even in a world like that, anachronisms happen."

"Yes. They do." She looked in his eyes, and saw Tezwa.

The Pa'haquel were furious. Deanna could sense it pouring off them in waves before she even entered the observation lounge. She strove to maintain a calm and relaxing presence as she entered the room, but Qui'hibra's cold, raptorlike gaze upon her made it difficult. Somehow his unwavering calm was more intimidating than the more overt rage of Chi'tharu and Tir'hruthi, the other two Pa'haquel he had brought to this meeting. His fury was something that would never overwhelm him, never cloud his judgment or diffuse his energies; it was something he wielded with stern efficiency, always a strength and never a weakness. All three of them wanted to snap her neck right now, but Qui'hibra would channel that urge into his words, his strategies, his arguments. That made him far more of a threat in her mind. She took some slight solace in the gentle warmth projected by Oderi, who had been brought along as an aide.

But Qui'hibra didn't even let Deanna sit before he spoke. "You will explain to me," he said, "how it is that the very telepath who handed the skymounts the means to defeat us is now being included on this mission."

Deanna's eyes widened. She resisted asking a question like *"How did you find out?"*; it would only serve to make them angrier if she treated it as a secret. Besides, Oderi's apologetic glance and empathic aura told the tale. Deanna looked at the little Rianconi in a new light and wondered which *Titan* crew member had allowed him- or herself to be seduced into revealing the facts about Tuvok's actions. She couldn't blame Oderi for being loyal to her allies, though. And she had intended to tell them anyway when the time was right.

"I assure you," she said calmly, "Mr. Tuvok deeply regrets what he was compelled to do under the star-jellies' influence, and wants nothing more than to make amends for it. We do have means to guard against it happening again."

"And we should trust the word of another telepath on this?" snapped Chi'tharu, a wiry veteran who had been chosen as huntsmaster for the expedition. "How do we know they are not influencing you now? It is sung in the ancient songs, it is known to all that the Spirit does not abide telepaths in the Hunt, for they compromise the stealth on which victory depends."

"With all respect, Huntsmaster Chi'tharu, this is not a hunt. We—"

"All life is a Hunt."

She went on. "We are trying to create a new kind of balance, one based on communication. Telepathic intermediaries are the only way to communicate with the sky-mounts."

"But *him?*"

Deanna explained her reasoning in choosing Tuvok, someone whom the jellies trusted and who could be valuable in advising them tactically. But Chi'tharu was unconvinced. "What do you know of tactics? You are an empath—a weakling, bled by others' wounds."

"She is not weak," Qui'hibra said, silencing the other with his quiet, simple sternness. "She worked tirelessly with the refugees. And she saved Oderi and others from the rampaging Fethet, striking a cunning blow against him and taking no pause for her safety." A look passed between him and Oderi, and she sensed something else between them too—nothing sexual, but a sense of trust and reliance. Oderi had his ear, had told him what Deanna had done, and was now gratified that her words had done their job. Her loyalty could be a two-way street, it seemed; she wished to do the best for everyone.

Or maybe to take care of everyone? Did the Rianconi see themselves more as servants, or as parents?

"Because of that," Qui'hibra continued, "I am willing to give you a chance to make this work. But understand that I do not indulge those who fail me. So you had best be very sure of this Tuvok—and of yourself."

"Let's be clear here," she countered, coming on strong in response to the implied threat. "Are you speaking of failure, or of betrayal? I am sure that neither Tuvok nor I, nor any other telepathic member of this crew, will act in violation of their duties." Regrettably, in some cases that would be because they would not be given the chance. She had sadly recommended that Orilly Malar remain confined to quarters for now, since she simply could not rely on the gestalt-starved Irriol's ability to resist acting under the influence of other minds—not when it was so much in her evolutionary nature to do so. As for the other psi-sensitives, they would all be on duty (where applicable) but under guard, and kept from high-security areas on *Titan,* though they might be assigned to work aboard the star-jellies on a case-by-case basis if and when that stage was reached.

"But I cannot promise you that this effort will be successful. We're trying something new here, and there are no guarantees. Threats and intimidation cannot change that. We will do our best. And if this plan does not work, then we will try something else. We will do so because we choose to and believe it is right—not because you growled at us or gave us an ultimatum."

Chi'tharu and Tir'hruthi grew angrier at her haughty tone, but Qui'hibra softened fractionally, and she even sensed amusement in him. "Well said, Commander Troi. We cannot shout the balance into shifting in our favor. We go to the Hunt with no guarantee that we will triumph—only that if we fail, it will not be for want of effort or commitment. That is what I require of you and your crew. And I hope that you will not fail me. I hope you will not fail the galaxy."

So do I, Troi thought devoutly. *So do I.*

"This plan is doomed to fail."

Jaza Najem had not met enough Vomnin to know whether repeating oneself was a common practice in their culture. Indeed, given how widespread their worlds were throughout the Gum Nebula, Jaza was certain they had no single culture. But at least it seemed to be a personal habit of Podni Fasden, the Vomnin scientist accompanying this mission. She was a member of Udonok Station's complement, sent as an observer on behalf of the Consortium which encompassed a plurality of the Vomnin-settled worlds. Her report would be reviewed by the Consortium's government as they deliberated whether to lend their resources in support of building a partnership between the Pa'haquel and the star-jellies. Given that, Jaza was actually glad of her skepticism; a report of success would carry more weight from someone who had not expected success. Of course, that would require the effort actually succeeding, and Jaza could not be sure that would happen.

Still, he tried to stay optimistic. "But if you're right, the jellies were engineered to serve as ships sometime in the past," he reminded Fasden. "And they must have accepted it, or been designed to accept it. Given their form of reproduction, their conscious error-checking of their genome, they wouldn't have kept those traits if they didn't want them."

"Their reasons for wanting them may not have been the same as those of their masters," Fasden responded, crouching on her haunches while her long arms reached up to tap at a console. Vomnin posture kept them a bit lower to the ground than most humanoids, and on their station the controls had often been at or near floor level. Fasden seemed to have no trouble adjusting to the equipment here in the science lab, though. "Warp drive, replication, more potent weaponry—these are clearly pro-survival traits for most any species. The artificial gravity, as you surmised, is beneficial to their metabolism. So they would have had no reason to eliminate these or other traits when they eliminated their masters."

Jaza wasn't quite convinced that the jellies' added traits had been given them by some other race. True, the Vomnin had been studying the question far longer than he had, and their genetic records—based on the accumulation rate of certain trivial mutations uncorrected by the jellies' error-checking—showed that these traits and their associated behaviors had been added or enhanced some eight million years ago, later than most of their other attributes. (Their sapience, telepathy, and more limited telekinesis had evidently been innate properties.) The Vomnin assumed the enhancement had been done to turn the jellies into ships for some ancient race, but Jaza did not feel the evidence ruled out Eviku's hypothesis that the jellies had independently chosen to adopt technologies they had observed. As Fasden said, they were beneficial survival traits.

But the question might never be answered. Despite the jellies' shared memories, Counselor Troi had reported that their recall grew hazier the further one went back in time. Even telepathically transmitted memory was a subjective thing, susceptible to alteration and forgetfulness, and with each duplication it blurred further. Past a certain point, it was no more reliable than oral history and legend.

For now, though, Jaza admitted that Fasden's theory was the more probable one, so he didn't argue the point. At least, not that part of it. "You're only assuming they turned on these hypothetical masters."

"What else do you suppose could have become of them?" She shook her wide-featured bronze head. "In our researches we have found the remains of more than one civilization which attempted to master cosmozoans and was destroyed by the effort. They are simply too powerful to control. One world attempted to harness a variant of the sailseeds to extract the vital elements from its system's asteroids and comets. They engineered away their migratory behavior. As a result, their whole system was overrun and its planets slowly disassembled.

"One great empire at war took a species of predatory cloud creature with metadimensional abilities, engineered it with warp capability and a hunger for humanoid blood, and turned it loose on its enemy. The creatures ended up nearly destroying both sides before they were stopped. And a few escaped to plague the rest of the galaxy, their fate still unknown."

"I think I'm aware of encounters with two of them," Jaza said, realizing that Fasden's tale could explain some of the anomalies about the "vampire clouds" encountered by James Kirk and the Klingons. "Both creatures were ultimately destroyed."

"That is good. But it does not mean I want to see a new scourge unleashed on the galaxy."

Jaza could understand her fatalism. The Vomnin's original technology had been left by a race which had colonized their world while they were still scavenger-gatherers, but which had died out in some ancient cataclysm. Upon learning of the region's hazards from the settlers' records, the Vomnin had mastered the remnant technology and used it to found many colonies of their own, most of them far from the Vela Association, to ensure that their species would survive any catastrophe. Along the way they had acquired more technology and knowledge left by other ancients, some destroyed, some regressed to primitivism, others apparently ascended to higher planes. Given the hazards of this region, it was even more littered with such ancient ruins (at least ones younger than several million years, and thus more likely to contain viable technology) than Federation space. The Vomnin had made a career out of harvesting such ruins, building their science and culture on the whispers of the dead. So a certain preoccupation with failure and destruction was understandable.

Another consequence of this history was that the Vomnin had little in the way of religious belief. The ancient settlers had appeared as gods to the primitive Vomnin, but discovering the truth—of their instrumentality and their mortality—had disillusioned them. On their travels they had come across relics of other religions based on beings they knew to be merely advanced civilizations. As a result they were skeptics and secularists, more concerned with making the best of this life than with anything after it. They indulged their Pa'haquel allies' faith in the Spirit of the Hunt, but Fasden had made it clear in private that she saw it as mere superstition.

But maybe that was the key, Jaza realized. "You keep talking about cosmozoans turning on their 'masters.' If that's true, maybe the problem is that they *were* mastered. Treated as servants instead of equals. Take it from a Bajoran—that kind of treatment has a way of provoking rebellion.

"And maybe that's why this can work. The Pa'haquel already feel great reverence for the star-jellies. They cherish them as a divine source of life. If we can redirect that reverence toward partnership with the jellies rather than predation upon them, it could help to ensure that they're treated well."

"How do you redirect an article of faith? Their divinity is a hunting deity, not one of peace and amity."

"They allied with you, didn't they?" Jaza reminded her. "There are as many aspects of the divine as there are believers to behold them. So faith can adapt to suit anyone's needs. If it couldn't—if it only applied to a finite number of people—it wouldn't be divine, would it?"

Fasden looked at him oddly. "I would not have expected such talk from a scientist."

Jaza smiled. "I think that's exactly my point."

• • •

"Well? Have you extracted the data?"

Fasden shook her fat-faced head. "No, Hunter Se'hraqua. Their computer security ciphers are extremely sophisticated and rely heavily on biometric identification. A consequence of their recent war, I suppose."

Se'hraqua hissed in frustration. "I do not care why, Vomnin. I only care about results. We must get that information!"

"There is only so much I can do without attracting suspicion. The information on your skymounts' sensor signatures has been encrypted, no doubt to guard against precisely what we are trying to do."

"Yes, yes, I do not need one of your lectures." Had the smug intellectual not been an ally, and would it not have drawn the attention of *Titan*'s security, Se'hraqua would have been sorely tempted to give her a head start, hunt her down, and rip her throat out. It would be a satisfying release for this frustration, this inability to achieve the holy task Aq'hareq had assigned him. The Starfleeters were being unreasonable, determined to keep the Pa'haquel from the sensor information they had given the skymounts—thus giving the lie to their claims of nonpartisanship. All they had to do was share the knowledge, and the Hunt could be resumed, the balance restored. All would be as it was—except Se'hraqua's status would be considerably higher. If he brought home a prize of this magnitude clenched in his jaws, Aq'hareq would surely reward him with a mount to command and a bride from a high family, perhaps Aq'ha itself. Indeed, since he had a whole line to repopulate, Aq'hareq might even reward him with multiple brides. Fathering so many directly would bring him to high status swiftly, especially with so many noble females to crew his mount and make it strong and swift in the Hunt.

But such triumph was contingent on his retrieval of useful information, and he had run out of ideas on how to retrieve it. His Rianconi servant, Ujisu, had been unsuccessful at seducing the ship's first officer, science officer and all the others he had propositioned. Perhaps he was not as persuasive as Qui'hibra's slut Oderi, or maybe the Starfleeters were more protective of this information, seeking to keep the skymounts from the honor of being righteously hunted. And now Fasden, as skeptical of Riker's plan as he and thus a potential ally, had failed as well. He wanted to command her to dig deeper, but he knew that was unwise. Her inquisitiveness to a point could be interpreted as the Vomnin's natural desire to scavenge others' technology, but if she dug too deeply or were caught trying to compromise their computer security, it could expose them to the Starfleeters.

So for now, Se'hraqua's only option was to watch and wait. As a hunter he knew the value of this, but at least in the Hunt he knew the waiting would culminate in a strike, and possibly the glory of a kill. In this kind of hunt, the hunt for hidden information, he was out of his element. He could see no way to make the strike, to claim the prize. No way to escape the disgraced state Qui'hibra had trapped him in and gain his rightful place as an elder. It made him want to rip something's throat out. Somebody's.

"Go. You are dismissed," he said to Fasden, before he gave into the impulse and did something . . . indiscreet. Once the soundproofed door had closed behind her, he let out a scream, though it did little to sate his rage. Maybe he should try that holodeck hunting program that the doctor had recommended, though hunting unreal prey would not serve the Spirit and could not ease his soul. Perhaps later he would take out some of his frustrations on Ujisu's body. Rianconi were always so obliging, and bore a suitable resemblance to the humans, Vulcans and others upon whom he would like to unleash his rage. He could only inflict such punishment up to a point, of course—even Rianconi drew the line at permanent damage—but it should be satisfying.

And perhaps someday, if the Spirit willed, he would be free to do the same to Riker and Troi and not need to hold himself back.

CHAPTER THIRTEEN

Christine Vale sat in a corner of the mess hall, nursing an orange-banana smoothie and monitoring the mood of the room. Jaza had been forced to postpone their just-friends lunch date—something she realized she was more disappointed about than she would've expected—but she'd chosen to remain in the mess hall anyway and keep an eye on things. It didn't quite feel right to be essentially spying on her own crewmates, but her peace officer's instincts died hard. Tensions were high in here right now. Several of the Pa'haquel visitors had gotten together with a number of *Titan*'s carnivorous crew members, including Ree, Huilan, and Kuu'iut, and were sharing a pair of tables, telling hunting stories in loud voices and laughing raucously. Many of the other crew members in the mess hall, particularly the herbivores, were acting disturbed and uncomfortable. A few minutes ago, Tylith, a Kasheetan engineer, had requested that they lower their voices, but as was usual in such cases, their compliance had lasted only a few minutes. Now Tylith was at a table on the far side of the cavernous room, trying to carry on a conversation but periodically glaring over at the carnivores. Vale expected that her silence wouldn't last; Kasheeta might be herbivores but they were not known for meekness.

Indeed, after another few moments Tylith and her tablemates rose and came over toward Vale herself. Vale noted that those with her were also herbivores: Lonam-Arja, the Grazerite sensor tech, and Chamish, the Kazarite ecologist. "Commander," Tylith said, "we'd like a word with you." Her wide-set yellow eyes stared out from under high bony crests, and the lips of her protruding red-brown snout were curled, giving her a haughty and irritated look. To some extent all Kasheeta looked like that by default, but in this case Vale could tell the illusion was accurate.

"Yes, Lieutenant?"

"I thought the carnivores had agreed to limit their mess hall activities to late night. They're not abiding by that agreement."

"They *chose* to do that as a courtesy to their crewmates," Vale told her. "It's not a formal policy. They have as much right to be here as you do. Besides, they're not eating."

"No, but they're *talking* about eating, and killing, and torturing helpless animals. It's put me quite off my appetite."

"And it's not just about eating," Chamish said. "Should we really be encouraging those Pa'haquel like this? Indulging their tales of brutality to nature's creations, laughing in celebration of their triumphs? I don't think the predators are serving Starfleet's ideals very well by doing that."

Vale stared at him. "Serving Starfleet's ideals? Listen to yourself, Ensign. 'The predators'? Is that any way to talk about your own crewmates?" She stood. "This is ridiculous. I'm not going to watch this crew get divided on some sort of carnivore-versus-herbivore lines. I mean, look at them," she said, gesturing at the Rianconi aides who sat near the Pa'haquel, listening politely to the stories. "Those herbivores don't have any problem coexisting with predators. So why are you standing here complaining about sharing the mess hall with your own crewmates? Come on, people. We're Starfleet. We should be the ones showing *them* how to get along."

Tylith and the others were lowering their heads abashedly, but that wasn't enough for Vale. She started moving toward the raucous crowd, gesturing to the others to follow. "I said come on. Let's not be rude to our guests." The steel in her voice got them moving.

As they approached the table, Vale registered that the Pa'haquel huntsmaster Chi'tharu was regaling the others with the tale of how his fleet had battled a Hoylean Black Cloud. "How do you kill a nebula?" Kuu'iut was asking.

"Ahh, it is not easy. You must destroy or scatter enough of the planetesimals that comprise its brain so that it cannot continue to function. But getting to them is the hard part. A Cloud contains immense voltages and can send vast lightning discharges against a fleet, as powerful as any technological weapon you have ever encountered. Even the gases that make up its body can hit you with devastating force when accelerated and concentrated by the Cloud's internal fields. The key is to infect its circulatory streams with radioisotopes. Injected in the right parts of its structure, they can interfere with its neural processes, leave it weakened, confused. But only if you can keep it from isolating the flow. It can cut off a damaged section from its neural network and keep functioning on the rest.

"For us, the slaying of this Cloud was a delicate,

lengthy operation. We would dart in to make a strike, to inject isotopes or fire on key neural nodes, to pierce through magnetic barriers and allow cross-contamination. But then we would have to race back out again before it could retaliate. It took us months of harrying the beast, wearing it away by slow attrition. But it wore away at us as well, sometimes getting in a fatal blow with its lightning, and it became a race to see who would run out first. It was a testament to our skill," he finished proudly, "that we only lost five mounts before the Cloud became too crippled to fight back anymore."

"Is that really something to celebrate?" Tylith asked in a challenging tone. "All that death and destruction?"

"We celebrate that there was not more," Chi'tharu explained.

"Still," Lonam-Arja said in his slow, deep voice, "all those people dying—isn't it hard to think about?"

The Pa'haquel hunter looked evenly at the Grazerite. "Those people were my siblings, my cousins, my friends. I lost a wife and my firstborn child. Of course their deaths came hard. But how can I honor their lives if I do not think about what they gave them for?"

Lonam-Arja lowered his bovine head. "I'm sorry."

"Don't you ever wish there was a better way, though?" Vale asked. "A way that didn't result in so much death?"

"In the long term, the quantity of death is always the same. All that matters is the quality of it, and the purpose."

"The quality of death," Tylith echoed. "As though it were a wine to be appraised and enjoyed. Necessary or not, bringing death, to yourselves or to others, is nothing to tell boastful stories about."

"Oh, really?" Counselor Huilan said with a small, mischievous smile showing around his tusks. "Tell us again, Tylith, about what you did during the Dominion War?"

His request was not hostile; he knew as well as Vale that the Kasheeta had been awarded the Medal of Valor for devising the means to destroy a Jem'Hadar fighter that had left her own vessel defenseless. But Tylith glowered at him anyway. "That was different. I only acted in defense, not aggression. And I take no pride in it."

"Oh, but it was such a clever solution to the problem! How did it work again . . . ? "

At Huilan's prompting, Tylith sat down at the table and began to spin her tale of how she had rigged her ship's tractor emitter to send false information to the enemy fighter's inertial damper relays, throwing it out of synch and causing it to amplify the fighter's accelerations rather than cancelling them. The result had been a messy but intact prize for the Starfleet Corps of Engineers to study. Chi'tharu reacted with interest, asking about the Jem'-Hadar's skills as fighters, about which Tylith had little to say. But the Pa'haquel female with him asked some cogent engineering questions, and soon she and Tylith were deep in shop talk, while the others at the table became engrossed in their own tangents to the discussion. After a few more moments, Vale slipped quietly away from the table, smiling. *And the lion and the lamb shall lay down together. And no help needed from Deanna.*

Soon *Titan* neared its destination, a star-jelly breeding world on the outskirts of the Vela Association. To repay Will for letting her name the first one Kestra, Deanna had suggested calling this system's star Kyle, in honor of his recently deceased father. At her recommendation, the ship was now taking up station just outside the system while she and Tuvok prepared to meld and make contact with the jellies. Qui'hibra had wanted to monitor the meld in order to guard against any tricks, but Deanna had insisted on privacy. She had reminded him that if they did engage in any telepathic collusion, he would have no way of detecting it. However, Dr. Ree had insisted just as forcefully that he at least needed to monitor them during the meld. She and Tuvok had both consented to this, and the doctor's presence had somewhat mollified the other predators.

Deanna found the doctor's presence somewhat comforting herself. She was unnerved at the prospect of surrendering herself so completely to telepathic influence, with no way to turn it off. But she did her best to manage her unease, for the mission's sake as well as for Tuvok's. She believed this meld would help him master his insecurities. She didn't want to burden him with hers.

Tuvok had spent hours meditating in preparation for the meld. Although he had the ability to meld without prior preparation, as he had done with Melora Pazlar, as a rule he preferred to get into the optimal mindset first. Indeed, given the harm his last meld had caused, reaching the state of equanimity took some doing.

However, she knew from his record that he had a good deal of experience with melding. That experience, combined with the natural psionic receptiveness of her own mind, meant that the meld came easily. At first it was just a level of communication which was second nature to her, a sharing of awareness and thought, but it quickly gave way to something deeper, a blurring of the boundaries between self and other. Part of her recoiled at the intrusion, but at the same time it did not feel like an intrusion, because the new thoughts and memories were *hers*.

But some of the memories, the perceptions—and yes, the emotions, for no Vulcan could hide them here—were distressing to experience at first hand. The distinctive flavor of a Reman mind, impinging on hers—*Vkruk!* No, she

(Tuvok?) reminded herself—*Mekrikuk*. The Reman prisoner who had saved Tuvok's life, befriended him, shared minds with him to aid his recovery and escape. It was a memory of a friend—nothing to fear.

Still, there was agony, rage and violence associated with the memory—the agony of weeks of torture, the rage at his captors, the violence of his escape. And now came another memory of violent anger—Melora Pazlar falling beneath him, her flimsy bones snapping, her grating voice silenced by pain until he bent it to his will. Deanna recoiled at the memory of the terror and helplessness in Pazlar's eyes, of Tuvok's satisfaction in it. But then she knew the shame and regret which Tuvok felt at the incident, at giving in to such impulses. The ordeal of the prison must have been horrendous indeed to leave him with such urges, such scars. As much as the ordeals that had shaped Shinzon, she reminded herself, or Vkruk— both of them raised as slaves, brutalized for decades, twisted by hate into monsters. It didn't excuse what they had done. So how could she forgive Tuvok, whatever the excuse?

Yet how could she not? He was as much a victim as she had been. This was how it was: cruelty was a virus, perpetuating itself, making its victims into carriers. Forgiveness was the only inoculation. The only way to break the cycle was to refuse to react to violence with more violence, hate with more hate. Someone had to let go.

She focused on that thought. That was the goal here: to end a cycle of killing, to make peace between mortal foes. That was their purpose, and they needed to concentrate on that. The thought, she realized, came as much from Tuvok as herself. She felt his rigid sense of discipline and purpose anchoring them. It gave her the courage to let go, to set her own mental discipline loose, let it be drawn in to merge with his. She felt naked, stripped of her psychological armor. But she felt him don it, felt that sense of discipline and purpose intensified by its strength, and that made her feel safe.

We are ready, he thought to her. As the one laid open, it was her place to reach out and make contact, to be the conduit. A renewed thrill of fear went through her, but there he was with her, anchoring her. And somewhere in the background was Will's presence too, grounding her further. Thus braced, she made the leap. *We are here,* she sent. *We wish to commune with you. There are urgent matters to discuss.*

Curiosity poured over her, then recognition, happiness. Too much, too fast, but she could not stop it. *Friends! Friends who [helped/rescued/freed] us! Great [joy/gratitude] once again!* A torrent of sensation and emotion inundated her as the jellies updated her on recent events. Many dead had been liberated from desecration, and finally returned to their breeding grounds. Many new lives had been conceived with the energies they left behind. They shared every one with her, an orgy of orgies. It was too much, it was unbearable, it was miraculous.

They sensed her distress at her lack of control, her inability to stem the flood of feeling. They pulled back, but it was with puzzlement and regret. To them, this kind of total openness, this absence of boundaries, was natural. This sharing was an act of giving, not domination. The thought of being without it was a desolate one, a thing to be feared, not craved. Deanna seized on that perspective, let it give her reassurance. She could not resist the influx, but she could trust it, embrace it. And she knew they would not harm her. Sensing that assurance, they resumed the sharing of their joy, but more gently, with care for her fragility.

Yes, came Tuvok's calming voice. *Your liberation is*

gratifying. Yet it comes at a cost. We need your help to remedy it. Curiosity and puzzlement came in response. Tuvok efficiently, methodically spelled out the situation.

Deanna was immersed in anxiety, terror and grief as the jellies witnessed the devastation wrought by the other cosmozoans, and shared their own experience of encounters with such beasts. They offered their commiseration at the loss of life, the grief of the survivors.

Your sympathy is appreciated. But there is more you can offer. You can help us combat the threat.

How [confusion/alarm]? We are not hunters. Fighting, they projected, was something you did when left with no choice; otherwise, you fled.

Tuvok explained the rest of the proposal. It met with alarm, distaste and no small degree of amusement. *Join with those who prey on us? Anathema/suicide!*

You need not fear. They can no longer hurt you. We gave you that. So it will cost you nothing to meet with them and hear their side. Their survival is at stake too. As is that of many other species.

Sad. But not our [concern/purview/capability] to stop.

Is it not? These creatures endanger your breeding worlds too.

We will defend them [determination/pride]. We always have.

If their populations are not kept in check, there may eventually be too many for you to defend against.

Then we will take our young and flee. There are other galaxies.

None within reach are as lush as this one, Tuvok countered. Deanna sensed him making an educated guess that Andromeda and Triangulum, the only other large spiral galaxies in the Local Group, were too far for them to reach. And the small elliptical galaxies making up most of the Local Group had few or none of the star-formation zones where cosmozoans could thrive. The jellies' options would be limited to the two Magellanic Clouds, which would be smaller, sparser environments for cosmozoans to inhabit.

But Deanna recognized that the jellies remained unconvinced. He was trying to reason with them, and they were creatures of passion. She knew that passion as her own; surely if anyone could know what would convince them, she could. She had felt their sorrow at the Shalra's plight, so she fed it to them anew—all her sensations, her experiences, all the empathic impressions of grief and desolation she'd gotten from the refugees. It was hard enough having no control over the emotions that came into her from without. Yet now she had to do something harder, to relinquish her control over the grief and pain within her, the full emotional impact of a tragedy too enormous to bear. She wrenched open the floodgates, let it all pour out of her, made herself confront it and not look away. The torrent could flow both ways. She poured her grief into them, made them feel it as their own.

Then she fed them her empathic sensations of the Pa'haquel's grief and horror at seeing so many of their fellows beamed into vacuum by the jellies. They had to learn to see the Pa'haquel as more than a threat. Making them feel some sense of obligation toward the hunters could help.

On top of it all, she fed them her own guilt, her complicity in bringing about this destruction. She reached for Tuvok's as well, but he resisted. *We must,* she told him. *It's the only way. Face your guilt. Use it. Make it a strength.* He acquiesced, let her feed it all to them.

This is what we have wrought, she told them. *Do you*

want your salvation to come at such cost? Is this the legacy you wish to leave your children?

Silence echoed back. If they were deliberating among themselves, they were not sharing their feelings with her.

Finally: *We will meet with them [wariness/unease]. After that, we shall see.*

Thank you, she told them—and Tuvok was saying it too.

Riker rushed toward sickbay, so swiftly that even Qui'-hibra's determined stride was hard-pressed to keep up. After Dr. Ree's message, nothing could have stopped him. *"Captain,"* he had reported, *"the star-jellies . . . are here. In the person of your wife. They are asking to speak with you and Qui'hibra."*

Imzadi? he called to her as he strode through the corridors. *Yes!* came her reply, but there was something more there, something he could barely sense. *Come to us!*

That sense of joyous anticipation intensified as he neared the doors to sickbay, and as soon as they slid open, there she was, hurling herself into her arms. *"Imzadi!"* She kissed him passionately. "We have missed you."

"Uhh . . . 'we'?"

Tuvok rose to face him. "Apologies, Captain. This is an unanticipated side effect of the mind-meld. Counselor Troi's unshielded mind is serving as a conduit for their communication." His manner was distracted, distant, and Riker realized he was still joined in the meld, himself a conduit for . . . whatever was happening here.

He grasped his wife's shoulders, looked in her eyes. "Deanna, are you still there?"

She laughed. "Deanna is with us, Imzadi. She feels

with us that it's a useful way to communicate. And exciting, too! All these strange senses." She looked around her with awe, breathed in the air, stroked his arms and chest as though it were all new.

Blushing on behalf of them both, he took her wrists and stepped back a bit. "Deanna, you did agree to this, then? It's consensual?"

"How else could it be?" She shook her head in puzzlement, still smiling. "You poor little ones, so apart from each other, so reserved." She threw a look at Tuvok. "All of you, you hide so much away from each other, from yourselves." Then to Ree. "You fight your urges for fear of not being accepted." Back to Riker. "It keeps you from truly knowing one another, leaves you lonely and unsure of one another." She moved close to him again. "You and Deanna, we have a hint of true communication, but still so much is held back, so much deferred. Why did we wait so long to share such joy?" She stroked his cheek. "Why haven't we made a child?"

He just stared at her for a while, then became aware that everyone was staring at him. "Um, right now I think there are other things we need to discuss." He stepped aside. "Uh, this is Qui'hibra, elder of the Clan Qui'Tir'Ieq of the Pa'haquel. I'm sure you two—or however many—have quite a bit to discuss."

Qui'hibra had been standing in the doorway, unexpectedly quiet. Now he strode slowly toward Deanna, who watched him warily. Hostility and suspicion showed on her face. "You are one of those who prey on us, and infest the bodies of our dead."

"I am a Hunter, yes." The elder spoke with a humility Riker had never heard from him. "My people do what we must to survive. Now that you know of us, you have done no less to us."

"True," Deanna said, lifting her head proudly and taking a confrontational step toward him. "And we will do it again if we must."

"To die at your will would be an honor, revered ones. But perhaps it will not be necessary. We are no longer in a position to threaten you, so you have no cause to prey on us."

"Perhaps. You would be wise not to test that."

"We have never sought to test your wrath, mighty ones. We owe you our very existence. We owe you our ability to defend the balance." The elder had not fully lost his clipped, businesslike delivery, yet it came now with a quiet poignancy Riker had not anticipated. He had believed Qui'hibra to be hardened, cynical, relentlessly practical—an old warhorse who had outgrown the idealism of youth and no longer believed in anything but the job. Riker had seen too many Starfleet officers become like that during the Dominion War and after, and he strove not to become the same way himself. But now he saw there was a sincere core of faith to the elder, and it brought him reassurance. "Please know," Qui'hibra went on, "that we have always conducted our hunts for you with the greatest of reverence. We believed that success in the Hunt was a sign of your favor and forgiveness."

"It was not. We didn't even know it was a hunt. We couldn't understand what had happened to our dead, that they would turn on us and break the cycle. You were a disease to us, a terror, unnatural."

Qui'hibra was chastened. "I truly regret that. It was our own folly—you could not forgive what you did not understand." He pulled himself to attention and spoke formally. "On behalf of the Pa'haquel Clans, I hereby ask your forgiveness for the taking of your lives and your bodies. Know that we pledge each of our kills to the holy balance.

That we have taken your lives, not for malice or for greed, but for the preservation of life, within our clans and among all those whom we protect. Accept our thanks for your lives, and for the boon of your bodies. We have sought to let your deaths serve life, and thus maintain the balance as the Spirit wills.

"That is our sacred prayer, passed on from father to son since the beginning. Now these words are mine. Forgive me if they lack grandeur. I am no poet, and to be truthful I have never had much time for the niceties of religion." He paused. "But every day of my life, I have had a full stomach thanks to your bounty and have slept securely in your warmth. I have raised dozens of children, seen them grow into strong hunters and leaders, nourished by what you gave them. Your strong hides and potent stings have kept most of them safe, and enabled the others to die meaningfully in defense of other lives. And so every day of my life I have given you my thanks, and my reverence, and my love. I have always hunted you with that in mind. My clan has never taken more than it has needed, or inflicted more pain than was unavoidable.

"And I am just an ordinary Pa'haquel. My life has been no different from any other's. So what I feel for you, what I owe to you, is the same for all. When I give you my thanks, and my reverence, and my . . . very belated plea for your forgiveness, I believe I can fairly speak for all Pa'haquel."

Deanna—or the star-jellies speaking through her—studied him intensely as he spoke. By the time he finished, many feelings showed on her face, but tears were among them. "That was truly felt, and well-said. We are willing to forgive you."

Qui'hibra was visibly relieved. "Thank you, mighty ones."

"But we do not want to go on being prey. Nor are we comfortable with you infesting the bodies of our dead, no matter how reverently. We want it to stop."

"At the moment, we have no other choice. But if we do as Riker suggests, if you allow us to exist inside your living bodies and join us in the Hunt as partners, then it might become possible to return your dead to you in time."

She frowned. "Deanna thinks that's a good reason to try this, and we tend to agree. But it still hurts us to see our dead in limbo, not returned to the soil that spawned them, unable to feed new life."

"If I may," Tuvok interposed. "Your dead are still serving the cycle of life. They feed Pa'haquel life, and defend other life that would otherwise be destroyed."

Riker picked up on that. "Maybe that doesn't directly support your own people's lives . . . but my people believe that all life is equally precious, that all of it is connected. And we have found that working alongside other life forms strengthens those connections, and makes us all stronger for it. It usually requires making compromises, and changing the way you think about certain things . . . but in the long run you're usually better off for it."

The look in those fathomless black eyes was pure Deanna. "All right, Will, don't oversell it. For the moment we'll set aside the issue of our dead. And we'll try this plan of yours." She turned to point at Qui'hibra. "But we'll be watching your people closely. So you'd better not try anything. Now that we know who you are, we remember when you first infested our young. You were greedy, taking too much from them, stunting their growth."

Qui'hibra nodded. "We were young too, and foolish."

"Your words now suggest that you've learned better. We'll be holding you to that expectation."

"And I will hold my people to it as well. I swear it to the Spirit."

"Very well." She/they paused. "Prepare your people. We will follow Deanna's ship and meet with you later. For now, Deanna is weary, so we need to leave her mind." Deanna made her way back to the exam table, where she sat while Tuvok placed a hand to her temple. Qui'hibra looked around, nodded to Riker, and left wordlessly.

After a moment, Tuvok slumped, and Ree helped him to another table. Deanna breathed hard as though exhausted, rubbing her temples. Will was by her side in an instant. "Are you all right?"

She nodded. "It was . . . intense . . . but exhilarating."

Riker grinned. "You're blushing."

"It was . . . embarrassing. But I felt safe with them, so it's all right."

He fidgeted. "You, uhh, said some things. . . ."

She shook her head, touched her fingers to his lips. "Don't worry about that. That's not really what embarrassed me."

"What, then?"

"It's just . . . all too often in the past, it seemed my job was just to be the mouthpiece for somebody's emotions. To tell the captain what a rival ship commander or negotiator was feeling. I've tried so hard over the years to become more than that—to be valuable for skills that weren't just an accident of birth."

"And you've succeeded. You're invaluable to this crew in many ways."

"I know that. But letting the jellies take me over like that, being just a conduit for them . . . it felt like a step backward."

"I don't see it that way. And neither should you. You are a woman of many talents, and your empathic ability is one of them. It's just part of the greater whole. Nobody can doubt that. And it's invaluable to me on this mission, along with all your other talents." He paused. "But . . . on the other hand, it was a little creepy. Will you, umm, have to do that again?"

She sighed. "I don't know. I don't think so. The Pa'haquel will still need me to interpret for them, initially at least. But I can do that without *becoming* the jellies. That only happened because Tuvok was, er, borrowing my mental shields. I'm not sure if that will be necessary again."

Riker turned to his tactical officer. "Tuvok? What's your status?"

"Nominal for now, Captain," he reported from where he sat on the exam table. "However, I am not currently under emotional pressure from the jellies. It remains to be seen how well I can function once direct interactions resume. But I am reluctant to subject Counselor Troi to such an ordeal again. Perhaps a more limited mental link would be sufficient to shore up my defenses while allowing the counselor to retain her own."

"I hope so," Riker said. "I'm going to need every crew member at their best." He threw a grim look at Deanna. "This was probably the easy part."

Chapter Fourteen

STARDATE 57202.1

The hardest thing to get used to was the heartbeat. Ever since Qui'chiri had been beamed into this live skymount, it had been there: the slow bass pulsation of the vast creature's circulatory system, a relentless reminder that she was now inside the guts of a living animal with a will of its own and, as yet, little patience for her presence. At first she had assumed she would grow accustomed to it in time. Instead, it was driving her crazy, so relentless was it. And it did not remain steady. It varied subtly as the skymount exerted itself at propulsion or transformation, changed with the skymount's moods. And so every time she had almost reached the point of not noticing it, the rhythm would shift just enough to draw her attention back to it. She was starting to think the great beast was doing it on purpose to drive her and her fellows into abandoning this mad scheme. But none of her other clanmates or crew members seemed as troubled by it as she was.

On the other hand, Qui'chiri thought, it was probably a

good sign if the acoustical ambience was the hardest thing for her to adjust to psychologically, because there were far more important adjustments she had to manage.

Certain problems had been immediately evident. In a live skymount, it would not be possible to excise unnecessary organs and brain components to create occupancy space, or to modify the circulatory and endocrine delivery systems for clan and crew use. Thus each skymount could not sustain as large a population as normal; Qui'chiri estimated a hundred fifty, two hundred at most.

Indeed, the clan and crew would have to share their space with other forms—the skymounts' internal maintenance and immune "cells," multitendriled gray-brown blobs near the size of a Rianconi, which swam through the circulatory passages and crawled over the vital organs. Working around these creatures would require revising a great many procedures. Then again, the maintenance cells did much of the work normally performed by crew. Thus crew sizes could be reduced, compensating somewhat for the occupancy reduction and allowing a larger number of clan members per skymount. But how would the Fethetrit, Shizadam and others react to having their numbers cut—particularly since many had nowhere else to go? They were useful allies in other ways, and it would be unfortunate to alienate them.

The skymounts' transformational abilities could prove another problem. Sometimes they would restructure their own innards to aid in a certain task—say, changing the distribution of respiratory corridors to provide more oxygen to their distortion generators or digestive systems. It would be difficult for clan and crew to navigate such a changeable environment.

But the biggest problem would be how to control the beasts, to direct their movements. It would no longer be

possible just to press and stimulate the proper nerve end-
ings to trigger the desired responses. Indeed, when she
and her work crew had made their first attempt at a propulsion test—nothing invasive, she had thought, but merely
a test of its sensitivity and responses—the skymount,
shocked at being made to move against its will, had reflexively beamed all its occupants away. At least it had shown
enough presence of mind to beam them to *Titan* rather
than empty space. Qui'chiri supposed she should take that
as a sign of its willingness to cooperate. But it showed
they would have a long way to go to learn each other's
boundaries.

After that incident, Troi had reminded her that the skymount was a living, telepathic creature with the innate
ability to respond to the desires of those who lived in symbiosis with it. All they had to do was think of what they
wanted, and it would oblige. That was the theory, anyway.
Initially Qui'chiri had managed to make good use of
Troi's advice. Rather than rewiring the sensory cortex to
install a sensation wall, she had simply asked the skymount to replicate one in a conveniently large open space
chosen as the command center. It had taken the specifications from her memory, and the sensation wall had materialized within seconds.

But at times, she had discovered, the skymount could
be too responsive. During maneuvering tests, it sometimes had trouble understanding the chain of command,
and when her father and some of his subordinates had different thoughts about what maneuvers to attempt, the conflicting desires would leave the skymount confused.
Qui'chiri was having similar problems with the females
on her work crews. The skymount had proven willing to
allocate available interior space and resources for various
functions—dwelling space, medical bays, workshops and

the like—but her department heads had differing priorities, leading to some structurally messy results. It did not help that this shakedown crew was assembled from various different skymounts, so the personnel were not used to working together.

At times, though, the mount grew tired of indulging others' wishes and sought to satisfy its own urges for nourishment, companionship or play. Particularly play. The creatures devoted an inordinate amount of time to it— flying around each other in frivolous acrobatics, experimenting with wild shapechanges, engaging in complex interactive light shows which Troi likened to singing, or simply caressing and rubbing one another with their tendrils and bodies. It had proven difficult to keep this skymount focused on maneuvering drills when its schoolmates swam near to tempt it, distract it, beg it to join them in play.

Qui'chiri doubted the skymounts could truly understand the work ethic that would be required of them in the Hunt. It was not something they could attend to casually when they felt like it; it was a lifelong commitment, a calling, a passion. She knew the beasts had fire in them when it came to defending their own, but could they be trained to devote their lives to it, and to summon the same fire in defending other species?

Worse, although her father and the other males shared her frustration at the skymounts' dilettantish attitude, they were hesitant to do anything about it. "They feel such reverence for the skymounts," she explained to Troi as they walked through the makeshift control center together. "Thus it is hard for them to stand up and tell it to behave."

She was concerned Troi might react badly to that, given how the empath was prone to resonate with the skymounts' emotions. Father had told her about the events in

Titan's medical chamber, and how Troi had effectively become the skymounts. At the moment, though, the connection did not seem that intense. Troi seemed more surprised than anything else. "That seems odd to me," she said. "I mean, considering that they don't have any difficulty hunting and killing them."

"Well, they are more used to that. It often takes young hunters time to acclimate to hunting skymounts. Either they are too reverential and hesitant to do what they must, or they are too bloodthirsty and must be taught proper reverence. This—it is a new balance, one they have not yet adjusted to."

"And what about you, and the other females? Don't you share the males' reverence toward the star-jellies?"

"Of course I do. I suppose. We females, we are too busy with practical matters to give much thought to the spiritual. It makes it easier to adapt to this. Of course, the most practical thing to do would be to euthanize this beast and rip its guts out like normal. Nothing personal, of course," she added, addressing it ceilingward. "But that is not the reality I have been given. This is the situation, so this is what we will adapt to." Qui'chiri chuckled. "It is rarely so easy for males, who must debate the spiritual and cosmic ramifications of it all, and make displays of dominance at each other all the time disguised as policy disputes. I tell you, if this is to succeed at all, it will rely on the females."

Troi smirked. "It usually does, doesn't it?"

"Of course. One matriarch to another."

Troi seemed surprised. "Oh, no, Qui'chiri. I'm not the matriarch of my ship."

"No?"

"Oh, no. As I understand the role, the closest equivalent on *Titan* would be the first officer, Commander Vale."

Now it was Qui'chiri's turn for surprise. "But . . . you are married to the captain."

"That's right. But in Starfleet we don't assign jobs based on family ties. In fact, it's fairly rare for married partners to serve on the same ship, at least in the command crew. I earned my post on *Titan* due to my qualifications and experience, not my relationship with Will Riker."

Qui'chiri looked at her in puzzlement. "I see little distinction there. Experience and qualifications are what you learn from your parents, your siblings, your cousins."

Troi nodded. "Yes, in a society like yours, where kin groups are the dominant institutions. My society does things differently, though."

"I can only imagine." She paused for a moment to check a work team's efforts at devising a circulatory bypass for their water supplies. She did not want to rely solely on the skymount's generosity to provide them with water, in case of emergency. "So . . . who *is* Vale married to?"

"No one."

"Really!"

Troi frowned. "Why so surprised? You aren't married, are you? I mean, you still use your father's family prefix."

"Now I do. When I was young I was briefly wed, and became Se'chiri. But my husband was killed soon thereafter, and I returned home." She reflected on the ill fortune of the Se'ha line. They had lost more than their share of sons over the years. They had lost their skymount in the battle that had taken her husband, and the survivors had had to take up residence on her father's mount at subordinate status, when formerly they had been one of the leading families. They had even lost their place in the clan name. Over the years since, they had regained much of the standing they had lost. But a few months ago, a battle with branchers had taken all the elder Se'ha males, catapulting that tiresome whelp Se'hraqua to a status he was ill-prepared for. She suspected the impetuous dreamer would lead his line to ruin, and she was glad that her affiliation with it had ended so long before. "Thereafter I became mount-wed."

"Mount-wed? You mean . . . you're literally married to your ship?"

"Literally, technically, symbolically—I do not know the nuances as a male would. What I know is that the mounts need a support staff they can rely on not to leap out of the nest when a suitor calls from elsewhere. Mount-wed females are the backbone of the fleet."

"You mean that mount-wedding gives you the social standing of a married adult female while still letting you focus on your obligation to your ship."

Qui'chiri mulled it over. "That is a strange way of putting it. I suppose so, though."

"It's not so different from people in my society putting family aside to focus on their careers."

"Perhaps not." The skymount lurched a bit, and her eye flicked across the sensation feeds. "Oh, no. The mount is getting playful again. Those other two keep trying to tickle it to distraction, and they are succeeding."

Troi laughed. "Well, that's one thing we'll never have to worry about on my ship."

"Will you, well, think to it? Tell it to stay focused?"

"I'm trying, but you'll need to learn to do that on your own. Maybe you can't hear its thoughts, but that doesn't mean it hears your thoughts any less than mine. Just . . . try to keep all your people concentrated on the goal. The jellies have a very collective psychology; they like to go along with the group."

"All right." She raised her voice. "Everyone, do you hear? Keep your focus on the goal, all of you, if we want it to follow!"

After a moment, the skymount shook off its schoolmates and resumed the drills, although it still seemed to have a certain insouciance to it. The thought somehow struck her as amusing, and Troi smiled, sensing it.

"So, about this mount-wedding custom," Troi went on. "What about children? With a dangerous lifestyle like yours, wouldn't mount-wedding remove a lot of potential mothers from eligibility?"

"Oh, no. Part of our responsibility is to mate with low-status males who cannot win brides of their own. Myself, I have had eleven . . . no, twelve children for other lines."

" 'For other lines?' They're raised in the father's family?"

"Of course, how else?"

Troi's eyes were wide. "So you've had to give up a dozen children?"

"Well, they are incubated in artificial marsupia once they are born, so I never had a chance to become attached to any of them. Just as well—I had too much work to do anyway."

The Betazoid seemed sad for her. "I guess it's easier that way," she said, sounding far from convinced.

Qui'chiri looked her over. "And how about you? How many children have you had?"

Troi grew wistful. "Well . . . technically, one. In a strange way. An alien energy being impregnated me so that it could be born as a corporeal being and learn about us. It . . . it was all over in a matter of days. Ian . . . the life-form was unable to survive for long in that form."

"I am sorry," Qui'chiri said. "Some of my offspring did not survive to term. And I have lost siblings who were very young. The Hunt exacts its price." She found herself growing somber. She tried to shake it off, but it lingered, calling up feelings of loss that she hadn't been bothered by for many years. Perhaps changing the subject would help. "So you have had no children yet with your husband?"

"No . . . no, not yet."

"Is that not the point of marriage in your culture?"

"Not the exclusive one. I mean, it's part of it, yes, but we've only been married a few months . . . it isn't the right time yet."

"How long must you wait?"

"Until . . . until the time is right."

Sensing her unease, Qui'chiri backed off. "I apologize. If I have impinged on some taboo . . ."

"Oh, no," Troi reassured her. "Nothing like that. It's just . . . not something I've given a lot of thought to yet. Although lately it seems to keep coming up." Troi smirked at something.

Qui'chiri found it amusing herself, somehow. "Then perhaps the Spirit is trying to tell you something."

Troi glared. "I thought you weren't spiritual."

"Of course I am. I just do not think about it much." She laughed. Just then the mount lurched again. "Oh, no! Are the ticklers at it again?"

"Yes, ma'am," said her assistant, who seemed very amused by it. Qui'chiri would have chastised her, but she could see the joke.

Troi was grinning too, but she seemed concerned as well. "Something strange is going on," she said. "All of you—your emotions are changing with the jelly's! When I grew sad, I felt it sadden in sympathy, and all of you grew more somber as well. And now the other jellies have come in to cheer it up, and we're all laughing!"

Qui'chiri started to laugh at that, but stopped herself. "How can that be? We are not telepaths!"

"I know. But there's no question—you're all emoting in synch with the star-jelly."

"Hormones," Dr. Ree explained, once he had concluded his examination of Qui'chiri and several of her crewmates. Now Riker, Troi and Qui'hibra had joined them in sickbay for his report. "I would call them pheromones, except they are internal to the star-jellies. Apparently Pa'haquel hormonal receptors are sensitive to the jellies' own hormones. I would imagine they shared their homeworld with the jellies for much of their evolutionary history, long enough for their biochemistries to be influenced."

Qui'hibra was puzzled. "The legends say our history began elsewhere on Quelha. That we only discovered the skymounts during our migrations."

"But your ancestral ecosystem could still have been affected by the jellies' breeding grounds—perhaps by runoff from their hotsprings."

"I'm more concerned with the here and now," Riker said. "Why did it take so long to detect this?"

Ree clacked his teeth thoughtfully. "The Pa'haquel have not cohabited with live jellies for millennia. Maybe it took time for their systems to reacclimate."

"Or maybe," Troi said, "it simply seemed natural for their emotions to correlate. The Pa'haquel would have expected to feel irritation or concern when they were having trouble working with the jelly, and satisfaction when things were going more smoothly."

"More importantly," Qui'hibra said, "what do we do

about it? How can we do our jobs if we cannot avoid breaking into fits of giggles?"

"I was able to manage it with an effort," Qui'chiri said. "I am sure the will of all Pa'haquel is at least equal to my own."

"No doubt," Ree said. "Still, perhaps some form of hormonal antagonist could counteract the effect."

"I will have my medical staff research it," Qui'chiri replied. "Although it would be so much easier if we could just convince them to let us hunt them again."

"Ahh, I have had the same thought," Ree told her. "But I have had no luck finding volunteers among the crew."

Ranul Keru couldn't tell up from down right now.

Free fall was one thing. That he could handle, having trained for it extensively as part of the all-encompassing security drills he required for his people. But the play of gravity fields around a star-jelly's distortion generators was much more confusing. Along the equatorial plane of the jelly, where the gravity vector reversed, one was technically weightless, but there was a sort of inverse tidal effect, a sense of one's head and feet being pulled in toward one's belly. It was particularly pronounced for a large man like himself. And right around the generators themselves, the gravity became considerably more problematic. Essentially each of the jelly's seventy-six generator nodes was the center of its own local gravity field, and "down" was toward it from any direction. As one drew nearer a node, the gravity vector shifted more and more toward it. It would be easy to get lost, except that all the respiratory "corridors" in the area fed into the nodes. Keru was assuming that the gravity shifts he was feeling meant that he was getting closer to a node, rather than getting turned around and heading away from the equator. But he could only hope it was the right node.

Truth be told, he wasn't even sure what he was doing here. Counselor Troi had suggested that he might be able to help the jellies adjust to the idea of living symbiotically with other sentient beings inside their bodies, by telling them something about the Trill experience with symbiosis. He did not consider himself an ideal choice for this, since he had never been joined. True, he had tended the symbiont pools for a few years, but his communication with the symbionts had been limited and intuitive at best, and he had no firsthand insights from the host's perspective. But there were no joined Trills on *Titan*'s crew, so it came down to him. Troi had heard his objection that he would have little to offer, but had asked him to do what he could anyway.

So right now he was tracking down a telepath. The jellies could read any thoughts he had to offer, but he could not sense theirs without an interpreter. Since the other psi-sensitive crew members were occupied, he had been assigned to work with Lieutenant Chamish. The Kazarite ecologist could only register their emotions, not their cognitive thoughts, but Troi felt that would be enough to allow basic feedback, and apparently in their case the distinction was blurred anyway.

Keru was happy enough to work with Chamish, since he'd been trying to persuade the Kazarite to help train his security force in tactics against telekinetic attack. The gentle ecologist had shown no interest in combat exercises, and had demurred that his powers were too feeble to present much opposition. Riker and Vale had not seen the proposal as important enough to make it an order. Still, Keru hoped to change the lieutenant's mind, feeling that any further edge he could give his people, however slight, would be worthwhile. Maybe it was impossible to save them all, but the more prepared they were, the fewer he'd have to lose.

A little TK might be useful for maneuvering right now, Keru thought as he stumbled onto the generator node at last. "Onto" was indeed the word, for he stood on the curving surface of the node, a seven-meter-wide sphere which glowed a warm red as the intense energies swirling within it shone out through its fleshy surface. The respiratory passages were wide and open here. The effect was something like being a giant standing on the surface of an ember-hot brown dwarf, though fortunately the node's surface was only warm. Keru started to walk along it in search of fellow crew members, and tried not to stumble as he went. To his eyes, it looked as though any step he took would take him downhill, and he reflexively adjusted to compensate; but the gravity field shifted with each step so that he was constantly on the "top" of the imagined hill. The conflict between expectation and reality made it hard to adjust. The red-on-red lighting scheme didn't help much either.

Soon enough, another crew member came into view around the curvature of the node. It was not Chamish, though, but Torvig. The cyborg cadet was traipsing along easily, no doubt using his bionic enhancements to compensate for the bizarre environment. "Oh, hello, Commander Keru! Am I in trouble for something again?" he asked, though his tone was affably inquisitive.

"Uhh, no. I was looking for Lieutenant Chamish, actually."

"Oh. He's on the other side of the node."

"All right." He paused. "What are you doing here, Cadet? I wasn't aware you were assigned here."

"I had some ideas I wanted to share with the star-jellies.

Ways they could enhance their distortion generators to accelerate their warp field initiation cycle. Shielding enhancements for combat scenarios. Ways of reallocating interior space to accommodate larger populations. It seems to me they have a number of body parts they could do without, or simply materialize on an as-needed basis."

Keru frowned. "Well. How did the jellies take your . . . suggestions?"

"Mr. Chamish says they're wary, but curious to learn more. I've got the schematics running as a subroutine in my brain so they can review them in depth while I work on other things."

"I see. Very well," Keru said with a harrumph. "Carry on, then."

Torvig blinked at him. "Commander, your tone of voice conveys disapproval. Do you now think I'm doing something wrong?"

"No. No, Cadet, it's not that."

"May I ask what it is, then?"

At least Torvig was learning to couch his relentless nosiness in slightly more polite terms. Keru sighed. "I just . . . don't like seeing this done to the jellies, that's all. Having their bodies altered to serve another species' purpose. It feels like . . ."

"Like Borg assimilation?" Torvig's gaze on him held steady.

"Frankly, yes. It just doesn't feel right to me."

"We know the jellies have probably been upgraded by others before. We are standing on one of the components added to their design."

"Yes, but if that's so, whoever did that to them isn't around anymore. And the jellies have been living free for as long as they can remember, which is probably millions of years. So I think if they were used by others, they probably weren't very happy about it. I think they decided they'd rather be free. Do we have the right to change that?"

Torvig looked surprised. "I don't follow your logic. Just because the Great Builders didn't stay with them doesn't mean they weren't wanted. They just moved on to other projects—the way they did after the Great Upgrade of my people."

Keru stared. "You mean . . . you assume this was done to them by the same race that made you into cyborgs?"

Torvig lowered his cervine head. "Apologies, sir, I should've couched that as a hypothesis rather than an axiom. I'm aware that the Federation doesn't share our belief in the Great Builders as the creators of all things."

"I thought Choblik didn't believe in anything that wasn't supported by empirical evidence."

"It is empirical that we were Upgraded to our current state millenia ago by some technological agency. It is also empirical that the galaxy contains many other life forms, worlds and phenomena that could not have come into being without technological intervention. And many of the fundamental mysteries of the universe can be resolved by postulating it as a construct of some entity or civilization existing on a transcendent plane. Given the power and pervasiveness that such a creative agency would require, it's logical to interpret all lesser creative agencies in the universe as aspects of the ultimate Builders."

Keru absorbed his words. "You mean . . . engineering is like a religion to you?"

"As I understand the term, I suppose so, although most religions seem to have less empirical bases and are hard for me to grasp yet. But yes, it's how I serve the legacy of the Great Builders."

"All right. But if you don't mind an . . . empirical question . . ."

"Not at all, sir."

"How do you know these Builders had benevolent intentions when they 'Upgraded' you? How do you know they didn't intend to use you as slave labor, or just as some kind of experiment that they abandoned when they'd learned what they needed?"

Torvig looked up at him and spoke softly. His synthesized voice was far more expressive than Keru had realized at first. "I can't see any logic in that hypothesis, sir. We owe everything we are to the Builders. In our native form, we are not fully sentient—simply relatively bright animals, small and weak herbivores who roamed the forests of Choblav, trying to avoid being eaten by various large predatory species. We had no speech, no arms, nothing but a simple prehensile tail." He waved his tail forward and flexed the bionic hand on its end, a smaller counterpart of the intricate, versatile grippers on his bionic forearms. "The Great Upgrade gave us language and reason, plus the ability to build and create, to protect ourselves, and to improve our lives. And the Builders stayed with us long enough to establish the infrastructure that lets our civilization continue, that lets us pass on these gifts to our young."

Keru suddenly realized he was curious about that. "How does that work, anyway? How can bionics be hereditary?"

"We have nanotech chromosomes which are passed on in our gametes and allow the self-replication of many of our internal components. Further enhancements are surgically installed in our young as soon as they are ready. We receive several successive suites of upgrades as we grow toward maturity."

Keru shuddered. "Sounds unpleasant."

"Oh, no, sir! It's a wonderful experience, to gain new

intelligence and abilities, to metamorphose into a new phase of being. These are celebrated rites of passage among my people."

The feeling in his voice surprised Keru. "I . . . didn't think you were the sentimental type."

"Less so than most, sir. But this is who we are. Is it sentimental to cherish the core of one's existence?"

"Hm." He was silent for a moment. "Even so, you can't assume that other species will have the same reaction to the idea of being . . . upgraded."

"Of course, sir. I understand. It's much like the Trill people's concerns about how symbiosis would be perceived. The fear that it would lead to rejection or persecution of the symbionts if other humanoids learned of them."

"Uh, that's not really what I meant. And it didn't turn out that way after all."

"Didn't it? Maybe not among other humanoids, but it seems that there was some serious intolerance toward the symbionts on Trill itself. I mean, considering the attempt to exterminate them and all." He paused. "That was about the time I entered Starfleet Academy, in fact. My family was reluctant to let me join, because they were afraid I might face persecution. We had only recently been contacted by the Federation, and their response to us had been . . . mixed. When the news about Trill came, many of us feared a similar genocide. But my studies of the Federation convinced me that you were better than that. Well, most of the time."

Keru was chastened. So many of the symbionts in his care had died because of the hatred of a few fanatics, because some people just couldn't accept their right to live the way they did. How could he stand here now and judge Torvig for the way he was? "I guess you must be pretty disappointed in us, then. Or at least in me."

"Oh, no, sir! I knew some discomfort and adjustment were inevitable. And you haven't tried to have me killed or anything. Indeed, I've learned quite a lot from our interaction. So it's all for the best, sir."

The big Trill stared at the little Choblik for another long moment. Then he reached out to shake the cadet's bionic hand.

CHAPTER FIFTEEN

Captain's Log, Stardate 57207.4

We are now four days into training, and the star-jellies and Pa'haquel appear to have established a comfortable working relationship. After the initial disruption, the Pa'haquel seem to be managing the jellies' hormonal influence on their moods effectively. Apparently the effect is not as strong as their telepathic influence. Meanwhile, more jellies have allowed themselves to be boarded by Pa'haquel, and practice maneuvers have been going well. This morning, Elder Qui'hibra led the school of jellies in a practice hunt of the plantlike sailseed creatures that pervade the region. The jellies took to it surprisingly well, tracking down two in the course of a few hours and destroying them both quite efficiently. So far, it looks as though the jellies will make excellent hunting dogs.

Now if only I could decide whether this is a good thing or not.

Qui'hibra looked around the control center, still unable to adjust to how empty it was. Normally, almost any place he went on a skymount was bustling with activity, as

clan and crew carried out the tasks that the live creatures'
own metabolism had done originally. But now the skymounts they occupied were live, and fully capable of
managing their own functions. Indeed, now that they
had adjusted to the collaboration, they could respond to
a hunter's thoughts faster than he could speak them, making for a greatly improved reaction time. He had been
able to spread out his skeleton crew, already only a
fraction of any one mount's normal complement, among
six livemounts (as many were now starting to call them).
The livemounts' performance in the hunting drill against
the sailseeds had been freakishly efficient, despite—
or perhaps because of—their frivolous attitude toward
it. They had chosen to treat the experience as a form of
play, and had taken to it quite eagerly. Qui'hibra was
not troubled by that; indeed, he welcomed their enthusiasm as a sign that they would take well to the Hunt. And
the enthusiasm they had induced in their occupants had
been good for morale, heightening the hunters' alertness
and energy rather than distracting them. The few people
with Qui'hibra in the control center had been a bit distracted by his uncharacteristic good humor, though, so
he had done his best to restrain his enthusiasm and maintain a properly stern visage. But inside, he'd revelled in a
sense of youthful predatory glee that he thought he'd lost
ages ago.

Now, though, Qui'chiri did not seem too pleased about
the livemounts' efficiency. "This is ridiculous," she said.
"This place is so empty. How can we support whole clans
this way? How can a mount be home to hundreds if seven
or eight can run the whole thing?"

"There is still much room for occupancy," he replied.

"Yes, many could live here, but what would they *do?*

How could they be happy without purpose? And what happens to all that youthful male aggression if it cannot be sated in the Hunt? This is why the sedentary peoples have so many wars—because they have nothing better to do with their hostilities. And when they do not war, they wallow in depravity and indulgence and the other sins of leisure. Must we see the Pa'haquel reduced to that?"

"There are other ways we can find to be useful. Look at the crew of *Titan*. They toil in science and learning, seek ways to better people's lives."

"Pfa. Most of it is sophistry, nothing anyone will ever need. They just imagine it keeps them useful. And it has caused us no end of trouble."

"Good point." He exchanged a small smile with his daughter—not mount-induced this time, but the genuine good humor that, since his last wife had died, he shared only with Qui'chiri. "I have no answer beyond hope. Hope and trust. I trust the Pa'haquel to find ways to lead lives of meaning, no matter how our circumstances may change. No matter what, we exist to preserve the balance."

"Well, females trust in the tangible. I will believe it if it happens."

Before Qui'hibra could respond, a hail came in from another livemount in the school. *"Elder,"* came the voice of Huntsmaster Chi'tharu. *"We have detected a group of spinners on the other side of this star system. I think they would make an excellent next test."*

"How many?"

"Four, Elder."

Qui'chiri appeared skeptical. "Spinners can be dangerous, Father. Perhaps it is too soon."

"Yes, they are dangerous," Qui'hibra said. "That is why we should not pass up a chance to kill them. If they have come to this system to procreate, we should prevent it. And the danger to a skymount is not that great."

"If the mount is accurate in its aim."

"I have confidence in these mounts. They have done their job well."

"Against things that cannot harm them."

"And now we must learn how they react when faced with things that can. I have made my decision, Chiri. And I advise you to think confident thoughts—for the benefit of our host," he finished, gesturing at the mount around them. Qui'chiri fell silent and nodded in understanding.

"All fleet," Qui'hibra said into the comm, "the hue and cry is given. Proceed to intercept the prey, maximum warp." He paused. "Mount, would you hail *Titan*, please? And ask Commander Troi to come to the control center."

A moment later, an image of Riker appeared on the sensation wall. "Riker. We have detected prey on the far side of the system. We are proceeding to engage them. I recommend you follow and observe." Even as he spoke, he felt the mount building up its energies to warp.

"What kind of prey?"

"Spinners. They are not sentient, so you should have no concern there. But they can be a hazard. They are vast sails of fine mesh, light in mass but as wide as fifty skymounts, rotating and given rigidity by a set of heavy nodules around their perimeter. Normally they travel propelled by light pressure, but the nodules contain maneuvering jets. The spin induces a magnetic field which they can also use for maneuvering, or to gather hydrogen for their jets. The mesh absorbs energy and can change its shape magnetically. If a starbeast or ship approaches too near and is too slow to dodge, the spinner will wrap around it, encasing it in multiple layers of sail, and drain its energy away."

Riker frowned. *"How great a risk does this pose to the star-jellies?"*

"Little, if they perform as well as before and avoid being caught. Spinners are flimsy, slow-moving things. The main peril is that they are hard to kill. Blast a hole through the sail and it is barely felt, since there is so much sail remaining, and the energy of the blast feeds it. You must strike the nodules, which contain its organs and what little brains it has. But they are small moving targets and there are eighteen per spinner. I would call it more of a challenge than a risk. The kind of challenge that would make excellent training."

Riker hesitated. Clearly the human was uncomfortable having his mate still aboard during a hunt. Not to mention the Vulcan tactical officer, who was aboard one of the other livemounts, assisting in the training. But he accepted Qui'hibra's estimate of the risk. *"Very well. It's your fleet, it's your call.* Titan *will follow and observe."*

It took a while for the mounts to cross the star system even at warp. Qui'hibra used the time to fill Troi in on the situation once she arrived. The quartet of spinners turned out to be on the far outskirts of the system's cometary belt, making it a somewhat longer flight. Qui'hibra ordered the school/fleet to maximum warp, knowing that *Titan* would need some time to catch up, but not concerned by the fact.

He was a bit concerned, however, by what the sensation wall showed when they came out of warp. Chi'tharu reacted to it as well, speaking over the comm. *"Look how fast they go! How did this happen?"*

His Vomnin scientist, Fasden, spoke. "They are still on the system's outskirts. They would not have been decelerated much yet by the star's light pressure."

"No, there is more," Qui'hibra said. "I have never seen spinners move this fast."

After a moment, *Titan*'s scientist Jaza spoke from his own ship, lagging behind but still in communications range. *"There's a pulsar seven light-years back along their course. Its emission cones sweep right through their path. They must have used that radiation to gain an extra push, and gotten a gravity boost from the pulsar as well."*

"Is this a problem?" Troi asked.

"It will take some work to match velocities," Qui'hibra said. "It makes for a more interesting chase."

She studied the sensation wall. "It looks to me like they're coming right at us."

"Yes, they are. Fleet," he commanded, "make backward thrust, and stand by to fire. They will overtake us before we can match velocity. We will meet them face-on and take what shots we can. All mounts, aim for the nodules around the outside, not the sail. And make sure to stay well clear of them once they pass."

"Wouldn't it be safer to stay out of their way and then approach them from behind?"

"That would let them gain more of a lead, and more time to react to our approach," he told the Betazoid. "Right now we are backlit to them, hard to detect—we have surprise on our side, and they will have more trouble dodging at this speed than we will."

"Firing range in five," Chi'tharu announced.

"Mounts, fire at will. Good hunting!"

But he felt that something was wrong. A sense of unease pervaded him, and no stings were launched. "What is wrong?"

"They're reluctant to fire," Troi told him. "The creatures don't pose an immediate threat to the jellies, and they don't want to provoke their hostility."

"Do not fear," Qui'hibra called to the mount around him and to its schoolmates. "We have trained for this, we are ready. The spinners react slowly. As long as you re-member your training, you will be fine. This is just an-other game! Try to hit the spinning balls! You can do this!" The optimum shot, of course, was to sever the radial cord which held the nodule in place, amputating it from the spinner. But that was a much harder shot.

His coaxing seemed to do the job. The livemounts moved into attack formation and began firing. Their first few shots went wild or pierced the sail uselessly. *"The star-jellies are unused to leading the targets,"* Tuvok re-ported from aboard his mount. *"I suggest the gunner crews concentrate on aim, and let their thoughts direct the jellies' fire."*

"Gunners, do as he suggests." With the gunners' expe-rience guiding the mounts, the shots began to fall truer, and one by one the nodules began to be blasted open, their hydrogen ignited. But the losses were fewer than they should have been at this stage, with the spinners nearly upon them. "Concentrate your shots on a single side of each," Qui'hibra commanded. "Unbalance them enough and they will spin out of control."

But there was too little time. A few more nodules fell, and one of the spinners began to wobble and drift off course. It instinctively tried to compensate by trimming the sail between its radial cords, changing the way it caught the light, but of course out here the light was too feeble to matter. Qui'hibra could tell from the way its sail was undulating that it was no longer a threat; it was too un-balanced now to stabilize itself, and the oscillations would build until it tangled and tore itself to tatters. But the other three were still intact and almost upon the school/fleet. "Evade," Qui'hibra called.

The mounts began to dodge, but one remained on

course, still firing. He focused his thoughts on it, knowing his mount would direct a comm signal there. "You are too close to its path! I said evade!"

A voice came back—Se'hraqua. *"We are off its direct path. Just a few more hits . . ."*

"Do not let it move to grab you!"

"This far out, the star's magnetic field is too weak to tack against!"

Idiot! Se'hraqua knew the physics well enough, but not the tactics. "You fool, they can tack off each other's fields!"

Even as he spoke, he saw the spinners repelling apart and knew it was too late. What happened next was almost too quick to see. The spinners swept by, and the sail of one caught Se'hraqua's ship. The force of impact wrapped that part of the sail around the livemount, and the spinner's momentum swept it forward. That sector of the sail began retracting along the radial cords, giving it slack as it wrapped itself layer by layer around the mount, trapping it.

Troi gasped, and Qui'hibra understood why. The trapped livemount was frightened, sharing its fright with the others, and their hormones fed it to him and his people. "Remain calm!" he urged everyone. "We can rescue them. Keep firing at the nodules, make it lose control of its wrapping! Se'hraqua, if you still live, fire out from inside, try to burn a hole through."

"They are pulling away too fast!" Chi'tharu cried. *"We cannot do it in time!"*

"Keep your focus, Huntsmaster! Keep the skymounts' emotions apart from your own! And mounts, do not despair! You can rescue your schoolmate, we will help you! But you must manage your fear!"

Someone was screaming now—it sounded like Se'hra-qua. On the sensation wall, livid violet stings were shooting out from the enfolded spinner as the captive mount tried to blast its way free. But the blasts were feeble, most of their energy absorbed by the mesh, doing limited damage. After a moment, the shimmer of the mount's teleportation beams began playing over the sail from inside, disintegrating its inner layers. But it kept wrapping more and more layers around the mount. Stings from the other mounts lanced into view as they tried to assist its escape. They were picking up speed, gaining on the spinner, which had been slowed some by the impact, falling slightly behind its two surviving fellows. When they grew close enough, they added their teleport beams to the effort. Soon, the livemount broke free and shot unevenly away from its tattered cocoon. Crows of relief and triumph from Se'hraqua and his crewmates sounded over the comm. The other mounts began moving to rendezvous with their schoolmate.

"No," Qui'hibra ordered. "We must engage them again. Finish this one off and take out the others!"

Troi shook her head. "They don't want to do that. They're had enough."

"Enough? This is nothing! No one has been lost."

"They're still new at this, Qui'hibra. Isn't this enough for one test run? Give them a chance to get used to it."

But suddenly he saw something on the sensory wall. "Everyone, hunt stations! The prey is turning to fight!" Or rather, one of the other two spinners was slowing, letting the school/fleet catch up with it. It must have pushed off its partner's magnetic field to get the deceleration.

Troi grabbed his shoulder. "The jellies want to flee, not fight."

He didn't need her to tell him that; he could feel the panic building inside him. He refused to give into it. "No. Hunters, we must master this fear! Stand and fight! A few more hits will cripple it! Keep firing!"

A few of the mounts, including his own, moved hesitantly toward attack positions, while others hovered uncertainly, torn between fleeing and aiding their schoolmates. The resultant formation was a mess. "Pull it together! We must act as one!"

"The jellies are conflicted," Troi told him. "They don't know what to do. They're starting to panic."

"Do all you can to keep them calm, Troi."

"They're not ready for this, Qui'hibra! Let them run!"

No. He could not do that. It would mean giving in to the cowardice he felt inside him. True, it was hormonally induced, but that was all the more reason why it must be conquered. Unless the Pa'haquel's courage could overcome the livemounts' timidity, the Hunt could never endure.

But just then, disaster struck. The livemounts' erratic courses had brought one too near the spinner's outer perimeter. A plasma jet shot out from one of its nodules, blindingly bright, the hydrogen heated to fusion temperatures. It sliced across the livemount's carapace, knocking it into a spin and leaving a glowing, blue-hot welt across its armor.

At that, the panic erupted through him at full force. He struggled to resist it, but to no avail. All he could think of was fleeing. He rushed to the nearest neural membrane wall, pushed at the nodules, not knowing or caring where he was going.

Then the ship shuddered, and a shroud fell across the sensation wall.

• • •

Riker watched in dismay as the star-jelly bearing Deanna and Qui'hibra began to be enmeshed. The school's members were panicking, flying every which way, and that one, in trying to escape the mostly intact spinner that was attacking, had shot off in the direction of the damaged one from which the other star-jelly had been extracted. Apparently, even though much of its sail had been holed and many of its outer nodules destroyed, it still had enough control to have untangled itself. It reached out and snagged the jelly, beginning to engulf it. Its movements were slow and erratic, and the jelly almost broke free, but the spinner managed to hold on and wrap more layers around it, holding it more and more securely. Stings shot out, transporter effect shimmered, but one jelly alone couldn't do enough, and the others were in panicked flight or crippled. "How soon before we get there?" he asked, striving to keep his voice level.

"Ninety seconds, sir," Lavena told him.

"Will, look." Vale gestured at another portion of the screen. The more intact spinner fired another plasma jet at a passing jelly, knocking it out of control, then fired a few other jets in the opposite direction in order to thrust a corner of it forward to snag the wounded beast. Now there would be two to rescue, at least.

On this vast scale, the attack came with stately slowness, so it was only moments later that Lavena reported, "Closing to engage, sir."

"Drop out of warp." Weighing the variables, he chose his target. "Target phasers on the damaged spinner. Sever the mesh around Qui'hibra's jelly." *Deanna's jelly.* Was he playing favorites? Maybe. But this one would be the easier target; it was wounded, slow-moving, its sail already damaged. They could deal with it quickly and have more time to tackle the other. He glanced at Vale; she nodded, supporting his tactical call.

Phaser beams lashed out, sliced through layers of sail. Wisely, Kuu'iut chose to cut where the jelly's sting had already burnt a hole through, widening the tear. Still, it was slow going; the mesh absorbed much of the phaser energy before it vaporized. "Tractor beams," Riker ordered. "Pull that slit apart." Kuu'iut split the beam in two and used it like a surgical spreader to widen the incision, tearing it further, slowly, laboriously. Finally the jelly wriggled out and shot away. *Deanna?*

We're all right, Will. Save the others.

"Helm, move to intercept the other spinner. Jaza, status on this spinner. Is it alive?"

"Yes, but its sail is pretty torn up and it's lost a lot of its nodules. It might not be able to recover."

Will frowned. Even though these weren't sentient beings, he'd still rather not play a part in killing them if there were an alternative.

The other jelly was now wrapped in considerably more layers of sail, with more being added. It would be hard to free in the same way, especially since it was inactive and doing nothing to attack the sail from within. Brute force might not be a viable option here.

Although that depended on what kind of force, he realized. He studied the way it cocooned its prey—not curling in from the edge like an enchilada, but doubling over in the middle and then rolling to pull the edge inward, something like an Argelian potsticker. And what could be pulled in could be pulled out. "Ensign Lavena," he said, "put us on a vector tangent to its rotation. Mr. Kuu'iut, as we approach, put a tractor beam on the retracting edge near the trapped jelly. Make it as wide a beam as possible—I want to unfurl that sail, not rip it." He leaned over Lavena's shoulder, caught her eye. "Once we have a grip, I want you to put us on a spiral trajectory, tracking the sail as it spins and pulling it straight out. Understand?"

She smiled, nodding. "Aye, sir.

The ship shook as the tractor beams engaged, and the stars on the viewscreen began scrolling upward as Lavena whirled around the spinner. "Lock the viewer on the captive jelly," Riker ordered. The view changed to an angle across the wide expanse of the spinner's surface, stars wheeling behind it. The enfolding of the jelly began to slow as the tractor beam pulled it back outward. Before long, the enfolded portion began to unroll.

But it was too slow. The creature resisted, struggled to hold onto its prey. "The sail is being held together magnetically," Jaza reported.

"Is there a way to demagnetize it?"

"If we heat the material enough, it should reach the Curie point and become demagnetized."

"Doesn't it absorb energy, though?"

"Absorbing energy means heating up. It must have limits on how fast it can shunt the heat away, especially with a portion clumped so densely."

"All right. Phasers to wide beam, thermal effect. Fire on the area around the jelly." A cone of phaser energy engulfed the clump of sail. Soon, it began to lose its grip and unroll. Before much longer, the star-jelly was released, flying off on a tangent. "Disengage tractor! Intercept that jelly, use the tractor to bring it under control. Then let's all get the hell away from these things."

●　●　●

Mercifully, there had been no fatalities in the battle, though Deanna and many of the Pa'haquel had needed Dr. Ree's ministrations and two of the star-jellies had been seriously wounded. Ree had had no idea how to treat them, but the jellies had taken care of it, using their replication abilities to repair the damage to their schoolmates. It was a time- and energy-consuming process, and they had now towed their mates inward to feed on the star's light.

Now Deanna stood up from the exam table and stretched, glad to be healed. Looking around sickbay at the Pa'haquel, though, she realized the damage to the alliance would be much harder to heal.

"It was a worthy experiment," Qui'hibra said to Riker. "And it was a privilege to commune with the skymounts for a time. But it is not in their nature to hunt. Their fear overtakes them in battle, and then it overtakes us, rendering us useless."

"Doctor," Riker said, "is there a way to block the effect of the star-jellies' hormones?"

Ree shock his elongated head, a humanoid gesture he had learned to mimic. "Not without disrupting the Pa'haquel's own endocrine systems. The two species' hormone receptors are too isomorphic. Suppressing the effects of the jellies' hormones would mean suppressing many of the Pa'haquel's innate emotional responses and behavioral instincts. They would be unable to function without, say, the fight-or-flight response or the desire to mate."

"Then there is no choice," Qui'hibra said. "The experiment is over. You will return us to our fleet, Riker."

"Where you'll do what?" Deanna countered, striding forward to confront him. "Try to go back to the old ways? Chase after star-jellies that you can no longer catch?"

"That is exactly what we should do," Se'hraqua interjected from his bed. "We will find new ways to take the prey. The Spirit is challenging us, and we will rise to the challenge and restore the balance."

"Hunter!" Qui'hibra barked, silencing him. The elder then turned back to Troi and Riker. "We will return to our fleet and regroup. We will assess other options. But this option is a failure. It is out of balance, and without balance there is no survival. We must find some other way. At the very least, we can still hunt other starbeasts with the sky-mounts we have left. So long as the livemounts agree not to try to liberate their dead."

"And how long will that last?" she asked. "Another few generations, maybe, but with ever-diminishing numbers. What then?"

"Do you have an alternative suggestion?"

"I'm still not convinced the alliance was a failure. You and the jellies were getting along very well after a few false starts."

"Only when we were not in combat. They have proven that they cannot handle that."

"Tell that to the thousands of Pa'haquel they've killed."

"They were in no danger from us—you saw to that. They can defend their own when they must, but when faced with danger they flee. This was an easy hunt, and they could not even rise to it."

"You pushed them into it before they were ready, Qui'hibra. You tried to fight against their emotions rather than working *with* them, accepting those emotions and directing them constructively." She drove the point in forcefully, aggressively, knowing he would respect that, knowing she had to push it through his tough hide. "Because you were too proud to tolerate being made to feel afraid and weak. You pride yourself so much on this cold, stalwart image. The great hunter, carved from stone, never bending, never losing control. So you tried to force your will on the jellies and you ended up spooking the herd. You fought so hard against a perceived loss of *self*-control that you lost control of the situation." He glared at her coldly—but he was listening.

So she went on. "Sometimes, Qui'hibra, yielding is necessary. Part of being strong is knowing when to trust in others' strength, to place yourself in their hands. It's part of any healthy relationship. A *balanced* relationship."

The elder remained silent for a moment, then spoke decisively. "We will return to our fleet and regroup. However, you and the skymounts may come with us, and we will explore the possibility of continuing the alliance, along with other options. But if you wish this alliance to resume, you must find a way for the skymounts to prove themselves equal to the Hunt."

Deanna exchanged an uneasy look with Will. Even if she could help the star-jellies meet Qui'hibra's requirements . . . was that really something she could forgive herself for doing to them?

Orilly Malar was so slow to answer her door that Jaza wondered if he would have to pull rank. But eventually the door slid open, and the Irriol looked up at him with her big, sad blue eyes. "Hello, Commander. What can I do for you?"

"May I come in?" Wordlessly, she acquiesced. When the door had shut behind him, he got right to the point. "Cadet, I've gotten stalled in my investigation of star-jelly evolution. I could use the help of a good exobiologist. Any idea where I could find one?"

"I am a fairly good exobiologist," she said matter-of-factly. "But I'm not a good security risk. Perhaps you should try someone else."

"Come on, Malar. You're not going to be made to attack me or anything. The star-jellies have no incentive to push you into that."

"No—but what if I learned something that they needed to know? Something that could further disrupt the state of affairs in the Gum Nebula, something the captain would not want the jellies to know?"

"I doubt there's anything in this line of research that could be harmful. If anything, it could be helpful to our current efforts. I'm trying to learn more, if I can, about how they were genetically modified eight million years ago. About whether it was done by someone else or by themselves. And about who else could've done it, and why. I keep thinking: back then, maybe five to ten million years ago, the main wave front of star formation in the Orion Arm would have been passing through what's now Federation space. Our home region would've been much like this region is today. It stands to reason that worlds there would've faced the same threat from cosmozoans. And it stands to reason that some forerunner of the Pa'haquel would've been waging this battle then. What if the jellies were engineered as part of that effort? What if they were used as ships for battling cosmozoans, and have instincts and abilities that they no longer remember they have? If there were some way of demonstrating that, it could help convince the Pa'haquel to try the alliance again."

Orilly pondered his words, then spoke uncertainly. "Pardon me for saying so, sir . . . but it can be unwise to start with a desired conclusion and search for evidence to confirm it."

"Yes, I know, science should never have an agenda. Personally I'll be happy either way—I just want to find some answers. I hate not knowing. But I've run out of places to look for evidence. I've had the computer searching through all our records, looking for scientific findings that might turn out to be connected to the star-jellies. Unexplained remains that could be star-jelly skeletons. Geological formations that were once their breeding pools. Ideally maybe the destroyed remains of a cosmozoan planet-killer with scars bearing the signature of star-jelly stings. But I've found nothing definite, nothing more than vaguely suggestive. And even that's probably just my own agenda making me read things into the data."

Orilly tilted her head, flexing her fingers thoughtfully. "It's a big galaxy, sir. And the star-jellies can travel very far. The odds are that they originated somewhere else entirely."

"I know. It's just frustrating not to have the answers. The best I can do is send what I've learned back to Starfleet, and maybe someday, some ship exploring another part of the galaxy will find more answers. But I might be long gone by then. And it'll always feel like I missed something . . . like I failed to know the star-jellies as well as I wished to."

"Evolutionary history is always fragmentary," Orilly said after a contemplative moment. "So much of the past is simply not preserved. So much of what we conclude is extrapolation and large-scale patterns, and many of the specific causes and pivotal events will never be filled in."

"And that doesn't bother you?"

"No," she said. "My interest in life-forms . . . is not about their dead ancestors, but about the living beings in the here and now. I wish to know them, to commune with them, to sense their part in the gestalt of nature, and . . .

and maybe feel a connection with them." She was quiet for a moment, but he sensed she wasn't finished. "A connection like I felt with the star-jellies. That was . . ." She trailed off. "Anyway, that is why I took up exobiology. Why I hoped I could make a career of it. To know life as it is, not as it was."

Jaza studied her. "In other words," he suggested, "what matters about a being is not what she did in the past . . . but what she does in the present, and in the future."

She stared at him. "That . . . is not quite what I meant."

"Maybe it should've been."

"But . . . what can I do in the present and future to atone for—"

"Ah!" He held up a hand. "As it is, not as it was."

She acquiesced. "What can I do in the present and future?"

Jaza smiled. "Well, you've asked the question. That's always the best place to start."

Chapter Sixteen

CLAN AQ'TRI'HHE LEAD SKYMOUNT, STARDATE 57211.9

This time, Qui'hibra had anticipated that the Conclave's vote would not go his way. Not only had Riker's plan apparently failed, but the membership of this Conclave was somewhat different from the first; they had moved closer to the heart of the starbirth zone, where there were more fleet-clans in range to join. The newcomers had not been swayed by his or Riker's arguments at the previous session—and the vote there had been narrow even with that persuasion. Additionally, there was the information Oderi had brought him, courtesy of her fellow Rianconi, who were ubiquitous, often ignored and always listening. "Hunter Se'hraqua has been speaking to many elders and family heads since our return, Elder," she had told him not long before the Conclave assembled. "Most are those who voted with us the last time. He has been trying to persuade them to approve aggressive action against *Titan*."

Qui'hibra was aware of the proposal to take *Titan*'s sensor information by force. Still, he had said to her, "I know he is discontented, but I question whether he would act against his own elder so overtly. It would undermine what little status he has left."

"Unless he had the backing of another elder, sir. He has been seen repeatedly with Elder Aq'hareq." Aq'hareq! A hunter so stubborn, tough and sour that Death itself had taken a taste and spit out the rest more than once. A fierce traditionalist who would never accept any of Riker's compromises. If he was guiding Se'hraqua, taking the youth's undeniable passion and eloquence and giving it focus, then there was indeed cause for concern.

So once the Conclave convened, it came as no surprise when Aq'hareq proposed aggressive action and Se'hraqua rose to second it. "We have been told," the youth said, "that the skymounts' new knowledge of our existence, their new ability to sweep us from our mounts and leave us to die in space, means that we must abandon the Hunt. That we must turn our backs on millennia of tradition, on the one act that defines who we are as a people. I do not accept this!" Aq'hareq could have been making this case himself, but he was apparently content to use Se'hraqua as his stalking-horse. After all, everyone already knew where he would stand, so for him to say it would be unnecessary. It would carry more weight from a new quarter, especially from one of Qui'hibra's own juniors, for that would undermine his position.

"These new developments," Se'hraqua went on, "are simply a new challenge to be overcome. Yes, they increase the danger of the Hunt. But we are Pa'haquel! Do we fear danger? Do we fear death? No! It is the danger that gives the Hunt meaning! It is by risking our own lives that we earn the right to take other lives, by dying that we repay the Spirit for letting us kill. Thus is the holy balance preserved."

"Do you say we were not in balance before?" Qui'hibra challenged. "We faced risk there as well. Even though the skymounts did not attack us, they could flee, or their armor could prove too strong. And failure in the Hunt could bring death." Even as he said it, though, it sounded hollow. The truth was, the Pa'haquel had held an unfair advantage over the skymounts. As a pragmatist, he had been satisfied with that; but a part of him had never truly accepted the rationalizations he made now, feeling that their advantage belied their claims of reverence toward the skymounts. On some level he had to wonder if Se'hraqua was right, if facing the mounts in a truly fair battle would do them more honor. He could tell that his voice was not convincing, for he was no politician.

"Certainly that was so once," Se'hraqua countered, surprising Qui'hibra with his diplomacy. Aq'hareq had coached him well. "But perhaps we have grown too skilled, too experienced. It has become too easy to kill skymounts, and we have grown complacent. That is why the Spirit sent us this challenge."

"We have no shortage of challenges, as any survivor of the Hounding can tell you." That, at least, he could say with conviction, and it reminded him of why battling livemounts able to defend themselves was not a practical course. "If we throw away too many lives, lose too many mounts in trying to take new ones, then we will be weakened for the other hunts, less able to keep the chaos at bay."

"Only if we are as weak and unsuccessful as you assume, Elder. If we rise to this challenge, yes, we will lose hunters and mounts, but the ones that survive will be stronger and fiercer than before. We will be hardened by the fire, and we will not have to suffer losses as severe as we sustained in the recent Hounding and brancher battle."

It was a good strategy, Qui'hibra realized: to capitalize on the elders' loss and pain, to promise them that it would not have to come again. But it also opened a weakness which Qui'hibra was quick to exploit. "How dare you say that all those brave hunters were lost due to weakness and complacency? They fell only because the prey was mighty."

"Or because there were too few of them," said Aq'hareq. "Where were you for the Hounding, Qui'-hibra?"

"I tried to reach it in time!" he shot back, furious. "We had taken too many losses. I was trying to rebuild our forces for the Hounding, but we were impeded."

"By the interference of *Titan!*" Se'hraqua cried. "A ship which you could have destroyed easily. Many of us pleaded with you to do so, Elder. Our own beloved matriarch advised you to destroy them! Instead you dallied with them and indulged them, and we were cheated of our chance for glory in the Hounding!"

"Is this true, Matriarch Qui'chiri?" Aq'hareq asked cagily—a question he would not have asked had he not already known the answer.

Qui'chiri had no choice. She could not lie to a venerable elder, and Qui'hibra would not forgive her if she did. "I did advise *Titan*'s destruction, Elder." A murmur rippled through the chamber. "But we could not have reached the Hounding in time even without *Titan*'s involvement, and any claim to the contrary is a lie!" The murmur grew louder, but fortunately Qui'chiri spoke over it rather than letting the Conclave grow distracted by the accusation. "And I now see that destroying *Titan* would have been unwise! They did not intend what happened, and they are our best chance to remedy it."

"Indeed they are," came Aq'hareq's smug reply. "And

we would not want their ship destroyed now—for only by taking it intact can we retrieve the knowledge we need from its computers, or extract it from its crew." A cruel laugh ran through the Conclave at the thought of how such extractions might be performed.

"The knowledge we need to do what?" Qui'hibra countered. "To resume hunting skymounts, to put everything back the way it was? That is a naïve hope. I understand the desire to go back to the ways we are used to. I share it. Tradition brings us comfort and certainty, and it is always easier to cling to it than to pursue change. But Riker was right—that which does not adapt does not survive. The balance *has* changed, and we cannot restore it by trying to force it backward. We must find a new solution."

"What solution?" asked Se'hraqua. "To fight alongside live skymounts? That has been tried and failed. As we all knew it would, for it is out of balance. Our life needs and theirs must compete; for one to live, the other must die. That is the way of the Spirit, the way of life."

"Life can coexist with life, as we do with our allies. We and the livemounts established a good rapport," Qui'hibra said to the Conclave at large. "It was . . . inspiring. Miraculous. I wish I had the words. It is not something I am sure I wish to abandon completely."

"But when you took them to the Hunt," Aq'hareq replied, "it was a disaster."

"They were untried. I admit I pushed them too hard, too fast. We cannot be certain it will never work."

"And how long must we wait until they are ready? How long before their nature changes to suit us? And how many worlds die in the meantime?" Cunning, to use Qui'hibra's own argument against him.

"We cannot afford to wait longer," Aq'hareq said, raising his voice. "We have talked enough, now we must decide. I call for a vote! The matter: that we give hue and cry upon the vessel *Titan,* take it intact and forcibly extract the information we need to counteract the skymounts' new advantages. And once we have that information, we make our kill, so that they can never interfere again."

"I second!" Se'hraqua called, predictably. A third came swiftly.

The voting went swiftly as well, and decisively. Aq'hareq's proposal passed with ease. Even many of the subordinates in Qui'hibra's own fleet voted for it this time. Qui'hibra exchanged a regretful look with his daughter, but he knew he was obliged to accept the will of the Conclave. He would do so with regret for Riker's people, and with concern for the future of his own. But he would do it nonetheless.

Still, there were other issues to be resolved, issues he wished he had managed to raise before Aq'hareq rammed the vote through. "I have already made arrangements with *Titan's* crew and the livemounts. We are to rendezvous at the Proplydian tomorrow. Troi claims she has new ideas to help us work toward hunting together."

Aq'hareq huddled with his advisors for a moment to discuss it. "Meet with them as planned, Qui'hibra," he said. "To cancel would make them suspicious. Indeed, this will be advantageous to the hunt. They could detect a force coming to attack them, but since you are invited they will be off their guard. That puts you in a perfect position to attack. And at the Proplydian there will always be other fleets close by as backup. Perhaps you can even capture Troi and their other telepaths, and we can get the information we need from them. At least, it will give us leverage over Riker. A threat to his mate may persuade him to surrender."

A matriarch raised a criticism. "If the livemounts can read our thoughts, will that not give the plan away?"

Reluctantly, Qui'hibra shook his head. "They cannot take what is not offered or consciously considered. So long as we guard our thoughts and emotions, we can retain stealth."

"Excellent," Aq'hareq said. "Then you are ideal for this task indeed, carved from stone as you are."

A laugh went through the chamber. Qui'hibra could see the ancient elder's malicious glee at making him the executor of a plan he had opposed. He burned with as much rage and shame as Aq'hareq no doubt wished upon him. But it was the Conclave's will, and it was a good plan. And for all he knew, it might even work. Maybe there was a way the traditional Hunt could be restored. He just wished that there were another way besides betraying Riker, Troi, and their people, for whom he had developed a grudging respect.

But he was a hunter, and that meant doing anything that was necessary to fend off the chaos for another day. It meant being willing to kill beasts that he admired and loved. It meant taking his wives, sons and daughters into danger and knowing that many of them would not survive. Next to that, betraying *Titan*'s crew would be a small thing.

Over the past few weeks, Will Riker's sense of the scale of living things had been broadened numerous times. He had grown somewhat accustomed to the idea of living beings a kilometer across. He felt he had made some progress toward wrapping his mind around the idea of a single organism the size of a small moon, such as the harvester. But nothing had prepared him for the sight of the Proplydian.

Well, not so much the sight itself; on the viewer, it appeared commonplace enough, an A-type giant star surrounded by a dense protoplanetary disk ("proplyd" in astronomer-speak). He had seen numerous such systems in his twenty-plus years in Starfleet.

But none of them had been a single life form.

Truth be told, he still wasn't fully ready to accept that was the case. After all, it wasn't a physically contiguous organism. But neither, Jaza had reminded him, were the thousands of chunks of matter that made up a Black Cloud's "brain." Though physically discrete, they interacted magnetically as a single collective organism. The Proplydian functioned on similar principles, with most of the planetesimals in its disk coated in bioneural compounds, exchanging stimulus and response through EM transmissions and functioning as a coherent nervous system. Together, they manipulated the systemwide magnetic field in order to turn the star itself into a propulsion system, triggering stellar flares and directing them as rocket thrust, ever-so-gradually altering the course and speed of the star, with the disk itself being pulled along for the ride by the star's gravity. They also used mutual repulsion to keep the chunks evenly distributed in a disk, rather than accreting into planetary bodies.

Jaza had reminded him that some nebular cosmozoans were larger even than this. But to Riker, it wasn't the same. A cloud of gas was one thing; this was a whole living *star system,* an organism with a sun as its heart. Trying to absorb that was making him dizzy.

The Pa'haquel or Vomnin could not quite say how such a life form had evolved, or where precisely it was motivated to go. This was the only such entity they knew of

(fortunately for Riker's mental equilibrium), and its travels were too leisurely to let them say much about its migratory patterns. It didn't seem drawn to energy sources like most cosmozoans; after all, it had an extremely powerful energy source at its heart, as much radiant energy as it could ever hope for. If anything, it seemed to direct itself through the densest parts of the interstellar medium, and was heading in the general direction of a dustcloud rich in organic compounds; presumably it sought to replenish its supplies somewhat through accretion, although the erosive friction of passage through those clouds would cancel out much of the gain. Perhaps, Jaza had speculated, it had no particular reason to do as it did; perhaps it was simply an evolutionary fluke, the spawn of an accidental convergence of factors. "Or maybe," the Bajoran had added, "it's a sign of some deeper meaning in the universe." Riker was content to leave that speculation to him.

There was always a Pa'haquel presence around the Proplydian, somewhere within a few light-years; they monitored it steadily, which was why Qui'hibra's fleet-clan and others from the Hounding had wandered this way since then, rather than staying around Udonok. They showed no interest in destroying it, however. "For one thing," Qui'hibra had explained when he had first told Riker and his crew about the Proplydian, "we do not know *how*. It is simply too vast. We know of ways we could detonate the star, but a supernova of that size would irradiate too vast a region. At least three inhabited worlds in range would be devastated."

Besides, the Proplydian showed little interest in coming near other star systems, perhaps wishing to avoid the gravitational disruption of its neural disk. It occasionally shed planetesimals which might have been reproductive spores, or might have simply been ejected by the chaos of gravitational interactions within the disk; the Pa'haquel captured or destroyed those to prevent it from infesting other systems. They kept watch on it for that reason—and because the Proplydian supported a whole secondary ecosystem of cosmozoans, living within it as symbiotes or parasites. Many species were drawn to the nourishing energy and hydrogen of its flare exhaust, to the rich stew of organics that pervaded its disk, and to the heavy elements that remained accessible as planetesimals rather than buried deep inside planets. Starpeelers swam in its wake, stealing hydrogen from its exhaust. Sailseeds attached to its outer cometary ring like barnacles. Spinners used its powerful magnetic fields to give themselves accelerational boosts. Crystalline Entities and other predators came here to feed on the rest. And star-jellies came to bask in its glow and dance through its disk—and perhaps simply to gape at the sheer wonder of it.

That was the other reason why the Pa'haquel let it be, according to Qui'hibra: It was the one cosmozoan even they didn't feel they were entitled to kill. It was just too far beyond their scope. "We revere all the beasts we hunt, and feel that we must earn the right to hunt them through our own risk and sacrifice. But how could we ever earn the right to prey on such a great embodiment of the Spirit of Life? Particularly when it may be the only one of its kind. This is a precious and holy place to us." More practically, because of its lure as a "watering hole," it was of more use to the hunters intact than destroyed.

On the practical side, though, the Proplydian had its drawbacks. Its intense magnetic field had ionized the dense local medium, creating sensor and comm interference. Plus some of the cosmozoans in the area might be dangerous—and Riker couldn't be certain whether the Pa'haquel fleets in the vicinity would see Titan as an ally or an enemy. The star-jellies, though, had considered it an excellent place to meet, and to recharge after the ordeal with the spinners three days ago. Meanwhile Jaza and the science staff were going crazy over the system's wonders. Riker half-suspected that if he gave the order to leave the Proplydian anytime soon, he'd have a mutiny on his hands.

But as amazing as the Proplydian was, Riker had to focus his own attention on other matters: specifically the star-jellies and the Pa'haquel, and what could be done to salvage their relationship—ideally without compromising Federation principles any further than necessary. Deanna had been working on a promising idea. It was not in the star-jellies' nature to actively seek out and attack prey, but it was in their nature to defend their breeding worlds against cosmozoan attack. Perhaps that behavior could be adapted to the defense of other inhabited worlds as well. It would not be as proactive as the Pa'haquel's method, but it would meet the goal of protecting intelligent life from the "chaos." As for the Pa'haquel's cultural need for the Hunt, that could be met using constructed starships, and the Pa'haquel alliance would still have the star-jellies' replication abilities at their disposal. Riker knew the Pa'haquel would have many objections, and he was skeptical about aspects of it himself; but at least it was a promising starting point.

"Sir," Jaza called from his console, interrupting Riker's train of thought. "We may have a problem."

"Explain."

"I'm detecting a group of Crystalline Entities approaching the system at over warp seven. ETA about forty minutes. I would've spotted them sooner if not for the interference. There seem to be . . . yes, there are four of them."

Riker's eyes widened. "So much for them not usually travelling in packs. Maybe Qui'hibra doesn't know them as well as he thinks. Any sign that the nearby Pa'haquel fleets have detected them?"

"No, sir. Both of them are farther away from the Entities, and they still don't have sensors as good as ours."

Deanna came up beside him, touched his arm. "Will, Qui'hibra's fleet is due within that window."

"We should abort the rendezvous," Vale advised. "Try again somewhere else."

Riker thought it over. "Things are tenuous enough as it is—I don't want to chance upsetting them by breaking the arrangement."

"I think they'd understand our reasons."

"But retreating could be taken as a sign of weakness," Deanna told her. "It could undermine our negotiating position."

After another moment, Riker spoke. "Deanna, I want you and Tuvok to beam aboard one of the jellies to wait for Qui'hibra. Take Keru and a security team just in case." With the interference, he wasn't sure the team could call for help if they needed it. But right now Riker judged the threat from the Entities to outweigh that from Qui'hibra. He felt he knew the elder well enough by now to trust in his integrity. And the jellies would be there to protect Deanna and the rest. "*Titan* will intercept the Crystalline Entities."

Deanna studied him. "And do what when you get there?"

"Attempt to communicate," he said grimly. "Without the Pa'haquel watching, we'll be free to try Data's graviton-resonance effect." He met her eyes. "God knows I'd like nothing better than to use that graviton beam to shatter them all to dust. But I have an obligation to at least try to make peaceful contact." He widened his gaze to include Vale. "And I'd like to manage to find a constructive solution to at least one thing in this whole mess."

Deanna smiled. "Good luck, Will." *I love you terribly, you know that?*

Actually I think you do it very well.

Throwing him an affectionate glare, Deanna made her way to the turbolift. *Just come back in one piece so I can keep in practice.*

Qui'hibra's arrival was right on time—but he came in more force than expected. The star-jellies notified Deanna when they detected his ships' imminent emergence from warp. *Dead ones come—many [alarm/anger]!*

Stay calm, Deanna advised as the lights dimmed and the heartbeat pulse grew stronger, indicating that her jelly was beginning to armor up. *Look more closely. Is it Qui'hibra?*

A pause. *Yes. And many more [suspicion/betrayal?].*

Please wait before you do anything. You know he was expected. Hail them for me, all right? Aloud, she addressed Tuvok, Keru and his team. "Qui'hibra's fleet is here."

A moment later, Qui'hibra's image appeared on the sensation wall, which the jelly had kept around for her benefit.

"Commander Troi. Where is Titan?"

"Not far. They went to make observations of a group of cosmozoans they detected in deep space not far from here." She could only hope Qui'hibra would not press the issue or attempt to scan for them. She had asked the jellies to position themselves on the opposite side of the star from the Crystalline Entities' approach vector; the intervening mass and EM field of the Proplydian would make detection more difficult. And she had emphasized deep space in the hope that the Pa'haquel would assume it was a non-warp-capable species, years away from endangering anyone and worth passing up for now.

Luckily, Qui'hibra seemed more concerned about *Titan* itself. *"And left you undefended?"*

She raised her chin. "The star-jellies can defend us and themselves, if necessary. Will it be necessary, Elder Qui'hibra? You seem to have brought your entire fleet. That could easily be taken as a hostile gesture."

"I appreciate how the livemounts feel about our use of their dead. But as we discussed, they must learn to accept it. We cannot instantly change our whole way of life or abandon our ancestral homes. Even if no new mounts are killed, we will still need the ones we have. They are a valuable resource in the battle against the chaos."

"Granted," Deanna said. "But I'm concerned you may be forcing the issue again."

"I am willing to accommodate the livemounts' concerns to a point, but accommodation must go both ways. The Hunt is an urgent calling, leaving no room for leisure."

Deanna gauged the jellies' reactions. They were unhappy at the presence of so many of their dead, but they were willing to tolerate it for now. It seemed they had begun to build a comfortable rapport with at least some of the Pa'haquel, and genuinely wanted to find a way to coexist. "Very well, Elder. In that spirit, why don't you beam aboard so we can discuss my proposal?"

Qui'hibra's expression showed that he got the subtext: while he was aboard one of the jellies, presumably the fleet would not attack. *"I will be there promptly."*

The sensation wall went dark. Within moments,

Qui'hibra shimmered into being near Deanna and her party. He looked around, not at them, but at the star-jelly around him. "It is an honor to be back here. Although I have my doubts that it can become the norm." She knew his appreciation was sincere; yet for some reason he was very reserved, his emotions even more tightly in check than usual. Probably it was unease at the prospect of their emotions overwhelming him again—a sentiment Deanna could sympathize with. Still, his reserve caused her hackles to rise. She knew predators were usually most dangerous when they were most still.

"You'd be amazed," Deanna said, "how often former enemies learn to work together as friends. Many of the Federation's founding members were once at each other's throats. And many of our greatest onetime enemies have become allies, or at least tolerant neighbors."

"Many of those in our alliance have battled each other at times. Sometimes they still do, when the threat of star-beasts is not so immediate."

"A common enemy can only do so much to unite people. It's the willingness to commit to understanding each other, doing the hard work of building and maintaining a relationship, that makes the difference. Not unlike a marriage," Deanna suggested.

Qui'hibra smirked. "I have had marriages that took endless work. And one that was nearly effortless . . . or so it felt to me, though probably only because she bore the burdens I placed on her with such grace. Qui'chiri is her issue, and her image."

What showed through his reserve made Deanna smile. "I can tell how much you love your daughter. If her mother was like her, you must have been very happy indeed."

"As happy as I think you are with your mate," he replied. "You work well together. I—" He broke off, and she felt his control clamp down again. "Well. All things are fleeting, and we must be grateful for what happiness we have, while it lasts."

Some of his pain slipped through despite his control. A sense of guilt too. Qui'chiri's mother had no doubt died in the Hunt, under his command, and some guilt was inevitable in that circumstance, even among a people as accustomed to death as the Pa'haquel. "I understand what you mean. During the troubles of the past few years, I became very aware of mortality, and of the real possibility of losing Will Riker. It was part of why we finally decided to get married. We'd waited far too long."

"And if death came to one of you tomorrow . . . would you feel you had been cheated?"

"No. I would've been happy even to be his wife for only a day, if that had been all we could have." She gave a small, wistful smile. "Although my mother would be sorely disappointed if I failed to give her grandchildren."

Qui'hibra stood silently for a moment, studying her, and something slipped through his mental armor. She realized that the guilt she'd sensed was not about the past . . . but about the immediate future.

Fortunately, she and Tuvok still had a partial mind-link, which he had been using to help him manage the jellies' emotions. She had been gradually weaning him off of it, letting his own mind learn to take up more of the slack, but enough remained to allow communication. *Qui'hibra's plotting something,* she told him. *Move discreetly behind him and be ready to act.*

Acknowledged.

"What about you?" Deanna asked. "You must have many grandchildren by now."

"And some of them have grandchildren. I have been blessed."

"No doubt you want your grandchildren's grandchildren to grow up in a galaxy where the Pa'haquel are prosperous and the chaos is kept at bay. I believe that the star-jellies can still help you achieve that. And they're willing to try . . . if you are."

"We all do what we believe is best for those we care about. I hope you understand that." Without warning, he whirled, and his taloned foot struck Tuvok's phaser from the hand that had just begun to draw it, leaving deep emerald gashes across the brown. Keru and his team began to draw their phasers, but Qui'hibra moved with uncanny swiftness, seizing Deanna before she could react. "Now," Qui'hibra barked into his communicator.

A second later, she felt a star-jelly transporter effect engulf her, and she and Qui'hibra rematerialized aboard his ship. He shoved her into the arms of a Fethet guard. "Bind her. Watch her. She is tougher than she appears. Propulsion team, move us out of the mounts' transporter range, now! Use the planetesimals as cover. Sting team, fire a few blasts to occupy them."

His team efficiently carried out his orders as the Fethet roughly wrenched her arms behind her and slapped shackles upon them. On the sensation wall, she saw the jellies recede as they retreated from the hunters' fire and as the hunters pulled away. Rescue would not be forthcoming.

Qui'shoqai, Qui'hibra's son and huntsmaster, came up to him. "Elder. The watchfleets have detected *Titan* on the far side of the Proplydian. It is apparently being pursued by a quartet of branchers."

The elder looked at him sharply. "Branchers! No doubt intending to communicate. He is a fool. Propulsion team, engage maximum warp and proceed to intercept. We must get there while there is still a *Titan* to seize. Are the watchfleets in range to rendezvous with us?"

"Not for some time, Elder. The prize will be ours alone."

Deanna felt the energy rumbling through the jelly's body as the distortion generators built up the warp field. Qui'hibra came over to her. "You can end this now if you give me the sensor and shield information which you gave to the skymounts. Show us how to counter their advantages and I will do what I can to see that your lives are spared." She said nothing. "As I expected. I apologize, Commander Troi. I must now take your husband's ship before he gets it destroyed by the branchers. I will pray for the Spirit's forgiveness . . . and I would hope you can grant me yours."

Her gaze seared him. "We were trying to help you, Qui'hibra. We are not your enemy."

"Not mine, no. But I am but one in the Conclave, and I abide by its judgments. This is how the balance falls."

"Then you'd better pray it doesn't lead to the downfall of your people, and countless others."

He held her eyes. "I already have."

Rage!

Tuvok reeled under the force of the star-jellies' anger. He had been largely insulated from their fear when the Pa'haquel fired on them; but now, with Counselor Troi being warped out of range, he felt the mind-link fading. Some telepathic effects (he reminded himself, striving to cling to analytical thought) were nonlocal quantum phenomena, acting independently of distance; but his link with Troi was not one of them, requiring the direct contact of a mind meld to initiate and attenuating with distance.

That was the cause. The effect was the rapid loss of his ability to insulate himself from the star-jellies' emotions *[fury/betrayal/disbelief/despair]*. No, not all his ability; this had been a weaker link than the first, allowing Troi to retain much of her own shielding ability while Tuvok used the rest to supplement his. He reminded himself that he still had some control of his own—even while the despair building within him fixated on Ree's prognosis that his control would never again be what it was.

Keru touched his shoulder, and Tuvok jerked away reflexively, not wishing to have to cope with the Trill's emotions as well. "Tuvok!" the burly security chief cried. "Come on, focus. We have to get after them!"

The words resonated with a desire he now felt crystallizing in the jellies. *Pursue! Pounce! Save Deanna! Sweep the parasites from our dead [avenge their treachery]!* He felt, both in body and mind, their distortion generators powering up for warp.

"Pursuit . . . is under way," Tuvok managed to get out. "Now leave me! I must concentrate." *Wait,* he told the jellies. *Restrain yourselves. There is danger there, both from the Pa'haquel and the Crystalline Entities.*

Don't care [afraid/going anyway]! We must save Deanna [sister/self]!

Fascinating. The star-jellies had accepted Counselor Troi as part of their collective identity. And because of that identification, they were willing to launch an attack to liberate her, even against enormous odds. When properly motivated, they could be fighters.

Tuvok felt in them the same manic determination and clarity that had driven him when he had attacked Lieutenant Pazlar and stolen the data. That same conscious choice not to care about the fear or the consequences because they simply did not matter as much as that one overpowering desire to act. In this case, though, the emotional imperative was acting in Tuvok's favor, in his crewmates' favor. Perhaps instead of fighting it, he could use it to his advantage. There would be no harm in letting it take him over.

No. Not again. Letting them have free rein would mean the Pa'haquel would suffocate in hard vacuum. It would mean ongoing conflict between the two species, and possibly untold death in generations to come if the cosmozoans were allowed to propagate too far. Tuvok would not accept that. He would not allow anyone else to suffer from his failures of control.

But how could he fight this? His mind was too weak, his shields inadequate.

Don't fight—yield. Deanna's mind, not through the link but an echo of memory. Something she had passed along to him in the meld was the concept that resistance was not the only form of strength. Sometimes being strong meant knowing when it was safe to yield, to trust in another's power and give oneself over to it. That trust could be hard to give if one had been hurt before. But without that trust, that yielding and acceptance, there could be no partnerships, no marriages, no crews, no federations.

But that was the key, wasn't it? Cooperation. The yielding went both ways. If he fought the jellies, they would fight him, and the struggle would deplete both their energies. But if he yielded to their passion, let it be a part of him, then his reason and judgment could be a part of them as well.

Very well, he thought. *We will pursue the hunter fleet. We will save Deanna. But we will do it my way. We will not beam the Pa'haquel into space. Instead we will disable their vessels.*

We will not fire on our dead. The jellies were adamant on that.

He shared their revulsion, and did not fight it. It did not

matter, because he could still achieve his goal through reasoned strategy. *That may not be necessary,* he told them.

He spoke the rest aloud for the security team's benefit. "Mr. Keru, hail *Titan*. Use the jelly's console; it will be out of communicator range."

Keru made the attempt, but only static came back. "I can't reach them. Too much subspace interference."

"Very well. We will make do. Here is the plan."

Chapter Seventeen

Riker was beginning to think Qui'hibra had been right about the Crystalline Entities. There was no mind here, no will to communicate—just pure, ravening hunger.

As *Titan* had neared the Entities, he had ordered Jaza to proceed essentially as Data had a dozen years ago aboard the *Enterprise*-D, generating a series of discrete graviton pulses from the tractor emitters, beginning at ten per second. The results had been the same as last time; the Entities had changed course and come to investigate the signal. Once he had felt they were close enough, he had ordered the pulses ramped up to twenty hertz, and as before, the Entities had come to a stop, seeming to look them over inquisitively. Riker had ordered the next phase, an increase to thirty hertz, at which point the vast crystal creatures had begun to respond with graviton pulses of their own. At this point twelve years ago, Captain Picard had grown hopeful that communication would indeed be possible, but Dr. Marr had sabotaged the effort, switching to the continuous beam that had destroyed the Entity. Afterward, Data had done his best to decrypt the signals they had received before its demise, but the translator had not had a sufficient baseline to work with. Riker had been hoping that this communication would add enough data to allow a viable translation matrix to be constructed.

But to the best of Jaza's and the computer's ability to determine, there had been little to the Entities' gravitic calls beyond a simple sense of acknowledgment and curiosity. After a few moments of hesitation and contemplative twirling in place—which Jaza suggested to be a means of scanning *Titan* through different facets to gain variant spectral readings—the Entities had begun to advance on the ship. "Try modulating the beam again," Riker had ordered. "Try forty per second."

The Entities had paused for another moment, then resumed their advance. It was no use—they were too hungry, and had nothing of substance to say to their dinner. Riker had ordered a retreat, and the Entities had pursued. Now he was leading them away from the Proplydian and the star-jellies, wondering what to do next. The fact that they were closing so fixatedly on *Titan* when the Proplydian offered a richer feast for them suggested to Riker that they were not guided by much in the way of intelligence, only instinct and immediate gratification.

He resisted the thought, though. Accepting that they were dumb animals would be too comforting, make it too easy to embrace his desire to lash out and destroy the things. What if he was wrong? What if their pursuit of *Titan* suggested just the opposite, that they were intelligent enough to be motivated more by curiosity than the prospect of a large meal?

On the way here, Riker had reviewed the research and records on the Crystalline Entities, and found only uncertainty. The first Entity had been brought to Omicron Theta by Lore, Data's twisted and malevolent prototype, who had then lured it to attack the *Enterprise* upon his discovery and reassembly. Lore had given the appearance of conversing with the Entity, but there was no other evidence to suggest that the life form was capable of understanding verbal communication. Only the graviton-pulse method had gotten any response from it at all. In Data's logs, he had speculated that Lore had actually used some other means to train the Entity to respond to the sound of his voice, in much the way that a dog or horse was trained—although given Lore's proclivities, Riker doubted his training methods had been particularly humane. Did that mean it lacked intelligence, though, or simply that its intelligence was not a type geared toward verbal communication?

Either way, though, it suggested that there was a way to train these beasts. Maybe it was time for a little negative reinforcement. "Activate the graviton beam again," he ordered. "Give them a continuous, oscillating pulse for five seconds. The same frequency Dr. Marr used."

Jaza and Vale looked up at him sharply. "Five seconds, sir?" Jaza asked.

Riker nodded in reassurance. "I just want to swat them across the nose."

"Swatting, sir." On the screen, the Entities wavered in their pursuit and came to a dead halt.

"All stop," Riker ordered. "Let's see what they do."

The Entities hovered there for a moment, then resumed their approach. "Jaza, another two seconds." This time they came promptly to a halt.

"It seems to be working," Vale said. "Now that we have the stick, should we try the carrot?"

He looked at her. "You mean the energy beam we tried before? I'm not sure I want to risk that yet."

Before she could answer, a beep came from the tactical console. "Multiple ships approaching," Kuu'iut reported. "It's Qui'hibra's fleet. Arrival in seventy seconds."

Damn. The subspace interference must have hidden their approach. *But what are they doing here?* "Hail them. Lavena, move us away from the Entities."

A moment later, Qui'hibra's face appeared on the screen. "Elder Qui'hibra," Riker said. "You were supposed to be meeting Commander Troi at the Proplydian."

"We saw you taking on the branchers, Riker. It is an unwise thing to do alone."

"We're managing just fine, thanks."

"So it would seem. I am curious to know how you got them to stop. Once we arrive, you can demonstrate your method."

Riker was reluctant to show them something that could so easily be used to kill the Crystalline—oh, hell, the branchers. "I think it's more important to resume negotiations with the star-jellies. Commander Troi will be—"

Will! She was there, in his mind. She was nearby. *They have me. It's a trap!*

Riker cursed himself for letting it throw him off. Qui'hibra's raptor eyes missed nothing; he knew Riker had been alerted. *"Commander Troi is my prisoner."* He gestured to someone offscreen, and a Fethet guard appeared, pulling Deanna roughly into frame. *"This can be easy, Riker, if you give me the sensor and shield data you gave the skymounts."* He paused, and proceeded with a grimace. *"Refuse, and Troi will suffer. Continue to refuse, and she will die, and we will take your ship. You cannot beat all of us, Riker. This will end with us having the information we want. Your choice is only of whether you, your crew and your wife are still intact afterward."*

"I can't believe you'd hide behind a hostage, Qui'hibra!" Riker barked. "You're a hunter, a warrior. This kind of cowardly tactic is beneath you."

That might have worked on a Klingon, but not here. *"I am a hound of the Spirit. I do whatever I must to survive and to stand against the chaos. And I will kill your wife today if it will save worlds in the future."*

Imzadi! Riker wanted to do anything to save her. But he saw the look in her eyes. If he traded the star-jellies' lives for hers, she would never forgive herself. Her thoughts came to him. *It's all right, Imzadi. Even a day together would have been enough.*

Steeling himself, he spoke. "Starfleet officers are trained to accept death before putting innocent lives in danger. I will destroy this ship myself before I let you have that information."

"Your nobility is foolish, Riker! Survival trumps all else. That is why I do this. That is why you should give me what I want, rather than letting your wife endure what I must otherwise inflict on her. It may interest you to know that the Fethetrit consider it an art form and a sport to dismember and consume their prey while prolonging its life and consciousness as long as they are able. Riathrek here has won trophies."

Riker traded another aching look with Deanna. "Please give me a moment," he asked Qui'hibra.

"Do not take long. Riathrek is impatient."

"Mute audio," Riker said, then turned to Kuu'iut. "Can we beam her out?"

The Betelgeusian shook his hairless blue head, gnashing his teeth. "They're generating a lambda hyperon field. Transporters won't work."

Their Vomnin scientists must have devised a countermeasure to the jellies' teleport beams. What if they could figure out the rest on their own, Riker wondered? What if he sacrificed Deanna and his crew for nothing?

But then another beeping interrupted his deliberations. "More contacts approaching," Kuu'iut said. "It's the star-jellies!"

"Elder!" called Qui'shoqai. "A school of armored skymounts has just emerged from warp! They are closing on us!"

Deanna didn't need to hear the words. She had sensed their arrival. *Sister/Self! We have come for you!*

No! Don't endanger yourselves! But they were determined—and very confident.

Qui'hibra was confident too. "They can do nothing. The hyperon field will block their teleport beams, and they will not fire on their dead."

"Still, they approach," Qui'shoqai said. "Should we fire?"

"Let them try their attack first. Let them see how futile it is. Hail *Titan*." A moment later, the channel opened again. "Riker—do not use this distraction as an excuse to strike. Remember what fate awaits your wife."

It frustrated Deanna to be so helpless. There was a time to yield, and this wasn't it. "Qui'hibra, you know this course is wrong. Let me go, and we can still work out a peace with the jellies."

"Silence her!" At the elder's command, Riathrek clapped his huge hand over her face, with nearly enough force to break her nose. She struggled to breathe.

"What are they doing?" That was Se'hraqua.

"They are bracketing us, above and below," Qui'shoqai reported. "It is like . . ."

"Like their funeral rites," Qui'hibra roared. "Fire on them! Break free, now!"

But it was too late. Even as the elder spoke, Deanna felt the jellies' somber satisfaction as they linked with the distortion generators aboard this one and began drawing out their energy. Almost immediately, the shipboard gravity field began to fluctuate and diminish, causing many of the hunters to lose their balance and fall. Luckily for them, the fall was growing gentler by the moment. Those who retained their balance grabbed at their controls, but the skymount's power was fading, the controls giving little response.

"Remain calm!" Qui'hibra commanded. "Sting team, dig in your talons and open fire! Power teams, divert whatever you can to stings!"

But Riathrek was not remaining calm. The Fethet was alarmed and unsure of himself, and his grip upon her loosened. Though her arms were bound behind her, she was not helpless. As the gravity continued to fall, she used a *mok'bara* move to break his hold, then swiftly kicked off the deck, propelling herself above the compass of his meaty arms before he could fold them shut around her. Flipping herself over, she pulled in her knees and kicked out hard at his bear-wolf muzzle.

The force of it was not enough to do any real damage, but with less gravity to give him traction, it knocked him back off his feet. Meanwhile, since her mass was considerably less than his, her acceleration was greater, so she soared across the room, well away from her captor. Her aim had been good enough that she collided with

Qui'shoqai and knocked him away from his controls. The collision bounced her back away from him and she settled gently to the floor, her weight reduced almost to nothing. She pushed herself up into midair to be ready for an attack.

But then she felt a presence in her mind. *Tuvok!* The meld had reestablished itself. His mind had actively sought hers out—and there were more minds too, the jellies, merged with his. *We have you now, Commander/sister/self. You are safe.*

She felt what was going to happen, felt the connection throughout her body. Of course—the jellies' transporter beams were part telekinetic. A strong enough psionic link gave them a lock that could overcome the hyperonic interference. (Was that reasoning coming from her own mind, or from Tuvok's?) Their awareness pervaded her, knew her every atom. In essence, they locked onto her from inside, and no outside interference could block that. Their love filled her, dissolved her, and then she was with them once again.

"Commander!" Keru was there, reaching down to help her to her feet. For an instant she almost recoiled from the huge, hirsute Trill, having a flashback to Riathrek. But she gathered herself, and realizing that the jellies had not beamed her shackles along with her, she grabbed his hand and pulled herself up.

"Can they send us back?" she demanded of Tuvok. "Me and the security team?"

"Back?" There was Will, his image on the sensation wall.

"Yes! I have to go back, try to talk some sense into Qui'hibra. He doesn't want to do this, Will. I can reach him."

The jelly shuddered. "They have opened fire," Tuvok announced. Qui'hibra's sting team must have successfully dug in their claws.

"You can talk to him later, Deanna. Right now let's get out of here."

"We may not get another chance, Will. He's wavering now. These tactics rub his feathers the wrong way. But get him caught up in chasing us—in hunting us—and it'll fire his instincts, harden his resolve. I have got to get back aboard that skymount now."

"Oh, Prophets." That was Jaza. *"We've got a new problem, everyone. The Crystalline Entities are closing in. They're heading right for the star-jellies!"*

Shit! Riker thought. The temptation of so many star-jellies must have overcome the branchers' fear of the graviton beam. "Hang on, Deanna. We'll come get you out of there."

"Sir!" Kuu'iut interrupted. "The hunters' skymounts are pulling away from the jellies. They're heading toward us at high speed."

Riker realized they must have recovered quickly once they broke free of the draining effect. The hunters came up fast, flipping their ventral sides forward to face *Titan* and cutting loose with plasma stings. The shields shuddered under the impact. Without Deanna as leverage anymore, Qui'hibra must have opted for a direct assault.

Mere moments later, the branchers came within range of the jellies and began firing their feeding beams. The jellies tried to break and run, but the branchers were too fast for them, swooping around them in a tetrahedral englobement, penning them in. A feeding beam swept across one of them, and Will could feel Deanna's resonant agony through their link.

"Lavena, close on the branchers! Tactical, target—" Another blow shook them, and another. Lavena tried to dodge around the Pa'haquel, but they kept themselves between *Titan* and the besieged star-jellies. The jellies remained trapped; each time one darted for an opening, a feeding beam struck at it, herding it back into the englobement.

"Riker!" Qui'hibra's image appeared in an inset on the viewer. *"Give me what I need and I will help you rescue your wife and crew. Refuse and I will prevent you from saving them."* Riker had been premature; Qui'hibra still had his leverage after all.

Again the branchers struck, and again Will felt the jellies' agony hit Deanna. "Kuu'iut, hit the Pa'haquel, hard! Get us past them!"

Phasers and torpedoes lashed out from *Titan*. Kuu'iut, no slouch as a predator himself, went for the jugular, his beams and salvos targeting the weakest points, the meridional fissures and weapon emitters. But the skymounts moved swiftly and dodged, and continued to pound at *Titan*. One was struck a crippling blow and drifted off, but the others kept coming. Kuu'iut knocked another out of the fight, but still the stings pounded the shields, eating away at their strength. One particularly direct blow knocked Riker off his feet. Sparks flew from the ops console, and Dakal recoiled from the discharge, shielding his face. No matter how much Starfleet improved the surge protectors, there were still fundamental physical limits on what they could absorb.

Riker climbed to his feet and checked to make sure Dakal was all right. His face and uniform were a bit singed, but he was back at work already, reinitializing the console, his tough Cardassian hide serving him well. So Riker took a moment to judge his own condition. He seemed largely intact, but had sustained numerous scrapes and had a very sore left elbow. Belatedly, he sat down in the command chair and activated its restraint harness, ignoring Vale's I-told-you-so glare.

And still the branchers' feeding beams ripped at the jellies' armor. The trapped jellies had begun returning fire, trying to blast an opening in the englobement. But they only succeeded in splitting two of the branchers into smaller units, which resumed their attack after mere seconds.

Meanwhile, the Pa'haquel's stings were still eroding *Titan*'s shields to critically low levels. The ship rocked under a particularly severe impact, and Riker was grateful for the seat restraints. "Starboard phasers are down!" Vale cried. "Starboard impulse reactor in emergency shutdown! Life-support alarms on decks four through six!"

This isn't working, Riker thought. *Titan* could stop the branchers with its graviton beam, if only it could reach the jellies. But Qui'hibra wouldn't let him get near them, and even if he could, there was still the question in the back of his mind of whether he could allow that knowledge to fall into. . . .

Wait. That was it! In a flash of insight, it all came together. The key was putting the knowledge into the *right* hands. Or rather, tentacles.

"Riker to Tuvok. Respond."

"Tuvok here, sir."

"Do you know the specs for the graviton beam we used on the branchers?"

"Aye, sir. I familiarized myself with it as a possible weap—"

"Never mind that! Just think about it. Focus on the

specs. Show them to the star-jellies! Show them how to use it to fight the branchers!"

Titan shuddered under more stings. The jellies screamed psychically under more feeding beams. But then: *"It is done, sir! The jellies are replicating the components now."*

Moments later, the branchers began to shudder and jerk away. Jaza superimposed a false-color effect on the viewer, making the gravity beams visible. Riker watched as the jellies struck at the branchers, holding the beams on them until they began to tremble. "Deanna, make them stop! That's enough!" Seconds later, the beams broke off. But the branchers had had enough. One by one, they slinked away.

Riker noted that Qui'hibra's fleet had stopped its attack. *"What just happened, Riker?"* the elder asked.

He met the Pa'haquel leader's eyes. "I've just solved your problem, Qui'hibra. I've just given you a way you can use the live jellies in the Hunt, and become even more effective hunters than before."

The raptor eyes narrowed. *"Explain."*

"We've just given the star-jellies a kind of graviton beam that allows communication with the branchers. As you've seen, it can also be used as a weapon against them. If the jellies had sustained their attacks, then the branchers would have been completely destroyed."

"So you offer us a better way to kill branchers? That is valuable, but it is not enough. There are too many other threats."

"You're not getting it, Qui'hibra. Look what happened here. We *didn't* kill the branchers—we *controlled* them." He exchanged a look with Vale. "And with that power . . . they can be herded. Possibly even trained. As you saw before, we also have a way to feed them energy. Reward as well as punishment. And maybe communication as well, up to a point.

"This is what I'm proposing. The Pa'haquel resume their efforts to work with the live jellies. But instead of using them as battleships . . . you use them as sheepdogs." Doubting the metaphor would translate, he elaborated. "They now have the means to control the branchers, and once I give them the specs for the energy beam, they'll have the means to reward them as well. You use those tools to tame the branchers. Herd them away from worlds with intelligent life, and focus their hunger on another rich source of bio-energy: the cosmozoans that you hunt. Make the branchers your hounds. That way the jellies don't have to go into combat themselves, and you turn one of your most powerful enemies into a powerful new weapon of your own."

Qui'hibra stared at him, standing silent for a long moment. Vale stared too. "Sheepdogs for hounds?" she muttered. "Let's hope your plan works better than your metaphors. The shields are critical and we can barely maneuver."

Se'hraqua came into the frame. *"Elder, you cannot be considering this! He insults us by suggesting we become herders, weaklings!"*

"Silence," Qui'hibra told him. But to Riker he said, *"The boy has a point, I fear. The Conclave will not think well of this scheme. It is not our way. I have doubts myself."*

"Is it so different from what you already do here, with the Proplydian?" Riker asked. "You don't destroy it, since it doesn't threaten planets. Instead you travel with it and use it to aid you in hunting other species. I've just given you a way to do the same with both the star-jellies *and* the branchers."

"It is very different. Trying to tame branchers, and hav-

*ing to hold the hands of live skymounts at the same time
... it is overcomplicated. Risky. The Hunt, the way of tradition, is proven by time. We know it works. Give us the
means to counter the skymounts' advantages and we can
restore it again."*

"I know you don't truly believe that, Qui'hibra," Deanna
said from her star-jelly. "You know that things have
changed forever, that a new solution must be found."

*"I thought I did at first, but many wise Pa'haquel be-
lieve otherwise. I am just a hunter, not a philosopher."*

"But you know the skymounts," Deanna said. "You
know them as living beings, better than any Pa'haquel
ever has since before your people left Quelha. You have
felt the rapport that can exist between your species, and
you know in your bones that you can be stronger as partners than you could ever be as enemies."

*"That is what I would like to believe. But the Conclave
has declared that the Hunt must resume. And the Hunt demands that I do what I must, not what I desire."*

"So you keep saying," Deanna fired back, her voice
hardening. "And I believe it. I believe that you will do
whatever you must in the name of what you think is right.
So if the Conclave says one thing, and you know that another thing is right, what does your loyalty to them matter?
What does their authority matter? What does your tradition and cultural preference matter?

"You keep insisting that nothing matters to you as
much as fighting the chaos, as much as preserving life
throughout the galaxy. Well, *here is life* for you to preserve! Here is a whole species that you have it in your
power to spare, right here, right now. A species that you revere and cherish, a species that is willing to forgive every-*

thing you've ever done to it and stand by your side as friends. A species that could be the greatest ally you've ever known.

"If they give you that, and you repay them with betrayal, with death—where is the balance in that?"

Qui'hibra was silent again for a long time. Deanna tried to read his body language, to strain her senses across space and pick up something from him, but she got nothing. Finally, he took a deep breath and let it out. *"Hunters! Stand down. There is no more prey here today."*

"What?" Se'hraqua challenged. *"You would defy the Conclave?"*

"You *would defy* me?" Qui'hibra's voice was softer and more dangerous than she'd ever heard it.

The youth seethed. *"I will stand down for now. But the Conclave will hear of this."*

"Yes, they will. I will tell them myself." He faced the visual pickup again. *"If you, Riker, and you, Troi, can prove to me that the branchers can be herded and used to hunt . . . then I will stand with you and prove it to the Conclave."*

"Thank you," Riker said sincerely, and Deanna felt his flood of relief. *"I hope this day will mark the beginning of a new era for this region of space."*

"Some things may change," Qui'hibra said, unimpressed by the rhetoric. *"But the Hunt goes on."* He paused. *"Commander Troi . . . once again I offer my apologies for what I believed the Hunt required of me. I hope that now you are willing to forgive me."*

She crossed her arms and thought about it. The jellies were willing to forgive worse, as she had pointed out so emphatically moments ago. It would be a bit hypocritical not to follow suit. Still, she had to ask one thing. "Would you really have let Riathrek eat me alive bit by bit?"

He seemed surprised by the question. *"Yes."*

She blinked. "Well, all right. Just as long as I know what I'm forgiving you for."

CLAN AQ'TRI'HHE LEAD SKYMOUNT, STARDATE 57221.8

The Conclave of Elders watched the sensation wall speechlessly as it showed a trio of branchers, herded by live star-jellies under the direction of Huntsmaster Qui'shoqai and his clanmates, made short work of a group of spinners basking in the light of the Proplydian's star. Deanna reached out with her mind, gauging their reactions, and found them too much in flux to let her judge how this would turn out. She turned to Will, who looked at her expectantly, and gave a fractional shake of her head.

"Now you have seen with your own eyes," Qui'hibra declared when the demonstration was concluded and the branchers were being led meekly away. "We have achieved this much after only a few days of training. Imagine how much more we can accomplish. We can still be hunters, even more effective than before. The balance of life and death continues . . . but we and the skymounts need no longer be on opposite sides of that balance. And we need no longer lose so many of our wives, sons and daughters, see so many worthy lines diminished or snuffed out in Houndings. Imagine how many of your kin would still be here today if we could have sent the branchers against the harvester."

Se'hraqua shot to his feet and spoke angrily. "You speak of the balance, but you do not understand it. The balance of life and death is not preserved if we no longer have the courage and commitment to sacrifice our own lives to the Hunt!"

"And how is it balanced," Deanna challenged, "if there is so much death on both sides, and so little life? Death will always be there—it doesn't need you to help it along."

"This blasphemer has no right to speak here!"

"She is here as my advisor," Qui'hibra countered, "and an honorary member of my clan. That gives her the right." He addressed the Conclave as a whole again. "And she speaks wisely. The more of our lives we throw away, the more we diminish our strength against the chaos. Consider it. Consult with your singers of history. Have we ever had so few in a Great Hounding before, or come away with so few left alive? Our old ways were not in balance— they gave too much of an edge to death."

Now Aq'hareq rose. "Our 'old ways' are our *only* ways, Qui'hibra! They were handed down to us by the Spirit, passed on from generation to generation pure and unchanged. They are the way we were meant to be. Follow this corrupt path and the Spirit will never forgive you."

"And what about the skymounts?" Deanna said. "In your tradition, you pray to them for forgiveness as well. And they are willing to forgive what you did to them when it was the only way for you to survive. But now it isn't the only way anymore. You have a new way, a better way that lets both you and them live in harmony and far greater safety. If you try to hunt and kill them now, when there is no need for it, they will not give you their forgiveness."

"The Spirit governs them too," Aq'hareq replied, unruffled by her words. "They stray from Its path by seeking to evade the Hunt, and they will be shown their folly in time. The branchers will turn on them, or they will sicken with disease from having Pa'haquel live inside them, or the hotsprings of their breeding worlds will grow cold. One way or another, the true balance will be restored."

"So it must be," Se'hraqua added, "for so it is written."

Deanna realized Aq'hareq was a lost cause, and probably Se'hraqua as well. For someone whose standard of truth was based solely on scriptural precedent, no argument based on reason or fact could ever be convincing. Fortunately, though, she sensed that other minds were more open. Her point about the jellies' lack of forgiveness had affected many of them, as she had hoped it would. For all their violence toward the jellies, the Pa'haquel felt genuine reverence and gratitude toward them. It was nothing personal. She pitched her next words for them.

"Aq'hareq speaks of balance. If you want to see balance, look around you. Look where we are. The Proplydian is the greatest starbeast in all of Vela. It's a symbol of the life force that pervades the galaxy, that sustains and defines you as a people. Do you have to kill it, or it you, to be in balance? No. You live alongside it, in symbiosis with it, in balance with it, as do countless starbeasts. It sustains a vast wealth of life, and does not need to die in order to do so. It pulses with life of its own, and does not need to kill to do so. Is this corrupt? Is this a path doomed to destruction? The Proplydian has lived longer than any other starbeast, longer than your entire species. It has earned your reverence and your awe. And it has done this without death. It has done this by balancing life with life.

"And now, here under the gaze of the Proplydian itself, the Pa'haquel can choose to do the same."

For some time, there was silence, broken only by a few furtive murmurs between elders and advisors. Aq'hareq clearly was not convinced, but sensed the mood of the chamber and stayed quiet. Se'hraqua followed his lead.

Now the youngish elder Rhi'thath rose. "If we made this change, what would become of our traditions as a people? How could we ever ascend to manhood or eldership without the blood of skymounts to anoint us?"

"There are still other hunts in which you can win honor," Riker said. "They don't all have to be against sky-mounts."

"But our most important ones do."

"There may still be a solution to that," Deanna said. "It was suggested to me by a fellow crew member, Orilly Malar. I'd like to ask her to tell you about it herself."

After a bit of prompting, Orilly diffidently stepped forward. It had taken some doing to convince the Irriol cadet to come here; she still didn't fully trust herself. But at the same time she had seen this as a way to help absolve her guilt, to offer something positive to make amends for the damage she'd done, and that had convinced her to come. "On my world of Lru-Irr," she began slowly, "we have our own balance, and all living things are attuned to it. When . . . when there is need, sometimes the sick, elderly or . . . or injured members of a species—even my own species, sometimes—may allow themselves to be taken by predators. So that . . . so that the rest of their members may be spared, and the gestalt served. I . . . we have suggested to the jellies—the skymounts, sorry—that maybe their sick and elderly members, those who are past healing, could allow themselves to be ritually hunted, and end their lives swiftly rather than slowly and in pain. They, ah, they were uneasy with the thought . . . but they said they would consider it. That maybe you and they could negotiate something . . . along those lines."

There was much muttering and discussion among the Conclave members. The empathic timbre was a mix of distaste and hope. "How can we settle for hunting the weak and feeble?" "We often take the weak and feeble as it is; there is no shame in it." "But only to hunt volunteers? Could there be enough?" "We should give thanks that the skymounts would consent to it at all." "And you saw how well they wielded the branchers. Imagine that power fighting for us instead of against us!"

Once the chatter settled, one of the matriarchs rose to ask a question. "What of the implementation of this? It requires telepaths for us to know the skymounts' thoughts and wishes. Will you of *Titan* remain with us indefinitely?"

"I'm afraid we'd have to decline that honor," Riker said. "We still have a mission of our own to resume. But there are other telepathic species in the region. The Vomnin are acquainted with several. You've excluded them from your alliance before because they were a security risk, but now that risk no longer exists."

"If I may, sir," Orilly said. She was terrified, Deanna could tell, but determined to get it out. "I'd like to stay with them," she finally forced out in a rush of breath.

Riker and Deanna stared at her. "Cadet?" Riker asked.

"No disrespect to you or *Titan*, sir. It's been an honor to serve with you. But . . . I think I can do more good here. I have a good rapport with the jellies . . . almost like the gestalt back home, except more conscious. These past few days, working with them to train the branchers . . . I've felt more content than I have since I left Lru-Irr."

Deanna knelt to bring herself to Orilly's eye level. "Malar, are you sure? You've worked so hard on your Starfleet training. And you have friends on *Titan*, you know that, right?"

One of Orilly's trunk-hands patted her shoulder. "I know, Counselor. But it might not be forever. The Pa'haquel travel all over this part of space . . . we may run into each other again."

Shortly thereafter, a vote was called. Many of the elders and family heads were slow to decide. The results trickled in slowly, and it was hard to get a sense of the outcome.

But finally Qui'hibra's proposal passed by a narrow but decisive margin. "So it is decided," Qui'hibra announced. "From now on, the Pa'haquel will hunt alongside the skymounts and the branchers. We enter this covenant under the gaze of the Proplydian, and pray that it grant us its blessing, and its guidance in finding this new balance."

But Aq'hareq, after a moment of building anger, shot to his feet. "My fleet-clan will not abide by the Conclave's ruling! It is blasphemy and cannot stand! My clan will find a way to carry on the Hunt. We will go on killing skymounts as tradition demands. And any Pa'haquel who stand in our way will die as well!"

"The skymounts will not forgive your kills," Qui'hibra shot back. "They will be tainted, corrupt. Your reanimations will fail, your clan will die."

"That is for the Spirit to decide. Now you will leave my skymount. Along with any elders who would abide by this corrupt ruling. Any who wish to join me in the fight to preserve the Spirit's traditions may remain, regardless of their clan."

The declaration brought many angry replies from the high elders. "Outrageous!" "No one else dictates to my clan!" "You claim to stand for tradition?" But Deanna sensed much division. Many of the junior elders and family heads were tempted to stand with Aq'hareq, and his prestige and seniority carried much weight. But for the most part, loyalty to their own clans won out. Most chose to follow their high elders and beam back to their own fleets, but a few broke ranks to stand with Aq'hareq.

Finally only the Qui'Tir'Ieq contingent was left. Deanna looked to Se'hraqua, expecting him to stand with Aq'hareq. He and Qui'hibra locked gazes for a long moment. "Do not be a fool, Se'hraqua," the elder said. "Do not defy the Conclave."

"The Conclave is nothing," Aq'hareq said. "It has grown weak and illegitimate. Come with us, Se'hraqua, and we will build a new Conclave, a new tribe. Come with me and you can kill a skymount of your own! Not some feeble old one that would have died soon anyway, but a vigorous, vital one, worthy to be the command mount of your own fleet, the birthplace of your own clan!"

Deanna felt his excitement. Aq'hareq offered him the fulfillment of all his desires, of the demands of his strongest instincts. But Qui'hibra's stare still held him, refused to let him go. "Would you truly wish to make your choice based on that, Hunter? On your own gains, your own ambitions? Is that a righteous choice in service to the Spirit?"

"I . . ." Se'hraqua faltered. "I wish to defend our traditions. To keep things as they were meant to be."

"I know you love our traditions, cherish the ancient ways. But you also love the skymounts, as much as I do. Possibly more, in your way—you are young, and your passions still burn hotter than mine. But I cannot tell you how deeply it has moved me to get to know the skymounts as living allies, to fight and hunt by their side, to feel them respond willingly to my needs and wishes. To know them, not as cold, dead machines, but as friends and partners. It has revived in me a love of the skymounts that I had almost forgotten. Imagine what it could be like for you, Se'hraqua.

"And imagine how it would be to go with Aq'hareq. To struggle to chase skymounts that could see you coming, that could brush off your attacks, that could drain your mounts of power and leave you stranded, unable to warp. And even if you could manage to kill one, imagine knowing that its spirit would never forgive you. Knowing that its body would only be a slave, not a gift. And knowing that you had chosen that path, not for love of the Spirit or the mounts, but for love of your own ambition and greed. Is that the life you would choose, Hunter? Is a clan of your own worth the price of your soul?"

Se'hraqua stood there, torn, for long moments more. Finally, Deanna felt him make his choice. It was a choice he still had doubts about, but he had made his decision and would abide by it. His eyes went to Aq'hareq's, held them for a time—and then he stepped over to stand by Qui'hibra and his clan.

"A foolish choice," Aq'hareq said. "And one you will pay for, Hunter."

"Perhaps," Se'hraqua replied. "But at least it is my choice."

"As you will. But you and your clan are no longer welcome on this mount. And neither are your people, Riker. All of you, know that if our paths cross again, it will be as enemies."

Qui'hibra ignored the other elder's rhetoric, and came over to Riker and Troi. "It seems we must go now. Thank you for all you have done—for my people and the sky-mounts, and perhaps the galaxy."

"Glad we could help," Riker said.

"But the burden remains ours to carry. As you said, you have your own mission to resume."

"We could stay with you a while longer," Deanna said. "Help you with the transition."

"No. This will be a difficult enough adjustment to make—if it is to work, the Pa'haquel must know that it is our own adjustment, not one imposed from without."

Deanna nodded. "That's very true."

"However, I would accept your cadet's offer to join us, if you will grant her leave."

Riker looked to Orilly. "All right—let's call it leave,

then. An extended leave, until you decide to come back to Starfleet. Granted effective immediately."

"Thank you, sir," Orilly said. "I'll try to do the Federation proud, as well as Lru-Irr."

"I know you will be an asset to the Hunt," Qui'hibra said.

That reminded Riker of the one thing that was still troubling him about this. "One more thing before you go," he said. "I'd like you to consider something. In the past couple of weeks, you've learned that you can coexist peacefully and beneficially with two species you formerly believed you had to kill. I hope you—and your people—will keep in mind the possibility that the same could be true of the other starbeasts. That maybe the jellies and the branchers are only the first in this new covenant."

The elder looked at him skeptically. "I am an old hound, Riker, slow to change. I may have reached my limit of changes by now." He threw a look at Se'hraqua. "But maybe younger minds are more flexible. And it may be the wish of the Proplydian, of the Spirit. I will pass along the suggestion."

"Thank you."

"I will pass it along as well," Orilly said. "On my world, living as one with our biosphere is second nature. Perhaps I can offer insights in how to coexist within the galactic biosphere."

Deanna smiled at her. "If anyone can, Malar, you can. Good luck."

Qui'hibra led Orilly over to stand with his group, and signalled his skymount. A watery shimmer came over them, and then they were gone. Riker looked around him one more time. "And I for one am tired of standing inside a corpse. Deanna—let's go home."

EPILOGUE

Captain's Log, Stardate 57223.6

Since the breakup of the Conclave, there have been several mutinies aboard various Pa'haquel fleets, as additional junior elders have chosen to reject the so-called Proplydian Covenant
and join Aq'hareq's dissident group. And there are still countless more Pa'haquel fleet-clans scattered throughout the Gum Nebula, clans that weren't involved in the Conclave and will have to
be persuaded individually to change—or to resist change. So
far, though, the majority are abiding by the Covenant, and Qui'hibra
believes that will continue. He's also convinced that the dissi-
dents are doomed to failure as they eventually run out of skymounts and are outcompeted by the new alliance. The process
could take generations, though, and I fully expect us to find
ourselves dealing with its consequences somewhere down the
road.

For now, though, things seem well enough in hand, and the
process will likely go better without further interference from us.
But we haven't yet said our last good-byes to the star-jellies. At their

invitation, we are returning to their breeding world in the Kyle
system for shore leave and scientific research—which I suspect
are much the same thing as far as Jaza and our science staff are
concerned.

T'Pel quirked a brow at Tuvok as she came out of the
bedroom to find him standing near the entrance to their
quarters. "Is it not time for your daily meditation?" she
asked.

"Yes. However, I wished to see you off."

"That is not necessary."

"No."

"But . . . I appreciate the support."

"As I have appreciated yours, my wife." Their fingers touched. "And I am certain that Dr. Ree, Nurse
Ogawa, and the Bolajis will appreciate your assistance
as well." After finding a sense of purpose in tending to
the Shalra refugees, T'Pel had proposed to Ree that she
could be of value as a sickbay assistant, taking some of
the responsibility for the care of the premature infant
Totyarguil Bolaji along with other duties as needed.
Ree had readily accepted her offer, and Ogawa had suggested that those other duties could include tending to
the needs and education of her own son, Noah Powell.
T'Pel had welcomed the opportunity to care for children
once again, and she displayed a palpable eagerness to
begin her work. Not that she was emotional about it, of
course; it was simply an accumulation of energy which
could be directed into her work. Eminently logical, as
always.

After she left, Tuvok darkened their quarters and sat
before his meditation flame, contemplating it, yielding to
peace and clarity. A sizable fraction of the crew was taking

leave on Kyle III right now, with others awaiting their turn, but that held no allure for him. To a Vulcan, to rest was to *rest*, to cease using energy.

The presence of the star-jellies on Kyle III was not a factor in his decision. He could detect their telepathic communications just as strongly here in orbit as below. But their ongoing chatter posed no obstacle to his ability to meditate. His melds with Counselor Troi had helped him recover much of his shielding ability, though it would never be as strong as it once was. And though some residue of the star-jellies' emotions continued to pervade his awareness, he was confident now in his ability to manage them.

But when he rose to respond to the door signal and found Melora Pazlar standing there, he realized he still needed to work some on managing his own.

"Mr. Tuvok, can I talk to you?" the Elaysian asked with apparent unease.

"Certainly, Lieutenant. Please come in."

She walked in slowly, leaning on her cane, her motor-assist servos whirring softly. She gladly accepted his offer of a seat. "I am gratified to see you regaining your full mobility at last," Tuvok said neutrally.

"Yeah, I'm almost there. Good as new." She took a deep breath. "Physically, at least. Tuvok, I'm going to be frank with you."

"I would expect nothing less."

A nervous laugh. "Yeah, I guess so. Look. Ever since the . . . since you attacked me, I've been—hell, I've been scared. I've . . . it made me feel so helpless, so violated, and I'm—I'm kind of nervous to be in the same room with you."

Tuvok yearned for the calm he'd had moments ago.

"Lieutenant, I cannot express how truly sorry I am for what—"

She held up her hand. "Screw the apologies, Tuvok. That's not what I need, not what I'm asking for." He raised a curious eyebrow, and she went on. "When I get afraid, the way I like to deal with it is to face it head-on. That's what I'm here for. Tuvok—I want you to teach me to defend myself."

Tuvok's head pulled back fractionally. "Lieutenant?"

"I know, I took the usual Starfleet courses, but they didn't quite know how to deal with someone as—as fragile as me. It basically came down to 'keep your phaser handy and try to stay out of the way.' But obviously that can't always work. And it's not enough for me, to be dependent on a weapon, on a machine, on other people. Because other people can't always protect me.

"I need to learn how to defend myself better against people much stronger than I am—which, let's face it, is going to be just about everybody. And I want you to teach me how."

"Lieutenant . . . I appreciate the request, but perhaps you would benefit more from a more qualified teacher. Commander Keru, perhaps."

"No. No, it has to be you. I understand, you're afraid of hurting me again. Hell, *I'm* afraid of you hurting me again. But that's why it has to be you, Tuvok. If I can learn to hold my own against you, then I can beat this . . . this emotional baggage you've saddled me with.

"Besides . . . we're crewmates, right? We're going to be working together for, probably for years. We need to be able to trust each other. So here I am . . . extending my trust to you. Do you accept it?"

Tuvok pondered. It was a very surprising gesture. He

would not have expected an emotional being to be so prepared to trust him after . . .

No. His surprise was not about her ability to trust. It arose from his difficulty trusting himself. Yet the starjellies had trusted him. Deanna Troi had trusted him with her mind. Captain Riker still trusted him as his tactical officer. T'Pel had trusted him enough to join him in his new life. And now Melora Pazlar was offering him her trust in spite of everything. With so much trust extended his way, was it logical to deny it to himself?

Tuvok rose. "I will meet you in holodeck one at 0800 tomorrow morning, Lieutenant. I expect you to be prompt. And I expect you to follow my instructions without protest and without distracting attempts at humor."

Melora gaped at him in disbelief. Then she shook her head and laughed. "You have a deal, Commander." She rose and stood at attention. "No *attempts* at humor."

Tuvok realized he was in for quite a challenge.

"May I join you, Christine?"

Vale looked up at Jaza's voice, surprised to see him in the mess hall. "Najem, hi. Uhh, sure. I thought you were down on the planet."

"I was, but there was some equipment I needed, so I thought I'd come up and grab some lunch before gathering it."

"Ah, okay." She let him eat in silence for a few moments, then spoke. "Najem, I need to ask you something."

"Sure, anything."

"You know how you've been this really good friend to me the past few weeks?"

He stopped eating. "I, um, I've tried," he said modestly.

"Yeah, about that, though. Has it really been about

being a friend to me? Or has it been about keeping yourself available to me and being really good to me in the hopes that I'd fall for you? Sort of a no-pressure romancing?"

It was a moment before he responded. "Actually it's both. Is that a problem? I mean, there is no pressure, you're right about that. And I'd sort of gotten the impression lately that maybe you might be open to . . . changing your mind about us."

"Well . . . I was."

He studied her. "Was. As in, not anymore."

"Yeah."

"May I ask what I did to change things?"

"Nothing. Pardon the cliché, but it's me, not you." She took a deep breath. "When the Pa'haquel had Deanna captive . . . Will was ready to sacrifice her for the greater good. I could see it was tearing him up inside. But he was able to make that choice. Thank God he didn't have to, but he was able to.

"And when I saw that, I realized . . . I don't think I could make that choice about someone I . . . someone I loved." She smirked. "In a weird way, it bothers me to realize that. The woman who inspired me to join Starfleet in the first place . . . when we met, she actually *killed* her own lover to stop him from killing me. I've always tried to live up to her example, and it's a bit disturbing to admit I can't in that regard. But at the time, really, I guess I thought more about her bravery than about what she had to sacrifice. I didn't know her as well as I know Will and Deanna, didn't know her lover as anything but a suspect. So I didn't *feel* it the way I did with Will. Now that I have . . . I just don't feel ready to put myself in a position where I might have to make that kind of choice.

"So I really need to *not* be in a relationship right now, Najem. I need to focus on my Starfleet duties, and not have to deal with complications like that. Maybe someday, when I've matured more as an officer, as a woman, I'll be ready. But not now. Okay?"

He placed his hand atop hers. "Okay. I understand. But I want you to know . . . whatever ulterior motives I may have had, the friendship is genuine. And it's there for you if you need it."

She placed her other hand atop his. "Thank you. I appreciate it. And we'll see how it goes. For now, though . . . for now you should get back down to the planet. Back to work."

He nodded solemnly, and removed his hand from between hers. They sat in silence for a moment, accepting closure.

But then he looked up. "Um, can I finish my lunch first?"

It was good to be the captain's wife.

Will and Deanna had discovered a perfect, idyllic nook tucked away between the body of a sessile young jelly and the shore of the thermal lake in which it sat. Will had exercised his authority to command everyone else to stay well away from the lake so they could have it all to themselves. Yet once she'd started to take advantage of their solitude and unfasten his uniform, he'd suddenly realized that the star-jelly itself would be a spectator. He'd hesitated for a moment, babbling something about contributing to the delinquency of a minor. She'd reminded him that this "minor" was nearly two hundred years old and shared the collective knowledge of its entire species. "Oh, great,"

Will had said. "You mean I have the whole species as an audience?"

"Don't worry," she'd purred. "Their perceptions of it will be filtered through me, so I know they'll be suitably impressed." She'd gone on to offer several less verbal and more persuasive arguments, and soon he'd gotten back into the spirit of the moment.

Now they were basking together in the afterglow, leaning against the firm, soft surface of one of the jelly's supporting ribs, resting their weight on a shelf it had materialized a little below the waterline for their benefit. "I've been meaning to ask you something," Will said after a while.

"I know," she said. He threw her a look of mild, amused annoyance before growing serious again.

"When you were in sickbay . . . merged with the jellies . . ."

"Yes?"

"When you asked why we hadn't had a child yet . . . was that the jellies speaking, or you?"

She didn't reply right away. She stood up out of the water, stretched, shook out her hair and leaned against the slope of the support rib. His admiration of the sight was palpable, but she could sense that it hadn't diverted him from the question. She hadn't really meant it to, but she'd needed a moment to build up her courage.

"It was both, I suppose."

"We haven't really talked about it much." He had to pause for a moment himself, but then he came out and asked it. "Do you want to have a baby?"

She smiled. "It wasn't something I'd really thought about . . . not consciously, anyway. I didn't even realize it had been on my mind until the jellies found it there. I think it started when I was first reaching out to try to contact them. My mind brushed across everyone in the crew . . . even little Totyarguil." She knelt by Will, took his hand. "The way his mind felt, Will . . . it had such purity, such perfect innocence. There's nothing quite like it. To feel a, a soul like that inside me, to know it came from a part of me . . . and a part of you . . . it would be more amazing than anything I've ever experienced."

Will thought about it. "That purity . . . it never lasts, though, does it?"

"No," she admitted. "But it's a good place to start from. A lot of it can be kept, cultivated, nurtured. And sometimes . . . even some of what's been lost can be gotten back."

"So are you saying you're ready for that challenge?"

"After all I've done, all I've learned in my life, I'm as ready as I'll ever be. And who knows if it'll last, Will? How many times have we almost lost each other? How many times before we even got around to admitting what we had? We've waited long enough as it is."

She could tell the prospect excited him, moved him. But still he hesitated, and of course she knew why. "Would it even be appropriate?" he asked. "Starfleet had enough trouble with a captain and his wife serving on the same crew. How great a conflict of interest could there be if my own child were on board?"

"I don't see any conflict. Your job as captain is to protect your ship, your crew."

"But if I kept worrying about my baby, let it keep me from making a sacrifice I had to make . . ."

"How is it any different if it's the Bolajis' baby, or Alyssa's son?" She held his gaze significantly. "How is it any different from being willing to sacrifice me?

We've both proven ourselves willing to make such hard choices."

He said nothing for a while, frowning. She offered another thought. "For the Pa'haquel, this is the way it's always been. Their ships are their homes, their families. They constantly put their children and loved ones in harm's way. And they accept it."

"Because they had to. Because they led a harsh life."

"Come look at the ruins of my mother's house on Betazed and tell me there's any life that doesn't pose the same risks. What matters is to do what good you can while you have the chance. True, it could be taken from you, negated at any time. But it might not. And if you don't even try because you're afraid it won't last . . ."

"Right. I understand."

She studied him. "Will . . . you haven't said if *you* want a baby."

"Can't you tell?"

"Not the point. Will, do you want to have a baby? I'm not asking you to commit to trying, I just want to know what you *feel* about it."

After a moment, he softened, smiled. "Deanna Troi . . . nothing in this universe would make me happier or prouder than to be the father of your child. Or children."

She snuggled up against him again, kissed him softly. "Thank you." Then they kissed again, for a much longer time. "So is that a yes?"

He pursed his lips. "Call it an agreement in principle. There are still a lot of things we need to decide—and there are definitely people we should talk to."

• • •

It was a long time before Christine Vale responded. "I think . . . I'd be okay with that."

Riker was surprised. "It wouldn't bother you? A captain having to deal with being a father as well?"

She studied him. "I think you've proven that you can balance those responsibilities. To be honest, you do it better than I could. I know that now. Yeah, there probably were some personal motives behind your decisions with the star-jellies. But you and Deanna didn't let those motives get in the way, and they meshed pretty well with the practical objectives of the situation. And all in all, your rapport with her made you a pretty effective team. You managed to resolve an ancient conflict and bring new hope to a whole region of the galaxy. And . . . I'd say that the Federation's ideals were upheld pretty damn well." He gave her a look of gratitude.

She smirked. "Of course, being a father can be a full-time job. I wouldn't even think of letting you do it if you didn't have a really amazing first officer to pick up the slack."

Riker smiled back. "I do, don't I? In more ways than one, Christine. Thanks."

He led her out of the ready room and back to the bridge. "Of course we aren't going to jump into it right away. There's still a lot to work out."

"Sure, I understand."

"Right now, we have a mission to get back to," he went on, pitching his voice for the bridge at large. "We've still got a lot of Bubblegum to chew." He ignored the groans that ensued. "Ensign Lavena, prepare to break orbit."

"Aye, sir. Course?"

Vale exchanged a look with him. "You know, after this marathon run to the Vela Association, we're a lot farther out from the Federation than we were scheduled to be by now. Should we go back, pick up charting where we left off?"

Riker thought it over as he took his seat. He traded a look with Deanna, who smiled. "No," he said. "We go forward. Always forward."

THE VOYAGES OF THE
STARSHIP TITAN

WILL CONTINUE

About the Author

At the age of five and a half, Christopher L. Bennett saw his first episode of *Star Trek*, believing it to be a show about a strange airplane that only flew at night. As he continued watching, he discovered what those points of light in the sky *really* were. This awakened a lifelong fascination with space, science, and speculative fiction. By age twelve he was making up *Trek*-universe stories set a century after Kirk's adventures (an idea years ahead of its time), but soon shifted to creating his own original universe. He eventually decided this was what he wanted to do for a career. Meanwhile, Christopher made two separate passes through the University of Cincinnati, thereby putting off real life as long as possible, and earned a B.S. in physics and a B.A. with High Honors in history in the process.

Christopher's published works include "Aggravated Vehicular Genocide" in the November 1998 *Analog;* "Among the Wild Cybers of Cybele" in the December 2000 *Analog; Star Trek: S.C.E. #29—Aftermath;* ". . . Loved I Not Honor More" in the *Star Trek: Deep Space Nine: Prophecy and Change* anthology; his first novel, *Star Trek: Ex Machina;* and "Brief Candle" in the *Star Trek: Voyager—Distant Shores* anthology. More

information and cat pictures can be found at http://home
.fuse.net/ChristopherLBennett/.

The author is not the same Christopher Bennett whose
father is *Star Trek* movie producer Harve Bennett, though
he is apparently a cousin of paleontologist Chris Bennett.
You can see why he uses the "L."

The third and final
chapter in the

STRING THEORY

ODYSSEY

E V O L U T I O N

by Heather Jarman

Coming in March 2005 from
Pocket Books

Turn the page for a preview. . . .

"Don't do it, Tom," Harry warned again, panic contorting his face.

Tom recognized the look. It was the same one Harry wore when Tom suggested that the captain really wouldn't care if he appropriated Chakotay's password to "borrow" from Tuvok's replicator rations to cover an unexpected gambling debt (unexpected because Ensign Tariq was obviously cheating: the way the chips landed on the wheel made a full-color quarto impossible!). Hypercautious Harry felt about risk the way Ferengi felt about loaning latinum. The irony of Harry's reluctance to wade into the unknown was that he, more than anyone else in Tom's acquaintance, was most likely to be mutilated, squashed, or killed, regardless of how careful he was. So why be careful? In Tom's experience, most of the risky situations Harry studiously avoided had a component of fun.

Tom liked fun.

And he was hungry. If room service had food, he wanted some. He twisted the door handle and pulled the door back to admit the visitor. "Come on in!"

Harry cringed, scrunching up his eyes as if expecting a photon torpedo to detonate where he sat.

A uniformed server, a man wearing gold-, purple-, and black-striped trousers with an antiquated military-style high-waisted solid-purple jacket sporting rows of shiny brass buttons, wheeled his covered cart past Tom and stopped in front of Harry. His black pillbox hat with gold braid (being a holoprogrammer who specialized in "vintage" designs, Tom had an eye for such details) featured an ill-fitting chin strap. The syrupy light from the clown lamp failed to illuminate his face, which was bowed toward the cart.

Luscious smells wafted up from the cart. Tom's stomach growled impatiently. "I hope you've got pepperoni pizza in there—" Tom began.

The server yanked the burgundy drape off the cart, revealing a tray of hamburgers stacked with bacon, tomatoes, and lettuce; mounds of chili fries sprinkled with stringy melted cheese; and two milkshakes as tall as Tom's forearm. "It's on the house, boys," the server said, meeting Tom's eyes and smiling predatorily.

"Q!" Tom's initial shock at Q's presence gave way to a back-door sense of relief. The illogic and seeming randomness of their current predicament, with Q figured in, made more sense in kind of a Q-like way. How else could he and Harry have taken a test flight using the tetryon transporter and ended up in this stinky dive? He reached for a milkshake and took a long pull on a red-and-white-striped straw. *Mmmm . . . chocolate malt.*

"Don't eat that, Tom!" Harry said, his eyes wide. "It's probably—"

Tom paused in midsuck. Harry had a point. But he was hungry, and this was the best malted milkshake he'd ever had; so what if it turned him into a tribble? He took another long pull, savoring the cold, icy sweet dripping down his throat.

"Probably what?" Q leaned over, nearly touching his nose to Harry's. "What kind of Q do you take me for? I'm insulted, Mr. Kim." He held his hand—thumb touching his middle finger, poised to snap—next to Harry's ear.

Harry pulled back. "I didn't mean—I wasn't—I, um . . ." he stammered. Sweat beaded on his forehead, and his face became a decidedly paler shade.

Q's eyebrows waggled a few times. "Gotcha." He glanced at Tom. "Is he always this easy?" he asked, jerking a thumb toward Harry.

Tom shrugged and reached for a chili fry. "Well, yeah," Tom said, hesitantly. "Pretty much."

"Have you missed me? I regret that I haven't stopped by since Q and I procreated, but the rigors of parenting and restoring order to the Continuum since the war have left me little time to socialize." Q took a seat on the edge of the bed beside Harry; Harry scooted over to put space between him and the higher being. "What, pray tell, is this?" He lifted his arm, jammed his nose into the armpit, then inhaled extravagantly. Withdrawing, he wrinkled his upper lip and said, "Do I offend?" Shaking his head, he answered his own question. "No! Kathy's clearly failing to teach her kids how to demonstrate proper respect for their superiors. But more than that, we have history. I thought we'd be backslapping like old buddies!" He smacked Harry between the shoulder blades; Harry eked out a painful grunt in reply. Leaning over, Q peered up into Harry's hand-covered face. "Are you nervous, Mr. Kim?"

Harry shook his head. "This has to be a dream."

Q crossed his legs, shrugged in, and looked over at Tom. "Regretfully not. Look, boys, I don't like having to involve myself in the troubles of lesser beings—"

Ply us with food, then start in on the insults. At least he's still the same old Q. . . . Tom rolled his eyes and reached for a burger. He might as well be full before Q ruined his life.

"Oh, don't start with me, Mr. Paris. There's nothing untoward about my intentions," he said snippily. "Fine. I confess: Toying with you lowly creatures can be amusing. But in this case I absolutely wish our rendezvous could come under more pleasurable circumstances. Inebriation, carousing, and other hedonistic pursuits might actually be fun with you two—" He glanced at Harry. "All right, maybe not him, but definitely you, Tommy. Let's wager half the galaxy and find ourselves some strippers from Plaranik V, shall we? I hear they're *very* flexible."

"What do you want, Q?" Tom asked. "Because, in spite of your food bribe—"

"I knew *that* would win you over," Q said, obviously pleased. "You're a creature of very fundamental desires. Speaking of which, how's the little Klingon spitfire?"

"—it's been a long day, and we're not in the mood," Tom concluded. "If there's no point to all this, send us home. *Now.*"

"Well, well! Your testy girlfriend's domesticated you, Tommy. Too bad. First Vash loses her sense of humor, now you're all work and no play. What's a Q to do?"

"Q," Harry said, raising his voice. "I'm with Tom. *Voyager*'s in trouble. We can't sit around here and make small talk."

Tom had to agree: Q's obvious enchantment with his own relentless prattling was testing his patience.

Q cocked his head and offered Tom a put-out sigh. "Fine. I'll send you back after we take care of a few problems. Your esteemed captain really needs to curtail her humanitarian impulses and focus on the task at hand: namely, getting all you miscreants home. *Voyager*'s getting a reputation for not being able to work and play well with others. Kathy needs to learn to stay in her own sandbox, or else there'll be a dustup." He paused. "Get it? Sandbox? Dustup? I keep throwing them, but you just stand there and watch the ball go by."

Tom suppressed a groan and struggled to stay on topic. "You're saying Captain Janeway caused a problem in the Monoharan sector?" he guessed.

Q smiled. "And it's a *doozy*. No half-measures for our Kathy! This time, she's managed to start the reversal of the Big Bang. Quite an accomplishment for such a primitive life-form, but nonetheless ill-advised in the grander scheme of things."

"Hold on there," Harry said, suddenly alert, shaking his head with genuine incredulity. "That's quite a responsibility to heap on—what was it you usually call us, 'ugly bags of mostly water'?"

"That wasn't Q, that was—" Tom said.

"The *point* is," Q interrupted, rolling his eyes, "your species is mostly insignificant, but every once in a while, you do something that makes your betters in the universal hierarchy take notice. Much the same way you might take note if a bunch of amoebas got together and built a tractor. Something audacious and daring, and in this case"—he sneered at Harry—"asinine."

Tom pulled a tipsy wood chair out from the desk where it was tucked and straddled it backward, facing Q. "Granted, astrophysics wasn't my best subject at the Academy, but I'm failing to see the connection between anything that *Voyager*'s done lately that would have such catastrophic ramifications."

A look of annoyance—or exasperation—flitted across Q's face. "It's always 'why this?' and 'why that?' with you corporeals. Patience, children. You'll have your answers soon enough. But we have to be on our way—"

Harry crossed his arms and exhaled loudly. "No. I'm not agreeing to go anywhere until you tell us where we are, what you want with us, and when we're going home."

Q sighed. "Think of this place as a suburb of the Q continuum. There. Satisfied, Mr. Kim? The sooner we leave, the sooner we get back to that tin can you call a spaceship. Let's go." Q grabbed Harry's arm and tried—unsuccessfully—to drag him to his feet. "Be advised: You are moments away from becoming a newt."

"A suburb—not the Continuum proper?" Tom said. "Why? We've been in the Continuum before. Saved you from Civil War last time we visited. Thought we'd be welcomed as heroes." Q's explanations weren't passing the "smell" test.

"The Continuum has a strict visitor's policy these days. No riff-raff." Q looked at them both disapprovingly. "Not to mention a dress code. Let's be on our way—"

A thought occurred. A wide, toothy grin split Tom's face. "You're in trouble."

"Am not!" Q said a little too quickly.

"You can't bring us into the Continuum because you don't want anyone to know. I'd say that puts us in a pretty good bargaining position. Say we help you and you send *Voyager* back to the Alpha Quadrant." Tom removed the burger platter from the cart and passed it to Harry. "You really ought to try one. The sauce is outstanding."

"Don't mind if I do." Harry selected a double-decker cheeseburger with a large onion ring sandwiched between patties and bun.

Q threw his hands into the air. "All right! I admit that my reasons for bringing you here weren't entirely altruistic, but you have to believe me when I tell you that there wouldn't be a problem if it weren't for Kathy."

"Still falling back on that tired excuse, Q?" Harry said between bites. "If you've got that explanation, I'm all ears."

Q snapped his fingers. With a flash of white light, an enormous ear appeared in place of Harry's head.

"You really need to work on some new material, Q," Tom said.

Q frowned as he considered Harry. "Too predictable?"

Tom shrugged and nodded.

Q harrumphed and snapped his fingers.